Firetender

Chalice
Book One

A Novel

By Erin Lewis

Full Quiver Publishing
Pakenham, ON

Firetender (Chalice Book One)
Copyright 2023 Erin Lewis

Published by
Full Quiver Publishing
PO Box 244
Pakenham, Ontario K0A 2X0
www.fullquiverpublishing.com

ISBN Number: 978-1-987970-48-7
Printed and bound in the USA
Cover photo: Erin Lewis
Cover design: James Hrkach and Erin Lewis

NATIONAL LIBRARY OF CANADA
CATALOGUING IN PUBLICATION

Published by FQ Publishing
A Division of Innate Productions

"In the struggle for existence, it is only on those who hang on for ten minutes after all is hopeless, that hope really begins to dawn."
G.K. Chesterton

"Come on; it's just a little farther."

Two boys scrambled uphill in the woods on the outskirts of town. They pulled a rusty red wagon behind them, reclaimed as an afterthought from the trash heap on the curb in front of Dallas's house. It held a few old glass bottles and tin cans, some wire, cardboard, and a BB gun. All but the gun had been scavenged along the way.

Channing was struggling with the wagon now, so Dallas took another turn. Over tree roots and around rocks they steered the squeaky metal toy, both of them far too big for it now.

"Are you sure this will be worth it?" asked Channing, huffing along behind.

"Definitely," Dallas responded.

"But you haven't tried it already yourself, have you?" asked Channing, gray eyes questioning.

"No, but I'll go first if you want."

They had reached the top. The reservoir lay spread beneath them, shimmering blue in the midday sunlight. Channing and Dallas had explored its banks before, gone swimming on the other side where the shore sloped gently into the water. This side, however, was new to them both. They walked along the ridge they had just climbed until they came to a steep, clear-cut path for the utility lines, and now both boys stood facing the lake, where the ground ended abruptly at a ten-foot drop-off to the water below.

"So it's deep enough right there, you're sure?" Channing squinted at Dallas.

"Yeah, I jumped off the edge when I was here last weekend and didn't touch bottom. I swam around and couldn't feel anything sticking up either, like rocks or sticks or anything. It'll be fine." Dallas exuded pure confidence and no fear.

Channing stammered, "Well… okay, it sounds like fun… but I'll watch while you go first."

They unloaded the wagon and piled the contents at the top of the hill, then Dallas centered it at the top of the path. He looped the end of a rope around his wrist, the other end tied to the wagon's handle. Sitting astride the rickety wagon, he adjusted its angle to line himself up.

Channing laughed at his 14-year-old friend in the too-small wagon. "This'll be hilarious to watch. I wish we had a camcorder!"

"Better to not have footage of what could be me going to my watery grave!" Dallas said dramatically. "Okay, here I go!"

Dallas shoved off with both feet and pulled his legs up. The wheels spun as he sped downhill, handle pulled back towards him to steer. The metal contraption bounced over bumps as it picked up speed, creating a terrific noise, and Channing, holding his breath, his eyes like saucers, watched as the wagon with Dallas aboard rocketed over the edge and soared out over the reservoir below, then broke the surface with a walloping splash. Upon impact, Channing scrambled down the slope. Dallas's head emerged from the water with triumphant cheers, and his eyes found Channing above.

"How was it?" asked Channing, perched at the edge of the earth at the sheer drop down to the water.

"Awesome!" shouted Dallas, kicking and pulling vigorously to the sloped shore beside the cliff, tugging the sinking metal wagon behind him. He found his footing and lugged at the rope, muscles straining as he brought it up from the water.

Channing had slid down to the wooded shore near the water's edge. The wagon finally emerged as Dallas used all his arm strength to haul it in, feet planted in the shallow water along the shore. Channing waded in to give Dallas a hand. They dragged the wagon onto shore, dumped out the remaining water, and manipulated it through the trees and shrubs to take it up the hill again, water dripping off the ragged hem of Dallas's baggy below-the-knee cutoff sweatpants.

Back at the top, Dallas extended the wagon's handle to Channing.

The younger boy hesitated. "I'm not so sure I want..." He took a step backward.

"Let's both go, then. Want me to drive?" Dallas sat in front and grabbed the handle, then glanced over his shoulder at his trembling friend. "Come on; I promise it's fun!" he coaxed. Channing squeezed in behind him. Dallas felt fingers digging into his skin through his shirt as Channing held on tight. "It's okay, Chan, I swear. You don't have to cling on so hard. We're wedged into this thing so tight; there's no way you'll fall out." Channing managed a slight nod.

"Here we go!" shouted Dallas, shoving off recklessly again.

The wagon accelerated, the additional weight like a magnet drawing them towards the lake. Channing, eyes clamped shut, mumbled self-reassurances into Dallas's back. The wagon clattered as if all the bolts might fall out at any moment, but then they were airborne, and the next thing either of them knew, they were underwater. Dallas immediately kicked to the surface above. Channing popped up sputtering a couple seconds later. Both boys were crowing gleefully.

"Wasn't that incredible?" Dallas cried.

"I thought we were going to die!" Channing returned, a mixture of excitement and terror in the grin across his face. He paddled rapidly to stay afloat. "Okay, I'm going to go alone this time. But I don't think I can pull the thing out of the reservoir by myself."

"I'll stay here to help right after you land," Dallas offered.

"Stay back, though. I don't want to smash your head in," Channing advised.

"Yeah, good tip." Dallas smirked.

Channing labored uphill in his waterlogged clothes and shoes, the heavy wagon following behind. Dallas waited in the deep water, treading water steadily.

"Are you lined up straight?" Dallas shouted up to Channing.

"Yeah," Channing called back.

"You just have to hold the handle steady is all," Dallas yelled back. "It might want to pull to one side, but just keep it straight. You can do it, Chan!"

Dallas treaded water as Channing stood still. "What's the matter?" he shouted up at him.

"I… I don't think I can do it," Channing stammered.

"Sure you can!" encouraged Dallas. "You just did! Get in and let it start rolling—I'm right here for when you land!"

Channing didn't budge. Finally, he pulled the wagon aside and sat down on the dirt, head on his knees.

Dallas stared up at Channing, who had become a solid friend to him over the past several months. *He needs to toughen up! Not having a dad around hasn't stopped me any. He's scared, just like he is of everything,* Dallas realized with chagrin, his insides squirming at the sight of Channing's disabling fear.

Dallas swam to shore and sloshed up the hill, stopping beside Channing. "Come on; I'll help you."

Channing looked up. "You'll ride with me again?"

"Don't you wanna do it on your own?"

Channing stared out over the lake, lower lip trembling. "I do, but…"

Dallas waited.

"I… I'm too scared," Channing mumbled, face pink under his shaggy hair. "I'm not as brave as you."

"Well, why don't you just sit in the wagon, see how it feels to be in it alone," Dallas suggested. "Take small steps until you feel confident."

Channing shrugged his shoulders, but he stood up. Dallas dragged the wagon to the top of the incline and pointed it towards the reservoir below.

"I'm not so sure..." Channing's face was paler than usual. His eyes darted to Dallas's and then down at his feet. "Can't we just go do something else?"

I can't let him feel so helpless like this! Dallas hardened his face and dug in his heels.

"You're gonna be *so* much braver after you do this alone!" Dallas's firmness was masked in excitement. "You'll feel like you're the king of the world, I *swear*, Channing!"

"But I already had to force myself just to ride with you..." Channing backed away slowly, eyes still focused on the ground.

Dallas narrowed his eyes. *I* know *he can do this. If he conquers his fears, he won't get picked on so much.* Dallas chewed his lip, considering other angles.

Channing glanced up, tears in his eyes. "I'm sorry I'm a wuss, Dallas. I don't *want* to be like this, but..."

"Okay, so here's what you do," Dallas said, adrenaline taking over his brain. "Come sit in the wagon with me, like before." Dallas sat astride the Radio Flyer with both feet anchored on the ground. Channing hesitated, then inched towards the wagon and lowered himself in, gripping Dallas's shoulders.

"First thing to do is you let go of me and hold onto the wagon instead," Dallas directed. Channing loosened his grip. Dallas felt his friend's rapid breathing down his neck.

"Okay, good. Now," Dallas continued, "I'm just gonna stand up a little, see, so you can feel what it's like sitting there by yourself." Dallas eased his lithe body up from the seat of the wagon and stood, still straddling it. "How's that?" he asked over his shoulder.

"Okay, I guess," Channing replied unsteadily.

Dallas stepped over the wagon with his right leg and turned to face Channing, feet cemented into the dirt and hands in a death grip on the metal edges. "Now try putting your feet up; see how that feels," Dallas coaxed. "I'll hold the wagon so it won't start rolling."

Channing's wide eyes met Dallas's determined ones. He sat like a statue and gulped.

"I've got it, see?" Dallas squatted alongside with both hands tight on the wagon. Channing tried to speak, but no words formed. He slowly drew his right leg into the wagon.

"There you go!" Dallas said triumphantly. "Now the other one, and you're in position to take flight!"

Channing kept his left foot on the ground. His face was cool and clammy. He swallowed and bit his upper lip.

"Here, I'll help you," Dallas said, taking hold of Channing's ankle and lifting it. Channing didn't resist. Now he sat in the wagon alone. Dallas smiled at his success, his own pulse thumping in his head. "Take the handle, practice steering," he goaded. Channing put one hand slowly on the handle. *It's working!* Dallas's brain nearly bubbled over. *He's doing it; he's gonna get past his fear!* The adrenaline of anticipation tingled down his spine as the force of gravity strained against his one hand, tugging at the wagon, heavy with Channing's waiting weight, teasing him to let go. Dallas's fingers twitched on the wagon, antsy for action. "Now the other hand… you're doing it, Channing, you're doing it!"

Wide-eyed and trembling slightly, Channing's mouth formed a partial smile, and he glanced at Dallas as if seeking approval.

Channing's slight change in body language did it. The adrenaline junkie demons inside of Dallas unleashed themselves, and he grabbed the back of the wagon with his free hand as he let go with the other, and he shoved it from behind in one coordinated motion, yelling, "Go, Channing, go! Yeeeeaah!"

The wagon took off, unable to resist the combination of gravity plus Dallas's strength. He jumped to his feet and chased it in his cheering excitement, skidding on the gravel path and nearly sitting down as he slid after Channing in the wagon. Halting before he tumbled head over heels, Dallas heard the air fill with Channing's deafening shriek. The high-pitched, agonized terror went like a knife to his stomach. It all happened in a matter of seconds. Dallas sat frozen, mouth hanging open, as the wagon reached the cliff's edge. *What have I done?* Channing's frantic wail echoed back up the hill, chilling Dallas's blood as the wagon smacked the water's surface.

Dallas slid to the edge of the drop-off as Channing's head surfaced for a second, garbling an attempted scream before going under again. His arms and legs were a crazed fury of splashing and thrashing. Dallas leaped into the water below, his heart pounding. He took strong strokes to where Channing struggled frantically.

"I've got you, Chan; it's okay!" Dallas shouted above the splashes and gasps. He put his arms under Channing's and felt fingernails dig into his flesh. Channing's unfocused eyes glazed with terror.

"I've got you now; calm down!" Dallas ordered, going under with Channing's pull. One of Channing's feet kicked him in the leg underwater. Dallas wrenched his head upward, spluttering on the gulp of water he'd just ingested.

Channing's entire body seized with convulsions, and his terrorized wails went to Dallas's soul as he fought to gain control over his friend's flailing body. Dallas threaded both arms under Channing's from behind. "I've got you; it's okay now," he murmured into his ear, wracked with guilt over what he'd done. Dallas pulled him towards shore as Channing's strength weakened. Finally, Dallas's foot hit bottom, and he staggered to his feet, lugging him in a bear hug into shallow water. Dallas collapsed, gasping for breath and dizzy from the exertion, their heads and chests above water. Channing sputtered and babbled incoherently. Dallas knelt in front of him and grabbed his shoulders, shaking him. Channing's eyes still registered nothing. Dallas shook harder.

"Channing!! It's me; it's Dallas! You're okay! We're out of the deep water; we're okay! You did it!"

Finally, Channing stopped wailing and sucked in gasping breaths, crying, shaking. His eyes focused on Dallas's with an expression of mistrust. He shrieked, then turned aside and threw up a few mouthfuls of lake water.

Dallas sat tense, staring at his friend's involuntary reaction. *What have I done?! What was I thinking?!* He loosened his grip on Channing's shoulders and pulled the sobbing boy close. Dallas's heart melted with an alien tenderness. Channing collapsed into Dallas, tears streaming and breaths heaving raggedly from his chest.

Dallas squeezed Channing tight. "I'm sorry, Chan; I don't know what came over me! Please, I didn't mean to do it! I was so excited that you were going to do it!"

Channing's breaths gradually relaxed, and Dallas pulled him to his feet and staggered to the shore with an arm around his shoulders. Dallas sat Channing on a log and squatted in front of him, but he couldn't look him in the face. Channing's eyes were closed, arms wrapped around his knees, and he managed to squeak out, "*Why?* Why did you *do* that to me?"

Dallas's cheeks burned. "I'm so sorry!" he repeated, his voice rising. "I won't blame you if you never forgive me! I'm so stupid, Channing! I can't believe I did that to you! I just wanted to help you be brave and strong, and I *completely* lost control of myself!"

Channing's eyes finally acknowledged Dallas. The fear was fading from his face, and his breathing had almost stabilized. A shudder convulsed through his body, and he heaved a sigh. Channing eyed Dallas with suspicion.

The accusatory look in his friend's eyes felt like a gut punch. Dallas pleaded for understanding. "I promise you, Channing, I'll never do something like that to you again. *Never*. It was crazy of me. Crazy, and... and just flat-out *mean*. I'm sorry," he choked out.

Channing finally spoke. "I... I'm okay. I know that... you weren't trying to be mean."

Dallas met Channing's eyes. "But I *was* mean. You weren't ready for that, and I was a jerk to think I could just force the fear out of you."

Channing's face softened. "I know you were just trying to help me," he said. "To help me be brave... I'm not brave, Dallas. I told you that, but I hope we're still friends..." He examined his waterlogged shoes, ears pink.

Dallas's mouth dropped open, and he snapped it shut. "Of course, you're my friend, my very best friend!" he said emphatically. "I'm gonna stick by you, Channing. I don't care how brave you act or not!"

"You want to hang out with a wimp?"

Lightning flashed in Dallas's eyes. "You are *not* a wimp. You went with me in the wagon, and that was plenty brave."

The remaining hesitation drained from Channing's meek face. "I know you didn't mean for what happened..."

They sat on the fallen tree, side by side for the next few minutes, silent. Then Channing turned to Dallas, voice unsteady. "You wanna... wanna ride down together again?"

"Oh no, Channing, you don't hafta..."

"But I *want* to," he interrupted. "It was fine when I wasn't alone. Really!"

Dallas looked away. "I'm sorry, Channing."

"I know. So let's go again together."

Dallas glanced up. "I can't believe you even trust me right now."

"You told me you'll never do it again, and I believe you." Channing stood up, scanning the water. "Where do you think the wagon went down?"

The wagon! Dallas had forgotten all about it. He stood alongside Channing and located the spot where he thought he'd last seen it. "I'll swim out and find it," he said, already trotting towards the water.

Channing splashed behind him. Dallas swam to where Channing had landed, took a big breath, and dove. He grasped around in the murky water, feeling for something obvious. *Not deep enough.* Dallas reemerged, filled his lungs again, and shot downward, stroking until he touched bottom. He swept his arms and legs around and, not making contact with anything that could be the wagon, came up beside where Channing dog paddled in place.

"Find it?"

"Nope," Dallas answered. He moved over a few feet, sucked in more air, and dunked under the water again. This time, his hand touched a wheel. Grasping with both hands, Dallas worked up until he found the handle. He gripped it in his right hand, then kicked and strained towards the daylight. When he broke the surface and lifted the handle in a clasped fist, Channing cheered. They dragged the wagon back to shore together.

I can't believe he wants to go again. Dallas shook his head as they climbed the hill. *I'm no better than those jerks at school! I should've known better.* Dallas glanced at Channing trudging alongside him. His face showed nothing of his recent terror.

At the top, Dallas turned to Channing. "Only if you're sure, okay?"

"I want to," Channing said, stepping forward with head held high. "Okay, you go in front again."

"You can hold on to me as tight as you want," Dallas offered, then added, "and it's more fun for both of us when we do it together."

Channing climbed in. Dallas double-checked the straightness of his projected path and pushed off. For the fourth time, the wagon shot into the reservoir with an impressive splash. As Channing broke the surface and gasped, Dallas gulped in a breath of air and swam alongside, observing Channing. A smile lit up his face. Dallas heaved a sigh of relief. The two of them gripped the rope and swam towards the shallower water, making quick work of hauling in their daredevil contraption.

They lost count of how many times they plunged into the lake, but eventually, their need for an adrenaline high was exhausted. At the top of the hill, worn out, they stripped off their shirts to dry in the sun. Soaked sneakers and socks were already discarded beside them.

Channing hitched up his loose jeans, heavy from the weight of the water, and turned towards a bush to hang his shirt. A dark yellowish-purple bruise stood out on his pale back. Dallas emitted a shocked gasp.

"What the crap—how'd you get that huge bruise?!?" He gaped incredulously.

Channing startled. "What bruise?"

"Right here, under your shoulder blade." Dallas touched the spot gingerly.

Channing recoiled, wincing. "How big is it?"

"Like as big as my fist!" Dallas spat. "Did your mom beat you again?"

Channing dropped his head, digging in the dirt with his big toe. "It's no big deal," he muttered. "It's just a bruise; nothing's broken or anything."

"I'd like to break *her*!" Dallas growled. "Or was it her boyfriend? Dammit, tell me, Channing." Dallas met the younger boy's eyes and locked there, not backing down.

"Okay," Channing said, flopping onto the ground with a sigh. "Yeah, it was Chuck this time. It was mostly my fault; I stole one of his cigarettes. I didn't smoke it, just burned it all the way down in the bathroom for fun. I hid it in the trashcan. I thought he and my mom were too drunk to notice, but I guess he smelled it. Once he broke the door, he found it right away."

Dallas punched his right fist into the palm of his other hand, seething. "That son of a…" He glowered. "That wasn't enough to deserve a bruise like that! What'd he hit you with?"

"Just his hands," Channing mumbled, keeping his gaze down. "I tried to escape through the window, but he grabbed my shirt and punched me in the back. He got me with his knee, too, and shoved me into the bathtub. Then he turned the shower on me and walked away, laughing. He's a jerk, just like all of them."

Dallas stared at him, not wanting to believe the awful truth. "Where'd he get you with his knee?" he finally asked.

Channing pointed to his upper thigh.

"Is it bruised bad too?"

Channing nodded. "Pretty much." He stood and brushed the dirt from his pants, then lowered them slightly to show Dallas the spot. "Impressive, huh?" he said with a weak grin.

Dallas jumped up and swung a foot at a nearby rock. With tight lips, he watched it tumble downhill, then turned to Channing with a huff. The thin twelve-year-old boy appeared closer to ten, whereas Dallas had matured early, amplifying the nearly two-year age difference even more starkly. "So can you stay at my house a few days, you think?"

Channing broke out in a wide grin. "I'd like that, yeah. Then my mom and Chuck can just hit each other instead of me." He rolled his eyes. "Come on, let's go shoot stuff."

Dallas grabbed his BB gun. They reloaded the wagon, then walked towards the other side of the reservoir to a clearing where they liked to go for target practice. Channing's bruise jumped out at Dallas like a taunting bully. *They're beating him bad, actually injuring him!* Channing's tales of his past spilled into Dallas's mind, all in clear focus now. Suddenly Dallas was paralyzed at having coerced Channing against his will, and he gulped for oxygen. *It makes what I did even more terrible!* He hung his head and closed his eyes.

"Dallas?" Channing paused and turned around. "What's wrong?"

Dallas mustered his resolve and forced his feet forward, averting his eyes from Channing's bruised back. "Nothing," he answered. *I'm gonna protect him. I can't let him get treated like dirt.* A surge of heat welled up in Dallas's throat. *Don't cry!* he ordered himself. *You don't cry.*

In the center of the clearing, Channing lined up the cans from the wagon along a board resting across two large rocks. Then he and Dallas took turns firing at them. Channing hit the first one he aimed at, sending it backward off the edge of the board. "Pow!" he said.

Dallas aimed, fired, and missed.

"You can shoot 'til you hit one," Channing suggested.

"Thanks, but that means you may be waiting awhile," Dallas ribbed himself.

After four more tries, Dallas hit the can he was aiming at. Channing took another two shots and blasted a can right in the center.

After five more unsuccessful attempts, Dallas picked up a rock and hurled it at a can, sending it flying. "Don't know why I can't aim worth a crap with that gun, but I can aim a rock just fine," he muttered.

Channing lifted the gun again and shot another can off its perch.

"That one was your mom's jerkface boyfriend!" Dallas jeered.

Channing gritted his teeth and fired a hole through another can.

"That one was your dad! And now for your mother." Dallas replaced the cans on the board and pointed out the one in the middle.

Channing hit it with deadly accuracy.

"Okay, my turn," Dallas said, pumped up with revenge. "That one on the far left, that's *my* father." He aimed and missed. Dallas grimaced and tried again. The BB hit the board, leaving the can untouched. Dallas stormed forward with a yell and swept all the cans off the board with one foot, then unloaded BBs into them at point-blank range, flinching to avoid any ricochet.

Channing jumped into the fray, hurling rocks and sending cans flying.

Dallas's anger gradually subsided until the two of them were overcome with silliness, smashing cans by dropping the biggest rocks they could find on them and turning the board into a catapult to launch cans across the clearing. Dallas dropped Channing on one end, but instead of sending the can airborne, his weight toppled the board. They collapsed in the dust, doubled over with laughter.

Channing gathered up all the cans again, standing the ones that would still stay upright along the board, then grabbed his damp t-shirt from the wagon and whipped it at them as he burst out in song, lyrics expressing both boys' thoughts over their absentee fathers with biting sarcasm. Dallas joined in chanting the final repetitive phrase as he kicked cans off the board and stomped them with loud crunches.

"Well, that felt good," Dallas announced, all the cans destroyed to their satisfaction. "In honor of our deadbeat dads." Dallas held up a badly damaged can in a mock toast, smirking.

Channing, breathing hard, nodded vigorously. He grabbed another smashed can and clinked it against the one Dallas held aloft.

"I wish we could go to Lollapalooza," Channing bemoaned. "Or the Jane's Addiction Show in Salt Lake City at the end of the month, so we could hear them perform live." Dallas didn't respond, thinking that even if they could afford concert tickets, they had no way to get there. *Being poor sucks.*

"Hey, there's a big concrete tunnel down by the edge of the reservoir." Dallas changed the subject. "I noticed it last week. Wanna see if we can go through it?" *It'll be exciting to Channing but not too high-risk scary.*

"Sure," Channing agreed.

A ladder led them down a pipe, and then the concrete tunnel went parallel to the ground. They ducked their heads and walked through it, sneakers slogging through the stream of water running through at the bottom. They met another pipe leading straight up, and they climbed metal rungs one after another, Channing going first.

"Whoa, Dallas, we're in the middle of the lake!" he called from the top. Dallas climbed the last rungs and hoisted himself up next to Channing, sitting on the concrete ledge. "This is awesome!" Channing continued. "I never knew you could get out here from under the ground!"

"Must be a drainage thing for controlling the water level or something," Dallas supposed aloud.

"Or a place to hide out, to spy on the Loch Ness Monster," Channing said.

Dallas rolled his eyes but said nothing. He was getting used to Channing's wild imagination.

Channing continued the fantasy. "You be the lookout, and if you notice a sea serpent, come after me, okay?"

Before Dallas could answer, Channing leaped off the pipe into the reservoir below. Dallas sat, legs dangling and swinging rhythmically over the edge, watching Channing below with his mind wandering elsewhere.

A few minutes later, he was brought back to attention by Channing's cries and a flurry of splashes that sent ripples out into the water beyond.

"Help, it's got me!"

Dallas stood on the narrow ledge and balanced halfway around the top of the pipe to the other side. Channing thrashed about like a maniac below.

"Kick it in the face!" Dallas didn't want to get wet again now that his clothes were mostly dry. "Sea serpents hate that, ya know."

"I can't, you gotta help me!" Channing yelped. He ducked under the water. Dallas glanced around for a long stick or something he could use to "save" Channing, but finding nothing, he relented and cannonballed over Channing's head and into the water below.

Channing went under again and reemerged, brandishing a short stick he'd found floating in the water. In a frenzy of jabs, he slashed at the water's surface while Dallas shoved water in waves in the same direction. With a loud battle cry, Channing declared them victorious, waving his stick high in the air and shouting, "Behold my sword, all besmirched with gore from the horrible creature's brain!"

"Be-*what* with gore?" asked Dallas in bewilderment.

"Besmirched," Channing declared again. "Besmirched with gore. Isn't that a great phrase? I read it in a library book, *The Odyssey*, when the cyclops gets stabbed in the eye."

"Sounds gruesome," Dallas said approvingly.

After swimming, the boys climbed the outside of the concrete pipe and sat again on the edge, taking in the scenery, each lost in his own thoughts. Channing broke the silence.

"So, what happened to your girlfriend?"

Dallas rolled his eyes and snorted. "She wasn't even my girlfriend," he began. "I mean, *she* said she was, sure. I know that's what she told you. But I didn't agree to it, and I just had to set her straight. Girls confuse me to death." He sighed while Channing waited for him to go on. "I mean, if our parents could screw up relationships so royally, how in the world could we do a good job with it as middle schoolers? Best not to get involved with girls for a long, long time."

Channing was silent. "She told me I took up too much of your time," he said. "After school, like a week ago. I just ignored her; I didn't think you guys were really together like that or anything. She was insisting that you loved her, though. Said you kissed her, too."

Dallas groaned. "*She* kissed *me*," he said. "I told her to cut it out. She acted like I was just kidding." He tilted his head in a mock attitude and mimicked her higher-pitched voice. "'You're so funny when you play around like that, Dallas!' she said. I felt rotten after that, but I got the point across that we weren't dating. Now she hates me."

"Yeah," Channing mused. "Girls confuse me too. I've gotten to know you better than I've ever known anyone, besides myself, that is."

"I… I've never had a friend like you before," Dallas said, fidgeting with the stick in his hands.

"Me neither," returned Channing. "I'm glad you're my friend. Really glad."

Dallas exhaled some guilt from earlier as the peaceful surroundings seeped into his soul. "This is a really cool spot," he said absently. "Wonder if anyone else ever climbs up this thing?"

"We could hide out in it all night and protect it from intruders," Channing suggested in all seriousness.

Dallas enticed him away with the reminder of staying over at his house for a few days. "And I think there's a box of Pop-Tarts in the kitchen."

A half-hour later, Channing and Dallas walked along the road's edge, clothes drying in the sun, wagon bumping along behind. "Can I store these glass bottles in your basement?" Channing asked. They'd collected several for Channing's art projects.

"Sure," Dallas agreed.

They entered Dallas's house through the basement and unloaded the wagon, then jogged up the stairs to the main level of the house. It was empty. Dallas picked up a scrap from the table and read the note jotted across it: "Dallas — be back tomorrow night. Buy yourself food." Fifteen dollars lay beside the note. Dallas pocketed the money and glanced at Channing.

"Your clothes all the way dry now?"

He nodded.

"Great, mine too," Dallas said. "Come on, let's go get some dinner and come back here. Maybe we'll have enough change to rent a movie." As they walked towards the convenience store two blocks away, Dallas felt a protective swell for the boy at his side. *I'm never going to give him a reason not to trust me again. Never.*

URGENCY
(Five-and-a-half years later… January 1997)

We've got to get out of here. Dallas stalked into his bedroom and yanked open a dresser drawer. He grabbed jeans and a few shirts and shoved them into a duffel bag. *We can't live here anymore. I can find a job somewhere, but what about Channing?* He couldn't even hold a job at a fast-food joint.

Dallas scanned the note on the kitchen table a second time, his gaze darting across words he'd already memorized. Unwilling to face its terse yet clear meaning, he quickly folded it up and slipped it into his wallet. *Is this why she was nagging me lately to get a steady job?* Fire leaped up inside of Dallas. Outside, dusk had fallen. Catching a glimpse of his angular reflection in the window, Dallas scowled at himself. *I have no control of my life.*

Flinging open the refrigerator and then pantry, Dallas appraised the contents with tightness growing in his chest. He slammed the pantry door and gave it a swift kick, his combat boot leaving a black mark on the door. *How are we going to eat?* the question echoed unanswered in his mind. *Where are we gonna live, and how will I get any money before I can find a place?* Dallas had spent most of his savings to buy the car from his mother over a year ago, and there had been little income from inconsistent job stints over the past half a year since Dallas had graduated from high school in June, class of '96. *If she's so desperate that she left for good, then she probably took anything that was left of my money with her. Why'd I trust her with it?* Contempt boiled inside of Dallas. The emotional distance between mother and son had only amplified with the passing years, but now… *I'm completely disgusted with her!* He slumped against the pantry door, face buried in his arms. *And myself.*

What about Channing? Dallas bit his lip. *Will we have to steal to survive? Anything but that…*

Just then, Channing clomped up the skeleton of steps from the unfinished basement, where he'd been working with his kiln. His thin frame cloaked in baggy maroon thrift-store corduroys, Channing carried two thick books under one arm.

Dallas met him at the top of the stairs and caught the title *World Religions* on one spine. He'd been racking his mind for how best to explain the predicament. *Keep it basic.*

Channing spoke first. "Hey, are we taking a road trip?" He eyed the Rand McNally Road Atlas that Dallas had picked up.

"Yeah, kind of." Dallas wavered, pulling at his earring and averting his eyes. "It's just that… well, my mom hasn't paid the rent. I'm not sure why, but it sounds like she's not coming back any time soon. So we need to leave." He paused, watching for Channing's reaction.

"Where will you live now?" Channing asked, brow furrowed.

"I haven't decided yet," Dallas responded, "but I want to just get out of town. No reason to stay around here." He tried to keep his voice laid-back in its typical casual tone.

Channing squinted, a question forming on his lips.

Dallas continued. "Channing, you know I want you to come with me. But, if you think you need to go back to your mom, well, I'd sort of understand that. But, man, I'll worry about you if you stay with her. I've gotta start acting like an adult. I don't want to boss you around, but…"

"Of course, I'm coming with you!" Channing asserted without hesitation, interrupting Dallas's attempt at a guarded explanation. "You're my best friend!"

Dallas saw the hopeful light in Channing's eyes. A heaviness settled in the pit of his stomach. *He has complete blind faith in me, even though I'm just fumbling around.*

"Why don't you go around the house and gather up clothes and blankets," Dallas told him as he evaluated the food left in the fridge. *A few slices of cheese, the last of the milk, half a jar of pickles, a few slices of ham — if they're even still good…* He was sure their food supply wouldn't last longer than two or three days. All that was in the pantry was part of a jar of peanut butter, half a loaf of sandwich bread, and a few Pop-Tarts. *When did she take all the food?*

Channing reemerged in the kitchen a few minutes later, carrying three blankets. Dallas packed useful items from the cabinets into a paper grocery bag.

"I was thinking…" Channing hesitated, brushing his chin-length wavy brown hair back from his boyish face. "Of course, I'm coming with you, but if you don't know when we'll come back, well, I should probably tell my mom I'm going. Just in case she wonders or something…" He followed Dallas to the bathroom.

"You wanna tell her, even though she hasn't cared where you've been all month?" Dallas asked. He grabbed their toothbrushes, his razor, and a bottle of shampoo and dropped them in a bag. "You know what I think of her," he added, an edge to his voice. *And now I know that my own mom's no better, clearly.*

"Well, I'll just tell her on our way out of town, if we can stop by there," Channing reasoned. He took the bag Dallas thrust at him and watched as Dallas added soap and deodorant to its contents.

"Okay, we'll go by there if you want," Dallas said, "but I still don't think you should bother to extend her the courtesy." He swept into his bedroom and grabbed a few pillows, then back into the bathroom for two towels. Channing paused in a doorway and followed Dallas's frenzy of activity with his eyes.

After making several trips to the car, Dallas found Channing sitting on the floor of the basement utility room, pouring the last drips of gasoline from one can to another. He capped the empty container as Dallas stood watching.

"What're you doing?"

"Consolidating," Channing replied, brow furrowed. He paused to wipe his nose on the cuff of his sleeve. "We have about three gallons."

Dallas had forgotten the gasoline stored near the lawnmower. Channing hadn't spilled a drop. Wondering if they would have room for it, Dallas picked up the toolbox.

"Yeah," he said. "We could use that for the trip." *There's only half a tank of gas in my car.* Dallas hadn't even considered the gas money yet. *This is worse than I thought.* He groaned internally, running his fingers through his cropped hair. He had already depleted most of his recent earnings from chopping up a neighbor's fallen tree into firewood last weekend. *We'll be leaving home with less than twenty dollars in my pocket!* But he wasn't going to tell that to Channing.

"I got the camping stove, too," Channing added. "In case we want to heat up some Chef Boyardee or something." He pointed to a propane canister. "But that tank's nearly empty."

"Yeah, we'll take it along, maybe get some more propane at some point," Dallas mumbled. He pictured the pathetically empty pantry and gritted his teeth. *We don't even have one can of soup or SpaghettiO's, nothing!*

Dallas and Channing carried the gasoline cans to the car's trunk. Then Channing loaded the tent and sleeping bags while Dallas sat in the living room, scrutinizing the road atlas, his square jaw set. *We'll go east, maybe towards Kansas...* Dallas couldn't process any further than that, and he closed his eyes tightly.

"Can I bring my kiln?" Channing's hopeful voice from the doorway interrupted Dallas's planning. "And my glass? And..."

Dallas glanced up and sighed. "Chan, we can bring what we can fit. The Isuzu isn't that big. We leave first thing in the morning. The rent was due last week. There's no time to do anything besides grab what we can and then split."

A few minutes later, Channing reappeared, smiling. "It fits in the trunk! I'll just bring the best of the glass. I can collect more when we get to wherever we're going."

"Let's think of anything else that might be valuable here," Dallas said. Disappointment filled him as he surveyed the pathetic options.

"I'm getting my books," Channing announced as he walked into the hallway. "Hey, Dallas, can I use that blue spray paint in the basement?"

"Sure," replied Dallas, wondering if he'd wake to find a painted wall in the morning. *Might as well stick it to the landlord to the fullest extent possible. And Channing's books—will they all fit?* With his almost-photographic memory, did Channing even need them?

Dallas stripped off his shirt. He flopped onto his bed and fell asleep, an escape from the depressing reality.

He woke to movement beside him what seemed like moments later, but it was the middle of the night. "Channing? What's wrong?"

"I can't sleep."

"Well, now I can't either with you breathing down my neck. Get off my bed." Dallas gave him a shove. He heard Channing slip to the floor and fumble around in the pile of blankets and cushions where he usually slept.

Dallas lay awake, guilt gnawing at him. *He's picked up on my anxiety. I've gotta hide it from him better.* Dallas gritted his teeth and tried to settle back to sleep.

The next morning, Dallas awoke to Channing breathing in his face. *It's like having a puppy dog,* Dallas thought in half affection, half annoyance. He stretched and went into the kitchen. He put the last two Pop-Tarts in the toaster and started the coffee, then stood with both hands flat on the countertop, staring at nothing. *I don't wanna do this.* Dallas waited for the dripping sound to stop. *But what else can I do?*

In a few minutes, Channing appeared in the doorway, rubbing his eyes.

"Are you making coffee?"

"Yep. It's almost ready." Dallas grabbed a clean shirt from the next room and slipped it over his head, complementing yesterday's jeans.

"Coffee is one of those wonderful things in life." Channing sighed as he pulled a chair from the kitchen table. "Good thing your mom left some. To get up and have a hot cup of coffee to start the day... just a simple little pleasure. And have you ever thought about how it unites us all around the world? Everybody drinks coffee and has since the 1400s!"

"How about the British?" inquired Dallas as he poured a mug. "I thought they drank tea?"

"I think they like tea better," Channing responded. He poured sugar into his mug and swirled it around with a fork from the counter. "But they drink coffee too, I'm betting. Coffee is a universal bond between us all."

Dallas had to smile at Channing's positive view of humanity and the things that connected everyone. Philosophy over breakfast had become commonplace when Channing was around.

Eating his Pop-Tart as he leaned against the counter, Dallas glanced down. "Your feet are blue, Channing."

"I know. I painted them after you went to sleep."

Dallas made a mental note to grab the paint thinner on the way out. He topped off both their mugs, then pulled out the chair next to Channing and sat, drawing on his boots.

Channing added two spoonfuls of sugar to his coffee, the last of it. He took careful bites around the perimeter of his Pop-Tart. Channing always saved the middle for last.

Dallas stuck the bag of coffee and two mugs into a paper bag, along with the toaster and coffee maker. "Is there anything else you need to get?" He scanned the kitchen, eyes resting on the microwave—it was a bit smaller than Channing's kiln. Dallas wouldn't try to convince him to make the trade. *I can't tell Channing how bad this really is.*

Channing carried the cooler and a pillow downstairs. Standing over the kitchen sink, Dallas drained his mug, then sputtered, spitting coffee across the counter as he caught a glimpse of movement through the window. The landlord was stepping out of a car in front of the house. Dallas dropped a profanity and the mug, then snatched the paper bag and darted down the stairs.

"Channing!" he hissed.

Channing paused and glanced over his shoulder.

"Don't go out yet," Dallas warned.

"What's wrong?" Channing frowned.

Dallas kept his voice calm as he grabbed the paint thinner from a shelf. "The landlord's out there, so we're gonna have to wait for just the right moment…"

Channing's eyes widened. "What will he do to you if he—"

"We're not sticking around to find out," Dallas interrupted. He peeked through the curtains of the window beside the lower-level door, eyes alert and focused. At the same moment, a sudden rapping sounded over their heads. Both boys froze.

A second knock and a commanding "Open up!" followed.

Dallas grabbed Channing by the upper arm and pulled him towards the basement door. "Wait. Stay calm…"

After the third knock, the kitchen door rattled, then opened. Dallas turned the knob to the basement exit and crept out, pulling Channing beside him. Heavy footsteps thudded on the floor above, and Dallas mouthed, "Now!" He and Channing ran for Dallas's Isuzu, parked on the road. Cooler, pillows, bags, and boys squeezed and tumbled into the sedan. Dallas had the key in the ignition and the car in gear before he got the door shut. The roaring engine sounded like an alarm in his ears as he pulled away from the curb and accelerated, glancing in the rear-view mirror.

"I see him!" Channing was squatting backward in the passenger seat, arms wrapped around the headrest and peering through the back window. "He's in the yard now!"

Dallas gritted his teeth and turned the corner. "Was he looking this way?"

"I'm not sure, but he isn't following us." Channing exhaled.

Dallas's body sagged. "He can't do anything to me anyway." He shrugged. "My name's not on the lease. Still, I didn't want to get into anything with him…" Dallas wasn't about to explain to the landlord that it appeared his mother wasn't coming back—ever--and that he had zero money to put towards the rent himself. *Especially not in front of Channing.*

The car crawled to a stop in front of Channing's house. He went inside while Dallas sat idling, studying the dilapidated building that was Channing's hell on earth. The paint was dirty and peeling. A few shingles had fallen off the roof, exposing black patches underneath. The large picture window was cracked—*from that time she threw the remote control at him and missed.* Dallas winced at the memory. With the driver's window open, he could hear the TV blaring loud and clear. He eyed a mangy-looking dog crossing the road, then scanned the yard: a pile of old bricks and cinder blocks heaped off to the side of the house, the same weedy gutter filled with trash just like the rest of the street, broken flower pots piled beside the tiny front porch where an ancient recliner sat facing the yard, stuffing coming out of rips on the armrests. Old beer cans lined the porch windowsill and littered the overgrown grass below.

Dallas glanced at his watch. *Five more minutes, and I'm going in after him.*

He didn't have to wait that long. Channing's mother's shrill shouting startled Dallas into motion. He turned off the car and sprang out of the driver's seat, pocketing his keys. He stalked across the brown, dry grass, leaped the steps, and threw open the door. Dallas's eyes narrowed, adjusting to the dim light. Channing's thin voice floated from the kitchen, followed by his mother's accusing, slurred words. *Drunk again.* Dallas paused to listen.

"Guess it won't be much different then, seeing as you've barely come around here lately. At least you won't eat up the food!" Her tone oozed with hostility. "Some son you are to treat your mother the way you do! All you come home for is to eat!"

"I don't want any of the food, Mom, I promise." Channing seemed to be pleading for understanding. *Does he think he's guilty?* "I just wanted to tell you I was going with Dallas, so you'd know."

"Go, then! Run off and waste your life away with your loser friend!" Her tone had turned sarcastic. "Who do you think bought you all those clothes, hmm? I've had enough of spending money on you without your rotten excuse of a father to help, so *good riddance!*" Something metal clanged against the linoleum.

That's it. Dallas rounded the corner just in time to see a spoon bounce off Channing's cowering figure. Next to the kitchen counter stood his mother, poised at the open drawer of silverware and surrounded by empty liquor bottles on the counter, along with multiple days' trash and dirty dishes.

Dallas's eyes blazed as he took heavy steps across the room. "What the hell do you think you're doing?!" he shouted, straightening up and towering over the sneering woman.

"Dallas, it's okay," whimpered Channing.

Dallas felt a gentle tug on the back of his shirt. He whirled around to face Channing. "No, it's *not* okay!" Dallas exclaimed to the boy struggling to keep a grip on an armful of clothing.

"Don't you *dare* threaten me, Dallas Malone!" slurred the voice behind him. Dallas whirled around.

Channing's mom pointed a table knife in his face. "I'll call the cops on you!"

"You call, and I'll show them the bruise you just put on your son's back with this spoon!" Dallas snatched up the utensil from the filthy floor, returning Channing's mother's threatening posture and glaring into her red-rimmed, drunken eyes. The two stood locked in battle formation as if ready for some bizarre fencing match.

Channing's nudge from behind relaxed Dallas's stance, and he backed off.

"Let's get out of here." Dallas's voice was low as he eyed Channing's mother. "You ready, or do you need me to stand guard while you get anything else?"

Channing gulped. "I... I'm ready."

Dallas glowered at the crazy woman wielding the blunt knife, then turned on his heel and grasped his friend by the arm, heading for the front door. Dallas forced it open wide with his foot, harder than was necessary. Channing kept his arms wrapped around his bundle. Dallas strode across the lawn and flung open the back door of the Isuzu, where Channing tossed the load on the seat before rounding the back of the car.

Sputtering sobs came from the house behind them, and Channing's mother appeared on the stoop, waving a donut box. "Wait, wait, Channing!" she called through her tears, her voice suddenly helpless and high-pitched, wavery, and... *concerned*? "Here, let me give you a donut for the road! You'll be hungry!"

Oh, no. Dallas fumed. *She's not gonna play him like this.* He crossed the yard again, blocking her at the bottom step.

"I'm not letting you anywhere near him again," he snarled, one arm extended. "I'll take it to him."

Channing's mother wrinkled her nose, staring back at Dallas, and gingerly passed the box to him. "Tell him," she said in a low voice, "that I love him."

Dallas's body tightened in fury. "You don't love him," he growled. Dallas swiped the box from her hands and marched back to his waiting car.

The door slammed behind him, and hysterical wails escaped from inside the house. Dallas set his mouth in a tight line and didn't look back as he slid into the driver's seat. Channing, casting a last wistful gaze across the dull metal roof of Dallas's car, caught a glimpse of his mother's shadow through the window. He sighed and climbed into the seat. Dallas gunned the engine and, as soon as the passenger door was closed, took off. He tossed the donut box onto Channing's lap.

"Well, at least I got the last of my clothes," Channing said a minute later, "and an empty sketchbook and a few pieces of old artwork. I told her we were leaving town and didn't know if we'd be back. I'm sure I made her madder than normal, because she was almost asleep when I first went in. She hates to be woken up when she's been drinking." He sighed again. "I guess I didn't expect any different with the way she is. But I feel like I've done all I could now. Thank goodness Tommy wasn't there. He'd be glad I'm leaving, I'm sure, but it's always better to avoid him."

Dallas shivered with the remembrances of the stories Channing had told him about abuse from his mother's endless string of boyfriends.

"And hey, it's exciting to be starting a new life, away from here!" Channing smiled.

How on earth does the guy stay so cheerful? Dallas glanced in his mirror. "What else did she throw at you before the spoon?"

"Just a fork," Channing said, as if this were a common enough experience to be unremarkable. "Her aim stinks when she's drunk. The spoon was a lucky hit."

Dallas shuddered inside at Channing's downplaying of the event. *My own mother just doesn't give a crap about me, whereas his mother despises him, hurts him! But that's all over now. She won't ever hurt Channing again if I can help it.*

They drove along in silence. Channing opened the box and took out the lone stale donut, the parting gift from his mother. He took slow bites, savoring each mouthful with closed eyes. Dallas glanced over at him and frowned.

Licking his fingers after his last bite, Channing asked, "So, where are we going? I'm so excited to be out of here!"

"East, towards Kansas." Dallas pulled onto the I-80 ramp. "So long, Crap Town!" he called out the window as they left their rural birthplace behind. "Surely we can make a better life somewhere new."

"Anywhere else sounds good to me," agreed Channing with a wide grin. "We're on a real adventure!"

Dallas gritted his teeth. *He has no clue that I barely have any money. Channing's still a minor, so he'd have to go back to his mother or into foster care if she won't have him or goes completely crazy again. Taking a minor across state lines without permission is probably a criminal offense, although based on her reaction, I have permission, sort of.* He shoved that worry to the back of his mind for now.

Changing lanes, Dallas accelerated until he reached highway speed. He settled back into his seat, resting his hand on the smooth steering wheel. Trees whizzing by beat a steady rhythm in Dallas's mind. The familiar, subtle scent of gasoline in the old sedan was a comfort. The car wasn't fancy, but it was his. The Isuzu's air conditioning hadn't worked since Dallas's mother had bought the car used. The 1982 model year car was now fifteen years old, but Dallas loved it—feeling the road beneath him, the car responding to his slightest move of the wheel, the power of the engine humming in his ears. In the driver's seat, Dallas was in control.

After a few hours, Channing reached for the paint thinner. He poured it onto a rag from the glove compartment and rubbed his feet clean.

Dallas wrinkled his nose. "Hey, hang your feet out your window or something!" He shook his head. *What possessed him to paint his feet in the first place?* When Channing was struck with an idea to paint something, it was pretty much impossible to stop him. "You're a pyromaniac, and I'm a *paintomaniac*," Channing had once quipped to Dallas.

A half-hour later, Channing pulled his feet back inside the car and cranked the window up. The secondhand Airwalks were a little too big for him, but with a thick pair of socks, they fit fine. After tying them, he rummaged through the assortment of music in the old shoebox under his seat and pulled out the Deconstruction cassette tape, an obscure favorite of his. It started on the song "America" when Channing inserted it into the tape deck. "Hey, Dallas, it's your theme song!" he announced. "It's what we're doing right now!"

Now that's what I call irony. Dallas bit his lip. *I still haven't come up with a destination...*

They pulled over at a rest area and retrieved the food from the back seat. Dallas and Channing each made a sandwich from the bread and peanut butter and sat at a picnic table. Dallas stared into the jar's depths before recapping it. *This isn't going to last us long. And Channing barely took any of it, anyway.*

While Channing sat engrossed in his falling-apart copy of Tolkien's *Lord of the Rings* trilogy, Dallas opened the road atlas. *I've got to make a plan for us.* The page taunted his indecision. Dallas sighed and put his hands to his forehead.

Channing lifted his head. "You haven't marked a route yet." He lowered his eyebrows at the open atlas. "You always plan out routes for our road trips."

"That's what I'm trying to do now," Dallas said. Channing was right that he was usually better prepared than this. An old route in faded yellow highlighter jumped up at him.

Channing noticed it too and pointed. "Remember this trip? When we drove all the way to Dumas, Texas, just to deliberately mispronounce the name of it around random people there?" He bent over and picked up some pebbles from the ground.

Dallas chuckled half-heartedly and said, "Yeah, real mature of me, I know. But that wasn't exactly the *reason* for going there..."

"So why do you always like to take road trips to new places for no reason and then just leave so soon after we get there?"

"Because..." Dallas struggled to answer without admitting his serious tendency for wanderlust. "Because it's all about the journey. And, it's fun."

"'All roads lead to Rome,'" quoted Channing, "'which is one reason why many people never get there.'"

"What's *that* supposed to mean?" Dallas cocked an eyebrow.

"I'm not sure," Channing said, lining the pebbles along the table's edge. "But I think... it's about something so big that we can't get our heads wrapped around it. Like something amazingly awesome at a destination that we can't quite reach." He swept one arm wide. "We don't quite know where to begin."

"I know where the roads begin and end," Dallas responded. "I'm the driver, and I've got the road atlas, remember?"

Channing said nothing to Dallas's outward confidence.

Can he tell I have no clue what I'm doing right now? Dallas furrowed his brow and bent over the atlas again, squirming at Channing's analysis. *What am I looking for, anyway?* Dallas did not know. He only knew, he realized with a sinking heart, that upon reaching his destination, he felt let down inside, disappointed, every time. *And this time, I don't even have a final destination. But I have to make a decision.*

Back on the road after putting two gallons of the gas they'd brought from home into the tank, the scenery flew by. Channing had fallen asleep. Dallas's mind wandered. Ideas of possible jobs he could take, where they could live before he earned some money...

As they approached the state border, Dallas reached over and shook Channing.

"Wake up," he said. "Channing, wake up. We're almost in Wyoming." Channing had always insisted that Dallas wake him when they crossed a state line.

Channing sat up and watched through the window for the sign. After a few minutes, he pointed. "We're in Wyoming!" sang Channing. "Although you know," he stated matter-of-factly, "that Wyoming doesn't exist." Dallas half-listened to his friend's diatribe, knowing it by heart at this point. He accepted that Channing couldn't be talked out of his wild theory, and sometimes he almost found himself believing that Wyoming didn't exist because Channing sounded so convincing. At other times, it sounded like Channing didn't believe a word he was saying himself. Dallas just considered it to be one of his quirks.

"Have you picked where we're going?" Channing turned to Dallas.

"Yeah," Dallas responded. "We'll go through Denver. Haven't been there before." He eyed the gas gauge warily.

Channing opened the glove compartment and pulled out a box of Band-Aids. He unwrapped them one by one, sticking them to the dashboard in front of him in a geometric pattern until he'd used the last one. Then he pulled the shoebox from under his seat and inserted the Eagles cassette into the tape player. Dallas sang mindlessly along to "Hotel California" as Channing stared at the passing landscape.

Three songs in, Channing said, "I wanna go back to Florida."

Dallas groaned. Every now and then, Channing would do this.

Channing droned on about the "amazing and poetical" trip they'd taken to Florida. Dallas tried to tune him out. This always seemed to happen when they listened to the Eagles album, arousing Channing's sentiment since it had been in the tape deck during their drive through central Florida.

As the fourth song began with no letup in Channing's verbal reminiscing, Dallas smacked the steering wheel. "Dammit, Channing, would you just cut it out?" he snapped. "Stop this sentimental crap! What the hell is so special about those stupid rinky-dink towns? I know you want to go there again; you've told me a thousand times. Why can't you let it go? Just *forget* it!"

Dallas ejected the tape and hurled it over his shoulder into the back seat, wondering in the back of his mind why he was so enraged over this. *Because this time we can barely make it to Denver, let alone Florida.* Dallas pushed that thought down quickly. By now, Channing was huddled up on the seat in a little ball like a roly-poly, trembling and mumbling to himself in a steady rhythm.

Not this, groaned Dallas inwardly. He rarely shouted at Channing. Oddly, this crazy Florida obsession was one of the strange things in Channing's life that had given him stability. It was like the trip had given Channing a validation for living in his belief in a euphoric place of perfection.

Dallas kicked himself mentally. *I keep failing at being a good friend. If something this simple helps him cope with life, as quirky as it is, I shouldn't get so mad at him. He really can't help it.* He would have to apologize to Channing and yet couldn't force the words.

As dusk approached, Dallas pulled off the interstate and parked in a truck stop parking lot.

"Let's sleep here," Dallas said. "You hungry?"

Channing took a slice of cheese from the cooler and nibbled it in silence. Dallas made himself a ham and cheese sandwich. Neither spoke for a few minutes.

"I didn't mean to yell at you earlier," started Dallas. "It's just that I'm tired of being pestered about Florida over and over. You know I don't go the same place twice unless I have to."

"I know," Channing answered, staring through the windshield into the field beyond the gas pumps.

Against his judgment, Dallas asked the question he'd been pondering. "I just wonder, every time you talk about Florida… can you explain why it's so amazing to you? I just don't get it. They seemed like the same little ordinary towns you'd find anywhere."

Channing furrowed his brow. "Well, it's hard to describe, because it's just this *feeling* I had when we were there. I don't mean to pester you over it, Dallas, but something is urging me to go there. It was so far away."

"So is that it, because it's the farthest you've ever gone from home?" Dallas asked. "It's the farthest I've ever gone either, come to think of it."

"It just seems like…" Channing pursed his lips. "Well, doesn't there have to be some place out there that's completely perfect? People always seem to be searching for something—something better. There must be *something* fueling that search for perfection."

Dallas chewed his lower lip. "I don't know that there can be any perfect place, Chan. We're all just stuck in life, and a lot of times it sucks."

"But there are so many good moments too," Channing countered. "Just ordinary things, like the complexity of a flower. It seems simple, and yet the intricacy of its design and the fact that it *repeats* itself in nature, millions of times over, always in the same detailed way - the stability of that is mind-blowing! Or roaming around on drives with you. Nothing special at first glance, but there's a rhythm to the roads, the predictability of certain things along the way, the comfort of traveling for hours without saying much... There's these moments that seem close to perfection. It just makes me think one day I can find it."

"And you think it's in Florida?" Dallas raised one eyebrow. *Channing can see beauty in anything, even hick towns in the middle of nowhere.*

Channing's eyes shone. "I know it might sound crazy. We had so much fun at the ocean, but still, it wasn't perfect. Those girls there nearly ruined it for a while."

Dallas remembered their argument at the beach, how he'd nearly traded in an agreement to read Dante's *Inferno* with Channing for frivolous banter with three girls they'd just met. *He called me shallow for hoping they might be interested in me.* Channing's sarcastic taunt still rang in his ears: *"Have fun impressing them with your fire-building skills!"* Dallas had just wanted to fit in. *I thought he was being impossible. It was a punch to my gut once I realized how much it had meant to him.* Channing had been like a helpless, lonely child, one who wanted to show you some trivial thing that means the world to him... *only Channing wanted to show you Dante. Channing wanted to share spiritual thoughts and classic literature and deep conversations.* A smile twitched at Dallas's lips over the memory now. Channing was the stronger one—he was confident enough not to care what those girls thought of him. *Channing's always true to himself. And he was right about me, too. He knew I wouldn't have fun with them and would've probably made an idiot of myself.*

"Maybe Florida is just an ideal," Channing mused, breaking into Dallas's wandering thoughts. "There's just gotta be perfection out there somewhere." Channing's voice had taken on a hushed, almost reverent, tone. "I guess it wouldn't make sense for it to be in Florida, though, because it must be something *not even of this world.*"

A moment of silence passed as Channing stared through the windshield, eyes rapt. "Will we ever go back?"

"Maybe sometime," Dallas said. *No, never. You can never go back.*

But Channing smiled at Dallas and reached into the back seat for his pillow. "And we could stop at the Florida Welcome Center again for the free orange juice samples!"

Channing's thrilled with the little things in life. Dallas went around to the trunk for the blankets. He tossed one to Channing and reclined back in the driver's seat. They got comfortable, growing drowsy.

"Dallas?" With his voice muffled by the blankets, Channing sounded even younger than usual.

"Yeah?"

"I don't think it's Florida at all. I think maybe it's… *heaven.*"

Dallas was silent, squirming in his seat. He tried to push the thought away, one of many regarding Channing's growing interest in religion. The night on the beach came back to him again, after their mutual reconciliation when Dallas had listened to Channing read the beginning of *The Inferno* aloud.

"But don't worry, I won't ask you to drive us *there*," Channing added, then chuckled. "Goodnight."

Dallas cracked a grim smile and rolled over. "Goodnight, Chan."

Dallas woke late the next morning after a restless night. He had racked his brain into the wee hours of morning for a plan, but with so little money, he'd come up with nothing. Gripping the ten from his wallet, he swallowed and tried not to think about the measly six dollars remaining. Ten dollars filled the tank above the three-quarter mark, and then they drove on, heading east. *At least this car gets excellent gas mileage. We can make it to Denver,* Dallas calculated, *and then I'll have to decide what to do next. Our food won't last much longer.*

Channing had a thick book open on the pillow on his lap. Dallas glanced over at him, distracted for the moment from his worries as he observed the frail boy. Channing, his best friend, the shy little artsy kid who had slowly warmed up to him, now the 17-year-old dropout who contemplated stuff most people never thought of and retained every word he read in that brilliant camera-like mind of his… Some of the stuff he'd been quoting in the past couple years was unnerving to Dallas, and he couldn't quite put his finger on why.

He's just a heck of a lot smarter than me. Dallas settled back into the seat. *I shouldn't overthink the things he says. It's funny — Channing doesn't seem to notice how brilliant he is.* That was a subconscious relief to Dallas's guarded ego. Being so absorbed in his intellect was probably why Channing hadn't registered how bad this was.

They'd driven about three hours before pulling off at an empty, middle-of-nowhere exit for a bathroom break. Dallas strode back from the bushes and grabbed the driver's door handle, then paused. The front tire had caught his eye. Brow furrowed, he squatted down next to it.

"Shoot, I think it's losing air."

Channing rounded the front of the car and stood watching as Dallas got out the tire pressure gauge and verified that the tire was dangerously underinflated. Suspecting a slow leak, Dallas hunted for a nail and finally found it.

"I can plug the hole, but then we'll have to find a gas station where we can air it back up," Dallas said to Channing, who sat reading nearby. "Can you get the spare?"

While Dallas extracted the nail and used the tire plug kit from his toolbox, Channing wrestled with the donut tire and finally maneuvered it alongside the front of the Isuzu.

Dallas took one glance at it and discovered the tire was dry-rotted. He rolled his eyes and kicked it. "Crap! I guess I'll have to hitchhike to the next exit with a gas station." He pulled out his road atlas, grumbling when he saw the distance. *So much for making it to Denver today.*

It took over four hours before they got back on the road. Glancing at his watch, Dallas decided to drive one more hour before stopping for the night. Walking a few miles with the plugged tire before somebody had picked them up for a ride to a gas station had worn him out.

It was after six when they pulled off the interstate again.

"Go ahead if you need the restroom," Dallas told Channing. "I'm putting in that last gallon." He opened the trunk and took out a gas can, grimacing as he obstinately poured it into the tank.

When Dallas entered the building a few minutes later, Channing was out of the bathroom, rearranging cases of soft drinks stacked up in a corner.

"What're you doing?" Dallas asked.

"Building a hobbit hole," responded Channing without looking up.

When Dallas came out of the restroom, Channing had created an opening like a little room in the stack of boxes. He peeped out at Dallas.

The tattooed clerk at the counter had noticed. "Hey, make him stop," he complained to Dallas.

"Oh, he's okay," Dallas excused Channing. "He's just been cooped up in the car traveling all day. He'll put them back." Dallas handed over the toothpaste he'd selected on the way to the counter. The tube they'd brought from home was practically empty. "Where's your ice?"

The employee pointed it out to Dallas, still scrutinizing Channing as he crawled between the boxes. "He's too old to play around with stuff in stores like that. What if he knocks the whole stack over? What's *wrong* with him, anyway?"

Dallas ignored the comments and gritted his teeth. It wasn't like Channing was hurting anything.

Channing emerged from the cavern he'd built and followed Dallas to the ice. Passing the self-serve drinks, Channing said, "Look, Dallas! I love gas station cappuccinos! Can we get some? Listen, I can imitate a cappuccino machine, just like those people in the Maxwell House commercials... whoosh, whoosh..."

"Hey!" the employee called at Channing. "Fix those boxes you messed up!" He rounded the counter, stalking in their direction.

Dallas's body tensed, and he stepped into the clerk's path with a sneer.

"Put them back now, or I'll call the police!" the man snarled over Dallas's shoulder. Then to Dallas, "Is he stupid or something?"

Fury rising, Dallas shut out the rest of the store and focused on the clerk. "No, he's not, and don't you call him stupid either. Let me pay you for this stuff, and we'll be out of your way. Chan, take the hobbit hole apart. Let's get out of here." Dallas heard Channing shuffle back to the stacks of soda boxes. He brushed past the clerk to the counter and begrudgingly set down the last bill in his wallet.

Channing was trembling and mumbling a verse under his breath as he forced himself to restack the boxes of soda properly: '*O! Wanderers in the shadowed land, despair not! For though dark they stand, all woods there be must end at last, and see the open sun go past...*' Shaking, he dropped a box and collapsed to his knees beside it in defeat, covering his face with his hands. Dallas pulled Channing to his feet, murmuring reassurances while shooting cold glares at the man at the register.

Dallas grabbed his change and shouldered the bag of ice.

Channing trudged ahead of him towards the door, head down.

"Freaks," muttered the clerk as they exited the store.

Dallas dumped the ice over the milk and cheese in the cooler. They climbed into their seats, and Dallas started the engine.

Channing was silent, wringing his hands in his lap and making snuffling sounds. Once on the interstate, he finally choked out, "Everybody thinks that about me, don't they?"

"Thinks what?" asked Dallas, keeping his eyes ahead and knowing full well what Channing meant.

"Like that man in the store just now... That I'm stupid. Or a crazy freak. He said so; you heard him! Does everyone think that? Do I embarrass you?"

"No, you absolutely *don't* embarrass me," said Dallas, his voice solid as a brick wall. "I know you heaps better than that idiot does, and you're the smartest person I know. And I don't care if people call either one of us a freak—you know I don't care what people think." *Mostly,* he added to himself.

"Everyone but you thinks I'm stupid, though." Channing slumped in his seat. "Everybody back home said I was weird."

"Screw that stupid town!" Dallas spat out. "Those people are clueless. People who insult you are just stupid and ignorant, Channing."

"Oh, sure," Channing huffed with a wave of his left hand. "That's why they all think *I'm* the stupid one. I'm the dropout, remember? Before I quit, I heard the kids in my grade say I was dumb behind my back all the time. What if... what if they were right? What if the objective truth is that I'm stupid?"

Dallas exhaled. "Channing, you are *not* stupid. Say that again, and I'll slap you. Well, of course, I won't really slap you; you know that." He took another breath and breathed out long and slow. "We've been over this before." Dallas shoved away the image of a group of three particularly nasty boys who'd made it their life's mission to make Channing know just how stupid they thought he was.

"Paul and his friends were always picking on me." It was as if Channing had read Dallas's thoughts.

"I know it," Dallas answered flatly. "And I'm still never going to tell you what the little jerk said about your mural either because it was too despicable to repeat. I still wish I'd beat the crap out of him for it. That's what I meant when I said it was probably better that you quit school. I sure hope neither of us will ever see those jerks again..." Dallas bit his lip, his desperate decision tightening his stomach into painful knots.

"Dropping out didn't fix it," Channing said. "At least, not at first. They still teased me around the neighborhood. Paul always said my artwork was stupid. Remember how he tore up one when I was painting in my yard?" Channing fidgeted with his hands in his lap.

Dallas sighed. "People in that town didn't appreciate creativity in guys. But... I like your artwork, Channing." Dallas's face grew warm at the awkwardness of offering direct praise, but Channing deserved to hear it. "You've got talent. And I wish I could entertain myself like you do with all the interesting things you come up with."

Another memory of the beach hit Dallas: Channing, alone in his own world, sitting in the sand in only his boxers, an absent-minded professor executing some masterpiece he'd planned out in his mind. Channing could see something clearly, laid out as if it were already real and complete, and then set out to create it from nothing: no sketches, no plans, no measurements. It just emerged from him and came to life as he'd envisioned it. *But then those girls noticed and commented about him having no pants…* Dallas blushed at the memory. *Why did I even care that some silly girls we'd never see again thought he was weird because he forgot to put on his shorts that morning, or when he told them to their faces that the Red Hot Chili Peppers sucked? Channing was so absorbed in his sand sculpture that he didn't even think, just walked out of the tent without his pants like you might walk out of the house without your keys… And I was irritated at him for never even having to give a second thought as to where a meal was going to come from.* When Channing got going on a project, he'd be engrossed for hours, and sometimes Dallas had begrudged Channing's flighty, artsy tendencies when he was left to handle life's practical logistics. But then Dallas would look at what he'd created and be blown away, or Channing would quote some deep passage from a book…

Channing's voice broke Dallas's trance. "Still, maybe it was dumb of me to drop out of school. Always getting bad grades made it seem so pointless."

Dallas pulled off at the next exit, where an empty stretch of road led into the endless desert. He parked the car on the shoulder for the night. They sat motionless, gazing up through the windshield at stars smattered across the clear night sky.

Dallas began again. "Listen to me, Channing. Most people don't know you like I do. Those kids thought you were stupid because you're so quiet. But you're *brilliant!* I mean, from what I can tell, you knew far more than your teachers ever did. If they wouldn't answer your questions, then it's no wonder you quit trying. But you were still asking them privately inside your mind. Just because you stopped playing their game and wouldn't jump through their hoops didn't mean you were stupid! Hell, I think it proves how smart you really are! Don't know what good it did me, staying in school all the way through, not caring about anything and barely graduating. You quit during freshman year *because* you're so smart. Staying in that rat race doesn't prove intelligence. You know how much you've learned on your own… I swear, Channing, I've learned more just from you reading aloud and telling me things you've discovered than I did in all my time at school. I'm serious."

"Yeah." Channing sighed. "I guess I just fall into doubt sometimes."

"Well, when you grow up hearing you're worthless for most of your life..." Dallas gritted his teeth. Heat surged through him, thinking about Channing's past. "You know what I'd like to do to your parents, Channing. The low-life, abusive... God help me, if your old man wasn't already dead, I'd kill him myself for all he did to you when you were little. And your mother..."

"You know how messed up she is," Channing interrupted. "It's really not her fault."

"Like hell, it's not!" Dallas shot back. "She *hurt* you, Channing! Hit you and threw stuff at you! You've got a bruise from her *right now*! That's the whole point of what we're talking about here! You have a hard time believing it isn't true sometimes because she called you stupid so often!" He bit his lip, fuming, as he remembered her final words on the steps. *Yeah, right.*

"I know," admitted Channing. "But I've forgiven her. It's not her fault my father beat her so much. And it's *wrong* to hit your mother, to want to hurt her as payback." There was an edge to Channing's voice. "It's wrong, no matter what wrong things she did to me."

Dallas exhaled, trying to cool his temper. "You know I have a short fuse sometimes. I'm sorry; you know I wouldn't do anything bad to your mom. I get your point, even if I don't understand your forgiving her when she's never admitted doing anything wrong to you."

"She doesn't have to," Channing replied. "But I have to forgive her for myself. And because she's messed up — we all are."

"Some are more messed up than others, Chan," Dallas said grimly. He stared out at the flat ribbon of road stretching alongside their car and into the desert beyond.

"You're thinking of my dad too, huh?" Channing said. "And yours?"

Dallas didn't respond.

"Because..." Channing paused. "Actually, I've decided to forgive my father, too. I feel sorry for him, dying without ever changing."

"*What?*" Dallas turned, jaw dropping, and stared at Channing. "Why would you want to forgive *him*, after all he did to you and your mother?"

"How would you feel if you found out today that your dad was dead, Dallas?" Channing tilted his head, eyes clear.

"Well," began Dallas, "I guess I'd feel like it served him right. He could be dead now, for all I know. You know I've never seen him once in my entire life. So I think I'd be feeling some kind of sick glee, like, 'Good riddance.'"

"Are you more angry at him than anything?" Channing asked.

Dallas squirmed in his seat. "I don't know. Hell, I don't spend much time thinking of him at all. I hate him for bailing on my mom and me, though. He *knew* she was pregnant, and she never heard from him again. I'll probably go to my grave hating him for it. So, yeah, I'm angry. That damned son of a..." Darkness threatened to swallow Dallas whole, and he shook his head. "I don't see how you can feel sorry for your old man even a little bit."

Channing gazed at the ceiling. "There's this quote that goes, '...to discover a plan for being merciful and also severe — *that* was to anticipate a strange need of human nature.'"

"What's that mean?" Dallas asked.

"That we need to combine mercy with severity, or else we'd go insane. Which do you think is right, Dallas — pardoning unpardonable acts or loving unlovable people?"

Dallas snorted. "Neither."

"Unpardonable acts are always flat-out wrong." Channing put his feet up on the dashboard and stretched. "But you can always love a person no matter what bad things they've done."

"And just why should either of us love our 'unlovable' dads, huh?" Dallas crossed his arms across his chest. "When did they ever love us?"

"That's what made them unlovable," Channing answered. "And partly why we have to love them. But the things they did to us — the 'unpardonable acts' — were *not* okay. We can renounce them with the utmost abhorrence!" Severity flashed across Channing's generally meek face as the big words tumbled effortlessly from his tongue.

Dallas rubbed the place between his eyes. *Here he goes again on religion and morals.* "It doesn't make any sense to love your enemies after they've treated you so badly," Dallas argued.

"That's just it," Channing replied, "it *doesn't* make sense, but forgiving him has made *me* feel better." He sighed.

"Even if I could forgive him, my father is still a scumbag," Dallas said resignedly. "But it doesn't matter — it's not like I'm ever gonna meet the jerk. And we can't change the past. Gotta just move forward. Anyway, I'm sorry to have brought all that up about your parents. I don't wanna upset you. But I don't want you thinking you're stupid or weird, that's all."

"Thanks," Channing said, leaning back against the headrest. "I guess I don't mind being weird — who would want to be the same as everybody else anyway?"

"Hey, and that life-sized sandcastle you spent over half the day making that time, hollowed out so we could get inside of it - now *that* was weird, in the most awesome way possible."

"It was pretty cool, huh? That guy back in the gas station should've seen *that*," Channing said, chuckling. "Then he'd be speechless!"

They exchanged a laugh, and Dallas tossed a blanket to Channing before reaching into the back seat again for his pillow. Channing lay back, gazing through the windshield with thoughtful eyes.

"You know, I'm okay with being myself," Channing said with a little smile.

Dallas fidgeted with the dangling keys. "You really have become so much more... I don't know, carefree. Since we first became friends, I mean." *To the point that I'm almost envious.*

"And, Dallas, I have to tell you this. Your friendship — the fact that you *like* being around me just because I'm me — you've helped me a lot, even if you don't realize it. And, well, I just wanted you to know that."

There was an awkward silence as Dallas pondered this. He wasn't sure what he found so likable in Channing, but their friendship came naturally to him. He had a soft spot for Channing despite his tough exterior, and Channing had seen the real Dallas right from the start.

As they got comfortable in the reclined seats of the Isuzu, Dallas said once more to reassure himself, "Channing? Tell me you think you're amazing and brilliant."

"I'm amazing and brilliant. *Not* stupid," he answered with a drowsy yawn. "And you are too. Thanks, Dallas. This is why you're my best friend."

"Shoot, nobody's perfect." Dallas stretched out, his muscles aching. *But I'm the stupid one. What's going to happen if I can't figure out a place to settle down and get a job soon?*

Channing's voice brought Dallas back from his worries. "I'm not perfect, but at least I'm brilliant!" he said with a flourish.

A wide smile spread across Dallas's face. The simplicity of Channing's light-hearted contentedness was something Dallas treasured. *I'd do almost anything to help him keep it.*

Dallas reached over and gave Channing a jab in the side. "Goodnight, Your Brilliancy."

"Goodnight, Most Gallant Defender of Self-Esteem."
A few more suppressed laughs, and sleep descended upon the friends.

Dallas awoke to Channing's head nestled between his knee and the gear shifter. Unsure how that could be comfortable in the least, he poked Channing awake until he lifted his groggy eyelids. Dallas blinked at the late morning hour displayed on the clock—yesterday's exertion had worn him out. They stretched and jogged around outside the car, shaking out their stiff legs, breath clouding in the icy air.

They ate the last of the food they'd brought, all but one spoonful of peanut butter. Dallas didn't tell Channing that the food was gone. He finished off the milk from the jug and pressed his lips together in a thin line. *Did my mother even think of me when she left this pitiful amount of food? And my money...* It was probably several hundred bucks. Dallas kicked himself again for not opening his own bank account. *Stop thinking about it. She's gone, and that money's gone with her.*

He put the car into gear. *I just need to take care of us. Channing's too frail emotionally—I can't let him be burdened by this. He's depending on me.* Rule number one in Dallas's book for the past several years had been to protect Channing. He narrowed his eyes. *And that's what I'm gonna do, no matter what.*

Dallas had turned south. He glanced at Channing, who was drawing an elaborate design on his right forearm using a Sharpie. The day had yet to come when Channing would help navigate a road trip. Dallas had long ago discarded the idea, knowing that Channing would be too flighty to check their route. That was fine by Dallas, who liked the control of being both driver and navigator. Driving was his addiction, and spontaneous trips had satisfied his urge. *This trip feels so different, though.* He chewed his lower lip. *It is different.*

With a knot in the pit of his stomach, Dallas glanced in the back seat at the plastic crate he kept there. It had every route and town he had ever traveled to carefully filed away, even though his sense of direction made this system unnecessary. Dallas loved maps and always had. He'd once lamented his wish to Channing that maps were their own school subject. Channing had replied, "They *should* be. Geography used to be one of the major school subjects. Anyway, it's found in most everything that's important in history." Dallas hadn't questioned how Channing knew this, but he didn't doubt the facts that Channing always had spilling out of his brain, because they were almost always accurate. Now, for the first time, Dallas was drawing a blank as he tried to formulate a concrete travel plan. *I have to choose a permanent destination — I don't know how to do that.* Channing's comments from the day prior taunted his indecision.

Just north of Denver, Dallas pulled off in a diner parking lot.

"Are we eating here?" Channing's lit-up face made Dallas feel about an inch tall.

"No, I'm just checking the tire pressure." Dallas stepped out and squatted by a front wheel with the gauge.

Channing slammed his door and rounded the bumper to watch Dallas in his near-obsessive maintenance of his car.

"Ready?" Dallas asked a couple minutes later, pocketing the gauge. "Or do you need to run in for the bathroom?"

Channing squinted into the winter sun low in the sky and drew aimlessly in the dust with the toe of one shoe.

Dallas pivoted back towards the car.

"Hang on," said Channing. "I'm going to treat us to burgers and milkshakes." He motioned towards the sign, which indicated the availability of both.

Dallas almost snorted until he realized Channing wasn't joking. "With what money?"

Channing slowly pulled a twenty and a five from his pocket. "This money," he answered, eyes cast towards the ground.

Dallas stared, dumbfounded. *Channing wouldn't steal from his mother. He's too... too good. But his mother surely didn't give him that much.*

Before Dallas could ask, Channing opened his mouth to explain. "I sold something."

"What did you sell?" Dallas asked, running a list of Channing's few possessions through his mind and quickly dismissing them as worth far less than this.

"Just one of those glass rings I made," he answered with a wave of his hand. "Got forty dollars for it, but I spent some already. I hung around that gas station on the corner back home. I figured I'd try it. You kept telling me I should try selling some art, and you were right. I never have much money; you're always paying for me. So let me treat you now!" Channing's eyes were pleading.

Dallas couldn't answer at first. *Channing has money! Twenty-five bucks! Maybe we can make it stretch...*

Channing, mind made up, turned towards the restaurant.

Dallas, frozen, considered his options. *He doesn't realize I have no money*

— none! Should I tell him? Their conversation about Channing's self-doubt from last night seeped into Dallas's heart. *He wants to show he's capable… and if I ask him to save his money, then I'm gonna have to level with him about how bad off we really are.* The tug-of-war inside Dallas ended as he impulsively shut his car door. *Let him do this; you saw how eager he looks.*

"Okay, yeah, sounds great," Dallas said, jogging to catch up.

They slid into the booth after the waitress led them to one by the front windows. Only a few customers lingered over their meals in the rural diner. Dallas was ravenous now that there was an opportunity for a full meal. He considered the menu options.

The waitress came to take their orders. Dallas glanced at Channing, menu unopened, bent over a paper napkin, sketching something on it. Dallas nudged Channing's leg under the table with his foot before ordering a cheeseburger with fries. Channing said, "I'll have the same. But no ketchup, please, and extra mustard and pickles. And Cokes for us both." He returned to his drawing. Dallas opened his mouth to protest the Coke, then snapped it shut.

When their drinks came, Dallas gulped in the sugary caffeine, savoring the luxury. "Hey," he said, gaze falling on Channing's drawing, "that's me. Man, am I really that ugly?" He flashed a crooked grin.

"Ha ha," Channing said flatly, his focus still intense.

"No, it's really good. That looks like me right in this moment."

The waitress had come with their burgers. "Wow, that *does* look just like him!" she exclaimed as she set down the plates. "You're good! How can you do that?"

"I just draw what I see," Channing said, eyes still on his work as he added to one of the hands.

"And he barely even looked at me while drawing either," Dallas said with an offhanded shrug.

Channing had added the final pen strokes to the portrait. Dallas struck a pose mimicking his likeness in the sketch, eyes cast slightly to one side, hands folded in front of him on the table's surface.

The waitress laughed. "Amazing! You boys let me know if you need refills or anything." She headed back behind the counter.

"She might be worried we're going to pay her with drawings," Channing said, finally noticing his food and drink.

Dallas chuckled. "Hey, your sketches are good, Channing. Might be something to consider. I mean, you sold one of your glass rings — that's great."

Silence descended over their booth as they ate.

"Saving any room for dessert?" asked the waitress when she returned to the table a while later.

"Yes," Channing answered as he pushed back his plate, burger three-fourths eaten. "A vanilla milkshake, please. What kind do you want, Dallas?"

Dallas asked for a to-go box, hesitated, and then ordered himself a peanut butter chocolate shake. They stood with them to leave. Channing left the napkin with the drawing under a generous tip on the table.

Following Channing through the parking lot, Dallas covered his face with his free hand and grimaced. *Stupid! You let Channing spend all his money! We really could've used that.* He stared at the never-ending road before him, hollow inside. *Just forget it. What's done is done.* Dallas got in and buckled his seatbelt. *We're no worse off now than before I knew he had that money.*

"Hey, thanks for the meal," Dallas forced the words.

Channing's eyes brightened. "Sure. It was fun to eat in a restaurant. I could have sat in there for hours."

"Yeah, maybe," Dallas said as he threw a glance over his shoulder to back up. "Waitresses don't want you staying around forever, though. You can't sit doing nothing after you've finished." Dallas was antsy to get moving again.

"It's nice just to sit around and think in a new and interesting place, slowly drinking your soda or your coffee... or milkshake," Channing added, taking a sip of his.

Dallas wasn't so sure he would call the little diner interesting. Channing was a paradox sometimes. *How can somebody who's so intelligent be satisfied by such simple things? But that's why I let him spend the money,* Dallas reminded himself. *It made him happy.*

An hour later, Dallas held his breath as he watched the gas gauge needle. *Almost to Denver — but then what?* They would have to find gas money somehow. And shoplift some food if he could come up with no better way. *Think, Dallas, think!*

"It's so huge!" Channing marveled as they headed into the heart of the downtown area.

Dallas took the next exit and merged into traffic on one of the busy downtown roads, the challenge of big city driving temporarily diverting his mind from his troubles. Channing rolled down his window and hung his head out, twisting his neck to see the tops of nearby skyscrapers.

A large, ornate church came into view.

Channing's jaw dropped open. "Dallas, pull over somewhere! I wanna go inside that cathedral!" Channing was already pulling on his Airwalks.

"Really? What for?"

"To see the windows," Channing replied. "Look at all that stained glass!"

"Well, I guess we can stop." Dallas decided to indulge Channing's whim. *I'm gonna have to stop any minute now anyway, whether I want to or not.* He grimaced as he found a parallel parking spot. Channing was already halfway up the steps of the Cathedral Basilica of the Immaculate Conception by the time Dallas caught up to him. They pushed open a heavy brass door, passed several statues before going through another door, and tilted their heads to the domed ceiling soaring above them, appearing to be miles away. Several people sat in the pews, and somebody was speaking into a microphone at the ambo.

Dallas grabbed Channing's sleeve. "Come on, they're having some kind of church service," he whispered. "Let's get out of here." Dallas turned back towards the doorway.

"No, let's stay!" Channing took a step closer. "I want to listen—this might be interesting!"

Dallas sighed and rolled his eyes. "Whatever. I'm going back outside. I don't know if you're allowed to just barge in like this."

"It'll be fine," Channing said in his ear. "Anyone can sit in on a Mass in a Catholic church. I'll just slide into that back row."

"Suit yourself," Dallas hissed through his teeth, glancing around for an escape. He eased through the doors, mindful not to let them bang shut. Dallas clomped down the steps outside and sat down on the bottom one. After a few minutes, he stood again and paced the sidewalk out front. *It can't last that much longer...* Dallas checked his watch.

Gazing at the high windows from outside, Dallas pondered Channing's fascination with stained glass. Several years earlier, Channing had tried to share his excitement in front of the class when he'd noticed a connection in the science lesson. He'd spent hours observing the glass frit going from a solid to a liquid when he melted it down in his kiln, a treasure he'd claimed from the dumpster when the school's art department had gotten a new one. Channing wanted to know things, really and truly *know*, and Dallas admired him for it. Unfortunately, in school, it had only resulted in him being labeled "quirky" and "distracting to the classroom environment" by teachers and earning him groans and scorn from his peers. Channing had withdrawn into his own head and classic books, dabbling in hobbies that had set him on the path of lifelong self-education. *How did his teachers never notice how smart he was?*

A half-hour later, the ornate front doors of the basilica opened. Dallas stood on the sidewalk, hands in pockets, watching for Channing. He didn't come. As the last stragglers made their way out, Dallas sighed and climbed the steps.

The church was empty other than Channing, who seemed drawn by an invisible force up the center aisle, tiny and insignificant in the enormous space. Feeling like an intruder, Dallas slipped into one of the back pews to wait. Suddenly Channing froze, head tilted upward, and dropped to his knees with arms outstretched at either side. He stayed immobile, transfixed, then bowed his head as if in hushed reverence. Dallas pushed aside that nagging thought again that his friend was having some kind of religious experience. *He's just in awe of the impressive architecture.*

Channing rose and walked between two pews, then paused at the base of a towering window, its mosaic of light streaming down and sprinkling his face with multicolored jewels. He stretched up a hand to caress the glass.

Channing's never been inside a church with stained glass windows before, Dallas realized. *Probably he's getting ideas for some wild project he'll be able to make look amazing.* Suddenly, footsteps echoed on the marble floor.

Dallas turned towards a figure emerging from a door behind the altar. Long black robe and white collar, rosary beads clicking together from where they hung at his side... *A priest.* Dallas tensed up. *I've never set foot in a church in my life. Channing said anyone could come to a Mass, but maybe it isn't okay to just hang out afterward.*

Channing, consumed in the majesty of the windows, started when he noticed the priest's approaching footsteps. The two at once fell into conversation, motioning towards the windows, then the intricate altar and ceiling. Though the priest didn't seem upset, Dallas jolted upright and moved closer. As Dallas slinked up the side aisle, the gray-haired priest handed Channing an embellished chalice that appeared quite old. The gold gleamed in the colored light filtering through the stained glass, and Channing accepted it in his thin hands, mouth gaping and eyes wide with reverence as he held it up, admiring the glinting garnet jewels encircling the base in a simple, stately pattern. Channing squinted closely, studying the craftsmanship of the antique. Bits of their conversation floated through the air. "Germany... seventy-five windows... Italian marble... communion rail..." Dallas exhaled as he saw that Channing was somehow already at ease with this stranger, asking questions as he motioned to different windows and then about the cup he still held with delicate fingertips.

As he gazed into the chalice's golden depths, Channing changed the subject. "One of my favorite authors was a convert to Catholicism."

The priest leaned in. "Oh? Who is that?"

"G.K. Chesterton," Channing answered. "I picked up a book by him, *Orthodoxy*, out of curiosity a few years ago. He was a brilliant thinker, so logical, yet he could still wonder about the everyday things that make life miraculous."

"Are you Catholic?" asked the priest.

"No, I'm not anything," Channing said. "But I've been reading a lot about religion over the past few years. I do believe in God," he added quickly.

"Chesterton isn't an easy read," the priest replied. "Have you read any of his other books?"

Dallas hung back. Channing's animated face lit up as questions and answers about Chesterton and theology bounced back and forth between them. Dallas half-tuned out the words, awkwardly outside of their conversation, until the priest made eye contact with him and beckoned him closer. "And your friend?" he said to Channing.

"Oh, this is Dallas." Channing introduced him as if he'd just remembered Dallas was there too.

"Dallas, Father Benedict," the priest said, his hand extended. Dallas shook it. A smile filled the older man's face, a disarming air of peace in his presence. Dallas relaxed. The priest wasn't demanding they leave, nor worse—Dallas considered—trying to convert them on the spot.

Father Benedict asked a few casual questions about where they were from, then ended with, "Feel free to stay as long as you like. There are no more Masses until tomorrow, so you are welcome to look around or to sit and enjoy the silence."

They thanked the priest, Channing finally handing back the chalice with a longing gaze. Dallas sat down in a pew while Channing wandered from one window to the next. The red light of prayer candles glowing inside their glass holders flickered in contrast with Channing's pale face as he paused to peer at them. Then the priest reemerged with a thick book in his hand. Father Benedict knelt and blessed himself as he passed the altar, then spoke a moment with Channing and handed him the book. Channing tucked it under his arm, and the priest disappeared behind the altar again. Dallas stared at those flickering flames, drawn to their blaze but reluctant to go nearer, as Channing continued his self-guided tour of the basilica.

A while later, Channing slipped into the pew beside Dallas. He set the book next to him and gazed up at the vaulted ceiling. "This place is a work of art," he whispered.

"What's the book?" asked Dallas. "More Chesterton?"

"It's the *Catechism of the Catholic Church*," answered Channing. "Father Benedict said it was an extra copy I could keep."

Dallas picked up the heavy book and flipped through it, noting the tiny print and hundreds of pages with numbered paragraphs. A small rectangle of thick paper fell into his lap. It was a holy card, creased with age, of the infant Jesus on his mother's lap, a prayer printed on the back. Dallas tucked it back inside and set the book between them on the pew again.

As he stared at the tall walls and delicate patterns in the windows, Channing began to recite in a whisper,

"All are architects of Fate,
  Working in these walls of Time;
 Some with massive deeds and great,
  Some with ornaments of rhyme.
 Nothing useless is, or low;
  Each thing in its place is best;
 And what seems but idle show
  Strengthens and supports the rest."

"Who's that by?" Dallas asked. He couldn't ever remember authors and poets without Channing there to jog his memory.

"Longfellow," said Channing.

"What's it mean?"

"I don't know for sure, but this cathedral makes me think of it," answered Channing. "There's more:

 In the elder days of Art,
 Builders wrought with greatest care
 Each minute and unseen part;
 For the Gods see everywhere.
 Let us do our work as well,
  Both the unseen and the seen;

Make the house, where Gods may dwell,
Beautiful, entire, and clean.
Else our lives are incomplete,
 Standing in these walls of Time,
Broken stairways, where the feet
Stumble as they seek to climb.
Build to-day, then, strong and sure,
With a firm and ample base;
And ascending and secure
 Shall to-morrow find its place."

"So it's about a cathedral?" Dallas asked. He was never sure if he was interpreting poetry correctly.

"Not necessarily," Channing replied. "I'm thinking it's more about how our lives can compare to how architecture was done with such a noble purpose long ago. People might call this building a frivolous waste, but it glorifies God to do your very best work, and to make your life beautiful too, like a cathedral. Same with that antique chalice the priest was showing me — did you get a look at it, Dallas? It was *gorgeous!* A breathtaking work of art, made by a creator now long-forgotten, because his only purpose was to make it for *the Creator!* So, yes, it's about this cathedral, but also about so much more."

Dallas scowled. "You can think outside the box better than me."

Channing replied, "Well, Chesterton had this to say about poetry: 'To accept everything is an exercise, to understand everything a strain.'"

Dallas chewed on that for a moment. "So we're not supposed to understand everything a poet writes?"

"To try would make us insane."

The silence anchored Dallas in the pew as they took in the detail in everything. *There's so much light.* The sheer enormity of the windows let in so much from outside, and firelight from beeswax candles flickered in every nook and corner.

"I could stay here forever." Channing sighed.

"You said that about the diner we ate at yesterday," Dallas reminded him.

"I did, true," Channing said. "And I meant that, too. But this… this is different. It's so peaceful. It's like being part of a work of art, being *inside* it. You can just tell that the people who designed all of this breathed their very souls into it, desiring to glorify their God by creating such a masterpiece. You should've stayed in here during the Mass, Dallas," he added, eyes dreamy. "It was… I can't even explain it. There were bells and incense and silence… It was *other-worldly.*"

Now Channing's getting all philosophical and spiritual again. "It is a magnificent building," Dallas conceded, but his nerves were tight with uncertainty.

"And you know, I had a sudden realization," Channing said. "That *Deconstruction* song is flat-out wrong."

"Which one?" asked Dallas, taken aback at Channing's direct criticism of one of his favorite albums.

"This one." Channing hummed a few lines to give Dallas the tune. "God's not gone from a place like this — it's just that people don't appreciate old cathedrals anymore, so maybe they can't find him 'cause they aren't looking. I hope it gets full in here sometimes and not so empty and echoey. Tons more people could've fit in here during Mass."

"I dunno," Dallas said, mindlessly lifting and lowering the kneeler with his foot. "I think modern man has maybe just gotten too intelligent to believe in God. The humans who built all those huge cathedrals hundreds of years ago were more primitive than us."

"Oh, no." Channing shook his head adamantly. "Modern man isn't really smarter. More skeptical for sure. Think about it, Dallas. We know practically *nothing* compared to all that there is! Did you know that of all the matter in the entire cosmos, we only know *four percent* of the universe? We have a good idea of how big it is, and yet ninety-six percent of it is unknown to scientists, of all the thousands of stars and galaxies we've discovered! *Think* of that, Dallas! That's why I'm thinking the song is dead wrong. God's still here in these cathedrals, and maybe people of the past were able to see that more simply than us, because they didn't have all their so-called 'enlightened' information to clutter their brains, making them lose their awe for all we don't know. *Somebody* had to have made everything in the universe…"

Dallas said nothing for a moment, then asked, "So you don't agree with lyrics on one of your favorite albums? Are you gonna stop listening to *Deconstruction* now?"

"I can still listen to words I don't agree with." Channing shrugged. "I agree with some intellectual ideas and disagree with others."

"You don't think you'll be influenced by listening to something over and over that you don't think is true?" Dallas asked.

Channing shook his head. "Nope. I like the music itself enough to appreciate the art of it. And it helps me understand what other people think, even if I think they're wrong."

Dallas thought this over. "Honestly, Chan, your analysis amazes me." Dallas just sang along to songs mindlessly without fully considering their meaning.

Conversation ceased as their eyes devoured the magnificence of the cathedral, but Dallas's mind spun. He felt he was missing something. *Get out of Channing's realm and concentrate on what you're good at: reality,* Dallas chastised himself. His mind went back to their dilemma. *Except you're doing a terrible job of that lately.*

Channing broke the silence. "Too bad we can't sleep in here tonight. That'd be amazing!"

Dallas snorted. "That priest seemed friendly enough; he might let you. I don't think these hard seats would make for a restful sleep, though. My leg's falling asleep just sitting here."

"We can go if you want," Channing said. "We must've been here a long time now."

Dallas glanced at his watch and agreed. They stood to leave.

At the back of the church, Channing halted, turned, and sank to his right knee in imitation of the priest's earlier action, then the two of them passed the baptismal font and silently slipped through the door.

"That was amazing!" Channing had a faraway look in his eyes. "Those windows... so much color and light! Hey, what's wrong, Dallas?" He turned to his friend.

Dallas's face was white as he turned the key and got no response from the car. The weight of the few coins in his jeans pocket was like a cruel joke. The needle pointed to *E.* It was obvious now. They had run out of gas. Dallas closed his eyes, leaning his head on his arms against the steering wheel. *We're just gonna starve here on the streets! Maybe I should figure out how to get Channing back home to his mother, just give up, waste away by myself. It's what I deserve!*

"Dallas?" quivered Channing again.

Dallas sat up. He couldn't hide this from Channing. "We're out of gas," he admitted.

Channing pointed out the window. "There's a station right over there. We can just..."

"No, Channing, that's not it," Dallas interrupted. "I mean, we're out of gas, and... there's not enough money to buy more." He stared through the windshield, unable to look Channing in the eye as he expelled the words that wanted to stick in his throat.

"But, Dallas, why didn't you tell me before I spent that money at the restaurant? Your mom didn't leave you anything this time?"

Dallas shook his head from side to side. "I… I'm sorry, Channing. I'm failing here."

"I would've used my money to buy gas." Channing furrowed his brow as he spoke. "Why didn't you tell me?"

Dallas forced his eyes to fall on his friend's face. "I knew you really wanted to buy us a meal. I couldn't take that away from you. And I just didn't want you to know…" *And now I look like a total moron.* Dallas's ears burned.

"That shouldn't have mattered if we had no other money," Channing insisted. "I would have given you all $25 if I'd known!"

"All right; it was *stupid* of me!" Dallas shouted as he banged a fist against the dashboard, startling Channing. "I didn't want to face reality, didn't want to admit it! I *know* you'd have given me your money, but I didn't want you to have to do that." Dallas hung his head.

"We'll just have to get some money then, is all," Channing said in his innocent way. "Hey, I know! Father Benedict will loan us some!"

Dallas's eyes narrowed.

Channing continued, "No, really — churches give people money when they need it. I'll just go tell him we need gas money."

"Channing, I don't want you to have to beg," began Dallas. *And this isn't some fairy tale.*

"I don't mind!" he responded, opening the door and hopping out.

Dallas got out and called after Channing, who was already walking towards the basilica. "Channing, really…"

"Be right back!" Channing waved him off.

Dallas sighed and leaned against the side of his car. *He's so optimistic. And so trusting.* Glancing side to side, Dallas crossed the busy road to the gas station. *If he's gonna beg, I can make myself do the same.* Dallas paced at the side of the building. He'd never begged for money before. Twice he began approaching customers entering the store but lost his nerve. Spotting a discarded fast-food cup on the pavement, Dallas picked it up and sat on the curb outside the door, cheeks pink as he avoided eye contact with customers passing his outstretched hand and grasping the empty cup.

Ten minutes passed. Then the Texaco door whooshed open behind Dallas.

"Hey, you can't beg here," the clerk boomed down at him.

Dallas jumped to his feet and backed away, muscles tense.

"Beat it!" yelled the man. Dallas trotted off, hands in pockets and head bowed.

That was humiliating! Dallas's cheeks still burned as he crossed the road. Channing was heading back towards the car, his gait light and dreamy. Dallas trudged towards him. Meeting his eyes, Channing flashed him a grin and held up a green bill.

Dallas's mouth dropped open as relief washed over him. "How'd you do it?"

"I found the priest and told him we needed gas money," Channing answered. "He tried to give me more, but I didn't want to be greedy. I did the math, and this is just enough." He extended his hand to expose a ten, a five, and two ones.

Dallas wrinkled his nose at the strange amount. "Seventeen dollars? Why not an even number?"

"I didn't want to take more than needed to fill up the tank," Channing said. "That wouldn't be right. This will just do it."

"How do you know?" Dallas asked. Channing had never once in his life pumped gas into Dallas's car—or any car.

"I saw the price per gallon." Channing motioned towards the sign across the road. "Your tank holds 13.7 gallons." He placed the money into Dallas's hand, beaming.

"How do you even… never mind; let's just take a gas can to get enough to start the engine first." Dallas unlocked his trunk as Channing came alongside him.

"It says in the car manual how much the tank holds," Channing continued. "I read it once, a few years ago." He relayed this information as if it were the most normal thing in the world to read car manuals and memorize the fuel capacity.

They crossed the road. Dallas turned towards the Citgo further down the street. The same price was displayed on its sign as the station in front of them.

"What's wrong with this one?" Channing asked, pointing at the Texaco.

"I'd rather go to the next one down," Dallas said, eyes on the sidewalk in front of him. Channing shrugged and jaunted alongside his friend.

After filling the can and paying for the two gallons, Dallas and Channing went back to the car, where Dallas emptied it into the tank. The engine roared to life at Dallas's command. He drove back to the

Citgo and finished filling the tank. Channing had been correct — the total spent on gas was just under $17. Over this hurdle, Dallas sank back into the driver's seat as they pulled back out on the road.

"Thanks," Dallas conceded.

"Sure," answered Channing.

Dallas's mouth was tight. Channing was more capable than he gave him credit for sometimes. *But we're still broke.* Dallas sighed. For somebody so shy, he was shocked with how Channing could suddenly take action. *He's sure grown up in the last couple of years. But to only ask for the exact amount…* Channing's moral compass was very exacting. *Of course, he wouldn't take more than he thought we needed. He doesn't know our food's completely gone. Because I haven't told him.* Dallas's conscience waged war with itself inside him. The instinct to shield Channing from their problems weighed on his soul. But something would have to give sooner or later.

Cruising along the interstate just east of Denver, Channing settled in with a notebook and Sharpies, lost in his own world. Dallas chewed his lip in serious consideration. His only viable idea for getting them some food disgusted him. *And I thought life was hard before. How clueless I was. I don't really know anything.*

Dallas's stomach was clenched in knots with the knowledge of his decision. He stared himself down in the rear-view mirror. *I take matters into my own hands when needed.* With his chest growing tight, he knew what he was about to do wasn't right. But he was responsible for Channing. It wasn't his fault his mother had left him with nothing.

TENSION

Dallas had ignored his creeping hunger pangs all the next day. They had finished off the last of Channing's leftover burger for breakfast, and Dallas had even pulled over to spend several hours wandering around a flea market to get his mind off food. Channing closed the cover of his sketchbook as his stomach rumbled. "I'm kinda hungry," he commented.

It's time. Dallas pulled into a Shell station and parked near the exit of the lot. He scanned the windows of the store, assessing the layout of the aisles. It seemed like a good location for the deed he was about to do.

"Stay here, and I'll be right back," Dallas said, voice nonchalant. Inside, his stomach did backflips, and his heart hammered in his chest. Dallas channeled his contempt over his mother's abrupt exit into a strong resolve as he shut the car door behind him. *It's her fault I have to do this.*

He entered the convenience store, eyes down to avoid the face of the clerk. One customer was inside. Dallas meandered to the back aisle and stuffed a package of crackers, a couple granola bars, and pre-packaged sandwiches into his jacket. Then he checked the beverage section. *No Josta — perfect.* He glanced furtively at the customer at the counter. *Stupid,* he criticized himself. *Should've picked a gas station that had only one car parked at it.* Dallas hesitated, quivering at his actions and doing his best to hide it under a confident exterior.

As the other customer left, Dallas's eyes darted up towards the counter. He took a deep breath. "Do you have any Josta?" he called.

"Any what?" said the cashier.

"Josta," Dallas repeated. "It's a soda made by Pepsi."

"Nah, we don't carry many of them specialty kinds of pop," she replied.

"Do you know of anyplace else that might have it?" Dallas asked, swallowing down the nervousness in his voice as he edged towards the door.

"No gas stations 'round here carry much of a different variety," answered the clerk.

"Thanks anyway," replied Dallas, and he pushed open the door, the food tucked out of sight.

When he got to the car, Channing was gone.

Dallas mumbled a curse under his breath. A panicky sickness crept into his gut, and his body screamed at him to flee, to get out of there with the stolen goods, but where was Channing? He tossed the food into the passenger seat after a worried glance back at the store, then slammed the car door. He scanned the area, pulse quickening and tingles running down his spine, and finally pinpointed Channing creeping around in the tall grass near the interstate on-ramp.

"Channing!" shouted Dallas. Channing gave no reply.

"Channing!" Dallas trotted towards him. "Hey, let's go!"

Channing stole silently through the grass, then paused and squatted down.

"CHANNING!" bellowed Dallas. His eyes darted over his shoulder again at the entrance to the convenience store. *I'm so bad at this!*

Channing stood up, holding something. Dallas motioned to him with rapid hand movements, and Channing ambled over to the car. Dallas felt tingles like jolts of electricity shooting under his skin in his agitation to leave.

"We gotta go," he said, going for the driver's seat.

"Look what I found," said Channing.

"What?" Dallas huffed, turning back to look.

"It's a kitten." Channing showed him. "It's so scrawny, probably homeless, and it might get run over on the interstate. Let's bring it with us!"

"No way," said Dallas, "we can barely feed ourselves. Put it down, and let's go!"

"But it's so soft and precious!" Channing exclaimed. "And it likes me. Listen, it's purring!"

The tabby was snuggled up against Channing's chest as he cradled it in his arms. It mewed in a high-pitched squeak and then bit at Channing's finger in play as he giggled, beaming down at it.

"It looks friendly, but now's not the time." Dallas's fingers were poised on the car door handle. "We can't afford to feed it. It'll be better off on its own."

"I suppose you're right." Channing sighed. He turned and went around the car, heading back towards the store.

"Where are you going?!" hissed Dallas, wild-eyed.

"To put it over there by the trees, so it will at least be away from the road," Channing answered. "Why, what's wrong, Dallas?" He studied Dallas's panicky face with a furrowed brow.

"Just do it quick," Dallas ordered. Internally, he wanted to grab Channing by the shoulders and fling him into the car after punting the darn cat across the parking lot, but he managed to control himself. *Just breathe. Don't act like a fool and attract attention. And remember, you don't want to burden Channing. Play it cool.*

Channing set the kitten between the building and the woods before climbing into the car. Dallas had the engine running already, and he eased the car out, breath held. Once on the interstate, the tension slackened from his jaw. *That could've been too close.*

Channing was examining the stolen goods he'd pushed aside when he'd climbed in. "How'd you buy all this food?" he asked Dallas.

"Oh, we had a tiny bit of money left," Dallas said, wincing internally. It wasn't fully a lie; he did have a few coins in his pocket.

They got off the interstate at a rural highway and headed south, then pulled off on a dirt road. Dallas surveyed the wooded area. No buildings were visible, so he parked under a few trees beside a small clearing.

"Can we camp?" Channing asked.

"It's too cold," responded Dallas, "but we can have a picnic dinner if you want." He forced a light-hearted attitude for Channing's benefit.

Channing got the crackers and sandwiches from the car. They shared the last of a two-liter bottle of Coke that Dallas had brought from home. It was flat and syrupy.

After dinner, Dallas lay back on the blanket, formulating how they'd get food the next day. The granola bars would be breakfast. *Maybe we can fish — there's a rod in the trunk. Anything but having to steal long-term...* Once they settled down somewhere, it would still be a challenge to find employment without having a home address — another thing Dallas hadn't considered before leaving but that had entered his mind during the drive. *There's a lot of things I didn't think of.*

As the sun set, Channing opened the back door to the Isuzu and rummaged through the back seat for a worn-out pair of sneakers. They were a pair found in Dallas's closet a few weeks previous, and Channing had asked if he could have them. From the glove compartment, he pulled a box of small nails. Without a word, Channing went to work on the shoes. Dallas glanced over at him, thought about asking why he was further destroying the shoes, then bit his lip and kept quiet instead.

"Finished!" Channing announced a short time later.

"What are they?" Dallas questioned, one eyebrow cocked. "Murder shoes?" The soles of both sneakers had the sharp ends of nails protruding from them in various places.

"They're like Curdie's shoes, from *The Princess and the Goblin!*"

Channing explained. "Don't you remember when I read it to you?"

Dallas recalled the name of one of Channing's favorite fantasy novels but had forgotten until now about the shoes the hero had used to help him to defeat the goblins.

"How are you gonna walk in those?" Dallas asked.

Channing shrugged his shoulders. "It'll probably just be like walking in soccer cleats, right?"

"Dunno. I've never walked around in soccer cleats," Dallas responded.

"Me neither," Channing acknowledged. He tried the shoes on, wiggling his toes and making slight adjustments to a few nails. Satisfied, he took them off and placed them on the floorboard behind the passenger seat.

Channing climbed into the front seat and curled up. Dallas bedded down as well, tossing and shifting restlessly, still uneasy from his shoplifting episode. It was late before his nerves settled, and he succumbed to sleep.

Dallas drove in the early morning light while Channing slumbered on. Jolting Dallas from the monotony, an odd noise banged from under the car hood. Channing startled awake. Dallas watched as the Isuzu's temperature gauge rose steadily.

Cursing and banging his fist against the steering wheel, Dallas pulled over on the shoulder of the road and got out. Channing stepped out on his side and stretched. An object glittered in the dust at his feet, and Channing leaned down to pick it up.

"Hey, Dallas, look — a quarter!" he exclaimed, holding it up.

"Good; we'll need some more food," Dallas said from under the hood, where he was already trying to diagnose the problem. "Grab a granola bar for yourself and then — look, that sign says it's a mile to Plainville. I'm gonna work on this. I'm pretty sure it was the fan belt, and thankfully I have an extra one in the trunk. Take the quarter, and maybe combined with this bit of change, you can buy some food — go in a grocery store and ask for stuff they had to take off the shelves; you know, food they couldn't sell by a certain date — expired bread, stuff like that. Get the most food you can with this." Dallas dropped the three dimes and a penny from his pocket into Channing's outstretched palm. Channing started down the road, whistling, and Dallas blew out a breath. Channing still hadn't asked about their food supply from home.

Channing hadn't been gone half an hour when a vehicle's engine rumbled behind Dallas. He'd lost himself in the repair work. Tires crunching on gravel announced the other car slowing close behind him, and he threw a glance backward.

Dallas froze. *A police car.*

He looked at the discarded stolen granola bar wrapper at his feet and cursed himself. *I can't even hide the evidence. And I'm littering.*

As the door of the police car opened, Dallas stiffened and kept his eyes on the job in front of him. He was certain the officer would be able to hear his heart pounding in his chest. Dallas gripped the wrench in his hand tightly, instinct egging on his fight-or-flight reaction, but his rational brain reminded him to keep his cool. *Just wait to see what he wants. Don't be stupid.*

The boots of the policeman clomped on the asphalt along the shoulder of the highway. "Having some trouble?" he asked, halting five feet from where Dallas stood.

"Uh, a little bit." Dallas tried to keep his voice steady. "Just a busted fan belt, but I can fix it." He glanced at the officer for a split second and then pulled his eyes away again.

The officer stepped closer and peered under the hood alongside Dallas. His left boot touched the shiny red granola bar wrapper, blazing like a huge flare in Dallas's guilt-ridden mind. *The clerk didn't see you take it,* rational brain spoke again. *She didn't notice two missing granola bars and send the cops after you. Calm down.*

"Need any help?" asked the man. "I'm not too handy myself, but I can call somebody for you."

"No, thanks. I've done this job before." Dallas turned back to his work, the automatic natural motions of his hands the only thing covering his internal storm.

"All right. Just wanted to be sure you were okay," the officer said as he turned to go. Then he paused. "You traveling all alone?"

Dallas bit his lip and lied. "Yep."

He waited for the officer to ask him more, brain fumbling for the made-up responses he'd not rehearsed. *Where am I from, where am I going... Surely he saw my Nevada tag already. Don't tell an obvious lie and arouse suspicion.*

But the officer only called over his shoulder, "Good luck. Find a phone and call 911 if it ends up you can't fix it, and we'll send a tow truck out."

Dallas mumbled a thank you and kept his eyes on his work. As the police car's engine roared to life, Dallas held his breath. Only when the car was down the road did he let it out, gripping the Isuzu's bumper with both hands, body convulsing with shudders. He gulped in deeply a few times, then told himself to man up and finish the belt job. The flashy red wrapper taunted him between his boots. Dallas snatched it and, taking the wrappers from last night's stolen sandwiches out of the front seat floorboard, he made a small pile of garbage at the side of the road and burned it. He watched it turn slowly to ash, melting plastic shrinking and graying under the power of the flame, emitting a disgusting stench. Then Dallas scuffed the pile of ash under the heel of his boot, scattering and spreading it into bits until he was satisfied the evidence was gone. Turning back to his car, Dallas steeled his will to get back to work. *Channing will be back soon, and he's depending on you. Don't let him down.*

Channing returned to the car three hours later.

"Where have you been?" Dallas cried. "I was about to come after you!"

Channing stared blankly, apparently oblivious to the passage of time.

"So, what took you so long? Was it hard to find a grocery store?"

"I found it, yeah," Channing began, "but first, I noticed that the library was having a used book sale — a bag of books for a quarter, can you believe it? I guess I stayed there longer than I thought. But, Dallas, the guy working there had read Nietzsche, and we had a friendly debate about..."

"Oh, no," groaned Dallas. "Don't tell me you wasted the last of our money on *books* when we have no food left?"

"No, I used *my* money on books," Channing answered. "It was my quarter 'cause I'm the one who found it."

"Channing!" exploded Dallas. He gave the nearby toolbox an impulsive kick, rattling the metal tools inside. "How could you throw our money away on some stupid books?! You already have tons of them! We can't eat *books!*"

"I *did* buy food," Channing said in a hurt tone. "I got two loaves of old bread, tortilla chips, cookies, and fruit punch, all for twenty-five cents, expired stuff, by doing just what you told me to do." He dropped the bags of food at Dallas's feet. "Here's your change." Channing plunked six cents on the roof of the car next to him and turned away.

Dallas rummaged through the bags. "You know, you could've gotten double this much food if you hadn't wasted that quarter on *books!*" he said in disgust.

"I don't want any of the food!" cried Channing, voice rising. "Eat it all, you jerk! If you really cared about me, then you'd stop treating me like I'm an idiot! You didn't even tell me all our food from home was gone! And after you just told me the other night that you don't think I'm stupid!"

"Channing…" Dallas averted his eyes and stared sullenly into the field to the side of the road.

Channing broke the silent tension. "Sorry," he quavered, fervor dying from his eyes. "I should've only bought food. But I was serious that you can eat it all. It's my fault if we starve, so at least you'll be better off."

"That's bull; I'm not gonna let you starve." Dallas sighed. He opened a loaf of bread and took out the heel, Channing's favorite. "Here." Channing hesitated, then accepted the bread.

"I'm sorry," Channing said again, eyes on the ground. "I shouldn't have said that a minute ago."

"Hey, I'm sorry too," Dallas put in, swallowing his pride. "I shouldn't have yelled at you. And I should've been upfront with you about our food situation."

"I get it; you're just trying to get us through this…" Channing's tight voice trailed off. He was crouched near the ground, arms wrapped around his knees to quell the involuntary shaking. The familiar recurring position reminded Dallas of Channing's damage from his past abuse. *I put too much responsibility on him,* he admonished himself. *And I guess he can't help it that the smell of old ink is practically a drug to him.*

"So hey." Dallas forced a light mood. "What books did you get, anyway?"

The brightness returned to Channing's face as he described what each book was about. Calculus, child development, ancient civilizations… The one he expressed the most enthusiasm for was called *Mere Christianity*.

"I've been hoping to find a copy of it," Channing explained. "But the guy working at the book sale was really critical of Christianity. He was trying to get me to buy this other book, *Beyond Good and Evil*, telling me how Nietzsche was such a 'free thinker.' I read that book, Dallas, like three years ago. I told this guy that Nietzsche was pretty misguided. I told him, 'If the whole world exists in ever-changing chaos, with nothing defined as being true, then what's the point, even?' It's not freedom to never define anything as right or wrong — it's just unsettling."

More religious diatribes. Dallas rubbed his temples and decided to hold his tongue as Channing continued his enthusiastic recounting of the conversation at the library. Dallas heard him but tuned out his meaning. *Maybe it's better that Channing has something else to occupy his deep thoughts, though, so he doesn't have to deal with the reality of what's happening to us.*

Dallas drowned his stress under the hood while Channing sat in the grass, indulging in his book. In the late afternoon, they both had some fruit punch and cookies.

"It's gonna take me just a little longer to fix this," Dallas announced. "Find us somewhere nearby to stop for the night." He threw the Rand McNally Road Atlas towards Channing. It smacked him squarely on the head.

"Ow." Channing rubbed the spot where the atlas had hit him, eyes never leaving the page of his book.

"Sometime before I finish, okay, Channing?"

"Okie dokie," Channing murmured.

When the repair was complete, Dallas put everything away. He mopped the sweat from his brow with his sleeve, relieved it had been something he could fix without having to buy parts. *At least I did one thing right.* He inhaled, chest inflated with a satisfied breath. "Okay, where are we gonna sleep tonight?" he asked, wiping the grease from his hands with a rag.

Channing, at the end of his book, put a finger to his lips.

"Earth to Channing!" Dallas ignored the call for silence. "Haven't you even looked at the map?"

"Shhhhh." Channing's eyes were glued to the book. Dallas folded his arms across his chest and watched him turn the page. Channing's face was lit up as he consumed the words. When he closed the book a moment later, the color and liveliness left his face as he lifted his chin and blinked at the real world. But as his eyes met Dallas's, he smiled with a contented sigh.

"Did you read that whole book?"

"Yes." Channing nodded, setting *Mere Christianity* aside. "You should read it, too. I think you'd…"

"I don't have time," Dallas interrupted with a wave of the hand. "I wish I could read as fast as you, but I'm not that smart. I barely skated through with my diploma. Lot of good it's doing me now."

Channing's eyes flashed. "You *are* smart," he said. "You just fixed the car—I could never do that. I can't even drive! And you're always thinking ahead, planning things. Here, I'll find a place for us to stop for the night now." He picked up the atlas and perused the nearby roads.

"Yep, with your intelligence and my practicality, we should be able to conquer the world!" Dallas joked. Inside he wilted. *And yet we have no home, no source of income, and now I'm a thief... I have got to figure something out for us.* Dallas burned with shame that Channing thought so highly of his life skills and common sense when he was, in truth, just barely holding it together for them. He scrutinized his filthy hands, aware that he and Channing hadn't showered in several days. *Once I decide where we should go, who would even hire me looking — and smelling — like this?*

"How about here?" Channing asked, holding up the map and pointing to an empty stretch of highway east of the next small town.

"Looks fine; let's go," Dallas answered.

The car ran smoothly again, and they pulled off the road for the night at a boarded-up gas station. Dallas drove around to the back side of the building alongside some overgrown bushes and killed the engine. In the last light of dusk, Dallas pored over the road atlas, trying to plan their route for the next few days. Channing pulled all his books out of the trunk and dropped them on the ground. Then he searched the back seat for a few more and squatted to organize the pile.

"Good thing we've never cleaned out the car," Channing said. "Look, Dallas, I found your library card."

"Mm-hm," said Dallas in a flat tone, eyes still on the road atlas.

Channing put all the books neatly into a cardboard box. Then he alphabetized the cassette tapes in the shoebox. While retrieving stray tapes from between the seats, Channing discovered his missing t-shirt from the Flying J Truck Stop.

"Look, Dallas!" he exclaimed, waving the shirt in the air. "I wonder if my Pilot truck stop hat is under here, too?" Channing pulled the t-shirt over his mustard-colored long-sleeved shirt.

"Probably," Dallas returned without looking up. "Everything's in this car." *It's only a slight exaggeration.* At least they had the car and everything inside it. There was a bit of consolation in Dallas's possession of the Isuzu.

Channing flopped down on the dirt beside Dallas and began tracing the Flying J logo in the dust in front of him. "When I own a truck stop one day," Channing fantasized, "we'll never have to worry about money again..."

Dallas glanced sideways at his friend and internally shook his head at another of Channing's oddities. *I don't get why he's so fascinated by truck stops.* Dallas recalled the time Channing had used the "professional truckers only" restrooms in the Petro station: he'd thought it was hilarious that he'd broken the rules by going into that bathroom.

As the still-unmarked route stared up at him from the atlas spread open in his lap, Dallas wrestled with the sinking sensation of having made a big mistake. *Why did I just start driving, anyway? Why not have stayed back in Nevada and tried to find a job there? We could've lived in the woods, camping, while I earned some money… No, it would've been too cold for that for a few months still. Or maybe we could've slept in the car there. But that town was so terrible. It would have sucked the life out of both of us if we'd stayed.* Still, how was this better? Dallas didn't want to have to resort to stealing food indefinitely. *We have to go south,* he decided. *Where it's warmer. Then we can camp, at least. Still not sure how I can be presentable enough to get a job.* Dallas reached up to touch his chin and the scraggly stubble of a beard that had been growing there. Remembering Channing's truck stop experience again, he thought maybe they could slip into one to use the truckers' showers there.

Stomach growling, Dallas retrieved the practically empty peanut butter jar. He poured the fruit punch into two cups.

"Want a skimpy peanut butter sandwich, Chan?"

"Is it crunchy peanut butter?" Channing asked, trotting over to Dallas.

"No, it's the last of what we brought from my house," Dallas replied, "creamy. You know I hate crunchy peanut butter. But if it was all we had," Dallas added, "then I'd eat it."

"I love crunchy," said Channing. "I wish we still had some cheese so I could make a cheese and mustard sandwich."

"Do you want peanut butter or not? I'm asking because there's maybe one spoonful left between the two of us, so we can each have a bit if you want." Dallas frowned, arms crossed as he waited for an answer.

"I'm not hungry right now," said Channing.

"You have to eat: you're borderline malnourished as it is." Dallas shoved the bag of bread at Channing, who hesitated and then selected two pieces of bread. Dallas passed him the peanut butter.

"Where's the mustard?" asked Channing.

"In the glove compartment," Dallas sighed.

They sat together on the still-warm hood of the Isuzu. Dallas was halfway finished with his sandwich by the time Channing had created his. One slice of bread, the heel, was slathered in mustard and folded in half. On the other piece, Channing spread the last of the peanut butter with his fingers. Then he alternated sandwiches with every bite, settling on only the mustard sandwich and leaving the other half-eaten on the roof behind him. Dallas finished it off for him and was still hungry.

As the sun went down, the temperature dropped drastically. Channing got his gray and maroon shirt and pulled it over his first two layers. He rejoined Dallas on the hood.

"I love this shirt," Channing said, pulling the cuffs over his hands. "It's so soft and cozy."

Dallas stared straight ahead and made no reply.

Channing spoke again. "How are we gonna get money, Dallas? Should we both get jobs somewhere? I could maybe sell more artwork if I make some things once we settle somewhere. We can't really earn money if we're driving from place to place."

"I know," Dallas answered. "We're looking for a good place now. We're gonna head south, where it's warmer, so we can camp until we can afford a place to live. I've been kicking myself for not being more responsible," he admitted, letting his guard down. "I mean, I should've gotten a regular job right after graduation, instead of piddling away my time these months since. More than half a year... I don't know what's wrong with me."

"You had a job," Channing reminded him. "At the car parts place."

Dallas remembered, and his voice lost its power. "Yeah, I should've kept that up." He'd taken the job late summer following his high school graduation but quit because he'd gotten bored with just working the register. "It was stupid of me to quit. If I'd kept that job — or gotten another steady one instead of wasting the past several months — then we could've stayed in Nevada. I could have earned some more money, and we'd be ahead of where we are now. Maybe." *Then again, I'd have probably trusted my mom with any money I would've made, meaning I'd be in the same place I am now, not being able to get my hands on any of it. What really happened to her? Should I try to find her? But I'm in no place to help her myself...*

Dallas paused, unsure of how much he should tell Channing. But the weight of this was something he couldn't bear alone, and Channing knew their dire situation now. "I guess as strained as our relationship was, I never expected my mom to just... *drop* me totally like she did. I wonder if she's in trouble somehow, maybe having to do with owing somebody money. But even if we had no house being paid for anymore, at least I'd still have a job..." Dallas's voice trailed off.

"I'm really glad we left," Channing said.

"Even if it was a boneheaded thing for me to do?" Dallas asked. "I just can't seem to settle down and be content."

"So many bad things happened to me in that town," Channing said. "Out here on the road, with you, I feel so… *free.*"

Dallas felt heat surging up inside him and quelled it by gritting his teeth. Because of the trauma of Channing's past, his holding a long-term job would be nearly impossible. Dallas was overwhelmed by his obligation to take care of him. *And I'm failing.*

Channing's chattering teeth prompted Dallas to notice his own numbness from the cold. They got in the car to go to sleep. Channing was out like a light the second he curled up on the seat. Dallas gently tucked a few blankets around Channing, then got the last one for himself.

"I think I hear it," Channing said, ear pressed against the smooth steel.

Dallas crouched beside him, laying his head along the track. "Yep," he agreed, the distant rumble reverberating deep inside his ear. "Still a ways off."

Channing squinted into the sun and swept his hair back out of his eyes, peering at where the track curved out of sight. "Wanna run alongside it?"

An approaching whistle sounded. Dallas stood with legs spread, one foot on each rail. One dirty shoelace hung untied, ends fraying. "Let's wait on the tracks as long as we can instead. And then jump off when it's getting close."

Channing's eyes widened. "*How* close?"

"Not too close." Dallas shrugged. "Don't wanna totally scare the engineer. Come on." Dallas turned and trotted down the track, keeping between the two parallel rails, gravel crunching beneath his shoes. Channing followed.

About fifty feet down, Dallas paused. "Okay, when the train hits that spot where we just were, we'll jump off to the left."

"And feel the breeze while the train roars right past us!" shouted Channing, eyes alive as he spun in circles.

Dallas was back on the ground, ear to the rail again. "It's getting close." Brushing the dust from his knees, he stood alongside the slight boy in the too-big shirt. Channing coughed and wiped his nose with the back of his hand, face alert and eager.

As they waited, they heard the faint rumbling and then the whistle blowing louder.

"Ready?" Dallas asked, and Channing nodded vigorously with a small gulp, tucking a thick strand of his mop of hair behind one ear and straining his eyes down the track.

The engine burst into view as it rounded the bend, rushing along the steel, barreling towards them. Dallas's body tensed, poised and ready to spring into action. Channing clutched Dallas's sleeve, not wanting to be out of sync with his best friend's movements. Their breath caught in their throats from the adrenaline as the powerful train blew its shrill whistle again, angry now, as they taunted it in what appeared to be a game of chicken.

Channing's fingers gripped Dallas's upper arm, and he nudged him, but Dallas stood firm, not budging from his stance.

"Now!" Dallas yelled a few seconds later, and he pulled to the left, but Channing's death grip stopped him.

Wide-eyed with combined thrill and downright fear, it was now Channing who stood immovable.

Dallas yanked him into action. One foot stumbling over the rail, Channing tripped after him, and both boys cleared the track, the train whistle screaming a warning at them. They turned and stared at its approach, a full twenty feet away but then immediately alongside them, the forceful whoosh of air nearly knocking them back as they stood exhilarated. The train passed by at a mere six feet's distance.

Channing spread his arms wide and closed his eyes, the wind whipping his hair, chin tilted up with a smile at the terror they had just faced. Dallas set his mouth in a straight line and crossed his arms over his chest, letting himself feel dizzy as his eyes tried to focus on each distinct car as it snapped past, inhaling diesel fumes.

The end of the train roared by and left a deafening silence in the surrounding air, the rumbling growing faint again. The boys stood motionless, staring after it until it disappeared far down the arrow-straight tracks.

Channing took off running behind, then halted and left the tracks to squat down in some nearby weeds. He pulled out a green glass jug, beaming, and returned to the track to wait.

Dallas approached, balancing on one rail with his hands in his pockets.

"Look, Dallas!" Channing lifted the jug high. The green color caught the light from the low setting sun, flashing across his face as he peered through it. "This color is perfect for my stained glass dragon window," he commented, waiting for Dallas's approval.

"Good finds today," Dallas said, pausing beside him. He reached into his back pocket and withdrew a small blue bottle Channing had picked up earlier.

"Yeah, such a brilliant blue—a perfect sky color!" Channing held the green jug beside the sparkling blue glass, brow furrowed. Dallas watched the gears turning in Channing's mind and then jammed the bottle back into his pocket.

They headed towards town, Channing bobbing along with the jug under one arm and Dallas following with a more reserved stride. Channing absently rubbed a swollen, bruised, crudely splinted right-hand pinkie. Dallas fantasized of all the vengeful things he'd like to do to Channing's mother and her boyfriend for it. He tried to push away the mental image of Channing, terrified and struggling to escape. *And just because he ate the last Pop-Tart!*

The thump of a rock landing nearby broke their contemplative single-file two-man parade. It had nearly hit Channing in the leg. Jeering laughter shattered the dead air, and Dallas pinpointed its source up the nearby embankment.

Three boys howled with laughter. One held another rock, poised to hurl it towards them.

Channing slipped behind Dallas, who sneered and took a swaggering step towards the boys. *Annoying little twerps.*

"The one with the rock, that's Jake," Channing said in a low voice. "And Paul and Brendan. They're the ones..."

"I remember," Dallas interrupted gruffly. "Those jerks are about to find out what they get when they mess with me!"

"Hey, big shot, get out of the way!" yelled Paul. "It's the pansy we're aimin' at, not you! Why don't you beat it and hang out with somebody your own age?"

Dallas crossed his arms over his chest and widened his stance, eyebrows lowered, daring them to try it again. He wasn't about to hand a sheep over to the slaughter.

Jake drew his arm back and let the rock fly. Realizing it was a perfect aim, Dallas flinched to the side and braced himself for the impact. The rock hit his upper arm, hard. Channing yelped.

The three high-fived, congratulating Jake on his hit.

Dallas stalked towards the group.

"Loser," Paul called, "guess you hang out with babies since you're so stupid you got held back a year!" It was true—Dallas had failed the seventh grade and had had to repeat it. "And you picked the wimpiest baby of all!" added Paul.

That's it. With a snarl, Dallas rushed up the incline and was on Paul in an instant, knocking him flat on his back.

Before either Paul's friends or Channing could react, Dallas and Paul were rolling down the embankment, a flurry of wild arms and legs, towards where Channing still stood. Dallas came out on top and pinned Paul to the ground and got in a few punches, tasting warm blood from the hit he'd received in the mouth as they struggled.

Jake and Brendan scrambled down the slope after the fighting boys.

Brendan grabbed Dallas by the back of his shirt and tried to pull him off. Jake kicked Dallas in the legs.

"Stop it!" cried Channing. Jake turned and shoved Channing hard in the chest. Channing stumbled backward, falling over the rail behind him. The green jug hit the ground with a crash.

Dallas's fury went wild at the sound. As he slugged a punch to Paul's eye, Jake shouted, "Let's get him like this — move, Brendan!" Dallas felt sudden sharp blows of rocks smacking his back, one after the other. He jumped off Paul as Jake and Brendan grabbed more rocks. Dallas dodged their next throws.

"You wanna fight dirty?" Dallas taunted them. "*Now* who's the pansies, huh? Hafta throw rocks instead of fighting like men?" He spit out a mouthful of blood-infused saliva. With gritted teeth, Dallas lunged at Brendan and rammed him in the legs, toppling him. Jake punched Dallas in the side and knocked the wind out of him, allowing Brendan to regain his feet, grab Dallas, and shove him onto his back. Dallas lay pinned with one boy holding each flailing arm as they knelt alongside him.

"Come and get him, Paul!" crowed Jake with sick delight. "We'll hold him while you beat the crap out of him!"

Dallas struggled to turn his head towards Paul, who was yanking Channing off the ground. Channing flailed his arms to get loose and took an elbow from Paul in the face.

"You bastard!" Dallas hurled the insult at Paul. "Why can't you just *leave him alone?*" Brendan and Jake tightened their grips on Dallas.

"Why're *you* callin' *him* that?" Brendan jeered. "You're the one ain't got no dad! Bastard yourself!"

Jake howled with laughter.

Paul let go of Channing and strode towards Dallas.

Channing's eyes darted between the altercation on the ground and Paul's hulking figure. As Dallas strained on his back, abdomen tight and legs kicking, Channing suddenly rushed at Jake and threw his weight into him, knocking him across Dallas and into Brendan on the other side.

Jake was thrown by the sudden blow and scrambled to recover his hold, but Dallas was already up again.

Paul stopped swaggering towards Dallas. His eye was already swollen and bruised.

Dallas stalked towards him, gnashing his teeth.

Paul glanced around, wide-eyed, then gave up and turned and ran away.

Dallas started to follow, but Channing's cry from behind halted him. He spun around.

Jake was twisting Channing's arm behind his back. When Dallas charged, Jake let go, moving side by side with Brendan and avoiding Dallas's swing. Together they faced him, backing up with ugly sneers on their faces as they teased, "Two against one—you might as well give up!"

Dallas stopped six feet from Jake and Brendan, waiting for one of them to make the first move. He stared them down, eyes full of fire. When Jake jumped forward with fists raised, Dallas caught him by an arm and spun him around, twisting his arm hard behind his back. "Now you see how it feels, huh, jerk?" he taunted.

Brendan hesitated, took one step forward, then paused again as his friend screamed in pain under Dallas's power. Jake struggled pathetically to get free.

Staring Brendan dead in the eye, Dallas snarled, "Get the hell outta here, or I'll break his arm."

While Jake whimpered like a tortured animal, Brendan stood wide-eyed and gaping, then turned on his heel and ran after Paul.

Dallas watched him a minute, then threw Jake to the ground. "You've got five seconds to follow your friends!" he threatened. Jake scrambled to his feet and fled.

Channing came alongside Dallas, whose breaths came rapidly, heart pumping in his throat. After the last of the tormentors had disappeared, Dallas sank down to the rail to catch his breath.

Channing plopped beside him. "That was low-down dirty of them to get you with the rocks."

Dallas nodded, still too worked up to talk.

"Thanks," Channing added. "I'm glad I wasn't alone."

Dallas rose and tested his sore arm. "Wish I'd have given them all black eyes so they'd match!" He withdrew the blue bottle from his pocket. "Saved your bottle for you. Sorry about the jug, though."

Channing's smile lit up his face as he accepted the blue glass. "It's a miracle," he whispered.

"No, it isn't. It's just science. Harder to break a smaller bottle." Dallas frowned at Channing's hand. "Hey, that jug cut you."

"You're bleeding, too." Channing pointed at Dallas's mouth.

Dallas shrugged.

They started side by side down the tracks.

"I hate those idiots for bullying you." Dallas seethed. Channing had to take longer strides to keep up with his heavy pace, Dallas's shoes kicking up a spray of gravel with each step. The tiny rocks rained down, pinging as they hit the steel of the railroad tracks. "But maybe I taught them a lesson now."

"Hey, Dallas?" asked Channing after a moment. "They make fun of you for hanging around me. Does that… bother you?"

"No," Dallas answered shortly, half-lying. "I don't care what jerks like them think."

The two boys fell silent again. They came to the edge of town and left the tracks. Dallas glanced around with heightened senses, wishing they would overtake the bullies so he could give them another thrashing. They paused at a street corner.

"Dallas, your mouth's still bleeding." Channing frowned.

"Yeah, I can taste it," Dallas said. "Tastes like metal."

"Think your tooth's loose?"

Applying pressure with one forefinger, Dallas tested his front top tooth for movement and winced. The sight of liquid red on his fingertip gave him pause. *Is it moving slightly?* The pain in his arm caused by the thrown stone was worse, so he shrugged it off. "It'll be fine. Hey, is your face okay where Jake elbowed you?"

Dallas examined where Channing pointed. A purplish bruise was surfacing on his left cheekbone. "I'm lucky it wasn't my eye," Channing commented.

"Yeah, Paul wasn't so lucky." Dallas smirked as he pictured the bruise he'd inflicted. "He deserves the humiliation, the jerk." Dallas spat on the sidewalk. The saliva had a pinkish tinge.

"So let's just go watch MTV or something," Channing suggested.

Dallas stepped into the road with his chin up, fists still clenched at his sides, refusing to look beaten. Channing shuffled beside him in silence, both shoelaces dragging on the dirty asphalt beneath his feet.

"Thanks for sticking up for me," Channing mumbled as they turned onto his street. "I don't like fights, but it's better than getting the snot beat out of me all the time." He sighed.

Dallas didn't reply. He twinged with the discomfort of how he'd feel if he wasn't strong enough to fight much for himself, like Channing. *It would crush me. But what else can I do—let Channing take the hits on his own?*

As they entered the unlocked house, the smell of unwashed dishes piled in a sinkful of dishwater greeted them. They deposited the glass bottle in Channing's room alongside other blue bottles stashed in the bottom dresser drawer.

"I have enough for the sky now!" Channing's eyes sparkled. "Wanna help me with it tomorrow?"

"Sure," Dallas agreed.

Stopping in the bathroom to check his mouth in the mirror, Dallas bared his teeth at his reflection.

"How's it look?" Channing asked over his shoulder.

"Fine," Dallas answered. "Not even bleeding now. But your hand needs help."

Channing stretched his palm out over the sink, revealing several cuts covered in dried blood.

Dallas turned on the hot water and stuck Channing's hand under it. He winced as the scent of blood filled their nostrils. "You got any peroxide or anything?" Dallas asked.

Channing shrugged.

Dallas opened a cabinet under the basin and rummaged to find a tube of Neosporin. He flipped it over, scanning it for an expiration date: 1989. "It's old, but better than nothing." Dallas squeezed out a small amount of ointment and offered it to Channing, who swiped it off his finger and dabbed it onto his cuts. He winced again.

"I think there's still some glass in there." Channing pulled the skin back and squinted at the deepest cut. "See that little fleck of green?"

Dallas pulled the hand closer to his face, examining it. The wounds had reopened, sticky warm blood trickling down Channing's fingers. "I can't see through the blood."

Channing rinsed the hand under the faucet and showed it to Dallas again, who acknowledged he could see a glinting bit of glass. Searching through a drawer, Dallas found some tweezers and attempted to extract the tiny sliver. Channing yelped and snatched the tweezers away.

"Here, let me do it." Channing's tone was annoyed.

I'm probably babying him. Dallas stepped aside to tend to his own wounds. He pulled off his shirt, back facing the mirror. Two ugly bruises the size of baseballs shone on his left shoulder blade and lower back.

Channing's tongue worked back and forth as he concentrated with the tweezers. "Got it!" The tiny shard glittered in the light as he held it up, clasped between the tongs. "Dallas, your bruises look bad!" He frowned, eyebrows lowered.

"Eh, I've had worse." Dallas brushed off Channing's concern. "Got a washcloth?" He ran the sink as hot as he could stand it and stuck the washcloth under the steamy water, then used it as a compress on the bruise on his shoulder. Wet heat radiated through the throbbing injury as he examined the bruise on his arm.

Channing noticed. "That would've been my head." He pointed at the bruise. "Hey, it's shaped like Australia!"

Dallas snorted as he suppressed a laugh. *Leave it to Channing to notice something like that.* He watched Channing apply a Band-Aid to his deepest cut. Dallas's slender but strong build appeared bulkier than it truly was when compared to Channing, side by side and shirtless. Dallas scrutinized his friend's scrawny frame, ribs jutting through tight skin. Only two or three inches taller, Dallas had about forty pounds on Channing. Channing's reflection, stark and small as he nursed his wounds, cut to Dallas's heart as he eyed the image in the mirror. A lock clicked deep inside. *I'd do anything to protect him from those jerks. I'd kill for Channing.*

Channing's voice broke Dallas's trance. "Dallas, if we have to have battle scars, then I'm glad we got them together."

Dallas returned a half-smile. "Well, school won't last forever. Surely people don't act like those idiots once they're grown up. Man, I can hardly wait to just be *done* with school. Only three more years, and four for you. And you'll get to be at the high school with me this fall." *Where I can watch out for him better.* Dallas picked up his shirt and flipped off the light.

They walked into the den, floorboards squeaking under their feet. Channing dug between the cushions for the remote. Cable TV was one bill Channing's mother never missed.

Channing pressed the power button, and he and Dallas collapsed into the numbness of music videos, an escape from reality, if only for a little while.

HOPE (AND COFFEE)
1997

Dallas and Channing woke to the sun slanting through the windshield into their eyes. Both stretched and got out to jog a couple laps around the car to warm up. *It's really, really cold.* Dallas's instinct to go south pressed heavily on him. Channing hopped up and down in place like a robin in the grass. After the engine had run a couple minutes, they climbed back in.

A few miles down the road, Channing spoke. "Dallas?"

"Yeah?"

"I'm sorry again for calling you a jerk yesterday," Channing said. "And for saying you don't care about me… because you're the *only* person who cares about me. You even gave me the extra blankets last night. You're always doing things like that for me."

"That's never gonna change." Dallas forced the words out. It felt like pulling taffy to say them. *But Channing needs to hear this.* "I'm always going to care about you." *And I* am *a jerk sometimes. A lot of times.*

Dallas turned on the radio. "See if you can tune in to any decent stations," he said. "I'm sick of this tape."

Channing turned the knob slowly until a familiar song came through the speakers. "It's 'The Rain Song,' Dallas! One of your favorites!" he exclaimed. "Wouldn't it be cool to learn to play the Mellotron?"

Dallas mentally added it to the list of Channing's many random ambitions, wondering what a Mellotron even looked like. *Channing probably knows.*

After the Led Zeppelin song ended, Dallas said, "Grab the King Crimson tape from under your seat if you want to hear more of the Mellotron. Remember how awful we sounded when we sang that on the beach?"

Channing laughed at the memory as he inserted the cassette. "Yeah, we couldn't remember all the words!"

For a while, Dallas was immersed in the mindless world of music amidst chatter about humorous memories they'd shared, a mental removal from their current plight.

They finished one box of cookies that morning and started on the tortilla chips. Dallas pulled over to look under the hood, checking that everything was still normal. *Over half the tank's gone now,* he realized, unsure of how much gas they would need to get to Oklahoma. He got back into the driver's seat and rubbed his eyes, leaning his head back against the headrest.

"Do you need to take a break from driving?" Channing asked. "Sorry I can't help by taking a turn."

"I'll just rest a few minutes, yeah. Maybe we should take a little walk," Dallas said.

"Let's go fish in that stream we just passed," Channing suggested.

Dallas figured it couldn't hurt to try to catch some food. They got the fishing pole and locked up the car.

As they ambled along the shore searching for a good spot, Channing said, "You really should read that book, Dallas. *Mere Christianity.*"

Dallas hesitated, wondering if he should allow his question out. He relented. "You gonna become a Christian or something? You sure have been reading and talking a lot about it."

"Maybe," Channing replied. "You know, I've been thinking about it since I read my first Chesterton book a couple years ago. This book was an easier read, but I see similarities to Chesterton in *Mere Christianity* for sure."

"Maybe I'll read it someday." Dallas shrugged. "But I don't know if I even believe in God at all."

"But... you're so *good*, Dallas!" Channing insisted. He'd stopped walking and stood with feet planted, talking to his friend's back. "You *have* to believe in God!"

"Yeah, well, how about I'm not so good as you think," Dallas snapped, turning to stare at the trees across the stream with hands stuffed in his pockets. "And if I do something good, then it's only because it's the right thing to do."

"But how do you know that something's right?" Channing asked. He was walking alongside Dallas again.

"Because it is," Dallas huffed, picking up a rock and skimming it across the water's surface. "I just know it's right to do good things." *It's why I'm so bothered by people picking on Channing.* The theft of the food gnawed at him inside.

"And who made you able to realize that being good is the right thing to do?" Channing persisted.

Dallas stopped walking and sighed, eyes on the spot where the stone had disappeared under the rippling surface. "I suppose you want me to say God?"

"Bingo," sang out Channing. "Really, Dallas, read the book. It makes so much sense out of something complicated. So amazingly complicated that nobody could have come up with it, *except* God."

"So, is this guy your new favorite author?" Dallas asked as he tested the footing near the bank's edge.

"No, Chesterton's still my favorite." Channing squatted down and turned over rocks, digging in the dirt with his fingers for worms. "There's something about his writing style I really appreciate. But they both write with so much, well, with what I'm starting to think is… *truth*."

Dallas pressed his lips together in silence. *Truth? Everything in the world is so mixed up. Channing didn't do anything to deserve the crappy hand he's been dealt in life.* Dallas didn't think he deserved the bad things in his life, either. *But I can handle it.* He shoved those unsettled feelings into a dark hole.

Channing had half-filled an old Styrofoam cup with dirt where three fat worms wiggled and writhed, tunneling down. He continued hunting along the shore while Dallas took the cup and hooked a worm. He cast the rod and watched the line arc fluidly over the water and then descend with a splash. He stood motionless, eyes consumed by the bobber.

"So if there *is* a God," Dallas mused aloud, "why is this world so terrible? Like, wouldn't he do something to make things better?"

Channing came alongside Dallas and dropped two more worms into the cup. He stood silent for a couple minutes, staring at the bobber. Just when Dallas started to think he wasn't going to reply, Channing quoted, "The world is indeed full of peril, and in it there are many dark places; but still there is much that is fair, and though in all lands love is now mingled with grief, it grows perhaps the greater." Before Dallas could ask, Channing added, "Tolkien."

Dallas thought the words over a minute. "But that doesn't explain why God would make a world and then let it go to hell," he declared.

"It's because we need suffering to really show compassion," Channing philosophized. "We have to *choose* to love. And God wants us to make that choice. If he made us like robots that were forced to do the right thing only, then we wouldn't be able to show we freely loved him or each other."

Dallas considered this a moment. "Maybe, maybe not." He shrugged. "If it makes you happy to think about it that way, then I'm glad for you." Dallas looked Channing in the eye. *Goodness knows Channing needs something to hold on to, something motivational.* But he felt a small hollow inside himself.

"I don't think it has to do with feelings, because those can change. Love has to be a *decision* and chosen not only when it makes you feel happy. I haven't got it all figured out yet." Channing paused, lips pursed. "Stuff still sucks when it seems unfair, when bad things happen. But there's this *hope* underneath it all. And it just makes me want to keep finding out more…"

Just then, they were distracted by a tug on the line. Dallas cranked the reel, and Channing craned his neck to get a glimpse at what both hoped would be an edible fish. As Dallas braced his feet, he felt the line slacken. *It got away.* Channing leaned forward until the line was reeled in, empty.

They tried again. And again. After three hours of minimal bites and losing their bait, they gave up and trudged back to the car. Dallas briefly confirmed their route to the south on the map. He started the engine and pulled onto the highway.

Channing, on a Tolkien kick now, recited, "The Road goes ever on and on, down from the door where it began. Now far ahead the Road has gone, and I must follow, if I can."

"Now ain't that the truth," Dallas muttered.

The next day passed in similar fashion. Their food supply dwindled, hunger pains growing from a lack of anything substantial. They were almost to Oklahoma, but this trip was taking forever with the stops for attempts at procuring more food. Several more tries at fishing had yielded nothing. *If we can't find another way, I'm going to have to steal again.* Dallas gripped the steering wheel and tried to push the thought aside, annoyed at their slow progress. They'd only gone a hundred miles in the last two days.

Channing's optimistic presence was a welcome distraction. "Maybe we'll catch a fish in the next stream," he consoled. "At least we still have a few slices of bread left!" Channing's words were reassurances, and yet the next moment, he wouldn't even seem to remember that they were broke. Dallas found Channing's attitude annoying and endearing at the same time.

They approached the state line. Channing announced their crossing of the border with his usual enthusiasm. He burst into a song by one of their favorite bands, singing the relevant lyrics.

Not a deep quote from a book or poem this time, and not needing some kind of religious analysis. This was more Dallas's speed. He joined Channing in wailing out the next lines.

"Good impersonation of his voice," Channing complimented Dallas. "Hey, you even look like him, like a combination of him and the greatest bassist ever..."

Dallas, already familiar with this comparison of Channing's for his stoic facial expressions, hoped this didn't mean the Deconstruction tape would be getting its millionth playthrough on his car stereo.

Instead, Channing reached into the glove compartment and pulled out Dallas's Discman and a pile of CDs, looking for the Toadies album. He opened it up and began prying the plastic jewel case apart, revealing a hidden photo under the piece that held the disc in place. "See?" he said, holding it up and pointing to the lead singer for Dallas to compare.

"Uh... I do?" he asked, one eyebrow raised. "Maybe we sort of have the same haircut," he acknowledged after another glance.

"You have the same earring, too," Channing noted.

Dallas didn't see an immediate resemblance, but Channing was the observant one; maybe he was right, although a little hoop earring could hardly make a real resemblance. Dallas hadn't even realized there was a secret picture hidden under the back of the CD case, but he wasn't surprised that Channing had noticed. *Channing notices everything.*

"Good to know that my look-alikes are two of your musical idols, I guess."

"Dallas, I *don't* idolize them," Channing said. "That would be *idolatry.* I just admire their musical abilities."

Dallas ignored Channing's hair-splitting over his word choice. "And you look like the singer in that Loud Lucy band," he said. "Do you still have that tape? You haven't tortured me with it lately."

"Yeah, it's here under the seat," Channing replied.

"Still think *that's* a great album," Dallas added, pointing to the CD case in Channing's hands.

"The disc's not in it," Channing said. "Did you leave it in your CD player at home?"

"Shoot, guess so."

"I'll find my tape of it, and we can listen," Channing offered, pulling out the shoebox of cassette tapes.

Music distracted Dallas for a while, but his worry over the dropping gas needle and a growing headache caused him to pull over after only an hour of driving. He tried to sleep it off while Channing explored in the surrounding grass.

After a restless night, Dallas finally fell into a solid sleep a couple hours before sunrise. He awoke at noon, his head still splitting with pain, and wondered if it was from a lack of caffeine. By now, every bit of their food was gone. Stumbling back to the car from a trip to the bushes for the bathroom, Dallas rubbed his forehead and squinted. "I've gotta have some coffee," he groaned to Channing. "This headache is killer."

"Do you wanna just suck on the grounds we brought?" Channing asked.

Dallas considered it seriously for a moment. "We have the coffee maker," he mused. "We just need to find an outlet and some water is all. Maybe there's one on the outside of a building somewhere." Dallas imagined how bizarre they would look, plugging in their coffee maker on the curb of some gas station.

"I could really use some coffee, too," Channing said. "How about we find a library? Ours back home had outlets outside the front door."

Dallas could guess Channing's real motivation for suggesting a library, but he also considered it a better option. *A library will be further from the road, less conspicuous. And homeless people hang out around libraries.* Dallas couldn't decide whether it was a positive that they'd blend in, or if it was depressing as it hit him for the first time that that's exactly what they were now: *homeless.*

Buildings emerged in the distance of the otherwise flat, empty landscape, indicating a town. Dallas sagged with relief when Channing pointed and said, "Look, a sign for the library!" They pulled up in front of the building, scanning the wall near the entrance. Channing motioned to an outlet with his right hand, his left already scooping coffee into the machine.

"Score!" cried Dallas in triumph, pulling into a parking space. "Now, you know you can't check out books here," he cautioned as they walked towards the door, carafe in hand.

Channing's eyes were drawn to the shelves like moths to a light as they entered the building. "Yeah," he sighed. "Can I just look around and read a few minutes while you brew the coffee?"

Dallas hesitated. "Okay, just for a few. I'm coming to get you if you're not back outside in fifteen minutes." They used the men's room, then filled the carafe from the sink. Dallas carried it back to the car and grabbed the coffee maker in his free hand while Channing wandered off amidst the stacks of books.

Dallas squatted by the outlet beside the library's entrance, plugged in the coffee maker, and poured the water into the back. A minute later, the first drops of liquid caffeine dripped into the carafe. The smell made his mouth water, and his stomach growled relentlessly. *This will take the edge off the hunger, even if just a little bit.* The library's main door opened, and Dallas glanced away, feeling scrutinized like a bug under a microscope. *Thief,* the word echoed inside his mind.

The second the coffee pot stopped bubbling and hissing, Dallas pulled the plug and transported it back to the car. He pulled out the mugs they'd brought and checked his watch. *Two minutes.* He tapped his foot, fighting the urge to gulp down the whole pot.

After two minutes had passed, Dallas locked the car and went in after Channing. He walked towards the back, scanning each aisle. Finally, he found him standing in front of a shelf, holding open Virgil's *Aeneid*, his eyes glued to the page.

"Hey," whispered Dallas. "Coffee's brewed, hot and ready."

Channing's eyes reluctantly followed the book back to where he slipped it onto the shelf, and then he was drawn by Dallas and the promise of a cup of caffeinated warmth.

They slid into the car, Channing careful of the coffee maker at his feet. "Let's stop at McDonald's or somewhere and get some sugar packets," he suggested. "And some creamer for you."

Dallas wrinkled his forehead and lifted one eyebrow. "Is that really necessary when we're kinda roughing it?"

"We can be extravagant!" Channing exclaimed. "Why not make the best of it? After all, the condiments at a fast-food place are one of the few things in this life that's free!"

"Well, when you put it that way…" Dallas started the engine and headed back towards the main highway through town. "You're right. Let's have a little extra enjoyment."

"I'll go in for them!" Channing offered with a grand gesture towards the door as they pulled into a McDonald's. The prospect of a perfect cup of coffee — or four — had a very uplifting effect on Dallas, and before he could respond, Channing was out of the car and jaunting into the restaurant. He reemerged a moment later, hands overflowing with creamers and sugar packets. Dallas poured each of them a mug and nestled them into the flimsy cupholders. Channing distributed the booty. Dallas stirred in four creamers while Channing dumped packet after packet of sugar into his own cup. Dallas pulled onto the road again.

"This is perfect," Channing said euphorically, steaming mug nestled in his cold hands. "I'm *so* glad we left Nevada. It's just you and me and coffee — what more could we want?"

Dallas sipped his coffee and savored the taste, anticipating the relief it was sure to bring to his pounding temples. "Well, food, for one thing."

"Mr. Practical," scoffed Channing in a silly voice. "But yeah, you're right, of course. Well, I can hold out at least the rest of the day now. I'm hungry, but that's okay. I mean, we have *coffee!*"

Dallas had to admit that this little thing was lifting his spirits tremendously. "Yeah, this feels really, really good," he admitted. "It seems like such a huge deal to have a few cups of coffee when we haven't had any for a few days straight now."

Having no way to keep the coffee hot, they drank cup after cup in quick succession. "That should tide us over a few more hours," Dallas declared.

As the sun got low in the sky, Dallas's stomach rumbled. He glanced over at Channing reading *Orthodoxy* to himself for probably the millionth time.

"You hungry?" he asked Channing. Dallas felt half-starved. Sitting parked in the McDonald's parking lot for several hours hadn't helped with that. By now, his headache had faded enough that he was ready to drive.

"Sort of," Channing replied.

"Do you think we should try to make it until morning?"

"I guess that's all we can do," replied Channing. "Unless we can buy some food for six cents somewhere. Maybe we should find a stream and fish again?"

Dallas pursed his lips and didn't respond. It just wasn't the best time of year to catch anything.

"Let's drive maybe one more hour and then stop for the night," Dallas decided. "If we cross a stream or something, then we could try fishing again. I don't think we need to head out of our way to find water, though. I'm getting a little concerned about our gas supply." Dallas glanced at the gauge, which showed just below a quarter tank.

The only water they passed was a mostly dry creek bed, so they continued until they came to the next town. Dallas saw a 24-hour Walmart and parked in the lot. Finding concealed places to stop was getting challenging. *We'll blend right in here in this parking lot, though.*

They tossed and turned all night. Hunger pangs woke Dallas multiple times. Channing half-woke with nightmare shrieks before Dallas shook him out of it. Channing would eventually wake from his nightmares, but Dallas always preferred to end them sooner for both their sakes.

Channing's hands trembled, and sweat beads stood out on his forehead.

"Was it bad?" Dallas asked, already knowing the answer.

Channing gulped and nodded, face as white as a sheet.

Dallas handed him a leftover sugar packet. "Eat this."

Channing scarfed the sugar down.

"Wanna tell me about it?" asked Dallas in the dark.

Channing closed his eyes, knees drawn up against his chest. "It was… they were fighting. He was choking me. 'Stop, Jeff, you'll kill him!' That's what my mom was yelling, over and over. It was… it was so real, just like in real life…" Channing paused, breathing in deeply, eyes still closed.

Dallas reached out and touched his shoulder. "Hey, you okay?" he asked. "If it's too much for you…"

Channing's eyes flew open, and he searched wildly for a moment, then focused on Dallas's concerned face. "If it's too much for you to hear, Dallas, then…"

"No, it's okay if you need to keep going." Dallas shivered. "But man, it's rough to hear. I imagine it feels worse to be the one remembering it…"

Channing stared at his hands wringing in his lap for a moment. "Yeah. I'm okay now. It's not real anymore… just a dream now."

"I hate it for you," Dallas muttered. His insides were tight, and he saw red over the abuse Channing's parents had inflicted on him.

Channing smiled at Dallas. "I'm safe now. I'm with you. Not my mom. My dad's dead. I'm okay now." Channing gathered the blankets up as he spoke and made ready to go back to sleep.

Dallas forced a weak smile. *But is he truly okay now?* The heavy load settled on him as to how much Channing relied on him and why he'd blindly followed Dallas away from home.

After Channing fell back into a fitful sleep, Dallas lay awake, the rumbling of Channing's stomach an added insult to injury. As soon as the eastern sky began growing light, he started the engine and headed south.

Then a new idea struck Dallas like lightning. *This town is probably large enough to have a food bank. Why didn't I think of the idea before?* Channing stirred as they came to a halt at a traffic light. Dallas turned off the highway and pulled over at a gas station. As Channing stretched, Dallas went inside and asked the clerk for directions to a food pantry. He sauntered back out to the car with a lightness in his step and heart.

As Dallas pulled the car into a parking lot next to a small brick building, Channing yawned and asked, "Why are we stopping here?"

"It's a food bank," Dallas explained. "I'm thinking they can give us something since we have no money. Dammit, they look closed. This sucks."

As they walked to the entrance for a closer look, Dallas felt hope draining. It was Sunday, and a sign on the door confirmed the food pantry was not open on weekends. Dallas stood staring at it, as if willing the door to somehow open anyway.

"Let's come back tomorrow." Channing tapped the posted hours. "Food box pickup at noon, see?" He pointed to the small print at the bottom of the sign.

"I guess waiting another night won't hurt us beyond repair." Dallas sighed. "We better find somewhere to spend the day."

They noticed a public park a few blocks down the road. "It's warm enough today," Dallas reasoned, "so let's just hang around here. Then find somewhere to sleep. We can last another 24 hours." He glanced at his watch and mentally changed that to 27 hours.

They strode towards an empty playground. Channing ran for the climbing structure and clambered up one of the slides. "The ground is lava," he called over his shoulder, referencing an old game of theirs.

Dallas leaped up the slide behind him, chased him across a bridge, and grabbed him from behind. Channing twisted and escaped Dallas's grasp, slipping into a tunnel. Dallas plunged after him and snatched him by one ankle, dragging him out. He wrestled Channing over to an opening above a ladder and dropped him onto the ground four feet below, both in stitches as Channing flailed arms and legs, pretending to be scalded to death by hot lava. *We haven't played like this in ages,* Dallas realized. *The last time was when we were going hand-to-hand on the shore at the beach, Channing flopping into the waves, rolling, laughing like a maniac...*

"Your turn," Channing announced as he brushed wood chips from his clothing. He bounded up some steps and was after Dallas, who had leaped on top of the tunnel and was balancing across the top to escape. Channing shimmied through below him and caught him on the next landing. Dallas fought to get free a moment, then allowed himself to be forced onto a slide, where he slipped down to the ground below.

"Scalded!" yelled Channing from the top platform, thrusting a fist into the air.

When another car pulled up, Dallas and Channing left the playground equipment and went for a walk down a path alongside a stream. They found a grassy spot and sat in the sun. Dallas's stomach growled like a lion. Channing got a cup from the car and filled it from a water fountain. He and Dallas slaked their thirst.

"We should find something to take our minds off the hunger," Channing posited. "Want me to read something out loud?"

"Sure." Dallas leaned back with his hands behind his head.

Channing pulled *Orthodoxy* out of his back pocket, where he so often had it stashed.

"Gonna read it to me instead of just quoting it at me?" Dallas joked.

"Yep," Channing said. "I thought of a part in here yesterday when we were enjoying our coffee, so I'll start there."

"I think you'll lose me if you don't start at the beginning."

"Well, okay," Channing agreed. "I'll let you know when I'm getting to that part." He opened to the first chapter and began: "'The only possible excuse for this book is that it is an answer to a challenge. Even a bad shot is dignified when he accepts a duel...'"

Dallas closed his eyes and tried to focus on the words. He'd always loved to listen to Channing read, although he wouldn't have admitted it to just anyone. Channing spoke so fluently, pronunciations and inflections coming naturally to him, but listening was a challenge today due to the gnawing sensation of extreme hunger. Dallas pushed down the discomfort and tried to lose himself in Channing's voice.

He thought back again to when Channing had read Dante's *Inferno* aloud on the beach. His dramatic reading had strung Dallas's imagination along, making the details come alive in a haunting description of hell. Dallas could still recite the inscription from the gate, which they had memorized together after Channing read with foreboding flair: *'I am the way into the city of woe. I am the way to a forsaken people. I am the way into eternal sorrow...' We thought it'd be a riot to stand outside the doors to the high school on the first day reciting that. 'Abandon all hope, ye who enter here!'* A faint smile at the memory contrasted with the uncomfortable thought that Channing actually believed in heaven and hell. *'I want to avoid hell at all costs!' he'd said after reading it, and he was dead serious. 'If we believe in it,' Channing had said, 'then we can try not to end up there. If we don't believe in it, then wouldn't it be ironic to end up in hell anyway?'* While Channing's succinct assessment had seemed rational, Dallas still wasn't sure what he believed himself. *If I even believe anything at all. So why does that Dante story still get me overthinking like this, more than a year later?*

"I will not call it my philosophy, for I did not make it," continued Channing. "God and humanity made it, and it made me." Hey, Dallas, this part's really good. When I first read it while sitting on the riverbank, maybe three or four years ago, and I started thinking of that word: *made.* I was made, everything and everyone was made, *created* somehow from somewhere. Matter doesn't just appear. And why would somebody make something if not because it had some purpose, some importance? I realized that this philosophy gave me meaning and value."

Dallas yawned, stretched, and sprawled on his back, shielding his eyes from the sun with one arm. "And you can remember thinking this when you first read it all those years ago? What made you buy such a complicated book anyway? You were what, like 13 or 14?"

"When I saw it at a garage sale, I bought it because I didn't know what the title meant. I like big words, you know."

Dallas knew. Channing's vocabulary was continually surprising him.

"See, I was watching the river flow past," Channing continued, "thinking how my life was like the river, wandering towards its destination. If our lives are real, like the river is real, then there must be a tangible source and destination. But unlike the river, our destinations aren't known yet. Books like this... well, they make me want to fully figure it out."

Dallas lay speechless, head muddled with Channing's deep ponderings. *And he worries he's stupid?* "Yeah, I... uh, that's too much for my brain to handle right now." *Or ever.*

Channing started reading again.

Dallas tried his best to pay attention. Finally, exhaustion won out.

"This is it, Dallas. This is the part I thought of yesterday!" Channing poked him in the back.

Dallas awoke abruptly, exhausted after nearly an hour of listening. He propped up on one elbow and yawned. "Sorry, Chan, I must've dozed off. I understood some of it here and there, before that..."

"Okay, ready?" Channing asked. Without waiting for an answer, he fired off, "'Humility was largely meant as a restraint upon the arrogance and the infinity of the appetite of man. He was always outstripping his mercies with his own newly invented needs. His very power of enjoyment destroyed half his joys. By asking for pleasure, he lost the chief pleasure — for the chief pleasure is surprise.'"

"I'm feeling a lot of humility myself about now," Dallas confessed. "I must smell like a dumpster. But yeah… I see what you mean, maybe. That coffee was kind of a surprise yesterday, and it was that much more enjoyable because of it." He stood up and stretched.

Channing beamed, delighted that his friend had gotten it. "That's why I've been trying hard to focus on the simple pleasures of life," he said. "It truly has made my attitude change. And yeah — you reek." Channing made a face and held his nose, collapsing against the ground as he pretended to pass out.

"You don't smell like roses yourself," Dallas shot back.

Channing got up on his knees and stretched his arms. Then he gave Dallas a playful shove towards the stream.

Dallas lost his balance and stumbled back, catching himself at the water's edge. "Hey, that's an idea," he said. "We can wash up in the stream."

"I'll get the soap," Channing offered, "if you give me the keys."

Dallas tossed them to him and sat down to take off his boots. In a moment, Channing was back with a bar of soap. The mid-50s temperature was unseasonably warm for January, and they rolled up their pants and waded into the water. Scrubbing their faces with soap was invigorating. They pulled off their shirts and did some more washing. Channing squatted down, turning over rocks on the sandy bottom of the stream to see if anything interesting was underneath. Dallas splashed him from behind. Channing turned around and got him back. Dallas lost his footing and sat down in the stream. With a whoop, Channing shoved waves of water at his face and then slipped and fell in. He rolled over on his back in the shallow water, laughing hysterically. Dallas dunked him under the water for a split second, and Channing came up sputtering. They floundered around in the water like kids half their ages.

"Guess our pants are clean now," Channing said brightly. "That means I can just keep wearing this same pair of underwear!"

"For some reason, I don't think you should sound as thrilled as you do about that," Dallas said with a mock look of seriousness.

They stepped out of the stream, and Dallas cast a glance towards the playground. *Is anyone staring at us?* Everybody seemed to be minding their own business. *We probably just come across as a couple of teenage boys acting like clowns. Which we are, after all.*

They knelt, scrubbing their shirts in the stream with the soap before walking out into the open to dry off in the sun. Channing shook his head, hair spraying droplets of water like a wet dog. Dallas ran a hand through his hair, making it stick up more than it already did. He squinted in the sun and pointed out a bench in a bright patch of sunshine. Channing perched on the backrest of the bench; Dallas lay on his back on the seat with knees bent, feet flat on the seat, soaked jeans dripping water through the slats.

They stayed in the sun for a couple hours, saying little. The playground cleared out as families headed home for dinner. Dallas sat up, pulled his socks back on, and slipped his feet into his half-zipped combat boots. Channing stepped into his Airwalks, which he never tied. He had gone back to the car for a dry shirt already. Their pants were mostly dry, but it was getting chilly as the sun sank lower in the sky.

"Aren't you freezing with no shirt on?" Channing asked.

"Getting a bit cold, yeah," Dallas replied. "Want to head out now?"

"Let's move around a little first and warm up some," Channing suggested.

Dallas pulled his dry shirt over his head.

"Who can get to that branch first?" Channing challenged. He scrambled and clawed to climb the trunk of a nearby tree.

Dallas stood on the bench and jumped for the branch, grasping it and hanging there. "Does this count?" he called.

Channing slid back down the trunk as Dallas started doing pullups on the branch. "Showoff," Channing teased, and he grabbed him by the feet and hung on.

Dallas struggled and pulled up both his and Channing's weights, barely getting his chin to the branch, and then let his arms go straight again, dropping Channing against the ground below. He let go of Dallas's legs, pulling one of his boots off in the process, and watched as he did a second pull-up with ease.

"How'd you get so strong, anyway?" Channing asked him in wonder. "I thought I'd at least stop you from pulling up, even if I couldn't yank you off the branch!"

"Dunno," Dallas responded. "I've just always had a lot of upper body strength." Dallas was lean and in good shape physically, but his wiry body frame wasn't overly muscular. He couldn't remember a time when he hadn't enjoyed a good set of pull-ups.

Channing attempted scaling the trunk again and scrambled to the first branch. From there, he climbed higher with the nimble skill of a squirrel.

Dallas kept up the pull-ups for a few minutes more, then lifted his body all the way up onto the branch, using one leg to get himself astride it. Channing was ten feet above him now.

"Have you warmed yourself up yet?" Dallas called up to him. "I've almost worked up a sweat myself."

Channing slipped down from one branch to the next. "Yep, let's go." They both dropped to the ground below.

"Gosh, what a fun day!" Channing exclaimed as Dallas started the engine. "It took my mind off being hungry."

Dallas agreed. "Yeah, that *was* fun. Made me forget about having responsibilities for a bit."

They drove back to the Walmart near the edge of town and parked in the lot for the night again. They tried to get comfortable under the blankets despite their hollow bellies. Even the mustard was gone at this point. All they'd had for more than 24 hours was a couple packets of sugar left over from their raid on the McDonald's condiment bar. Dallas readjusted his pillow and tilted his seat back farther. Glancing over, he noticed that Channing had that Catholic holy card out, eyes mesmerized as if under a spell in the dim light. Then Channing slipped it into his back pocket and curled up to sleep.

Dallas awoke after seven from a jab by Channing's elbow as he turned over in his sleep. *Only four more hours and we'll get some food!* His mouth watered. He adjusted his blanket and stretched his legs against the floorboard, but the pangs were so bad now that Dallas had to withdraw into a hunched position.

When Channing woke up, Dallas was staring at the ceiling, arms wrapped around himself and tucked against his tight stomach. After asking what time it was, Channing groaned, "I don't think we can make it! I mean, I know we *can*, but I can't remember the last time I've felt so starved."

Dallas cringed. *I was so convinced that it was in Channing's best interest to come with me, and here I am, unable to even keep him from getting hungrier than he's ever been in his life.* Dallas couldn't look at him.

They drove to a Burger King where Dallas got ketchup, mustard, creamer, and sugar packets from the condiment counter, shutting out the torturous smell of fries and grease. They sat in the car parked outside the food bank, greedily slurping them down. "This is pathetic," Dallas ridiculed himself.

"It's okay, we've almost made it now!" encouraged Channing, sucking on a mustard packet.

The moment it hit 12:00, Dallas and Channing approached the front door, vulture-like. A volunteer met them there.

"Uh, we need some food," Dallas began, eyes darting to the side as he rubbed the back of his neck. "We have no money…" His voice trailed off. *What else are you supposed to say in this type of situation?*

"Hang on, I have to go check with somebody," the young volunteer said and turned away. She returned with a man who appeared to be in charge.

Dallas explained again about their lack of money. The man asked where they lived, and he had to answer "nowhere."

"We have a screening process to make sure people qualify for regular food pickups," he said, his face wary.

"We're just passing through," Dallas explained. "This won't be regular."

"I'm sorry," the man replied. "We are only authorized to hand out food boxes to families who have been screened and fall below a certain income." He crossed his arms over his chest as if to show he meant it.

"So there's nothing you can give us?" Channing piped up.

"I don't like to turn people away, but if you stay around town awhile, fill out this form…" He handed Dallas a piece of paper. "I'm sure you'll qualify if you have no money or residence. Let me tell you where the men's shelter is."

He jotted down directions and pointed out the way from the parking lot.

"Do they have any food at the homeless shelter?" Dallas asked. "That's what we really need. We've got shelter," he said as he jerked a thumb over his shoulder towards his car. "We've barely eaten anything in two days - more than two." Dallas blushed at how desperate he probably sounded.

"Look, I might be able to give you a few cans of soup," the man said, torn between following procedures and helping them out. "And yeah, the men's shelter does one meal a day, if you register with them to stay there. You're both 18 or older? They won't take minors, but I can give you the women and children's shelter address if you…"

"No, we don't need that one," Dallas put in quickly, not even wanting to consider having 17-year-old Channing separated from him. *Who would protect him then?* "But the soup sounds great; we have a camp stove in our car."

The man went down the hallway and returned after a moment with two cans of tomato soup and a box of cereal. "I'm not supposed to do it, but take this for today," he said. "But you can't come back here begging like this. You have to follow protocol. If you aren't going to stick around, get yourselves into the shelter or make some effort... What I'm trying to say is that I don't want to hear that you've been back here again just because I gave you this stuff. This is a one-time deal, unless you fill out that form and get into the shelter, understood?"

Dallas took the food and nodded, throat tight, and he and Channing turned to go. *Do we not look homeless?* He glanced down at his clothes, in decent shape — *not what I'd think of a homeless person wearing.* Channing's clean-scrubbed face was marred only by a tiny dribble of mustard at the corner of his mouth. The man's scrutinizing stare burned into Dallas's back as he dragged his feet to the Isuzu, dirge-like, following Channing's trailing shoelace. This was not at all what he'd expected.

"At least it's something," said Channing as they got into the car.

Dallas didn't respond, deflated. He had been so sure they would be given a big box of food. This would feed them for maybe two days if they stretched it. The dull ache in his stomach wasn't hunger anymore. *It's fear — the cold fear of hopelessness. I don't know what the hell I'm doing.* Dallas glared at his miserable self in the mirror and mechanically put the car in gear.

Channing tore open the cereal box, poured some into an empty cup, and passed it to Dallas. "Mmm, it's delicious," said Channing. "Cinnamon Toast Crunch! I've only had this kind once before."

The cereal stuck in Dallas's dry throat as he drove south along the stretch of road before them. The realization that he would have to keep stealing food squeezed his chest like a vise, and he struggled to suck in a breath. *I'm* not *going to continue doing such a crappy job of providing for us.* He tried to rationalize the need to steal. *We can't just starve, after all. Ignore the guilt.*

Not wanting to run out of gas again, Dallas only drove for a half hour before stopping. His bad mood followed him, and he spent the afternoon trying to bury his disgust with himself by tinkering with his car. Channing lounged in the back seat with his books.

That evening, Dallas pulled out the propane stove and a can opener.

They had eaten a little more than half the box of cereal between them, and Dallas was ashamed he was still ravenous.

Channing bounded beside Dallas, giddy at the idea of "camping." "I'm going to sleep outside tonight!" he announced. "Can we set up the tent?"

Dallas was hesitant about the tent. "Look on the map." He showed Channing. "There's this wildlife preserve on a lake here in Texas. If we can just get ourselves there, then we can camp all you want, and hopefully, we can catch fish and live in one place for a while, while I take a job in one of these neighboring towns." Dallas pointed to each spot in the road atlas as he spoke. "It's still too cold here to camp reliably each night, but another 200 miles south should be warm enough. But we don't have enough gas to get there, so I'm not sure yet what we're gonna do."

"I can hold up a sign on the side of the road," suggested Channing.

Dallas considered this. "Yeah, we'll have to do something."

As the sun set, they warmed the two cans of soup on the stove. Each of them drank a can, and finally, a little relief settled in Dallas's stomach.

"If you build a fire, we'll be warm enough tonight," Channing said.

Dallas bit his lip. He didn't want anyone to notice the smoke and brushed the idea off. "Maybe another night."

The following day, they ate a few bites each of the remaining cereal. Watching the gas gauge with a grim expression, Dallas drove a few miles to a rest area. In the bathroom, he washed his face in the sink and stared into the mirror, face blank. *What are we gonna do? I just want to give up.*

When Dallas came out, he noticed Channing standing by the ramp leading into the parking lot, holding up a piece of cardboard to the passing cars. Dallas started to go to him, but a prickling made him hang back. *Let him try to help.* He remembered the boost to Channing's competence from having sold the glass ring he'd made. Dallas sat in the car and watched Channing through the window, planning to give him a half-hour before telling him to give up.

Only five minutes later, a pickup truck slowed down and came to a stop beside Channing. He bent to talk to the driver through the open window, and a moment later, he was jogging towards Dallas in the parked Isuzu.

Breathlessly, Channing said, "Dallas, follow that car to the next gas station—he says he'll fill up our tank for us!" Channing was already in the passenger seat and buckling his seatbelt. He dropped his "NEED MONEY FOR GAS" sign on the floor beneath him.

"Channing, you're too trusting. How do we know for sure he'll do it? Why wouldn't he just give you some money?"

"Because," Channing answered, "he said he only has a check card on him, no cash, and he'll pay for it that way if we follow him. There he goes, come on!"

Figuring it was their best bet, Dallas put the car in drive and pulled out after the black truck. When the driver of the pickup signaled, Dallas turned in behind him. He waved them on to a gas pump with an arm extended through the open driver's window.

Dallas was on guard as he pulled up to the pump and stepped out of the car, stance wide. The driver of the truck approached. He was a middle-aged man with white hair, and he wore overalls that were remarkably clean. "You just fill it on up," he drawled. "Your friend says you boys are out of money and need some gas to keep goin'. No problem for me to help you out. I have three sons myself, all grown now. Every one of 'em ran out of gas at least one time when they was younger. I remember those days." He flashed a grin, nostalgia glowing in his eyes.

"I appreciate it." Dallas unscrewed the gas cap and removed the nozzle from the pump. Tension drained out of him as each gallon of relief flowed from the pump into the tank of the Isuzu. His car had always been his ticket to freedom, and for the first time, it had seemed to be becoming a burden, as he wondered whether he'd be able to afford to keep it going. When he'd bought it from his mother shortly before his 18th birthday, Dallas had relished a deep sense of satisfaction at being able to drive anywhere he wanted, any time. *My mother…* He lowered his eyebrows. *I'd thought maybe she would've given it to me, like a gift, but no, she wasn't even home on my birthday that year. She was gone so much by then, to who knows where.*

The older man paid for the gas and shook Dallas's hand, wishing him good luck and offering a fatherly reminder not to leave home without some extra cash in his pocket next time.

Dallas watched him drive away, still swirling inside with thoughts of his mother.

Channing leaned out the window and grinned up at him. Dallas flashed a smile back. "Thanks, Chan. You must've charmed him, holding that sign like a sad puppy dog. I'm blown away by how fast it worked."

Dallas started the car and watched the needle climb to the *F* position on the gauge. He tapped it with his finger and said to Channing, "Yep, the little things. Now *that* is a sight that makes me blissfully happy right now!"

Channing settled back comfortably in the seat. "All's right with the world," he sang out.

Not exactly. Dallas hid his frown as he checked his blind spot, although he was more hopeful than he had been a half-hour prior. *Can we pull off begging for food, too?*

Channing must have been thinking the same thing. They finished the cereal as they drove. After nearly an hour, they came to a tiny town, and Channing said, "Let's hold up a sign asking for food. Here, let me stand on that corner to try."

"I should do it this time," Dallas said, ready to humble his pride. He pulled over in a parking lot near the intersection.

"No, I look more pathetic," Channing reminded him.

He sounds almost cheerful about the fact. Dallas watched him bound out of the car with the sign. On the back of the cardboard, he had written: HOMELESS — NEED FOOD, PLEASE.

Channing stood on the corner for two hours. Several drivers passed without giving him a glance. One man yelled at him, "Get a job!" through his car window. Chin down, Channing slunk back to the car when Dallas motioned to him.

"Maybe that one guy who helped us was just a fluke," Dallas said as Channing got in. "Wonder what it would be like to have parents who bail you out when you run out of gas."

"Yeah, I couldn't picture my mom coming to help me out," Channing answered wistfully. "She only gave me money when she got to feeling guilty about hurting me, like that time she let me keep the change after I went to the corner store and bought her cigarettes after she'd forced the door down and it hit me in the face..."

Dallas bit his lip as he saw Channing's mother in his mind, crazed eyes and unkempt hair. He was beginning to feel like more of a failure than she was.

"Hey, Chan," Dallas said, letting down his guard. "Your mom... well, at least she usually fed you. Like, I know things were bad, but at least, well, you had food most of the time, huh?" Dallas stared through the windshield and poked at a hole in the cuff of one sleeve with his index finger.

Channing sat up and turned to face Dallas. "Are you trying to say that you think I shouldn't have come with you?" He didn't blink.

Dallas shrugged slightly, unable to make eye contact.

"You know," began Channing, voice going into thoughtful mode, "there's a distinction, and I think it's an important one. Sure, my mom usually bought food for us, but she yelled at me or hit me if she thought I ate too much, and there was no pattern to it. So it was always really, well, chaotic."

Dallas chewed on this for a few seconds. "So you're saying she didn't care whether you ate or not, and I do."

"Exactly," returned Channing. "You have good intentions, and that's what matters."

"Yeah, well, here's a quote for you, and a religious one at that—the road to hell is paved with good intentions." Dallas's tone turned cynical. "What matters is that we can survive, period."

Channing sighed. "Well, that's not how I see it. I still think coming along with you was the right decision. I don't think my mother will ever overcome her mental illness…"

Dallas studied his hands gripping the bottom of his steering wheel. *I have to get more for us to eat. I can't stand it if Channing is worse off now than he was back at home!* He started the engine and exited the parking lot.

After trying a few more street corners over several hours, Dallas decided they should give up. With nothing to show for their day of begging, they proceeded east, where they would join up with another rural highway that would point them south again.

At dusk, Dallas decided the time was right. He pulled over at a lonely gas station—one with only one car parked outside it this time.

"Wait here while I use the bathroom."

Channing nodded, eyes focused on his sketchbook as he copied the minute details of the infant Jesus's face from the holy card resting on one knee.

Dallas slunk into the store towards the refrigerated section, consoling himself that Channing seemed oblivious to what he was planning to do. He instantly sized up the male employee on duty: *I'm bigger and stronger.* He'd noted the clerk's position at the checkout counter and automatically knew which aisle to hit. Dallas wasn't sure what to think about the rapid pace at which he was gaining the stealth to shoplift, so he buried the subject and focused on his goal.

Scanning the shelves, he prepared to pocket a few canned goods. His hands hesitated as his heart rate increased. *You're the risk-taker, remember? You love a thrill. Just do it.* But his stomach churned over a bold act of theft. Finally coercing himself, he slipped two cans of Chef Boyardee ravioli into his jacket pockets. Beef jerkies… peanut butter crackers… *Better stop.* He didn't want his pockets to be obviously bulging.

Just as he was pretending to look for a drink in the refrigerated case, the clerk called out, "Can I help you find something?"

Dallas jumped at the unexpected question. He'd been hoping to just slip back out of the store in silence. "Uh… yeah," he called back in a voice that shook like Jell-O in his own ears. "It doesn't look like you have any Surge, do you?" *Please let me sound more confident than I sound to myself,* he begged with closed eyes, still facing the array of canned drinks.

"No, we don't carry that," answered the man behind the counter.

"Oh, uh, okay," Dallas responded. "Guess I'll just use your bathroom if that's all right…"

The clerk nodded at him and turned a page of the open newspaper on the countertop. Dallas stepped into the single bathroom and jerked the lock into place, then slumped back against the door with his heart pounding in his throat. He splashed cold water over his face and stared himself down in the mirror, willing himself to get a grip. He was doing this for Channing. They had to eat, and they needed more than cereal. This was protein. It was okay to take it. *Just look cool. Walk out of here at a normal pace, and everything will be fine.*

Dallas reemerged from the bathroom, his only goal the door dead ahead as he strode forward with laser focus. As he pushed through the exit, the clerk's "Have a good evening" chased him out. Dallas fought his instinct to run, taking methodical, slow steps, then opened his car door and got in. *Easy does it…* He started the engine. Channing had dozed off while waiting for him. *Good.* He eased the car onto the road.

Dallas constantly checked his rearview mirror as he drove into the night. Not a single car came into sight behind him as he put distance between himself and the theft. Adrenaline finally slackening, he found a small road to turn down and park for the night, well concealed behind a collapsing barn, nature reclaiming it.

Channing stirred beside him and mumbled, "Where are we?"

"You can go back to sleep," Dallas replied. "We're stopped for the night now."

Channing said something incoherent and turned over, tucking his feet under him on the seat. Dallas grabbed his pillow and their blankets. After double-checking that the doors were locked, he beat himself up mentally until he finally dropped off to sleep.

Channing sat up the next morning and rubbed his eyes. Dallas leaned over the open road atlas across his lap. The sun shone, and a symphony of birdsong serenaded them from the surrounding trees. Suddenly, Channing scanned the evidence of Dallas's crime from the previous evening, stashed on the floorboard of the driver's seat.

"Hey, how'd you get that food?" he asked.

Dallas looked away. He didn't answer, lips drawn tight.

"You… *stole* it?" Channing's eyebrows shot up.

Dallas still didn't respond.

"You stole it," Channing repeated softly. "You did…"

"Yeah, I stole it!" snapped Dallas. "We have to eat. I've dragged you way out here to nowhere, and I'm not gonna make it worse by starving you. It's not wrong if we can't get food otherwise, and we've *tried*. I don't like stealing, but I have no other choice." Dallas knew he sounded more angry than convincing. *Angry and bitter.* To his surprise, Channing's eyes were merciful.

"It's okay, Dallas," he murmured. "I know you're doing the best you can right now." Channing picked up one of the beef jerkies and opened it.

Dallas hadn't expected this. He opened one himself. "It's only temporary," he said with a sigh a moment later. "Just until we can figure out something better. When we get settled in one place, we can see if we can get on the list of a food pantry and get food that way until I earn some money."

"This is hard," Channing stated.

Dallas could only nod.

Dallas stirred at the sound of hands fumbling for the tent flap zipper. He'd come out of his sleeping bag entirely, sprawled across every inch of available space. Channing threw a leg out of the way as he tried to get out.

"What's happening?" Dallas grumbled.

"Sorry, gotta pee," said Channing. "Be right back."

Dallas was fully awake when Channing returned and dove back into his sleeping bag, tucking the inside blanket snugly around himself.

"How can you be outside your sleeping bag?" Channing's voice was incredulous. "Aren't you freezing to death?"

Dallas shrugged. "I can't stand to be confined like that."

"Your leg was on top of me." Channing giggled. "It's a three-man tent, but you're taking up the space of two and a half of them."

"Good thing you only take up the space of half a man," Dallas quipped back.

Just then, a strange chirp came from somewhere outside, muffled by the tent walls.

"What was that?" Channing tilted his head to the side.

"I heard it, too." Dallas sat motionless, straining to listen. Something rustled through the underbrush nearby.

"It sounded like a bird," whispered Channing, "but that movement's too big…"

"And what bird would be out at night, anyway?" interrupted Dallas, slipping into his boots.

"A nighthawk," replied Channing matter-of-factly, "but they don't sound like that… Dallas, are you going out there?"

"Yeah. It's probably nothing, but I better make sure."

"I don't want to stay here alone!" Channing yelped, groping in the dark for his shoes. "Wait up!"

Dallas, flashlight in one hand, turned and paused.

"What are you gonna do if it's… *not* nothing?" Channing gulped.

"I've got my knife in my pocket." Dallas was self-assured. "I'll stir up the fire and add more wood. If it's an animal, that'll keep it away."

The harsh tent zipper pierced the quiet of the night. Dallas stepped into pitch blackness, Channing at his heels. They crept a few paces forward, pausing beside the fire. Embers glowed a dull orange from the center of the ring, the last life from its previous blaze. Dallas felt his left pocket for his lighter. The noise squeaked again. Dallas turned towards it, narrowing his eyes as they adjusted to the environment. The sliver of moon didn't do much to illuminate the dark woods around them.

Dallas switched on his flashlight and swept it across the trees in front of him. A sudden scrambling came from that direction, something big moving through the bushes. Dallas silently handed Channing the hatchet that lay alongside the fire ring and motioned for him to stay still, then prowled forward, all his senses heightened. The knife, open in his right hand, pointed straight ahead. Dallas's fight-or-flight instinct was strong, and though he often wasn't sure which one to follow, he typically went with the former.

Fifteen paces past the fire ring, Dallas froze. His light shone straight into the glowing eyes of a full-grown mountain lion. The sleek animal stared him down, unmoving, a terrible beauty. The sight of the powerful muscles sucked Dallas's breath from him. *It could be on me in one pounce. They rarely attack humans… Don't run… Channing…*

It seemed much longer than the several seconds Dallas stood immovable, hair raised on the back of his neck, poised for reaction as he stared into those animal eyes. He wanted with all his being to turn tail and run, but that could be a deadly decision. Unblinking and with heart hammering in his chest, Dallas took one slow step backward.

The big cat emitted a low growl.

Channing stood frozen as the sound plus Dallas's lack of action communicated danger.

"Don't move," Dallas whispered from the side of his mouth. He took another step back, knife and flashlight still pointed forward. Another step back. And another, cautiously, over the low rock wall they had built surrounding their campsite a few hours before sunset. The mountain lion took one stride forward and growled again—longer, more menacing.

Dallas dared not turn towards Channing, but he could picture how he must appear. *The hatchet's raised halfway in his left hand. He's three steps from the fire ring.* Dallas calculated the paces needed for Channing to get to the tent. He took another reverse step.

"Get a really long stick that's red-hot on the end," coached Dallas, voice steady. One foot inched back. The mountain lion prowled forward, just on the other side of their low wall now. Dallas heard Channing moving for the stick, but he kept his determined eyes trained on the cougar. His body was tensed, ready to fight at the first sign of attack. Positioned where he was, Dallas was a willing martyr for the cause of Channing.

Another two paces back, and he was within Channing's reach. Groping behind, Dallas found the middle of the extended stick and drew it forward, sword-like, grasping it and his knife in the same hand. Another step back. Channing's rapid breathing was like a blacksmith's bellows behind him now. Dallas's pulse hammering in his ears was the loudest sound of all.

They remained deadlocked, boy facing mountain lion, for an eternal minute. Dallas hadn't blinked once since his flashlight had found those wild eyes.

Finally, Dallas spoke again. "Keep the hatchet raised. Back slowly inside the tent, but don't zip it. *Don't* turn your back."

Channing gulped. Dallas heard his movements and compensated, keeping himself centered between the lion and his friend. *It'll have to get through me first!* The surge of warrior-like adrenaline coursed from a primal place deep inside. Eyebrows lowered, lip curled, arms poised and ready on either side of him, Dallas was alone in the universe with the threatening big cat.

Channing took another step. And another. Dallas remained unflinching, frozen. He heard a muffled footstep on the tent fabric and knew Channing was crouching to duck through the doorway. He dropped the flashlight and withdrew the lighter from his pocket in one swift motion. With a deft flick, a flame illuminated the dark as the flashlight's beam bounced off uselessly to the side.

Channing had withdrawn into the tent, and Dallas held the flame from the lighter against the hefty stick in his hand, coaxing it to ignite. The glowing orange tip brightened as the flames licked the bark below it, and then the branch was on fire. The flame grew, Dallas skillfully manipulating the lighter to create as much fire as possible.

He could see the mountain lion again now. It snarled and cowered as the flames leaped higher. Dallas bit his lower lip, his brow furrowing as he worked, then boldly stepped forward with the flaming torch extended. The wild cat slinked away several yards, then crouched low and hissed. Dallas took firm strides and hopped the wall. He waved his flaming weapon and screamed at the animal.

It turned and bounded into the bushes.

Dallas followed, brandishing his fire stick and emitting deep, guttural, menacing sounds he hadn't known could come from himself. He couldn't see the mountain lion anymore and paused, listening to a distant cracking sound as it ran through the bracken.

All adrenaline and power, Dallas stalked back to the fire ring. Keeping his eyes alert to the place where the cougar had disappeared, he piled more tinder on the fire from bits Channing had shredded earlier, touching them off with the flaming stick and adding kindling simultaneously, and then set to work building the fire back up quickly. It roared to life under his attention until he had flames leaping as high as his chest, sparks flying from the top. Dallas stood with hands on hips, watching the raging fire he had birthed.

Channing's whimpering voice from behind jolted him from his trance. "Is it gone now?"

Dallas scanned the perimeter of the campsite. "Yep." He pulled the long stick back out of the fire ring and held its blaze aloft. He patrolled the campsite, illuminating the darkness all around, peering out into the stillness of night.

Channing watched from the open tent flap.

"Come warm up," Dallas offered.

Channing crept to the fire ring in the light of Dallas's torch. Squatting close to the flames, a contented smile spread over him as the heat warmed his skin. "Ahh, this feels nice!"

Dallas stood beside him. "I'd just like to see that mountain lion *try* to get close to our site again," he boasted with a sneer.

"You think it'll stay away now?" queried Channing.

"I *know* it will."

Channing put a finger to his chin. "Yeah, with flames this big, wild animals won't come near. Unless… unless they have rabies…"

Dallas waved a hand in dismissal and scoffed. "We're fine now. I'll build it back up in a couple hours, and it'll be good until sunrise. I'm not afraid of a mountain lion in the daylight."

Channing shivered despite his proximity to the flames. "*I* am." He watched Dallas poking at the flaming sticks with his long one, pacing halfway around the fire and studying it from that side, pausing now and then to warm his hands momentarily before adding more logs to the blaze. "Were you scared, Dallas?"

Dallas's brown eyes concentrated on the flames before him a moment before meeting Channing's gray ones through the fire. "Yeah," Dallas confessed. "But I couldn't think about that in the moment." He put one more log on the fire. "You warm enough now?"

Channing nodded and dove for the tent opening.

Dallas paused at the tent door, one final glance around him before backing in through the flap. Channing was already deep inside his sleeping bag.

Dallas lay back, hands folded behind his head. As he watched the glow of flames through the tent wall and heard their crackling, his body trembled, and the danger crept over Dallas now that it was over. He shivered, blew out a deep, shuddery breath, and pulled his blanket up to his chin.

Channing poked his head out of his bag. "You okay?"

Dallas, face towards the tent wall beside him, nodded in the dimness, the night less black around them as the fire threw its light from ten feet away. "I am... *now.* I was *terrified,* Chan. That was *terrifying.*" He swallowed. A weight descended on Dallas, all the worst possible outcomes assaulting his mind at warp speed. *And Channing was out there alone, completely unaware... How close was he to the cougar without even knowing it? Don't think about that!* he chided. *Nothing happened to him.*

Channing shifted closer. "You scared it good, though. We're okay now." Dallas felt the gentle pressure of Channing's shoulder against his involuntarily shaking body. The unsettled trembling gradually subsided.

Dallas turned his head towards Channing. "Good thing you shaved up all that extra tinder. Made it easier to get the fire going again."

Despite their heart-stopping scare, Channing was asleep within a few minutes. Dallas dozed fitfully and stirred an hour and a half later, slipped out into the darkness, and stoked the fire, bringing it back to a roaring blaze. After prowling the perimeter of their camp, he crawled back in the tent and finally crashed, soon enveloped in deep sleep.

Dallas woke to morning birdsong and stretched. Channing was still a sleeping ball of fabric crammed next to him. Dallas poked the layers of Channing's cocoon, to no avail. He slipped outside to build the fire back up.

A few minutes later, Channing emerged from the tent, wrapped in his blanket.

Dallas sat entranced before raging flames. *Create fire, give it life, make it powerful...* Dallas broke away from communing with the fire and started a pot of water for coffee.

Channing huddled as close as he could without getting burned, color returning to his cheeks. He held a stick strangled with the remainder of last night's canned biscuit dough over the fire while Dallas fried eggs.

"I'm gonna have more marshmallows." Channing stuck six of them onto a forked stick, caught them on fire, then blew them out and singed his fingers as he pulled them off. Dallas wrinkled his nose while he watched Channing cram several into his mouth at once.

Channing pointed out birds as he licked his sticky fingers. Dallas half-listened to his litany of mountain bluebirds, downy woodpeckers, and mockingbirds while polishing off four eggs and then wiping out the pan. He poured himself the last of the coffee.

They spent the morning exploring huge, lichen-encrusted boulders near a slender, flexible tree dubbed "the catapult" with which they could launch pinecones far distances. Midday, a rumble of thunder warned in the distance. By the time they returned to their campsite, rain pelted in fat drops, and they crawled inside the tent just as the sky opened up in a downpour. They nestled in with blankets and sleeping bags.

Channing held up two books: *The Everlasting Man* by G.K. Chesterton and *Around the World in Eighty Days*. Dallas pointed decidedly to the fiction novel over what looked to him like a deep philosophical text. Last summer, when they'd tired of exploring out here, Channing had read from *The Princess and the Goblin*, a long-time favorite of his. A year before that, while hanging out along the river, it had been *Tom Sawyer* and *Huckleberry Finn*, in between Channing's bursts of inspiration to build a raft out of sticks that promptly sank ten feet off the bank. Dallas was learning to appreciate the value of classic literature and the vocabulary workout the novels were giving him.

After Channing had read aloud a while, the sun broke through the clouds. He unzipped the tent. "C'mon; it's stopped raining!"

Dallas, lulled into a dreamy state from the steady beat of the rain on the tent as accompaniment to Channing's reading voice, murmured, "Sure, give me a minute." In a minute, he was sound asleep.

Twigs snapped in the distance. Dallas awoke with a start. He rubbed his eyes. *What time is it? Nearly 4:00.* He pulled the tent flap aside and squinted in the bright light slanting through the treetops. Channing wasn't far off, lost in his own imaginative world, propping long sticks against a tree. Dallas rummaged around for his shoes, then emerged from the tent and stretched. Channing was no longer visible, so Dallas trotted towards where he'd been, eyes scanning his surroundings.

Suddenly, Dallas tripped. Flat on the ground and clutching the knee he'd banged against a rock, he spied the culprit: a rope tied between two trees, four inches off the ground.

"Channing, what the crap?" Dallas grumbled, eyebrows lowered. He was halfway up when Channing barreled towards him from one side. Dallas's balance was thrown, and he was eating dirt for the second time within the same minute, now with Channing on his back, trying to wrestle him to the ground and attempting to grab his hands and tie them together.

"Oh, you wanna play rough?" Dallas threatened, flipping Channing over and glaring at him with flinty, intimidating eyes. He pinned his friend's wrists to the ground. "Give up?"

Channing struggled hard, but it was futile. Dallas usually let him have the advantage, at least for a while, but he was annoyed by the unexpected tripwire, still groggy and harboring leftover reactive instincts from last night.

"I got you with the rope, anyway!" Channing taunted. "My fortress must be protected pretty decently from invaders, if I was able to catch you!"

"You didn't catch me!" Dallas wrinkled his nose in disgust. "But you sure pissed me off!" Suddenly Dallas gripped Channing in strong arms, wrapping him in a bear hug, eyes squeezed shut and pulse pounding in his head. *What if I'd lost him to that lion last night?* The delayed reaction was suffocating, and Dallas struggled for a gulp of air. *I wouldn't be able to live with myself!*

Dallas let Channing go quickly and sat back on his heels, eyes on the ground.

Channing pushed up on an elbow, brushing some stray leaves from his wavy hair. He hadn't flinched at Dallas's sudden outburst of brotherly affection. "Nope, I caught you," he continued. "I just couldn't *capture* you 'cause you're too strong for me." Channing met Dallas's eyes.

"Okay, I'm not mad about tripping over the rope anyway," Dallas said. "Any*more*, that is. I guess I'm still on edge from last night."

They sat silently on the ground, Dallas fiddling with a few pieces of pine straw and Channing picking leaves off his clothes.

"Hey, Channing," Dallas said without looking up from the pine needles in his hands, "did your dad ever— before he left— did he ever play-wrestle with you?"

"If he had, I would never want to play-wrestle again." Channing's voice had gone flat and defensive. "When he was rough, he wasn't playing."

Dallas regretted having even mentioned Channing's abusive father. He had wondered if it was something all dads did, and the question had just come out.

"I guess neither of us had anybody to rough and tumble with." Dallas sighed.

"But now we do!" Channing leaped on top of Dallas again. Rolling and wrestling in mock aggression, the boys tested their strength within the assuredness of their friendship. Channing bound Dallas's hands with a small section of rope and made him walk on his knees towards the stick structure. The impressive cage-like shelter had a doorway on one side.

"Into the dungeon," Channing ordered, and Dallas complied.

"Don't I get to speak with a lawyer or something?" Dallas joked.

"Nope, you're a prisoner of war."

"Can I bribe the guard with a promise of pizza?"

"That's a possibility," Channing considered.

"I'll throw in some slave labor of taking down that tent and carrying it back to the car," Dallas added.

"If you provide facilities for us to get cleaned up before going for pizza, then you've got a deal," Channing bargained.

"Wellll..." Dallas deliberated. "I don't know. I might make you go out smelling like dirt and campfire smoke."

"Then you're sentenced to being imprisoned here forever." Channing spread his arms wide. "Just you and the mountain lions."

"Okay, okay, I'm begging for mercy," Dallas played along. "You can have first shower, and soap will be provided."

"Okay, your term's up early then." Channing pulled aside the makeshift bars and untied Dallas's wrists. They got to work stuffing their belongings into their bags and taking down the tent.

Dallas had found a twenty on the kitchen table when they returned to his house to get cleaned up, and now he and Channing were seated in a booth along the back wall inside Marino's Pizza.

Channing inhaled. "It smells so good in here!"

Dallas agreed, stomach growling as they waited for their food.

Channing noticed Dallas's fingers drumming subconsciously on the table. "Hey, we've seen the music video for this song on MTV, remember?"

Dallas paused and listened. "Yeah, it's the Toadies, right?"

As the next song came on, the distinct vocal wail elucidated that

Marino's was playing the album straight through.

Several songs later, their order came out, hot and steaming, as Channing was calculating the total plus tip and whether it would leave Dallas with extra money to put towards purchasing the album they both agreed would sound awesome playing in the car.

The pizza was a warm paradise following their overnight in the woods. They were two explorers, back in civilization after an unexpected fright. Dallas was suddenly frozen in time, unblinking, unbreathing, staring at his best friend across the table: Channing, completely absorbed in twirling a stretchy string of cheese around his left index finger. The wicked eyes of the mountain lion burned in Dallas's memory, and he felt hot all over, stomach reeling, one line of the music suspended in midair, hanging... *This is the one person I care about more than anyone else in the world. I would* die *to save Channing. I know I would.* The split second dragged while an imprint of the reality surrounding him was engraved onto his soul. Dallas would recollect the burning inside him and the warmth of the restaurant, the smells, the tastes, and the sounds paired with this snapshot of Channing for the rest of his life: the moment he was astonished to know he was capable of unconditional, sacrificial love.

FALL APART

Dallas double-checked the route, atlas lying open to the Texas pages. It wasn't far to the lakeside wildlife refuge he'd been eying. Most of the stolen goods had been consumed over the previous day, in between stopping for several futile attempts at begging for food or money, and now Dallas needed to make one last raid somewhere before finding a semi-permanent camping location. *We're about an hour away and have enough gas,* he estimated. Dallas didn't want to beg or shoplift in the little town where he would then be searching for a job. He plotted it all out in his mind as he tucked the atlas under his seat and put the idling Isuzu into drive.

Now that Channing knew he had been stealing, Dallas had nothing left to hide. *He seems to understand, but still, I wish I could've shielded him from how desperate this has become. But he probably knew, deep inside. He's so smart. And I wonder what he really thinks of me now. Stealing is opposed to the Christian values he seems so into lately.*

Dallas glanced over at Channing in the passenger seat. He held a little metal Matchbox car, flicking the wheels and watching them spin as he held it in front of his face, lost in the spinning of his own world. Dallas was ever-aware of the childish appearance of his best friend and struggled to hold down the jealousy that Channing didn't have to be — *couldn't be* — the one to make the tough decisions. As Channing stared at the toy, transfixed, Dallas wondered if he truly did think that this was the actual car his father had heartlessly thrown away when he was six.

Channing had told Dallas about the incident years ago when they'd first become friends. He'd been running the little blue car along the dashboard as his father drove along Highway 225 in their hometown. Channing would still point out the exact location every time Dallas drove past the spot. His father had become enraged at the repetitive action and had snatched the car from Channing's hand and thrown it out the driver's window in one swift movement. Channing had stifled a whimper and dared not show any further reaction. Later that night, unable to suppress his sorrow over the loss of his favorite toy, he had broken down sobbing into his pillow. When he failed to make his cries silent, Channing had endured a severe beating after his father had heard him. He still had a faint mark above his left eyebrow from that night, where he'd been slammed against the edge of a bookshelf.

Dallas winced inside as he caught a glimpse of the scar out of the corner of his eye, a physical reminder of all the abuse his friend had endured. His father had abandoned Channing and his mother for good soon after. *Probably the day any last dream of a normal childhood went out the window completely,* Dallas reflected as he watched Channing clutching the tiny diecast memory.

Dallas recalled the occasion much later when Channing had pulled this toy car out of his pocket and showed it to Dallas, beaming. "I got it back!" he'd exclaimed. "My very favorite car, that my dad threw out his truck window. I found it again!" His smile had stretched so wide across his face that Dallas hadn't tried to talk him out of his unrealistic belief. Channing had been wandering the booths of a flea market when the little blue BMW car had caught his eye. He described it to Dallas as a miracle, the toy coming back to him after all these years. Now he clung to it as if it were his same Matchbox car, and he was still that six-year-old boy.

The rumbling of Dallas's stomach jolted him back to the present reality. The mental pep talk he'd given himself that morning jostled in his head, coaxing him to bury his guilt and focus on what was best for Channing. *I have to take care of him,* the mantra droned. *It's not wrong if we're starving, and it's only temporary,* he convinced himself for the hundredth time. Dallas narrowed his vision to the goal of survival with everything else pushed far into his periphery.

Dallas pulled the Isuzu into a Shell station parking lot, filled with unfeeling determination over what he was about to do. As he opened his mouth to tell Channing to sit tight, Channing interjected, "I'm going in with you. You'll need help."

"No, I'm gonna do it myself," Dallas replied with a scowl. "I don't want you in trouble."

"You need more hands!" Channing insisted. "We talked about how we need a little more this time, this *last* time, so we can live on it a week or two until we can line up a better way, an *honest* way, to get food. I'm coming in with you, Dallas. You can't stop me." Channing finished tying his shoe.

Dallas sighed and leaned back against the headrest. He closed his eyes and tried to think of what else he could say to convince Channing to stay put. "It'll be more obvious if we both go," he started.

Channing stared at Dallas and said nothing, unblinking clear eyes communicating that he'd follow him to the ends of the earth.

Dallas blew out a long breath. "Okay, I see what you mean about needing more hands. Even though we spent nearly all day stopping and begging, we don't have enough food to last more than a few days. And we need solid calories, not the little stuff a few people have given us in their pity." Dallas eyed the half-eaten Christmas-patterned gift bag of leftover caramel popcorn that a well-intentioned elderly lady had dug out of her car and handed to them earlier that morning. "All right, so you go into the bathroom first. I'll sneak a few things while you're in there. Come out after just a minute or two, and then pick up a couple things as you walk down the back aisle, only when you're *sure* the clerk isn't looking. Put them deep into your pockets. And be ready to do whatever I say immediately, if necessary." Dallas's words were heavy weights as he miserably gave Channing a few more tips on how to be stealthy about pocketing food.

They were ready. Dallas and Channing closed their car doors and strode towards the store, side by side, hearts racing, Dallas's eyes darting in every direction. Channing entered first and walked straight to the bathroom. Dallas followed and stood in back, browsing the shelves and studying the clerk in his peripheral vision. He snuck some things into his jacket. Antsy jitters bubbled inside of him. *Granola bars, beef jerky, a couple cans of tuna...* His senses were on high alert, taking in all degrees of the store as if feeling everything through the sight of a gun. *Channing can't get caught.*

The bell on the door jingled like a warning alarm to signal the arrival of another customer, but Dallas dared not look behind him lest he appear suspicious. Then Channing exited the restroom. Dallas glanced at his friend, and the tightness in his chest grew as he saw the blood drain from Channing's face. Channing averted his eyes and scurried into the next aisle, slipping something into his pocket and then making frantic eye contact with Dallas. "*Get out, get out* now!" Dallas could read it on his face as plainly as if he had spoken the words. He risked a peek over his shoulder and nearly choked when he saw what had Channing so unnerved. An Oklahoma State Trooper had entered the store.

Dallas froze as the blood rushed to his ears like the roar of a train engine in his head. His hammering heart seemed to stop suddenly in his chest, and he was outside of himself, watching a scene between other people about to play out. Barked orders screamed in his brain. *Get a hold of yourself! Play it cool!*

Dallas glided around the far end of the aisle to Channing's side. *Don't get separated! Channing is your main concern. Get the hell out of here, fast!*

The trooper was speaking in hushed tones with the clerk at the counter. As if in an urgent conference concerning dire matters of state, the two men's eyes darted over and went like ice into Dallas's soul. *They've seen something!* insisted his conscience. He glanced into the first aisle, where he'd picked up the items now concealed in his jacket. The trooper's car was parked on the other side of the window, right outside the building. Dallas inwardly cursed himself. *How could I miss hearing that car pull in?* Had the man seen him stealing through the window of the store? Or had the clerk noticed and was telling the trooper now?

"Keep walking, eyes on the floor," Dallas mumbled at Channing through the side of his mouth. His eyes were laser-focused on the door as Channing gave a small nod of compliance. Their feet propelled them forward, driven by the wild animal of instinct. There was no stopping now.

Almost there. A few more steps…

The trooper was suddenly between them and the door. "Boys, you'd best show me what's in your pockets if you know what's good for you," he ordered. Eyes narrowed and hand hovering above the pistol on his belt, he stood squarely in front of Channing, blocking his path to the exit. The trooper's hand slid the weapon from its holster.

Rational thought fled from Dallas. Self-preservation took over. The swaggering state trooper holding his gun was all Dallas saw, a threat to his promises made to Channing. Protective instinct raged like a wildfire and triggered the defensive fight in him. *He can't get Channing; he WON'T!*

"Run, get out!" Dallas barked at Channing, grabbing and shoving him past the trooper like a running back dodging a tackle. Channing barreled through the door at Dallas's command, not looking back.

The next few seconds were a blurry storm that would later replay constantly in Dallas's mind as if watching a movie scene in slow-motion: a confusing horror movie in which he was the monster, the reality of the bang from the gun ringing in his ears.

"We can't stay here!" Dallas was a raving maniac, pacing the ground distractedly, deep in the wooded area off the uninhabited side of the lake, voice frantic. "We have to leave the area and get as far away as we can!"

Channing sat wide-eyed on a large rock, staring at Dallas with his knees drawn up to his chest, hugging them to himself. It was the small, scared look of the much younger version of Channing, the one Dallas had first met years ago. *Is he afraid of me? How will he ever trust or believe in me again?*

"We should go back and confess," Channing said in a timid voice. "Explain that it was an accident. Dallas, it was an *accident*! You didn't mean for it to happen! We won't be in as much trouble since it was an accident!"

Dallas stopped pacing and stared Channing in the eye. "We were in the act of committing a crime," he said in a cold, quiet voice. "The time to confess has passed. The second he stopped us - *that's* when I should have cooperated. But like a crazy idiot, I reacted! And if we turn ourselves in, I'm going to *prison*, for a long time... or maybe worse." Dallas swallowed hard and looked down. The crimson of dried blood around his fingernails threatened to drown him, and he jerked his head back up to face his friend. "They'll put you in juvenile detention! I won't let that happen to you, Channing, I *won't*!" Dallas gripped Channing's shoulders with both evidence-bearing hands, eyes wild and furious.

"Dallas, no! You can't go to jail!" choked out Channing with a sob as he slid down from his perch on the rock. "You *can't*! What would I do without you? And how could you stand it?!"

Dallas wrestled with himself to gain control of the disastrous situation. "We're gonna have to find a fast way out of here. We have to ditch the car. That clerk ran outside as we were driving away, so he might've gotten the license plate number." Dallas was pacing again, brow furrowed, reasoning everything out and talking with his hands. "We'll have to hitchhike, find somebody going as far away from here as possible. As *soon* as possible. Before they get our faces all over tomorrow's news. I'm such a moron—I didn't even check for a security camera first!" Channing had filled him in on that detail as they sped away.

"Dallas," cried Channing, still sniffling nearby as he helplessly watched his friend's manic pacing, "we didn't mean for it to happen this way! We didn't want it to all go wrong; we just wanted some food! You're a good person, Dallas, a *good person!*" His distressed voice trailed off, and he sat back down on the rock again, body racked with sobs as he buried his head in his knees.

The sight of Channing falling to pieces was like a kick in the face to Dallas. He sank to the ground in a squatting position, reeling from dizziness. It all played back again in slow motion: the scuffle between himself and the trooper, seeing the back of Channing as he ran out the door, the state trooper's drawn handgun, Dallas's struggle to get loose from the tight grip, the deafening close-range blow of an accidental gunshot, the sight of another man's blood trickling onto his hands. The trees whirled all around him, and Dallas resisted an overwhelming urge to throw up.

"I killed him." Dallas forced the repulsive words out of his mouth. A hoarse whisper, repeating the awful truth: "I just wanted to get away, but I killed him."

I can't crouch here like a frightened, wounded animal. There isn't time to kick myself for my hot-headedness right now! Action is called for now, prompt action. Channing'll be eaten alive in juvey! A burning fire rose inside Dallas, an iron will not to let anything happen to his friend. He couldn't waste a moment worrying about anything else. *Right now, all that matters is protecting Channing. And that means protecting myself.*

Dallas was throwing open the car trunk in an instant, rummaging through his toolbox for a screwdriver. He squatted at the back bumper, took off the license plate, and wrapped it up in a plastic bag. His shirt, soaked through with blood, came off over his head and was crammed into the bag in a wad. Dallas was nauseated at the sight and smell of it.

"Get your clothes, all that you can," he urged Channing. "Pack up anything important that you can carry in here." Dallas threw an empty backpack at Channing, who took it and silently obeyed. There was a duffel bag on the back seat, and Dallas dumped its contents and rabidly sorted through the clothing, stuffing the bag with essential items.

"Dallas?" whimpered Channing.

Dallas ignored him as he packed frantically.

"Dallas, are we going to be okay?" Channing's lower lip quivered, and he appeared very, very small.

That look shattered Dallas. Reality slammed him, and he dropped to his knees in front of Channing and broke down.

"I'm not going to let anything happen to you, okay?" he choked out through tears. "This is all my fault, and you're *not* going to suffer for it! I swear, Channing." Through his anguish, Dallas's promise was like steel, convincing.

"I trust you," Channing said, unreserved. A calm covered his face as he met Dallas's brown eyes, eyes Dallas had never until now allowed Channing to see dampened with tears. A wave swept through Dallas, firmly cementing his purpose.

After locking the car, Dallas pocketed the key. They shouldered their bags. Dallas swallowed a lump in his throat as if he were leaving an old friend behind as he stole one last glance at his car parked beneath the trees, silvery in the moonlight.

At the shore, Dallas dropped his bag and waded into the shallow water, washing his hands, arms, and bare chest with the bar of soap. He nearly scrubbed his skin raw, and still he was filthy, the smell of blood filling his nostrils. He pulled a clean shirt over his head before they schlepped up the shore of the lake, breathing heavily as they hiked towards the road in the distance.

When they crossed a bridge across where the river yawned open into the north end of the lake, Dallas threw the tied-up plastic bag, now full of rocks along with the evidence, over the side. They watched it disappear into the water below, a dark secret swallowed up by the lake. They edged the road, Dallas's eyes everywhere at once, all his senses of awareness heightened to a superhuman level.

"So we're gonna hitchhike?" Channing asked.

"Yeah," Dallas said. "And we need to take the first chance we get. Let's hope nobody who drives by knows anything from… from back there," he finished with a gulp. He clung desperately to the hope that the tragedy hadn't yet been reported on TV or the radio.

The headlights of a car illuminated the pavement from behind them. Dallas pulled down the brim of the hat he'd grabbed from the car and turned to face the oncoming vehicle, his thumb extended. He never wore hats. The car gave them a wide berth and sped past.

Channing adjusted the bag on his shoulders. It was bulky with his clothing, some art supplies, and the camp stove. The rolled-up road atlas stuck out of the opened zipper at the top, and a few books were jammed wherever they fit.

Dallas's bag was stuffed to bursting with the tent, clothing, the stolen food, a few tools, and some old rags. Without time for discernment, he'd grabbed all he could carry. They each had a sleeping bag with a blanket and pillow rolled up inside tied to their bags with rope. Dallas had his knife in his pocket and the coffee press tied to his bag by its handle. Channing had a small hatchet and a flashlight hanging from his belt. *We must look a sight.* Dallas wondered if they appeared too insane to get picked up by anyone.

They didn't have to worry for long about finding a ride. The next driver that passed pulled over at their signal. It was a small pickup truck headed in the same direction they were walking. Dallas's eyes locked on the truck's Ontario tag on the bumper, and he held his breath. *Plenty far from here.*

The driver stuck his head out the window. "Where are you guys heading?"

"North," Dallas replied. *Beggars can't be choosers. And neither can killers...*

"You're in luck then," the driver said. "I'm on the way to Canada. That north enough for you?"

A small weight lifted from Dallas's shoulders. "Sounds good," he answered.

"I live a little north of Minnesota," added the driver. "Name's Patrick. You'll have to get comfortable in the back," he said with a motion towards the truck bed. "One of you could fit up here if you'd like."

"We'll both ride in the back, thanks," said Dallas. They slung their bags over the side and climbed in. "Lay low," Dallas advised Channing. They nestled down in the bed of the truck with their heads on their bags, out of view of passing vehicles. Patrick pulled back onto the highway under the star-smattered sky.

Channing gave Dallas a small smile. "This worked out perfectly," he whispered, "to have somebody pick us up that's going so far from here." Dallas could only give a silent nod. If only he could catch just a bit of Channing's habitual enthusiasm.

"I need to forget all that's happened," Dallas said numbly as he stared into the passing landscape in the darkness. "Start again. This isn't even real to me."

"I'm sticking with you," Channing said in a decided whisper. "I've been thinking a lot, and you know what? That state trooper should *never* have pulled his gun in that situation. We weren't threatening him — you didn't even have a weapon on you! It wasn't your fault. It wasn't your gun, and you didn't pull the trigger, either. It was an accident!"

Dallas pressed his lips into a tight line. He knew he was at least partially complicit for the tragic outcome of the altercation in the convenience store. And deep down, Channing knew it too, Dallas was sure.

Run, run! came the overpowering instinct screaming inside his head. *Your only choice is to get away — far, far away.*

The truck traveled on into the night, reverberations of the vehicle's frame like some nervous new mother trying to bounce her colicky infant to sleep, taking them towards a hope for a different life.

TRUCK STOP

Channing sat on the curb alongside the building. A 16 oz. Styrofoam cup with yellow and tan letters proclaiming "World's Best Coffee Blend" steamed inside his quivering hands. Baggy maroon corduroys cloaked his legs in the 40-degree weather. A steady whir of cars sounded from the embankment, traveling along the Kansas interstate from which Patrick's pickup had exited in the dark hours of morning. That same interstate led to the scene of the crime from which they had fled. In the opposite direction, it stretched away from a past Dallas wanted to erase from his memory.

He bounced up and down on the balls of his feet on a parking tie in front of Channing, the cold wind whipping through his jeans. He glanced at his watch, then around the corner towards the door. Patrick had gone inside to the restaurant mid-morning. It had been after two a.m. when he'd pulled off at this exit so he could get a few hours' sleep before continuing his drive. Dallas and Channing had stayed hidden in the back of the truck, huddled together wrapped under sleeping bags and blankets for warmth, trying to sleep themselves. Channing had already logged several hours by the time they'd stopped, lulled to sleep by the movement of the truck and the steady pace of Dallas's pounding heartbeat.

Patrick had invited them inside with him for breakfast, but Dallas had quickly declined, saying they would just eat their own food. *Our* stolen *food, a measly amount that ended up costing a man his life,* Dallas thought bitterly. Patrick had insisted on at least buying them some coffee. They'd accepted the hot drinks, then retreated outside and around the side of the building to where they now waited, basking in the bright midmorning sun and ingesting the liquid warmth.

"I hope he finishes quick," Dallas grumbled. "We need to be as far away as possible." He glanced down at Channing and saw the younger boy studying him, and he turned away again, shoulders hunched, still horrified at his impulsive actions the evening before. "Uh, is the coffee good?"

"The best," Channing said, face brightening. "How nice of him to treat us. It's good to get warmed up before we get back in that cold truck."

"We should walk around to get warmer," Dallas suggested. Being cramped all night in an open section of a moving vehicle on a metal surface in January had chilled them both to the bone. Dallas, usually like a furnace when he slept, still could not get warm enough. *I barely slept, anyway. But I'll feel like less of a sitting duck if I'm in motion.*

Channing rose, cradling his coffee close to his chest in both hands. "Let's go look at the trucks!" He turned towards several 18-wheelers parked in the overnight lot.

They walked briskly along the first line of big rigs. Channing paused to look at one that had just pulled in at the end of the line. The truck gleamed in the sunlight. Channing brushed a strand of his hair out of his eyes, mesmerized by the sleek cab, lights aligned in rows along the sides. The chrome sparkled as it caught glints from the sun's rays. The hood of the Freightliner concealed the powerful engine that roared in their ears until the driver withdrew the key and began to climb down from the cab.

Dallas instinctively pulled Channing from his enchantment, backing between two trucks and out of anyone's sight. *Being inside the building just long enough to use the bathroom and get the coffee was bad enough.* Channing had wanted to linger and look at the cheesy souvenirs as usual, and Dallas had rushed him through.

As Dallas led the way to the next row of parked trucks, Channing pointed out the little differences in each type of rig. Dallas tried to let Channing's recital of information distract him from his worries, but the words floated past his ears, meaningless. As Channing turned towards the third row, movement near the gas pumps caught Dallas's eye, paralyzing him. His breath stuck in his throat.

Two police cars had just pulled into the parking lot.

"This way!" Dallas hissed, backing behind the nearest truck's trailer. Channing was right beside him, eyes wide.

The boys peered around the trailer and watched as police officers stepped out of the cars and convened near the front door, engrossed in conversation. Each turned in place, eyes up, alert to the area surrounding the pumps and front door. Dallas held his breath.

They watched from their position of almost a football field's length away as the two officers approached people who entered and exited the truck stop building, conversing briefly with each one they stopped.

The way they seem to be asking random people for information… could me and Channing be the subjects of these cops' investigation? Quickly, Dallas squatted beside the truck, pulling Channing down with him.

"Get under the trailer!" he commanded. "Behind the wheels!"

Channing obeyed, setting his coffee underneath first and scrambling in on all fours. Dallas followed. They crouched on the asphalt, concealed by the rear tires, breathing heavily.

"Dallas, do you think they're looking for... for *us*?" Channing gulped in a whisper.

Dallas's face was grim. "They're definitely looking for something," he murmured, eyes zeroed in on the two men, arms taut as he gripped the inner tire. *Please, Patrick, don't go back to your truck and leave without us - or worse, walk out right now and get stopped and questioned by the cops.*

Dallas's heart nearly stopped a few minutes later. The law enforcement officers were walking towards the parked trucks, right where Dallas and Channing were hiding. They squeezed tighter to the large dual tires. The officers stopped at the first row of trucks. Dallas strained to listen to the noise of banging on metal.

"They're knocking on a sleeper cab door!" he whispered frantically to Channing, whose eyes were round with fear.

Dallas and Channing dared not move as the officers made their way down the line of big rigs. They could hear distant voices in conversation but couldn't make out any of it. Dallas wracked his brain as he surveyed the flat landscape. *We can't just make a run for it — where would we go? What if we're seen?*

Dallas swallowed hard as thuds against pavement announced the approaching footsteps of the two policemen, almost to the second row of trucks. Channing put his hand over his mouth to stifle a gasp as four shiny black boots entered their line of vision, walking alongside the very truck beneath which they were concealed. The boots halted beside the cab, and the entire truck vibrated above Dallas and Channing with the jarring knocks of the officer's fist against the side.

The sound of a metal door creaking open came from above. A man's voice said, "Yeah, can I help you?"

One of the officers spoke. "We're just doing a search. Mind if we take a peek in your cab?"

"I suppose I don't have a choice, do I?" the trucker's voice joked. "What you lookin' for?"

"Two suspects who fled the scene of a shooting in Oklahoma," returned the voice of the police officer. "We're checking along the main highways." His boots disappeared as he climbed the steps into the sleeper cab. The other man's boots remained stationary on the pavement, less than twenty feet from where Dallas and Channing huddled, hearts in their throats at the words they'd just heard.

"You see anybody looking like either of these young men?" asked the officer who remained outside the truck. "Not the clearest pictures, I know, but if either of them looks familiar at all…"

Dallas reached up to touch the hat he'd intentionally worn inside the truck stop despite his hatred of how it felt and looked on him. Channing's fingernails dug into Dallas's tightened upper arm. The tension was like a taut rubber band, and Dallas was close to snapping.

"Nope," returned the trucker, "and I'm headin' south, so I haven't been through Oklahoma yet. You got reason to think they came this way?"

"We're just checking along all major roads in the surrounding states," the cop stated. The other officer climbed back down from the cab, his search complete. "If you see or hear anything, please contact the local law officials. We believe they may be traveling in a car with Nevada tags, a gray sedan. We thank you for your time."

Dallas had inserted himself between the officers and Channing, backing them both around the rear edge of the inner wheels. Dallas watched the men round the front of the truck and stop at the next cab. Not moving a muscle, they crouched in complete silence until the officers had moved on again and several more minutes had passed.

Dallas's mind had been racing through every possible scenario. Now he motioned with a finger for Channing to remain where he was as he dropped to his belly, flat against the pavement. Dallas commando-crawled towards the other side of the trailer and peered out. He could see the officers, spotting their telltale boots, several trucks down — *at least six*, Dallas estimated. He shimmied back to where Channing cowered and snuck a glance around the tires. Daring to lean out, Dallas did a quick visual check to be sure the sleeper cab door was closed again. It was.

At that moment, Channing jabbed Dallas in the back and pointed. Patrick was walking towards his parked pickup truck. Dallas made a rapid mental calculation as he eyed the pickup, which was parked facing them, fifty yards away and roughly equidistant from both Patrick's position outside the building and the boys' precarious hiding place.

Dallas stole a glance back at the building, now at Patrick, now at their common destination: his truck. One last scramble to the other side of the trailer for a look down the line of trucks — the officers were still far away. Dallas was back at Channing's side in half an instant. It was now or never.

"Leave your coffee. Stay beside me," Dallas breathed the orders rapidly in Channing's ear. "Jog, don't run. Don't look scared. Straight for the pickup."

Dallas and Channing were moving, a straight shot for their promise of escape. The twenty-second action stretched into eternity. They finally met Patrick just in front of the bumper, nodded a quick acknowledgment, and Dallas smoothly guided Channing around the bed of the truck, where they hoisted themselves over the side. Dallas pushed Channing in farther as Patrick opened the driver's door and asked, "You boys ready to head out again? I'm planning to drive a full ten, maybe twelve hours before stopping to sleep again. Should be into Minnesota by then."

Dallas gave a quick yep and a nod. He pushed a blanket towards Channing, who understood and slipped most of the way underneath.

"Taking a stroll around the lot, eh?" Patrick asked, jovial. Inside, Dallas was about to explode. *Get in, drive away, move!!!*

"Just looking at the trucks," Dallas answered, and he slipped down into the bed of the pickup, making as if arranging his bag. *Please, please, don't let him think we look suspicious, like we're running, please don't let him see my terror,* Dallas begged silently to the air around him.

Patrick climbed into the driver's seat and started the engine as his door slammed shut. Dallas moved close and pulled the blanket over Channing's head. Forcing himself not to sneak a glance over the side of the pickup bed, he covered himself with the other blanket. One frozen moment as the truck halted at the exit of the parking lot, waiting for an opening in the oncoming traffic… Dallas held his breath. Next to him, Channing trembled and murmured something steadily to himself. Dallas adjusted the blankets to fully conceal them both and caught sight of Channing's hands, clutching his Marian prayer card tightly. The tension threatened to tear Dallas apart as their getaway vehicle remained motionless, the clicking of the turn signal nearly deafening and the smell of oil from the front of Dallas's shirt smothering as he hung suspended in time.

Finally, the pickup lurched into motion as Patrick turned out of the lot, onto the road, and then the gentle acceleration of merging onto the interstate ramp. As Dallas sensed each familiar movement, he began to breathe again, the truck vibrating beneath them, taking them away, taking them north.

THE SHELTER

Dallas had to do it. He swallowed the last shred of his pride as he and Channing slunk into the building marked "Ericsburg Men's Shelter." *I give up. I'm finally gonna admit to myself that I can't do it all on my own. I can't. I still have to keep us from being found, and that's exhausting enough, the hiding. It'll just be for a little while, having to live here.*

Dallas had already decided to lie about Channing's age. He'd convinced Channing it was just rounding up if he claimed he was 18 — after all, his birthday was only five months away now. He couldn't bear the thought of them being separated. Imagining what strangers in another shelter might do to Channing without Dallas there to stick up for him made him sick to his stomach.

When asked if they had any identification, Dallas lied again and said no. His Nevada driver's license pressed uncomfortably against the sole of his foot, tucked inside his sock. It wasn't a lie for Channing — he had no form of ID. They listened as the rules of the shelter were explained and then signed paperwork agreeing to them.

Their beds were in a large room, two among a row of cots. Dallas sized up the place, sweeping his eyes from face to face of the strangers they'd have to sleep among. *I can't trust anyone.* But this was the best option for now. Both breakfast and dinner were served daily here, and that alone was a huge burden off him.

"Come with me to the bathroom," Dallas muttered after they'd tucked their bags under their beds.

"Why?" asked Channing.

"Because I don't want to leave you by yourself in this place," Dallas whispered. "I want you to stick close to me, all right? Grab your toothbrush. I've got the soap — might as well get ourselves cleaned up."

Dallas felt almost like a normal person again once he'd showered and shaved. *Why didn't I just take us to a shelter in Nevada in the first place? Then this whole nightmare would never have happened.* He glanced at Channing, snuggled under the covers on his simple metal frame bed, sketching something in the notebook he'd brought. *No use beating myself up now; what's done is done.* Hardening his heart, Dallas refused to think about the accidental death of the state trooper. Any time the memory surfaced, he pushed it into another compartment and locked the door.

Following a warm breakfast the next morning, Dallas and Channing headed outside. The shelter kicked everyone out by nine, and they couldn't reenter until five, dinnertime. Dallas was on the offensive now, determined to find a job. They walked along the sidewalk, moving quickly in the frigid air. *Should I suggest Channing get a job, too?* Dallas couldn't picture that working out. *What if he has an anxiety attack, or starts talking about one of his quirky interests? But where will he go all day?* Their breath steamed in puffs around their faces as it hit the icy northern air. Snow seeped through their shoes when they stepped in the mounds along the road.

Dallas shifted the strap of his bag on his shoulder and paused, analyzing where to search first. He motioned towards the downtown area, and Channing fell into step alongside him again.

They had to carry all their belongings since the shelter was first come, first served each evening, with a maximum allowance of thirty days' stay total. Dallas walked with a lightness in his step, his successful evasion of the police plus this new start in a heated facility with regular meals boosting his confidence again. He started to whistle as they passed storefronts along the main street.

As Dallas stepped off the curb to cross the road, Channing stopped short and tugged at Dallas's sleeve. He pointed to the sign in the door of a business behind them: *Assistant Mechanic Wanted.*

They entered the shop's lobby. Bells startled Dallas as they jangled against the glass door. The room was wood-paneled and smelled of coffee and gasoline. A few customers sat in chairs, one flipping through a magazine. Dallas shuffled towards the counter, eyes down, self-conscious that these people would judge them because they were carrying sleeping bags, a telltale sign of their homelessness.

A man emerged from the bay, wiping his oily hands on a rag. "May I help you?"

Embarrassment heated Dallas's face as he rubbed at the back of his neck. *Maybe this was a stupid idea. It can't be good for business, hiring a homeless guy.* He swallowed and extended a hand, forcing his old independent self-assuredness to the surface as he introduced himself.

"Dallas, nice to meet you," the man returned. "I'm Mitchell."

"This is Channing," Dallas offered. "We're… I'm looking for a job. I know a lot about cars, and I've specifically done a lot of work on an old Isuzu I used to have." The "used to" brought a lump to Dallas's throat, and he swallowed it down quickly.

Mitchell glanced them over, his eyebrows lifting and the side of his mouth twitching in an almost smile, but he made no comment.

"Why don't you step into the office, and we'll chat about what the job involves." He held the door wide. They entered and sat in folding chairs alongside a desk.

Something in the man's demeanor made Dallas trust him. "Mitchell, I want to come right out and tell you that we're currently living in the homeless shelter. But I want to change that, so I'm willing to work as hard as I can at an honest job so we can save up and do better." Dallas held his breath, hoping his polite and commanding personality would make an impression.

"How about you, Channing?" Mitchell asked him directly.

Dallas glanced at his friend, whose eyes were on his shoes.

"Channing's like a brother to me, and I'm responsible for him," Dallas said. "I'm not sure what he should do while I'm working. It's too cold for him to just hang out on the streets. I'm not sure if you need anybody to do extra stuff around here, sweep up and such…"

"Nah, we do that ourselves. It's not much," Mitchell replied. "Channing, you don't look old enough to get a job anyway, but I'll tell you what. The library is just down the road, out the front door to the left. It'd be a fine place to spend time, until you get registered for school. I presume he'll go to the public high school?" Mitchell addressed this question to Dallas.

"Uh, that's something to consider," he answered noncommittally, knowing he'd never subject Channing to that.

Channing had registered nothing after the word "library." Turning to Dallas, he said, "Going to the library is a great idea. Can I go right now?"

Dallas had to chuckle. "Okay, sure. I'll come looking for you after I'm done."

Mitchell walked them to the door and pointed out the building in the distance to Channing. Then he and Dallas returned to the back room.

"What is he, 14 or 15?" asked Mitchell.

"He's older than he seems, but he can't handle a job just yet," Dallas admitted. "Channing's a little bit, well, unhinged, because of past abuse by his parents. He's childlike in a lot of ways. I mean, the guy will still pick up a stick and run it along a fence as he walks, just to hear the bumpity sound, and he's thrilled with things like the ice cream truck. It's been his way of coping, like living the childhood he never could when he was younger because he was so busy worrying about staying alive.

He's brilliant, though, so one day, I'm sure he'll find something that's a great fit for him." Dallas paused, unsure of why he was spilling all this to a stranger. "Anyway, my primary concern is getting myself employed so we can rent someplace and get out of the shelter. I have to take care of him."

"Tell me more about your car repair experience," Mitchell said.

Mitchell agreed to hire Dallas as an assistant mechanic. The good fortune of a job that paid above minimum wage and started the very next morning had Dallas walking on air as he and Channing left the library.

Back in the shelter and following a satisfying dinner, Dallas related the details of the job to Channing, sounding like his old self for the first time since they'd left Nevada.

"This is perfect, Dallas!" Channing encouraged him. "You love working on cars!"

"I'm determined to bust my tail, work harder than I've ever worked before," Dallas vowed, cracking his knuckles. "I have to be responsible and get us back to a normal life." Inside, Dallas ignored the nagging concern over being on the run from the law. *We've escaped now*, he reassured himself quickly.

Dallas buckled down immediately, getting to the shop early and throwing himself into the work. It helped that he loved it anyway. Being able to get under the hood and even drive vehicles in and out of the bays every day helped assuage Dallas's regret for the loss of his car. He sought out extra ways to help around the shop, trying to earn Mitchell's trust and approval.

"You have a natural ability for car repair," his new boss told him his second week there. "The way you automatically know your way around the underside of a vehicle is impressive, Dallas. I hope you're planning to stay on a good long time."

"As long as I can, absolutely," Dallas replied.

By the end of two weeks at the shop, Mitchell was pulling Dallas in to help him on engine work and other jobs requiring more skill. He'd shown himself competent at rotating and replacing tires, flushing radiators, and even changing out an axle without help. He felt capable and useful and, most importantly, responsible, again. His returning dignity was like a drug to Dallas. *I'm earning money and taking care of myself and Channing like any self-respecting man would do.* He exhaled as he started work on Friday, his first payday. He was breathing easier, cautiously optimistic about releasing his fear of letting Channing down.

Dallas stayed until closing to help clean up. He focused on each detail as he cleaned the toilet and sink and then mopped the bathroom floor thoroughly. He sprayed down the storefront windows with Windex, putting some elbow grease into giving them a good shining with a rag. The squeaking sound of clean glass was satisfaction to his ears.

"Dallas, I was wondering." Mitchell stood at the counter, checking over the logbook for the day. "With you living in the shelter, is there a safe place to keep your money?"

Dallas paused in his enthusiastic cleaning and turned towards his boss. "I'm not sure," he pondered. "I don't want to just cash it and carry it around in there with me, though."

"Do you need some now?" Mitchell asked. "Or would you like me to hold it for you here?" His boss set the paycheck in Dallas's hands.

Dallas considered this offer, fingers gripped tight on his prize. He ran one hand through his lengthening hair. "I want a little cash for now, yeah, just so I can get my hair cut. Can I cash it and leave it here with you and take a little as needed? I've gotta save as much as possible to put towards renting a place."

Mitchell took back the check and handed Dallas a twenty, mentioning a nearby barbershop and telling him where he could cash the paycheck tomorrow. Dallas's outstretched hand trembled invisibly as the offered haircut money was placed in his palm. With a trusting and grateful heart, he headed out into the dark night.

Snow was falling again—a regular occurrence in Minnesota this time of year—and Dallas trotted, the thick tread of his boots crunching on the salty sidewalk. An overcast sky revealed no moon. Dallas glanced at his watch under the glow of a streetlight and hoisted his bag further up his shoulder. It was nearly 6:00. Dallas's stomach growled for dinner, and his work-weary body craved a good night's sleep before a full day tomorrow, which would earn him overtime. *That barbershop visit can fit into my lunch break.* He eagerly anticipated a haircut, being about three weeks overdue for one. Dallas considered the wisdom in buying a new electric hair clipper instead, like the one he'd had back home but had forgotten to bring with them. *It'll save money, and I need to be as frugal as possible.*

When Dallas dropped his bag on the bed next to Channing's, he knew that something had happened. His friend hunched small and still, all but his fidgeting hands. Dallas flopped down on his bed facing Channing, their knees almost touching as he leaned in closer. "Hey, what's up?" he asked in a low voice.

Channing shifted on his bed, nervous eyes darting up for a second, and said nothing.

Dallas surveyed the room, eyes like lightning, suspicions racing through his mind about everyone in the place.

Finally, Channing spoke. "That guy, Rex, over in the bed under the window," he whispered, trying not to look in that direction. "He made me give him my dinner. I was waiting for you to eat, but they told me to go ahead, and then nobody else saw what happened, and…"

Rage bubbled up inside of Dallas like lava. "Did you get anything to eat at all?" he asked, eyebrows lowered.

"Yeah, a bowl of soup," Channing quivered. "He took my roll, and my sandwich, and my dessert - a cookie."

"Why'd you let him?" Dallas spat out in a hissed whisper.

A hurt expression flashed across Channing's reddening face.

Dallas immediately regretted his question. "Well, did you tell the kitchen staff?"

"No," Channing whimpered. "I was too scared. He said he'd *cut me* if I told anyone. Said he'd do it while I was sleeping."

Fire blazed in Dallas's eyes. "With what? They won't let us have blades in here!" Dallas's knife and hatchet, initially stashed out in a planter along the street, were now stored in a drawer in the back office in Mitchell's shop.

"I don't know, Dallas," Channing said in a thin voice. "He might've smuggled something in here. Or maybe he'd use anything sharp he can find! Like a lid from a tin can, out of the garbage."

So much for my good night's sleep. Dallas gritted his teeth. If this type of thing had happened in Nevada, before Dallas was concerned about drawing the attention of the law, he would have called out and challenged any tormentor of Channing. In fact, he would have relished it. But now… there was too much risk involved in walking over to that scumbag and pummeling him. Instead, Dallas took Channing by the shoulder and walked him over to the on-duty staff to tell them what had happened.

The employee on the night shift, Tom, didn't come across as very understanding.

"Why didn't you report it right away?" asked Tom. There was silence as Channing stared at his shoes, blushing.

"He's really shy," Dallas tried. "I should've been here to stand up for him."

"He needs to stand up for himself," Tom sniped. "Rex will push you around if you let him."

Dallas scrubbed a hand over his face and huffed, "Okay, just let Channing wait to eat until I get here from now on, okay?"

"Nobody made him eat," Tom said. "It was just a suggestion. Why don't you two come in together each evening if he's that helpless?"

"Fine." Dallas sighed, giving up more easily than was in his nature. Against his judgment, he refrained from mentioning Rex's threat of cutting Channing. *Yet again, I'm the only one who cares about him.*

"Come on, Chan." Dallas filled up his tray just as the kitchen was about to close for the night. They sat at a table, where Dallas tore his grilled cheese in half and handed one piece to his downcast friend. *I used to assume one day Channing would be fine on his own, once he's an adult anyway, but...* Dallas still couldn't picture that happening. He scarfed down his half-sandwich and sat brooding.

"I'm sorry, Dallas," Channing said dully.

"Sorry for what?"

"Sorry that I can't defend myself," came Channing's deflated answer.

Dallas grimaced as that old uncomfortable wondering crept in, of what he'd think of himself if he were as defenseless as Channing. He tried a small smile to boost Channing's confidence. "Hey, I get it. I know you're shy with strangers. But I need to go to work so we can get out of here, and then you won't have to worry about things like that happening, okay? Let's come in together tomorrow. When the library closes at 5, just come over to the shop. I'm sure Mitchell won't mind if you hang out in the lobby 'til I'm done."

Unsettled in the pitch blackness following lights-out, Dallas shifted on the thin mattress. Sleep never came easily now — the still quiet of night always made room for the time and space to be reminded of the horrible accident — but tonight, his concern for Channing's safety had him on edge.

Well after midnight, Dallas was finally on the verge of slipping out of conscious thought when a noise jarred him awake. *Channing's having a nightmare.*

Dallas was out of bed in an instant, trying to stifle Channing's thrashing and cries from waking everyone up. He shook him hard and jabbed him in the side with his fingers, hissing in his ear.

"Channing, wake up, wake up! Channing!"

Channing bolted upright and blinked, bleary-eyed, at Dallas in the dark.

"It was… we were in that convenience store… the gunshot!" Channing clamped his hands over his ears and cowered.

Dallas went cold at Channing's description. "Shhh, just a bad dream," he whispered. "We're here in the shelter, remember? Go on back to sleep, Chan. I'm right here next to you, okay?"

Channing gave a semi-conscious smile and lay back down again on the edge of his bed, facing Dallas's. Dallas sat up a while longer in the dark, rocking slightly and watching as Channing reentered deep sleep. All his muscles tensed and taut, the scene from the death of the trooper played through his mind on repeat: the man's tight grip on him, Dallas pulling and shoving to get away, one hand of the trooper holding the drawn gun, the continued struggle, the sound of the gun firing as the trooper's hand was pressed into his own abdomen in Dallas's frantic push to free himself. In his mind, he saw Channing freeze outside the building at the blast, wheeling around in the parking lot and meeting Dallas at the door, the look of shock on his face as he stared past Dallas at the man in a crumpled heap on the floor, blood pooling… saw himself grabbing Channing as he barreled out of the building, leaping into the Isuzu and peeling out of the parking lot with the pedal pressed to the floor. Dallas held his face in his hands, willing himself to stop caring and to just focus on moving forward, but he couldn't block out the consuming horror of it. *I can't just sit wallowing in my wretchedness!* He darted up, hoping a walk to the bathroom and back might reset his brain.

He almost ran into somebody as he turned away from his bed. The figure was a shadow in the dark, looming a few inches taller than Dallas and much broader. Drowned in his guilty memories, Dallas hadn't heard anyone approach. He took a startled step back and, fists automatically at the ready to defend himself, allowed his eyes to adjust in the dimness as he stared at where the man's face should be. The hulking figure took a heavy step towards Dallas, and he knew it was Rex, Channing's dinner thief.

"What do you want?" demanded Dallas, hushed tone hostile. Rex took another step towards him, and this time Dallas stood his ground, the potential fight his only focus.

The bully snickered in a low voice, "Saw you and your friend snitchin' on me earlier. You gotta learn that ain't the way things work around here." Another step forward, and he was up against Dallas, who stared back into the man's now-visible face with iron in his darkening eyes.

"If stealing people's food is 'the way things work' in here, then you gotta learn that I don't play by unfair rules," returned Dallas, a wolfish instinct rising inside.

The man raised both eyebrows, and Dallas realized that he was probably used to successfully intimidating people. But Dallas was stubborn. *And maybe stupid, too.* This wasn't going to be an evenly matched fight by far.

"You give me part of your dinner every night, and I'll leave you both alone," Rex growled, "but if you don't…" He took another step forward, pressing against Dallas.

Dallas made himself taller and refused to back down. "You're not getting one bite of our food!" he snarled.

Then everything happened at once. Curses rang out, hands grabbed and shoved, and Dallas was knocked to the floor. Scrambling to regain his footing, he took a fist to the side of his face and staggered at the power of the punch. The overhead lights burst on, glaring bright fluorescent, a stunning contrast. Rex towered over Channing's bed, yanking him from under the blanket by his collar. Occupants of other beds began stirring, and two employees shouted from across the room, running in the direction of the commotion. Dallas's fury flamed beyond his control, and he was on Rex's back, hands around his neck from behind, squeezing, clawing, anything to stop him from whatever he was going to do to Channing, blind with rage and frantic over the threat to cut him. The attack produced sputters and gasps from Rex, but Channing's startled cry was all that Dallas had registered.

"Let him go!" Dallas demanded, cursing and choking Channing's aggressor.

The next instant, Dallas's clutching hands were pried off Rex's neck, Channing was led away from the altercation, and three shelter employees were wrestling the large instigator into submission. Dallas's sharp eyes scanned Rex's hands for a makeshift weapon, his reactionary senses at full volume until he was sure the threat was contained.

Dallas stepped towards Channing, but Tom still restrained him by both wrists. "Hold it!" he ordered.

"He came after us!" sputtered Dallas. "I told you, he already conned Channing out of his dinner, and now he wants to intimidate us into letting him keep doing it!" Dallas jerked his arms away from Tom's grip.

"Stop resisting!" barked Tom. Another staff member now flanked Dallas's other side. "Kevin's going to step in to help me if you get aggressive again."

"It wasn't me!" Dallas exploded, wrenching his arms free again. "I had to defend myself after he attacked me!" Tom and Kevin pulled him back again.

"Dallas, he hit you!" Channing gasped, face paler than normal.

Dallas touched the spot along his jawbone. Gauging by the tenderness, he would be sporting a nice bruise there by morning.

By now, the whole room was abuzz with confusion, from murmurs to angry outbursts. Rex had been dragged from the sleeping quarters into an adjacent room. They could still hear his protests through the wall. "Look at the marks that jerk put on my neck!" he was shouting.

After a brief assessment of what had happened, both Dallas and Rex were ordered to leave the shelter. If they wouldn't go peacefully, the police would be called. Rex gave in, grumbling, and was given his bags at the door and ushered out into the cold night.

Dallas, still shaking with adrenaline, raved in protest. "But *he* attacked *me!* Then ripped my friend out of bed by the neck! I wasn't gonna just stand by and take it, and watch him beat up Channing too!"

"I'm sorry, Mr. Malone, but you're going to have to leave now," Tom reiterated calmly. "You signed the papers with the understanding that we have zero tolerance for fighting. If you use violence on anyone here, you're gone. Channing may stay, but if you don't take your things and leave, we *will* call the police."

Dallas stood staring, fuming. *This can't be happening!*

Channing came alongside him and murmured, "Come on, Dallas, let's go."

Dallas hesitated, glowering at Tom and Kevin. *Should I make Channing stay? Would that be better for him, safer?* Dallas turned to his friend and opened his mouth.

Channing spoke first. "I'm coming with you if you're kicked out," he said firmly. "I don't wanna stay here by myself, even if Rex is gone."

Dallas wasn't ready to relent. "So you're gonna just turn us out into the night with Rex, so he can come after us out there instead?"

"Nobody is allowed to remain in this shelter after getting into a fight like that," Tom repeated, voice rising. He picked up Dallas's bag and held it out to him. "The soup kitchen on 4th Street serves a hot lunch every day at noon. But we don't want to see you back here again."

Dallas snatched the bag with a sneer and grabbed his sleeping bag and pillow. Channing followed suit. They were escorted to the door and stepped into the icy Minnesota night air, the door clanging shut behind them. They stood side by side, paralyzed with uncertainty. Dallas scanned the parking lot and beyond with penetrating eyes, alert for any sign of Rex.

Channing's small voice shattered the silence. "Where should we go?"

Dallas fought to swallow the lump in his throat. "I have no idea. Come on." He trudged down the side of the building, hoping that Rex had gone in another direction.

Channing and Dallas tramped through the snow for a half-hour until they came to a wooded slope by the side of the interstate. Seeking shelter under the trees, Dallas flicked on his flashlight and swept its beam across the trunks.

"Come on, let's pitch the tent in here," Dallas decided. He found a flat area on the ground and opened his bag.

Channing helped. "Good thing it's not still snowing," he commented.

Hesitating, Dallas pulled out his lighter. "I'm gonna build a fire first, though. We need to warm up as much as we can. See if you can find any dry wood." He pulled back branches of some nearby shrubs. *No luck.* Everything under the bushes was damp from the snow.

Channing returned to Dallas's side with a couple of slightly damp sticks. He set them on the ground where Dallas had cleared back the snow and ice.

A few pine trees with low branches stood sheltering the area, and Dallas shimmied up into the closest one. "Catch," he called out, and Channing stood below to retrieve the pinecones Dallas dropped.

A few minutes later, Dallas crouched over the small pile of sticks and pinecones, fraying the end of his rope and extracting fluffy strands to use as tinder. *I hope there's enough lighter fluid in this thing.* Dallas flicked the tiny steel wheel and held the flame against the bits of cotton.

The fire smoked more than it flamed with tiny dwindling flickers. Dallas stared at it contemptuously. *I'm a failure.*

"Warm your hands as best you can," Dallas advised. "The wood's too wet to make it bigger, but at least we can warm our fingers a little before we get in the tent. Here, you take a turn while I get it pitched."

Dallas chose a spot against a large tree with only a thin layer of snow on the ground and scraped away what he could with the sides of his boots. He and Channing worked quickly, alternating turns at the struggling fire and getting the tent up with the skimpy tarp underneath. *That's not gonna give us much insulation.* Dallas bitterly surveyed the area, spotting some dead leaves piled up under nearby trees. He inspected them, knocking off the top snowy layer.

"Let's gather up a few armfuls," he instructed Channing. "We can pile them in the tent to help keep us warm."

Channing nodded vigorously. "Like squirrels would do! It's too bad we can't go into torpor to conserve energy while we sleep. Chickadees do that, and even then, they still have to eat all day long. Or groundhogs —did you know their body temperature drops to 38 degrees when they're hibernating?"

Dallas, all action, shoveled up scoops of leaves in his arms and stuffed them inside the tent rather than trying to understand Channing's science lesson.

A few minutes later, they huddled inside the tent on top of a thick layer of leaves, wrapped in sleeping bags and blankets, trying to regain sensation in their frozen bodies. They wore extra socks over their bare hands, pulled on over the pathetic flame of Dallas's fire that was now cold ash outside the tent.

Channing, motionless except for his shivering, watched Dallas's face with a small frown in the dim glow from the flashlight switched on at their feet.

Dallas sat upright, glowering at nothing. Channing silently scooted up alongside him. Dallas gave no acknowledgment.

"Dallas?" Channing whispered. Getting no response, Channing continued. "Come on, let's just go back to sleep now that we're settled here. So you won't be too tired for work in the morning."

Dallas almost snorted in response, then bit his lip and sighed instead. "I'm still too worked up. You can lie down. I'll just sit up being mad awhile."

Channing studied Dallas's face, stern and unmoving. He tried again. "Dallas, don't let it keep you mad. It's over now."

Dallas jerked around to face his friend. "I can't *help* but be mad!" he spluttered with a scowl. "That guy could've pounded us both! I suppose you're going to say I should just 'turn the other cheek' or something. And now, even though it wasn't our fault, we're out here where we'll probably get frostbite, or hypothermia, or..." Dallas swiped at the leaves piled before him, scattering them with his fist.

Channing said nothing for a minute. Then, shifting inside his sleeping bag, he added, "I just thought you would feel better if you let go of the anger." He curled up tight and laid his head down on his pillow, looking up at Dallas with clear eyes. "Do you remember in *The Divine Comedy*, where Dante meets the wrathful in *The Purgatorio*?"

"Maybe." Dallas remained noncommittal. The book Channing referenced was in the trunk of Dallas's Isuzu, back in Texas.

"I was thinking of the footnote that explained how wrath blinds the reason like smoke," Channing continued. "The Italian phrase mentioned by the translator, the one that means 'to lose the lamp of his eyes...' Well, I don't want that to happen to you, Dallas."

Dallas's instinct was to snap back in response, but he held it in. *I shouldn't dump my rage onto Channing. He's just trying to be helpful in his own way. But I can't help being wrathful! I can't relax,* his mind raced helplessly, *not when everything's going wrong, everything's against us! Wrathful, yeah! I wish I was burning in hell now, where at least we wouldn't be freezing to death.* But for Channing's sake, Dallas shot him a tired attempt at a grin before switching off the flashlight and said, "Yeah, okay. I'll let it go and just get some sleep."

Channing, seeming satisfied, pulled the covers over his head and burrowed down. Dallas lay awake, bombarded by their problems, coldness seeping into his bones. He was suddenly overwhelmed by this latest setback now that nothing else required his diligence. *We can't just sleep out here in the subzero weather night after night! What are we going to do?* The wrath melted away as despair crept in to take its place. The tightness in Dallas's chest grew, and he wrapped his arms miserably around himself. *I can't do this anymore; I can't!* His shoulders shook, and Dallas couldn't hold back the hot tears that flowed down his cheeks. He gasped, trying to stifle his sudden uncontrollable blubbering. *Channing would've been better off with his mother!* Dallas berated himself. *I can't do anything right! I've ruined our lives!* Dallas could no longer pretend everything was fine. The defensive outer shell he'd fought so hard to keep up had cracked. His body shook, racked with wrenching sobs.

Channing sat up and scooted closer to Dallas, laying a hand on his back.

"Dallas." Channing's soft voice was surprisingly steady. "Dallas, it's okay. It'll be okay."

"I'm... sorry," was all Dallas could choke out between sobs. He was ashamed, defeated, engulfed.

Channing hugged Dallas from behind, through the sleeping bag.

Dallas's heaves gradually subsided until he lay like a statue, numb.

"Dallas, it's okay," Channing repeated. "Tomorrow's a new day. You have some money now, and you still have your job. We could get a hotel room on the coldest nights. We won't freeze to death!"

Channing's optimistic words rang hollow in Dallas's ears. "Maybe. But that'd run us dry real fast. Mitchell's holding just under $400 for me. That's a lot, I know, but it won't last long if we spend a few nights at a hotel. I guess I can check around tomorrow and see what the cheapest rate is."

"Then let's just try to stay warm enough tonight," Channing replied. "At least we have these good coats from the shelter. That was nice of them to give them to us, wasn't it? We could still camp some nights, when it's not sleeting or snowing."

Dallas wasn't so sure. He'd hoped to avoid February in the north by going south. But now they had to just play with the hand that had been dealt to them.

"Okay," Dallas relented. "Here, get under the blankets and sleeping bags with me. We need the body heat." He shifted, unzipping his sleeping bag, still unable to make eye contact with his friend after his display of weakness.

As they hunkered down, Channing whispered, "I wonder where Rex went, and how he's keeping warm all alone?"

Dallas almost felt sorry for the man. He scowled. *But not quite.*

Shivering back to back, Dallas and Channing finally fell asleep.

Channing sat waiting in the lobby of Mitchell's shop, coffee in one hand, tattered paperback in the other. He'd picked up a couple of books at an estate sale earlier that morning with a five-dollar bill Dallas had given him. Mitchell and Dallas were completing a brake job before closing time.

"Channing's coming into the shop a lot lately," Mitchell commented offhandedly, positioned in the driver's seat and pumping the brakes.

"I hope that's okay," Dallas said, bleeding out all the air with the valve on the caliper until brake fluid squirted onto his hand. "I mean, is it a problem? I know how it looks, him sitting in there with a sleeping bag and backpack stuffed with all his belongings..."

"I was more wondering if everything's okay with him," said Mitchell. He stepped out of the car and inspected Dallas's work as he connected a new brake line. "And you," he added, and Dallas could tell he was studying the remains of his mostly faded bruised jaw. He had brushed it off as nothing when Mitchell had noticed it the morning after Rex had attacked him, five days ago now.

Dallas took a relenting breath and described what had happened to Channing at dinner that day and how it had resulted in the middle-of-the-night confrontation. "So we got kicked out of the shelter, even though this other guy provoked the fight. And I'm worried that Channing could bump into him somewhere, out alone during the day. He's been going to the library, but I worry about him until he's back in my sight. I have to earn enough to get us a safe place to live." Dallas pivoted the caliper back into place and ratcheted the bolt down until it was snug.

"Where are you staying at night now?" asked Mitchell as he rolled the wheel alongside the car and grabbed the impact wrench.

"We have a tent," Dallas answered, his face growing hot under the grease from the afternoon's work.

"You're sleeping in a tent in the snow?" Mitchell was incredulous. "It got down to four degrees last night!"

"We stayed in a hotel last night," Dallas added quickly, the luxury of a night in a real bed still delicious in his memory. "When it was over 15 degrees, we camped."

"That's still way too cold. You guys need shelter."

Dallas made no reply. He fiddled absently with the leaky brake cable they'd removed, winding and unwinding it around his fingers.

"So, do you know where this Rex character ended up?" Mitchell asked.

"No idea, which is why I'm more concerned for Channing than usual," Dallas answered.

"You're good to take care of him. You said he was abused by his parents?"

Dallas nodded, gathering up the old brake pads they'd removed and setting them aside while Mitchell reattached the wheel.

"Man, that's rough," continued Mitchell. "Makes my blood boil when a kid is treated like that. There's plenty of people out there who would give anything to have kids, and then you see some of these people who don't even deserve to be parents. It's pretty sickening, if you ask me. So is that why the two of you ran away, ended up in the shelter? What about your own parents?"

Dallas focused on the wrench he was wiping off and tried to formulate a response.

"It's okay if you don't want to talk about it," Mitchell added quickly.

Dallas nodded, absorbed in cleaning up. *How much should I tell Mitchell?* He thought of the story Channing had told him about his mother's first mental breakdown when he was five years old. She'd torn his room apart, searching for a pair of his overalls while calling Channing by his father's name, cursing and flinging clothing around the room. Channing had actually been wearing the overalls but hadn't been able to make her see that, so he'd retreated to his place of refuge: the roof. He would get up there by climbing a tree that grew close to the house. When his mother had dragged a ladder out to climb up after him, he'd crawled back down and shut himself in the bathroom. Dallas couldn't fathom the confusion and terror Channing must have felt as a young child. The police had eventually been called by a neighbor, and his mother was taken to a hospital. Channing had been found huddled in the bathroom after the police officers had broken down the door to get to him.

Dallas broke out of his trance, aware that Mitchell had been studying him with furrowed brow. Dallas decided he owed it to him to reveal just a little more. *He seems to trust me, and I want my boss to think well of me…*

"The reason we left home," Dallas explained, "is because my mother disappeared. She left me a note saying she wasn't coming back. So we had to fend for ourselves. Channing, he wanted to stay with me rather than with his crazy mother, so, well, we left, and we've just drifted around a bit, trying to start over." Dallas shut his mouth in a tight line and hoped not to have to say anything further on the matter.

Mitchell's eyes were soft. "You know, I feel terrible, you guys out in the cold at night. You've been such a hard, reliable worker in just these first few weeks, and you've hit on some hard times. I'd like to pay you in advance for the next month, help you get on your feet faster so you can get yourself a place, so I can keep you working for me. You have a real knack with cars, Dallas, a real knack. And I admire how responsible you are for your friend, wanting to take care of him along with yourself. You're a respectable young man. I can see that."

Dallas almost couldn't believe what he'd heard. *A month in advance?* He'd already earned two weeks' pay and his second paycheck was due in another week.

"How about it?" Mitchell was asking Dallas now. "With two months' pay in your pocket, do you think you can find a place? And until then, you and Channing are staying at my house. I can't have my employees losing their hands to frostbite, now, can I?"

Dallas gaped at the surprise. "Thank you," he stammered, his throat dry. "It's more than I deserve, for sure, but wow. I don't know what to say. I don't want to intrude on you, though. We can camp again tonight now that yesterday's snowstorm has blown over. I'll just be so relieved to get Channing and me into our own place!"

"You won't be intruding," Mitchell insisted. "It's gonna hit below zero tonight. My wife is out of town for the week visiting her mother, so it's just me at the house right now. Stay tonight, and I'll help you look into some possible rentals."

Dallas could only nod, his breath shuddery, and accept the stroke of good fortune.

Dallas told Channing the news as soon as the tools were put away.

"Tomorrow, we're going to go and look for a rental, a cheap one, but a place of our own. It's finally happening — we're starting over again!" Dallas tried to make himself believe it could be like old times when he and Channing were more carefree.

Channing's demeanor lightened, and he grinned his infectious child-like smile. "That's great, Dallas!"

Cautiously optimistic, Dallas smiled back, trying to force himself to feel positive, to keep pushing back the worries and guilt that he carried with him perpetually, hidden deep within himself.

PROFESSION OF FAITH

Dallas reached across the rickety wooden table for the sandwich bread. The open jar of Skippy peanut butter sat alongside—the crunchy kind, Channing's preference. Dallas spread a glob onto a piece of bread with a plastic spoon. He was sick of eating the same thing for every meal over the past few days. He took a bite and grimaced. *At least I get my next paycheck this week. And the rent is paid; the utilities are covered.*

The midday sun streamed through the window above the sink. Dallas stood, ingesting his sandwich bite by slow bite. Channing hammered in the backyard, constructing a "squirrel park," his latest hobby. A series of squirrel feeders, ramps, tunnels, platforms, and bridges crisscrossed the yard. Dallas watched with jealousy-tinged admiration as a squirrel scampered up to Channing's outstretched hand and took the corn kernel he offered. *I thought it was crazy, but apparently, the squirrels love it.* Ever since Channing had designed the park with scrap lumber he'd found in the crawl space, the little critters hadn't left the yard.

Dallas ran one hand along a splintered section of the window frame. The one-bedroom house showed its age, but it was what they could afford and certainly a step up from the homeless shelter. *The accident in Oklahoma changed our course so fast. It's been a hard few months, but things have ended up better than I hoped, and with a job I love, too.*

Dallas finished his sandwich and kept staring out the window, stuffing his hands into the pockets of his jeans. He pondered Channing's figure, childlike as he crouched in the dirt, bent over his creation. Oblivious to everything outside his own little world, he swept a lock of his chin-length hair behind his ear, only to have it fall back into his eyes a moment later. *Channing doesn't seem to have a care in the world. I wish I could be that at ease.* Dallas sighed. Despite the exterior stability of their current life, he constantly second-guessed himself for having dragged Channing into such a mess. *At least the trauma hasn't seemed to put him more on edge, especially since we've gotten settled here. He trusts me too much. But isn't that what I've been trying to do? To absorb the stress so he won't feel it the way I do?*

Dallas closed his eyes and tried to picture his life prior to Channing. He couldn't. Never one to have many friends, Dallas was a loner by choice. *But it's always been different with Channing.* Dallas's instincts about the boy had only grown stronger all these years later. *It's weird how I gravitated towards the kid everyone else picked on, because I know I could sometimes be a real jerk back then. And after everything that's happened, I'm even more sure of this—I'd die for Channing in a heartbeat.* Dallas's conscience piped in, *You already killed for him.* A reeling dizziness hit him, and he shook the tragedy from his mind. He lowered his eyebrows in determination. *As long as Channing's okay, that's all that matters.*

Dallas took a sip of his coffee and studied Channing's mannerisms from the window as he dragged two boards to a partly constructed bridge for the squirrels. *He really seems content. Maybe I haven't wrecked his life after all and should cut myself some slack.* He heaved a deep sigh.

Dallas's thoughts shifted to his mother. *Was she really in bad trouble, or just sick of supporting me?* He pictured her weary, stoic face, worn down over years of solitude, and tried in vain to remember the last time she'd hugged him. He wondered if he should have done something differently. *But I was just a kid.* He clenched his teeth. It was because of her they had begun their trek across the country, their search for a job and home, and… Dallas stopped short. *Stop thinking about the accident!* He screwed the lid on the peanut butter.

We're safe now, and we've started all over. This is a place where we're both happy, thriving even, and if we can just keep from being found... Dallas paced the kitchen. *We're over a thousand miles away. It's finally getting warmer here, and we're fitting in, living like normal people.* Dallas's endless mental tug-of-war game threatened to tear his sanity apart some days. He'd almost begin to believe his pep talk, and then something as minor as a police car driving past would send the adrenaline surging through his body again.

Channing stood up, brushing the dirt from his hands on the seat of his corduroys. He raised his hand to cover a cough and then picked his way across the yard. He entered the kitchen as Dallas was wiping down the counter. Channing went to the sink to wash his hands.

"How're your squirrels?" Dallas inquired.

"Oh, they're doing well overall," responded Channing. "The first three that came—Travis, Bill, and Jack—they're starting to become friendly with the newer ones. Seems like they're buddies with the other Jack and Peter now. There's a new one today; I named him Clement. But Linus is limping—it looks like he hurt a hind leg somehow."

"Poor Linus," mused Dallas mindlessly, wondering how Channing could even tell them apart. *And he sure comes up with weird names for squirrels.*

Channing laid two slices of bread on the table. Then he opened the refrigerator and peered inside.

"There's nothing in there, Chan," Dallas said.

Channing paid him no heed and took out the mustard. He spread it onto the bread with his fingers, then delicately placed three gummy worms on the sandwich. The candy had been their one splurge item, a treat bought when Dallas had cashed his last paycheck.

Dallas wrinkled his nose. "How can you eat that?"

"It's good!" As Channing picked up the sandwich, mustard oozed onto his fingers.

Dallas scrutinized his friend's bony frame, frowning. Channing's diet had never been nourishing. Last week, he had been sick with some kind of stomach flu. The virus had attacked Channing's frail body, and he'd had a hard time getting rid of it. *I still can't let my guard down. I have to keep earning as much as I can. What would we do if he got seriously sick and needed a doctor?* Dallas would just have to continue putting one foot in front of the other now. *Being an adult sucks, but what other choice do I have?*

Late that night, Dallas woke with a start. Drowsy and disoriented after a few hours' sleep, he wondered what had disturbed him. Then he heard Channing yelling out from his bed on the sofa. Dallas was out of the bedroom and beside him in an instant. *One of his nightmares. He hasn't had any since we moved in here.* Dallas shook him, gently at first, ducking to avoid Channing's thrashing arms. He shook him harder.

"Channing, wake up," he commanded.

Channing cried out, "No! Help me!" and rolled over violently.

Dallas continued shaking him until Channing suddenly sat up, breathing hard.

When he recognized where he was, Channing drew in a long breath and let it out in a shuddery sigh, then began breathing normally again. "Just a nightmare," he said, tucking his knees under his trembling chin.

"Was it about… in Oklahoma…" Dallas's voice trailed off as a pang from his guilty conscience pricked him.

"No, not that this time," Channing responded quickly. "I was in my old house, and I couldn't get out. There were no windows, no doors, and I was trapped. Something was trying to get me, and I couldn't figure out how to escape. But you woke me up in time, before it got worse. Thanks." He reached for the pillow he'd knocked off the couch. "Sorry I woke you up," Channing added, voice back to normal.

"No problem," Dallas said. "You okay now?"

"Yeah, I'm fine, thanks," Channing said through a yawn.

Dallas wandered back to his bed and lay down under the covers again. He never had nightmares. Instead, he couldn't sleep, as nightmare-like worries consumed him mentally. *I'm the one who needs reassurance. Reassurance that I'm still me — still the same person I was before the accident and not some monster.* But Dallas couldn't ask Channing for that. *I need to be the strong one.* Channing's nightmares were very real, physical reactions lingering from what he had endured in the past. *I can't burden Channing with my guilt.*

After passing a restless night, Dallas arose at 6:30 to get ready for work. He took a quick shower and threw on some clothes. Channing stumbled sleepily into the kitchen and sat at the table, where he pulled on his socks with the yellow stripes at the tops. Dallas handed him a vitamin C tablet.

"Why do I have to take this dumb vitamin every day?" Channing complained.

"Because it'll help your cold go away," Dallas answered.

"No, it won't," Channing said. "I have a permanent cold."

"Well, it's good for you anyways," Dallas said as he chewed a vitamin himself and wondered if he believed his own words. "I'll be back from work at 4:30 or so. I get my paycheck today, so maybe we can go out to eat tonight."

Channing's eyes lit up at the prospect. He opened a cabinet and took the last bagel. Gnawing on it, he waved goodbye through the doorway as Dallas walked down the gravel driveway.

Dallas trekked briskly along his route to work, a mile away by road. The rental house shrank in the distance as Dallas walked the narrow, unpaved side street, grateful that at last the snow and slush had disappeared, hopefully for the season. Buds on the trees were opening, and birds sang and flitted around in a frenzy of activity. Dallas held a slight grudge about having to live so far north, but he was starting to feel better about it now that spring was arriving.

Dallas entered Mitchell's Garage through the back door and checked the appointment book. There were only two customers scheduled for that day — Fridays were often slow.

Mitchell greeted Dallas and went over the itinerary. "You can probably head out around 3:00 today," Mitchell told him. "There's not much to do once these jobs are complete. There's a good article I want you to read in here," he added as he handed Dallas an automotive magazine flagged with a post-it note.

Dallas organized equipment around the shop in between the car jobs.

After replacing the transmission on a station wagon, he was done for the day. He said goodbye to Mitchell and walked across the street to the small grocery store, the only one in town, where Dallas cashed his paycheck at the bank inside.

Channing was outside when Dallas got home. The full sun made the near-50-degree temperature pleasant for Minnesota. Dallas gathered a few sticks to build a fire in the ring of stones he'd arranged in the yard.

Channing darted across the yard, wearing his Flying J t-shirt and making big rig noises, and pretended to talk into a CB radio.

Dallas watched him wonderingly while standing beside the fire — *this is the same seventeen-year-old whose favorite authors are Chesterton and Tolkien, who makes works of art effortlessly. Once he's done with his game, he's likely to attempt a deep intellectual discussion with me.* Channing was an enigma, and there was no better way to put it.

Dallas tried to ignore Channing's "Breaker, breaker, what's your handle?" lingo and concentrate on the article that Mitchell had asked him to read. After a few minutes, small twigs and pinecones rained down around him.

"Target in sight... clearance for attack? Clearance granted... aim...missile launch... attack successful, target destroyed!"

A pinecone hit Dallas on the knee and bounced off. He pretended to fall out of his lawn chair. "They've shot me down!" he wailed, then stretched out flat on his back alongside the fire and continued reading, magazine held at arm's length above his face. Another pinecone hit Dallas's elbow.

Channing threw himself to the ground nearby and shouted, "Duck and cover drill! The Cubans are attacking! Air raid!"

Dallas squinted at the print as Channing crept across the yard and occupied himself elsewhere. He finished the article a few minutes later and propped himself up on one elbow. Channing was in a ditch near the tree line, and Dallas could hear him saying something about 'trench warfare.' He thumbed through the magazine and began another article, distracted after a few minutes by Channing reciting a poem, one he had liked for many years now. Dallas paused in his reading to listen, eyes closed. He could hear the phrases in his mind as he caught them coming on the breeze from where Channing dramatically proclaimed them:

'"Forward, the Light Brigade!'
Was there a man dismay'd ?

buildings, and landscape in my kingdom. I'll paint murals on the walls, all I want, and nobody will mind. And of course, you'll have to help me make stained glass windows for the buildings..."

Channing's lilting voice fluttered on about his favorite form of art. He had started a new glass collection when they'd settled here, although without the kiln, Channing had been unable to make more glass artwork. Dallas half-listened as Channing elaborated on the history of stained glass. *This is why he can't get a job.* Channing just wasn't quite anchored enough in reality, not reliably enough for steady employment, anyway. *They'd fire him from any job in a heartbeat if he started daydreaming about a magical kingdom, much less if he talked about it to anyone. It's kinda wild what the abuse did to him. I wouldn't wish his past on anyone, but he wouldn't be Channing if he were any other way.* A lump rose in Dallas's throat.

"I wish we had some marshmallows," Channing said wistfully. "We haven't roasted any in forever."

"Going out for dinner will be our treat this time," Dallas replied. "Marshmallows have zero nutrition. Maybe in a few more months, once we save up."

"I don't eat as many at once as I used to," Channing said solemnly.

"Right, ever since you read about the gluttonous circle in *The Inferno,*" Dallas said. "So, do you want to go to dinner now?"

"Maybe once you get another car, we can stop at the Stuckey's for ice cream," Channing said, a gleam from the dancing flames reflected in his eyes as he gazed into Dallas's fire. "We passed it when we came here, only a few exits away."

"Sure, sure," Dallas replied, tapping his foot. "Don't get off the subject. The question now is where we should eat tonight."

"Okay, Katherine's Kitchen," Channing decided.

"Fine with me," replied Dallas. "Let me change my clothes, and we'll go."

"Wait a sec, Dallas." Channing stopped him. "Looking at your fire reminded me." He was rummaging through a stack of books on the back step of the house and pulled out the thickest one. "Lemme read you something first."

As Channing sat down in the grass beside the fire ring, Dallas craned his neck to get a glimpse of the book. "Is that a Bible?"

Channing flipped through the pages and nodded. "Got it at that estate sale a few weeks ago. I've been reading through the Psalms, a little each day, and I read this earlier. Here it is." He cleared his throat, glancing up to see that Dallas was attentive.

"Lord, you have made your decrees with justice and absolute truth," began Channing in his clear voice. "Your promises have been *tested in the fire,* and your servant delights in them. I am not strong, no one respects me, but I have not forgotten your precepts. Your justice is justice forever, and your law is truth. Trouble and suffering are my lot, but your commandments are my delight. Your decrees are righteous forever. Give me understanding, *and I shall live.*"

Channing raised his head after his dramatic ending towards his friend across the flames, as if asking him what he thought of it. When Dallas made no comment, he said, "I thought you might like the fire imagery. It made me think of you when I read it. But the whole thing also makes me think of myself, too. Of both of us, really."

"It's not true that no one respects you, though," Dallas pointed out. "I respect you."

Channing broke into a wide grin. "I know it. Something in it just made me want to read it to you. I love the last line especially."

Dallas was silent at this, staring into the leaping flames. *Give me understanding, and I shall live...* If there was meaning in the words, it eluded Dallas. *Trouble and suffering...* Dallas shifted, and his stomach fluttered.

They sat a while longer, watching the fire slow to an ashy glow. Hungry, Dallas spread out the remains of the fire with a stick so they could get ready to go.

Dallas leaned back, every crumb from his plate devoured. A half-empty pot of coffee sat on the table between them. Channing was folding the napkins into origami-style shapes, the last of his order of three cheese biscuits untouched. Dallas helped himself to the rest of Channing's food.

As they lingered over their coffee, Dallas cleared his throat. It was like pulling teeth for him to bring up his weaknesses and worries, even to Channing, but deep inside, he'd been floundering with his opinion of himself as a man, and Channing's earlier talk of a fantasy world had touched a nerve.

"Channing, I need to ask you something," Dallas began, voice low. He glanced around the restaurant, then took a deep breath. "I need to know, well... When you were talking about your dream of a kingdom where everything's perfect, and you said you wanted good people there, like me, but you also said there'd be no crime. You know that I'm... I'm a *criminal.*" Dallas sputtered out the last word disgustedly. "I messed up, big time."

They had avoided discussing the accident until now. The truth festered just under the surface lately as the comfort of their new life sank in.

"I'd definitely want you to be there!" Channing insisted. "You're my best friend, and you treat me better than anyone else ever has. You respect me. You accept me for who I am. You forgive me when I mess up and do careless things. You make sure I have basic necessities — food and shelter and even those gross vitamins, Dallas! You *care* about me! You..."

Dallas cut him off. "Did you not hear what I said, Channing? I'm a criminal. A *criminal!* If you want a place free of crime, I can't be there. I don't like to remind you of something so awful," Dallas grumbled, hands scrunched on his temples. "But it's been eating me up inside, and keeping it bottled up is pure hell! I *hate* myself for it! I was just trying to help us survive, and then I go and commit such a heinous crime..."

It was Channing's turn to interrupt. "Dallas," he said, glancing up to be sure the waitress was still back in the kitchen, "don't talk about yourself that way! It was an accident! You were *trying* to do the right thing. A criminal — you? I've never thought of you that way! I mean, I know what you did; I remember, and it was terrible what happened, but you didn't *mean* for it to end up that way! We had to eat; you didn't want us to starve! And you're sorry, Dallas. I *know* you're sorry for what happened! That means there's hope for you, and since I know you're sorry, of course, I'd still want you in my dream world! You don't always have to be perfect as long as you're trying, knowing right from wrong!"

Dallas had his face buried in his hands, shaking his head back and forth. "Sometimes I wish it'd been me that died back there," he whispered.

Tears streamed down Channing's face. "See, that's because you *are* a good person! I know you would give up your life protecting me!"

"But I did the *wrong* thing!" Dallas said, his voice rising. "That's the whole point! I'm an impulsive, quick-tempered punk who can't control myself!"

"You didn't mean to!" Channing insisted. "It all happened so fast! If any little thing had been different, it would've come out another way. We aren't completely innocent, but intent is important, too, and I know you didn't *intend* it to happen that way! We tried to get food in honest ways, and we couldn't! Dallas, stop saying you're a criminal, *please!*" Desperation flashed in his eyes as he clawed Dallas's hand across the table. "You didn't threaten him. You didn't have a weapon! He *never* should have pulled his gun on us!"

"Channing," Dallas said, leaning forward over the table and looking him straight in the eye, "we escaped, and we're far away now, but do you know what will happen if we get found? I've just been pretending that can't happen, but I can't keep ignoring reality. No jury is gonna find me innocent if I do get found someday." Dallas swallowed. "And my worst fear is that you'll have to take some of the rap too. I can't let that happen. You're the one who got caught in the middle."

"But that's where I would want to be," Channing insisted. "We were in a desperate situation. If you're guilty of anything, then I'm guilty right there with you. I shoplifted too!"

Dallas winced. *Channing would never survive prison! Now that he's almost eighteen, that's where he would go for something this serious, isn't it?* Dallas felt fire in his face as he thought about anyone hurting Channing.

"I'd never let you take any of the blame," Dallas protested, folding his arms across his chest. "I'd rather lie, say that you didn't take anything, didn't know I was stealing, even. That's how I wanted it to be in the first place." He set his jaw and stared at Channing, daring him to argue.

Channing fell silent. He cast a long look out the window and then turned back to Dallas with a sigh. "At some point, you've gotta let me show you how much you mean to me, Dallas. I couldn't ever repay you for everything you've done for me, but I can accept it and marvel at why you'd ever want to sacrifice yourself for *me*, and I can only stand by you and take the punishment alongside you, if it comes to that. You *have* to let me have that choice. What sort of friend would I be if you covered for me while I abandoned you and went free? I wouldn't be able to live with myself! I'm partly to blame too, and I'm truly sorry for it."

For the first time, the hook Dallas hung from loosened just a bit. His tense muscles relaxed as what Channing was telling him sank in, a burden lessened. *Channing has that right...* the right to make his own decisions about his role in their friendship, the right to take on responsibilities and decide what he was willing to live with, the right to show Dallas what he meant to him as well. Dallas closed his eyes. *And I have to accept that from Channing. He really is capable of more than I give him credit for.*

Channing stacked and unstacked extra coffee creamers, eyes on his task. "You want to know something?" he asked. "You might not like hearing this, but, Dallas, your friendship and how you're always making sacrifices for my sake... well, you've taught me so much about God."

Dallas's jaw dropped, dumbstruck. *Me teaching anyone about God? God, who I might not even believe in?*

Before Dallas could think of how to fill the silence that hung in the air, Channing added softly, "But God gave his creation free will to love him back. He paid the ultimate price for us, when we didn't deserve it at all, just like how I didn't do anything to deserve your friendship. God lets us show him we love him back. Just look at the early Christian martyrs who died gruesome deaths out of love for their faith! You're not God, Dallas…"

At this, Dallas snorted. "Of course not," he interjected. "Not even close."

"So you can't make a perfect sacrifice," Channing continued. "But you're trying to make the best sacrifices you can. Humans aren't perfect, and it backfired when you tried to help us all by yourself. But, since you're *not* God, you also don't have to bear the whole brunt of this sin on your shoulders. You've gotta let me take some of it. I *have* to, to show how grateful I am that you care so much about me," Channing finished. "I've told God I'm sorry, and if there are consequences, then I need to accept them with you."

Dallas didn't say anything for a long time. The two of them refilled their coffee mugs and sipped in silence as the waitress brought out a fresh pot and cleared away their empty plates.

Dallas stared into the darkness outside, wrestling with the inadequacy of his decision-making skills, or lack thereof. *Channing's so much smarter than me. He was right—we should've turned ourselves in immediately! It would've been better for us then.* But that little stubborn part deep inside of Dallas wouldn't let him relent completely.

"Okay, Channing," Dallas finally said. "We're in this together. You and me. We'll stand together or fall together. I still just want to protect you, but you're right. You're practically a man yourself now, and I should start treating you more like one. Like brothers." He looked up and reached a hand across the table to where Channing clasped it back, arm-wrestling style.

"Like brothers," Channing repeated softly. "Man to man."

Though the gravity of the crime still hung over them, a warm peace settled inside both boys.

"I think I want to become Catholic." Channing looked up from his coffee. "Actually, I *know* I do."

Dallas almost dropped his fork, and then a smile played at the corners of his mouth. "Where'd that come from?" *Leave it to Channing to drop in a big announcement like that.*

"You've probably guessed it's something I've been thinking about for a long time." Channing glanced up at his friend's face. "And I was just talking about God, you know, so it's not such a random time for me to bring it up."

Dallas flipped through files in his brain of Channing's many attempts at discussion about his religious encounters. *Yes, the signs have all been there.* Dallas had assumed they were part of Channing's fantasy world, things he planned to maybe do one day but would never really come to fruition. Dallas studied Channing's earnest, rock-solid expression across the table. *He's dead serious. I probably should've seen this coming.* He hadn't wanted to think about it and thus had dismissed the signs as unimportant.

"So why?" Dallas asked what he thought was the obvious question. "Do you think it's going to make you happy?"

Channing replied, "It's what I think is *right*. It's not about feeling happy… well, not in this life, not in the way we tend to think of happiness. But yes, I *do* think it will bring true happiness, which is true peace. Even when life is hard."

Dallas bit his lower lip, then blew out a deep sigh. "There's no Catholic church in this town, Chan. So what's next?"

"That's partly why I hadn't told you," Channing answered. "I'd have to take classes for several months, then get baptized and confirmed at Easter. That's when they typically do baptisms, although sometimes they'll do it sooner. Actually, in a dire emergency, *anybody* can baptize another person, even if they haven't been baptized themselves. Catholic parishes usually start holding classes in September. That's only a few more months, so maybe, if we have a car by then, I could go to the nearest Catholic church. So, you won't mind, Dallas, if I become Catholic?"

Dallas wondered if Channing meant that he'd mind feeling left out. "It shouldn't matter what I think." He shrugged. "I mean, this is for you. It's your decision." Dallas looked Channing in the eye.

Channing refilled his mug, then stared at the carafe with pursed lips. "Want some more?" he offered.

Dallas nodded. *This might be a long night.*

"I guess what I mean is that I care about what you think," Channing said, carefully pouring the coffee. "I respect your opinion. But I've also never been surer of *anything* as this. I know it had to be from God when I chanced across that copy of *Orthodoxy* all those years back. And it led me to Chesterton's other books, to Dante, to C. S. Lewis, to books opposed to Christianity that I read and just *knew* in my gut were dead wrong, to the *Catechism of the Catholic Church* that Father Benedict gave to me, and I've just been able to put it all together, and… it just makes sense! It's right. It's *true*."

There's that word again. "How do you know what the truth really is?" Dallas asked. His adrift, constantly restless mentality had been Dallas's norm for most of his life. He didn't see how what was true could be so easily determined.

"You know through reason, but you also have to have faith," Channing answered. "Chesterton said, 'Reason is itself a matter of faith. It is an act of faith to assert that our thoughts have any relation to reality at all.'"

As usual, Channing's intellect was several leaps ahead. Dallas found it easier to just move on rather than try to seek some kind of deep meaning.

"So," he asked, rubbing a hand across his face, "what made you choose Catholicism? There's some other Christian churches in this town that you could get to easily enough."

"Catholicism is the original Christian faith, the one founded by Jesus Christ himself," asserted Channing. "You can literally trace back through the popes all the way to the apostle Peter. The Catholic Church contains the fullness of Christian truth. And it's the only one that's never changed its core beliefs."

"Never changed, huh?" Dallas cocked an eyebrow. "In what, almost 2000 years, for an institution to never change? That's impossible."

"Well, it's like this: you have a beautiful, ancient building, right? And you add to it over the years, but you never tear down the original—that part stays the same because it's already perfect. Or a snowfall—more layers can be added, but they don't disturb the foundational layers. What's added always has to be supported by the original foundation. For example, there are lots of technologies now that weren't around in Jesus's time, so when Catholicism clarifies the morality of these new things, it's always through the lens of the original, solid beliefs. Like birth control: no Christians accepted it until less than a hundred years ago. Even when birth control pills were made easily available, the Catholic Church stuck with their position against it, based on respect for the human person's dignity and the purpose of sexuality."

No birth control? Dallas bit his lip rather than argue with Channing that it was a stupid and archaic idea.

"Catholicism has always been able to find truth because God himself, as Christ made man, founded the Church to work that way," Channing continued. "The Holy Spirit guides the Church to teach the truth unerringly and unchangingly. The Bible says the gates of hell will never prevail against Christ's Church."

Channing's voice was so convincing, ringing with power behind his words. *Could he be right about this?* It was quite possible, given how smart he was. *Or is he brainwashed? Is this another of his quirky obsessions, a childish fantasy?*

"The Catholic Church hasn't compromised what it believes just to match the times," Channing continued. "Catholicism has only clarified teachings to shed light on modern occurrences. Because God exists outside of time and space, you see, so why would his foundational teachings have to change to keep pace with the world? They should be relevant to all people on earth at all times. Or else they wouldn't be truth. Truth can't change, because if it did, that would just result in chaos." Channing gave a contented sigh. "I just love the stability in truth."

"Is that why there are so many different Christian faiths?" Dallas asked. "Because people changed things here and there, and they broke off from the main faith?"

"Yes," Channing replied, "and sometimes they were trying to fix real problems, but once their belief in Christ's sacraments, especially the Eucharist, was lost, then, well..." Channing shook his head. "Some people's worship of God moved further and further from the beliefs of the earliest Christians, resulting in disunity. And some people want to pick and choose which things suit them best at a certain time and never really decide on one faith to stick with, but there's no real stability in that. I *need* stability — everyone does, really. C. S. Lewis — who was Anglican, not Catholic — said, 'The hall is a place to wait in, a place from which to try the various doors, not a place to live in... Are these doctrines true? Is holiness here?' They *are* true, Dallas, *all* the teachings of the Church in that *Catechism* the priest gave me. They all make *sense*, Dallas! I've read the book repeatedly. They're true for *all* humanity and all time. It's amazing! I wish I could explain it better. You should've sat in on that Mass with me in the cathedral. It was so beautiful, and it made a lot of things so clear to me, like the True Presence in the Eucharist... but once you realize it, the beauty and power of it just hits you — like a ton of bricks."

Dallas was still. *He's a hundred percent serious, completely sincere.* He stirred his coffee and took a sip. "So it sounds like you've thought a lot about this. How often do you have to go to this class before you can join?

Sounds to me like you already understand it all." *I sure don't.* Dallas fidgeted with his spoon.

"The classes usually meet once a week starting in fall and going through Easter," Channing answered, "but, Dallas, there's still so much more to learn. They want to make sure you're committed."

Dallas nodded. "Seems reasonable. We can figure out how to get you there if you're this dedicated to the idea. So, do you want me to become Catholic too?"

Channing's eyes nearly popped out of his head. "You... you would *want* to?"

"Not really, no," Dallas replied. "I'd be doing it for you. I still don't feel like I can believe in anything myself, but I want to support you."

Channing was taken aback. "That's *not* the way it works, Dallas."

"Okay, so I won't." Dallas shrugged. "But if you think you should do it, yeah. Then I think you should, Chan."

Channing smiled his broad infectious grin. "I'm glad to finally be making a decision on this," he sighed. Channing pulled the holy card from his pocket and gazed at the Christ child in Mary's arms. "It's miraculous that it's the answer to everything. I even have a true mother — the perfect mother..."

He trailed off, and Dallas wondered if he was going to start crying. *Maybe this all comes from his lack of a good mother. Or maybe there's more to it than that.* Dallas pressed his fingers to the place between his eyes. It was too much to process. *This is Channing's thing, and it's okay if I don't understand it.* But Channing's private connection with the card left Dallas alone, excluded. He bit his lip and told himself it was stupid to feel jealous of Channing striking out on something that seemed so... important, somehow. *I don't believe in God, so why should it even matter to me?* Dallas buried the discomfort and emptied his mug. He studied Channing across the table, prayer card in one hand and coffee mug raised in the other, staring at the holy image in rapt attention.

A few minutes passed before Dallas broke the silence. "That's like your fifth cup," he jibed. "Are you planning to drink your weight in coffee tonight?"

"That wouldn't be too difficult," Channing returned, slipping the card back into his pocket. "In fact, I'm probably more than halfway there." He grinned at his own joke.

The waitress had already brought the bill, and Dallas picked it up. Channing said, "$12.42. Leave a dollar and eighty-six cents for the tip."

Dallas had long ago stopped double-checking the math because Channing was never off in his effortless mental calculations. But he laid down an even two dollars before walking over to the register. Channing finished off his last sip of coffee and followed Dallas to the counter, movements awkward from his choice of footwear, the mangled shoes with nails sticking through the soles.

As Dallas pulled his wallet from his back pocket, the waitress behind the counter said, "Okay, I've been wondering all evening and have to ask now that you're about to leave—what's with the shoes?" She pointed at Channing's feet.

"They're for stomping goblins," he said, straight-faced. "Goblins have tender feet, you know."

Dallas, biting his lower lip to stifle any expression, handed the money over and received the change. The waitress eyed them as if they weren't quite right. As soon as they got outside, both boys doubled over in hysteria.

"The look on her face was priceless when you said they're for stomping goblins!" Dallas howled.

"Yeah, that was awesome!" Tears streamed down Channing's face with his laughter. "It was worth walking all the way here in them just for that. My feet are aching so bad!" He slipped out of the shoes and held them up under the glow of the parking lot lights. One of the soles was falling off, and some of the nails had come loose. "Well, it was fun while they lasted." Channing carried the shoes to a nearby trash can.

"Guess you'll have to leave the goblin-stomping to what's-his-name," Dallas said.

"Curdie. Curdie's *amazing*," Channing put in. "I wish I could be Curdie."

Dallas was pretty sure Channing was at least half-serious about that last comment.

As they walked in silence side by side into the surrounding night, Dallas thought over the evening's conversations. *Maybe Channing will become a monk or a priest. Maybe that's the type of job for him. Not that I know anything about how that works or if they even get paid. And then he'd have to move away from me and into a monastery or something.* Dallas quickly pushed the thought out of his mind.

When they got home, Channing took a shower. Dallas lounged on the couch, his head still swimming with everything they'd talked about. *But maybe things are heading in the right direction for us now.* It felt good to trust

Channing as an equal, although that fierce, protective instinct for him still burned in Dallas. *I suppose it always will.*

Channing emerged from the bathroom, rubbing his wet hair with a towel. He grabbed a pair of sweatpants and pulled them on, then flopped down on the couch next to Dallas.

"Can I paint the cabinets however I want?" he asked.

Dallas had taken the kitchen cabinet doors off the hinges a few days previous so they could be painted, and Channing had volunteered for the job. "Sure," Dallas responded. "There's a can of wall paint in the closet. Use your acrylic paints that you brought with us too if you want."

"It'll make this place more home-like to get them painted," Channing said, cocooning himself in a blanket. "I like this little house, even if it needs work."

Dallas wasn't sure how to organize his thoughts on Channing's newfound faith. He opened his mouth, then paused and clamped it shut. Finally, he blurted, "Don't Catholics say some kind of prayers before meals and bedtime and stuff? Are you gonna start doing that?"

"I already have been," Channing replied. "There's the Our Father and Hail Mary. I say them in my head, and then I just sort of talk to God. There are lots more prayers — like the Rosary; I don't know how to pray that yet. Why do you ask?"

"I don't know," Dallas mumbled, picking at a tear in the arm of the couch. He couldn't admit the loneliness he imagined at knowing Channing was in his own head in this unearthly communion with something spiritual, leaving Dallas anchored to earth all by himself. "I mean, I guess, if you don't mind... I might like to hear you say your prayers. Like, it'd probably be kinda relaxing, like listening to you read aloud. Seems like a soothing way to end the day." *And maybe praying would soothe my guilty conscience.*

"You can say them with me if you want!" Channing's eyes lit up. "I'd like that. I haven't ever prayed with anyone before."

"Well, I haven't ever prayed before at all," Dallas said, "so I don't know how to do it right."

"I don't know if I'm doing it right myself, but God probably understands," Channing replied simply. "Here, I've memorized the prayer on the back of this holy card — it's my favorite so far. You can read along, and we'll say it together."

"Should I say it with you if I don't even know if God's real or not?" Dallas asked, raising one eyebrow.

"Even more reason for you to say it," Channing answered.

Dallas realized Channing wasn't going to explain the rationale behind his statement. "Okay," he answered slowly, taking the prized possession that Channing held out to him, holding his friend's generous trust delicately. "I feel a little weird, though. But I suppose I should learn some about it, for your sake."

The warmth in Channing's eyes conveyed a spark of something new and deep between them. Dallas was willing to follow Channing's lead on this, even if only to be supportive and united.

"Okay," Channing said, pulling the towel off his scraggly brown hair and brushing it back from his face. "Get comfortable."

Dallas raised one eyebrow. "Why, how long does it take to say bedtime prayers?"

"As long as you want," Channing answered. "I usually fall asleep saying them. You're right that prayers can be soothing. I've been praying for our situation over the past several months as I go to sleep, even back when we first left Nevada. I really do think it's given me more peace."

Dallas considered this. "That sounds like a nicer way than I fall asleep most nights."

"So if you want to, come sleep in here." Channing tossed his pillow onto the small sofa, dragged a blanket over behind him, and nestled down into a cozy position. He motioned to the larger couch. "You take that one. You're taller than me."

"Okay, thanks." Dallas went into the bedroom for his pillow and blankets. As he sprawled out on the couch and arranged his covers, Dallas remarked, "This is a lot better than that thin mattress. Are you sure you have enough space on that little couch?"

"Yep, you know I sleep curled up anyway," Channing said.

"Don't know why I've not been sleeping out here all along then," Dallas chuckled.

"It's like a sleepover!" Channing said dreamily. He turned off the light switch on the wall above his head. A sole lamp provided the room's only light. "Ready? Just read along on the card. Then we can repeat it phrase by phrase. It isn't long, so you'll have it memorized in no time."

Channing's confidence in Dallas made up where it was lacking in himself. He wasn't a natural memorizer the way Channing was, but he'd try it. *What do I have to lose? If God doesn't exist, he can't very well be mad at me saying a prayer to him.* Dallas flipped the card over and saw it began with the words, "Remember O most gracious Virgin Mary." *Okay, so if the Virgin Mary isn't really the mother of Jesus, then I still don't have anything to lose.* Either they'd both be pleased at his attempt, or they wouldn't even hear him. But he knew it would please Channing, so Dallas called out, "Okay, I'm ready. We're praying to Jesus's mother? Not to God, or Jesus, or whatever? They're both God, right? But Mary isn't God too, is she?" Dallas wondered why he was encouraging Channing with all these theological questions, but somehow he couldn't help asking.

"Right. Mary's not God," Channing explained. "She's his mother, and for the Jews, the queen was the mother of the king. So Mary, as the mother of Christ the King, is like the queen. But still, she's not the one to be worshipped. Mary's like the moon — the moon reflects the light of the sun, right? So Mary reflects Jesus's light; she's always pointing us back to him. And Jesus listens to his mother's requests because he honors her, so we can ask her to take our prayers to him."

What if her requests are bad? Surely, Channing had thought of this himself, having a mother who had made so many destructive choices. *But maybe, being the mother of God, Mary wouldn't ask her son to do anything bad. Maybe God wouldn't even let her try. Does she have a choice, or is she like a puppet of God? Surely, she had free will like the rest of humanity if she was a person and not a goddess…* Dallas didn't know what was getting into him. *Stop overthinking this. Just say the words and relax.*

Channing began, and Dallas read along: "Remember, O most gracious Virgin Mary, that never was it known that anyone who fled to your protection, implored your help, or sought your intercession was left unaided. Inspired by this confidence, I fly unto you, O Virgin of virgins, my Mother. To you I come, before you, I stand, sinful and sorrowful. O Mother of the Word Incarnate, despise not my petitions, but in your mercy hear and answer me. Amen."

They read it through another few times, then Channing said, "Okay, now put the card down, and I'll say a line, and you repeat it. It's a good way to learn something by heart, and it will put us to sleep in no time."

Dallas wasn't sure you were supposed to intentionally use prayer recitation as a sleep aid, like counting sheep, but it sounded good to him if he could fall asleep gently to the rhythm of the words rather than to the nightmare of a reality that would be playing through his head like a movie otherwise. He passed the card back to Channing and watched him retrieve his pants from the floor and tuck it back into the pocket. Dallas settled in and closed his eyes.

"Remember, O most gracious Virgin Mary," began Channing.

"Remember, O most gracious Virgin Mary," echoed Dallas.

Their voices trailed off sleepily into nothingness somewhere into the seventeenth repetition of the Memorare.

END

Dallas's watch alarm woke him early the next morning for work. He jolted upright, remembering last night. *It worked!* He'd fallen asleep peacefully for the first night in months. He started the coffee, letting Channing sleep on. He ate a bowl of cereal and made a sandwich to take for lunch.

Dallas got to the shop right at 8:00. Anna, a part-time employee, was entering information into the computer when he came through the door.

"You look bright-eyed and bushy-tailed," Mitchell commented. "Ready to tackle that truck?"

"Let's do it," Dallas agreed.

They worked nonstop on a Toyota Tacoma with engine problems. Past noon, they stopped for lunch.

Dallas and Anna made small talk as they ate their sandwiches in the back while Mitchell worked at the front counter. The jingle of the bells on the door set Dallas's teeth on edge as they announced a customer's arrival. *It's just some dinky bells...* He was the only one who always startled at their jangle and couldn't pinpoint why the sound grated on his nerves. Mitchell's friendly voice at the front desk lowered and became serious suddenly. Dallas and Anna fell silent, listening through the crack of the door.

"Dallas has worked here a couple months now," Mitchell was saying. "A good kid, a good kid. He's real reliable, a hard worker. I can't imagine he'd be in any sort of trouble."

Dallas bolted out of his chair. Sweat broke out on his forehead. Trembling, he stepped to the side where he could glance through the window blinds separating the backroom window from the main part of the shop, revealing two uniformed men who stood inquiring about him to his boss. *Could they... How?!* Dallas was frozen, a panicky sickness washing over him from the inside out.

"We have a warrant for his arrest regarding a case in Oklahoma," said one of the officers.

Dallas didn't wait a moment longer. "Channing," he whispered through quivering lips and silently glided towards the back door.

"But, Dallas," Anna said, "you can't just..."

Dallas was already out the door. His boots pounded the pavement as he flew across the back lot. *I've gotta get to Channing before the police do, before they see me! Or have they already been to the house?! Do they already have him? Not now, not when everything's finally started going so well for us!* Dallas tore through the woods behind the shop, his heart racing. He emerged from the trees on the gravel road not far from their driveway, a streak of motion powered by raw terror, the mailbox in the distance his seemingly unreachable goal.

"Channing!" he shouted, voice frantic. "Channing, quick! *Channing!*"

Channing was in the yard. Spatters of paint covered his clothing and hands, and a couple of smudges adorned his face along with a blue streak in his hair. Surrounded by two open cans and several smaller tubes of paint, the artist carefully daubed his brush against one of the biggest cabinet doors, creating a grassy outdoor scene. He waved and called out, "Look, Dallas! Won't the kitchen look great when..."

Dallas plowed into his friend and cut him off. "Channing, we've gotta go — NOW!"

"Where?" asked Channing, squinting and tilting his head to one side. "I've gotta get my shoes..."

"No, *now!*" ordered Dallas, pulling Channing towards the woods. "They've found us, Channing! The *cops* are looking for me! We've gotta run!"

Channing's eyes clouded in fear. "The cops - for us?" his voice quivered. "I thought we were safe here..."

"They came to the shop with an arrest warrant for me! They didn't see me, but they were questioning Mitchell, and they're probably on their way here *right now!*" The explanation tumbled from Dallas as he and Channing strode across the yard. "We have to go into the woods, *now!* If we go down the street, we could run into them!" Dallas's adrenaline-fueled reactions were a runaway train speeding ahead of his reason. *Run through the woods, head across town, hitchhike again with the first car that's heading out of here...* It was a replay of a few months previous, but this time there wasn't even time to grab any of their belongings. *Will life always be like this now?*

They stumbled around the back corner of the house, the urgency in Dallas's voice and face maniacal. Abruptly, Channing fell to his knees and jerked his arm from Dallas's grasp, crouching low to the ground, shaking and crying with his hands over his head as if taking part in some bizarre duck-and-cover drill, body in lockdown. Dallas flew beside Channing, down on one knee, pleading with him to get up and run.

"I'm so scared, Dallas!" He sobbed. "Are they going to get us?"

Dallas's mood was grim as he leveled with Channing. "I don't know! I'm going to do everything I can to prevent that. But you have to move, *now!* Come on!" He pulled the terrified boy to his feet and coaxed him a few steps alongside the house.

Without warning, Channing lunged at the faucet sticking out from the back wall and clung to it for dear life, screaming hysterically. Face flushed, Dallas tried to wrench his hands free, but Channing kicked and thrashed, shrieking indiscernibly. Dallas's heart pounded in his chest as his barked orders melted into pleas with Channing to let go and come with him.

"Channing, are you *crazy*? Come on! Please, get up and come with me before it's too late, *please!*" Dallas's desperate grasps couldn't get a grip on Channing's wild eel-like maneuvers.

Channing yanked at the knob, and the water turned on, a gushing hiss from the faucet. He begged in a frenzied panic, "Baptize me, Dallas, please, *please!*" It was an anguished, hysterical pleading. "I need it, NOW, *PLEASE!*"

Dallas's jaw dropped. "WHAT?! Channing, not now! We have to MOVE *NOW!* They'll be here any minute!" He wrenched Channing's left hand free from the faucet and tried to drag him towards the forest.

Channing broke loose and scrambled madly back towards the running water, unrelenting. "Please, Dallas, *please* do it! Splash the water on my head and say the words, PLEASE! It's an *emergency!!*" His desperate cries mingled in the air with the gurgling rush of water from the free-flowing spigot.

"Channing, *let go!* I'm *begging* you!" Dallas was beyond desperate. He tugged at Channing, but his boot slipped in the slick mud that was forming beneath their feet, and he lost his grip again.

"Just splash the water over my head, and I'll come, I *promise*; I'll do anything you want!" Channing screamed. "Just do it three times, and say the words! Say, 'I baptize you in the name of the Father and the Son and the Holy Spirit,' *SAY* it, Dallas!!"

I should just leave him, the temptation flashed through Dallas for a split second, *and save myself!* Guilt smacked him over the head before the idea had fully formed. *I have to get Channing to come with me — nothing else is more important!* Running his hand quickly under the gushing stream, Dallas flung water over his friend's head, where it trickled down into his hair, running down his face and into his eyes and mouth. Dallas frantically scooped another handful of water, and a third, racing through the words, "I baptize you in the name of the Father, Son, Holy Spirit. GO! *Now*, to the woods!" He grasped Channing's hand with an iron grip and yanked him up from the ground, feet racing, heart pounding, running as he'd never run in his life, a dripping, paint-spattered Channing whipping behind him like a child's pull-toy.

They slipped into the margin of the woods, chests heaving. Dallas caught a glimpse of a law enforcement vehicle pulling into their driveway as he and Channing disappeared into the depths of the trees.

"I think they saw us!" Dallas cried to Channing as they shot like arrows through the woods. "Faster!"

Dallas and Channing flew, dodging trees and bushes. Dallas's mind raced as he tried to formulate a plan, but everything was happening too quickly. *Run, escape, get to the interstate...* The shouts of the cops goaded them on in flight, barked orders to halt issuing from the two men not far behind on foot. As they neared the end of the woods, the gray geometric edges of buildings appeared.

Channing gasped, "They might *shoot* us, Dallas! God, please help us, God!"

They exploded from the woods behind the dry cleaners. Channing's feet, muddy and bare, bled from cuts where sticks and pinecones had gouged them. They both heaved heavily for air. Shouts rang out behind them, clear in Dallas's ears: "Stop! This is the police! Stop running!"

We can't stop! screamed Dallas's possessed impulsive demons, holding any shred of reason hostage. *Run, protect Channing, escape!* The main street stretched before them, and Dallas shouted, "Towards the interstate!" It was their surest escape, the one thing Dallas could come up with in his frenzied flight. Channing nodded, feet slapping pavement, hair streaming wildly, and eyes glazed with terror as his body followed Dallas's risky race in complete abandonment.

They rounded the corner in one motion, Dallas hugging the curb and Channing beside him in the road. That same moment, a huge Mack truck barreled down the narrow street. Channing took the turn wide and couldn't stop. There was a skid of wheels, an ear-splitting airhorn, but it all ended as quickly as they had turned the corner. The massive truck plowed into him headlong, crushing his tiny body and instantly ending his life.

"NO!!" screamed Dallas, skidding on the sidewalk. "CHANNING! NO!" The screeching big rig brakes reverberated in Dallas's head, and people rushed out of shops along the street as he fought desperately to get to Channing. The pursuing officers jumped on Dallas from the side and wrestled him to the ground, handcuffing his arms behind his back, his cheek scuffed against the cold concrete. "Dallas Malone, you are under arrest. You have the right to remain silent..."

But Dallas didn't hear them through his sobs. "Channing, *Channing!*" He struggled to his knees on the sidewalk, vision blurring with the flood of tears, a lunging, snarling wild animal.

"Who was that guy?" asked an onlooker. Nobody seemed to know.

"His name is Channing!" Dallas hollered, his voice anguished as he struggled against the officers behind him. "He's an artist! His beautiful stained glass... He's *brilliant!* He's going to become Catholic—he needs a priest, a Roman Catholic *priest*, somebody, please! *Please!*" Dallas gasped as he was forced to the concrete, chest pressed against the curb with an officer's knee on his back to subdue his resistance.

"He's dead," said one cop as they pulled Dallas to his feet and struggled to propel him towards a nearby police car.

Dallas choked and heaved as the officer confirmed what he'd already known, and his legs buckled beneath him. The sidewalk reeled and spun as Dallas sagged on his knees. "H-he's my b-best friend!" cried Dallas through his sobs. The officers dragged Dallas a few steps. He couldn't grasp the enormity of his world thrown out of orbit in the last unchangeable seconds. Suddenly he lunged against the handcuffs again. "Please, *please,* I've gotta see him. I need to go to Channing! There's something in his pocket—I *have* to have it!" Dallas strained frantically towards the crowd around the truck.

"Settle down!" the other officer ordered. "Anything on him is evidence now."

"But I have to have it," wailed Dallas, "I *have* to! It's nothing to anyone else! It's a little prayer card; he always has it in his pocket, *always!*"

The officer's voice softened, sympathetic. "I'll write it down in the report. But you can't go over there."

"Please, let me go to him; let me *see him!*" Dallas wailed in hysteria. His body dragged between the two officers as they supported him. He couldn't breathe as sobs racked his body. This was worse than the worst nightmare. They were almost to the police car. Dallas and the two officers passed beside the wreck, and he strained to look in front of the immense tractor-trailer at Channing's mangled body crumpled on the pavement. His crimson blood added to the paint colors already marking his body.

An ambulance siren sounded in the distance. Dallas turned towards the curb and vomited, his body heaving out sobs along with his lunch. He staggered with dizziness and shook violently with chills from head to toe. The officers moved him along firmly, though not as roughly as expected.

"Channing," Dallas cried as he strained against the handcuffs, his resistance weaker now. "*Channing!* I have to tell him goodbye; I *have* to!" Dallas made a last-ditch effort to get to his friend's body. "Channing, I'm so sorry; I'm *so so sorry!*" The words gushed out in agonizing wails.

The officers hauled him to the car, one shouting orders that didn't even register in Dallas's animal brain. He resisted with raw desperation until they shoved him into the back of the police car and locked him in. He scrambled madly against the door panel despite being handcuffed, desperate to get to Channing, refusing to believe the awful truth. The last thing Dallas saw of Channing was a sheet being pulled over his body as law enforcement milled around the accident scene, holding back the crowd. He beat his head against the glass of the window and howled, a torrent of fresh tears flooding his view as the car drove away.

Dank and crowded, the county jail echoed with people up and down the halls, clanging in and out of cells. Dallas crouched alone against the wall of a tiny cell, regretting, mourning, turning events over in his mind, blaming himself again and again. Two days he had been like this, eating next to nothing. Dallas barely recognized what was happening. He muttered to himself while he sat for hours, rocking the back of his head against the wall in a dirge-like rhythm: "What are they doing to him, to his body? A burial, and who will come?" or "Channing was right; he was always right. He could've done great things, and I ruined it! I ruined his entire life!" and "My best friend... what kind of rotten friend am I, getting him killed that way, that awful way? So much blood..." Dallas couldn't catch his breath, his body a wreck of jittery shivers. He didn't cry now. To cry would have been to relieve his pent-up anguish. Dallas was living in his own personal hell. Everything he'd tried so desperately to protect had vanished in an instant. And it was all his fault.

Through the bars of the next cell, a man snarled, "Shut the hell up! What's wrong with you, talkin' to your damn self?" The man seemed mentally off himself, but Dallas didn't notice. He didn't notice anything, a stark contrast to his normal state, but he didn't care. He couldn't feel. Dallas made no reply, eyes staring at nothing.

"You on the way to the loony bin for sure," the inmate continued. "Whatcha in for?"

Dallas stared at the blank, grimy walls as they closed in on him. His head spun with images of squirrels, books, stained glass windows, 18-wheelers, and wonder-filled gray eyes lit up with a burning new faith. *Why?!* The question screamed in his mind. *Channing, why Channing? Why not me instead?* Dallas closed his eyes and gulped deeply for air.

"Hey, I said what'd ya do?" repeated the man. "Must be bad—I hear they're takin' you out of state for it. Whatcha in for?"

Dallas opened his bloodshot eyes and slowly raised his head. He forced his cracked lips to spit out the ugly and disgusting words that had become his reality. "Killing my best friend," he whispered numbly.

NUMB

"You've *got* to get it for me."

Dallas's voice was pleading. He sat in a brightly lit room on a folding chair, facing his state-assigned lawyer. Dressed in an Oklahoma state penitentiary uniform, hands cuffed, gaunt face with dark circles under his eyes reflected in the dull sheen of the metal table in front of him, Dallas was practically a specter of his previous self. Just when he'd started to almost breathe normally and relax again, life had turned upside-down. Now he had nothing. Nothing except this desperate hope for this one small piece of Channing.

"I'll see what I can do," the man responded. "If the prosecution has no use for it, then I can possibly get it for you, if they even kept it. It's a long shot, you know. I don't want you to get your hopes up."

Dallas would have to be content with that answer. Nothing was in his control any longer. All decisions were now made for him.

Dallas had nearly gone insane in the hazy nightmare since his arrest, an intense desire to see Channing one last time plaguing his waking moments. He'd finally resigned himself to the fact that his last memory of his best friend's body would be that awful death scene. He had longed to take care of him one last time, to clean his wounds, to give him a decent burial. Being locked up, prevented from helping his friend in this final way, was the worst agony Dallas could imagine now. Channing was dead, and Dallas couldn't even say goodbye.

"So what'd they do with his body?" Dallas rocked in his seat, his face in his hands.

The lawyer shuffled through some papers in front of him and adjusted his glasses. "Channing's next of kin was contacted, his mother. She declined to have his body sent home."

I'm not surprised. Even in his death, she can't be bothered to care about him! Dallas clenched his fists under the table. "So who buried him?" He jerked his head up, voice rising. "Somebody better have taken care of it! They don't just dump people's bodies somewhere…"

His lawyer interrupted. "Oh, no, of course not. There are burial plots reserved for these situations. Usually, the spot is marked with a simple plaque with name and dates. Records are kept so the place can be located by family and friends."

"So would it be back in Minnesota, near where he died?" Dallas barely remembered the ride to Oklahoma; life had sunk into a fog over the past several days.

"Most likely," the lawyer answered.

Channing won't even have a funeral. But he'll be laid to rest in a place where I can visit when I get out of here. If I ever get out… The thought only brought him a shred of comfort.

He just wanted to have that holy card. He remembered the prayer — Channing had been right; it had been easy to memorize. Dallas couldn't bring himself to say the words aloud or even run them through in his mind. All his thoughts were stifled. But that simple piece of paper and a deep desire to get back that one little connection to Channing — it was all he had left to hold on to.

The lawyer went over the details regarding the previous day's arraignment, but Dallas barely registered what was being said. He would be tried for kidnapping and manslaughter, among the more minor crimes of fleeing the scene of a crime, theft, two counts of fleeing and resisting an officer… The list rattled off by the lawyer sank Dallas lower into the abyss as he clutched his stomach. Oklahoma allowed the death penalty. Dallas didn't care about that now. He wasn't even sure he wanted to live. *What's left for me in this world anyway? Nothing.*

"I hope to get you off with an involuntary manslaughter charge rather than voluntary, a sentence carrying a minimum of twelve months up to eight years. And you know the kidnapping charge is ludicrous, anyway. Just a way to stack everything they can against you."

Dallas knew. It had been like a knife to the gut to hear that one, but he and his lawyer had already gone over why it was nearly guaranteed to be dropped since Channing had come with him willingly.

"But what if I just want to plead guilty to manslaughter?" Dallas asked through one hand covering his face.

The lawyer's eyebrows went up in surprise. "Why would you do that? Then there's no chance for a lighter sentence."

Dallas put his head on his arms against the cold metal surface of the table. "I *feel* guilty. I can't avoid the inevitable anymore. I took a man's life…" — *two men's lives,* he added silently to himself — "Albeit involuntarily. And ran off instead of owning up to it."

"And that's why I can show your culpability to be lessened — because you didn't intend the death," the lawyer explained. "The fact that the trooper pulled his gun out and had his finger on the trigger of the weapon that killed him — this shows that his poor choice in pulling his gun as he did was a direct cause of his death. This will almost certainly result in a lighter sentence. I don't even expect you to be given the full eight years. The surveillance video of the incident helps your case."

Dallas didn't care about getting a lighter sentence. *I deserve the stiffest penalty and then some,* he berated himself. *But I just want the trial over and done with.* Dallas sighed. "Okay, whatever. You decide what's best to do."

"Let's go over any information we need to discuss so we are on the same page," the lawyer said, all business.

Dallas told his lawyer everything he could to help speed things along, answering all the man's questions in a dull monotone. Going back through all the details again was mental torture.

After his lawyer left, Dallas was escorted back to his cell. The correctional officer removed his handcuffs and locked him in. Dallas sank onto the bed and closed his eyes. He couldn't block out the nightmare of his reality unless he slept — and sleep had been fleeting since his arrest.

Each day passed the same as the one before it. Dallas barely ate, barely slept. When he did sleep, he wakened in a split second of unawareness, almost beginning to open his eyes and think Channing would be there with him, and then the avalanche of truth would tumble down on him, a tight squeezing in his chest that suffocated him. He feared sleep, desperate to avoid that terrible letdown that would crush him as soon as he awoke. The tug of war between using sleep as an escape and not being able to stand the terrible reminder of what had happened every time he woke threatened to tear him apart.

The court date arrived. Dallas awoke and paced his cell, jittery. He rehearsed the answers his lawyer had prepped him for, as simply and truthfully as possible. His stomach was in knots as he anticipated being asked difficult questions involving Channing. Even the thought of having to talk to strangers about him made Dallas sob - or fill with white-hot fury. *What right do these people have to know anything about Channing?*

Following his fifth humiliating strip search since his arrest, Dallas trudged into the courtroom, stone-faced. He recognized the convenience store clerk among the witnesses. Detective Jack Parker, the one who'd pieced all the clues together to track down Channing and Dallas, sat near the front. A woman Dallas presumed to be the widow of the deceased state trooper glared at him, and he ducked his head. Dallas felt no emotion towards any of them. He shuffled across the room and took his seat, hollow. He listened in a fog as the charges were brought against him and witnesses spoke. Finally, Dallas was called to the stand. *Let's get this over with.*

Dallas felt empty as he watched the surveillance footage of his struggle with the trooper. It was a black-and-white, low-quality recording, but the horror of it was clear, and Dallas hung his head. His only consolation was that the footage made it obvious that the man had pulled the gun out before Dallas had even pushed Channing past him towards the door.

Channing. There he was, displayed for the entire courtroom, running, moving... *alive.* Dallas couldn't take his eyes from the screen as it was shown in slow motion a second time: *Channing, fully alive.* A tear ran down Dallas's cheek, and an anguished ache welled up in his throat.

He answered questions from his lawyer easily enough. Then the prosecutor stood.

"Mr. Malone, did you attempt to flee after Trooper Schmidt asked you to show him what was in your pockets?"

"Yes," Dallas forced his answer through his misery.

"And did you push your accomplice past him in order to help him escape?"

"I did."

"Next, Mr. Malone, is it true that you tried to dodge the trooper, and that as he was trying to restrain you, you fought and struggled to get free?"

"Yes," Dallas responded, monotone.

"And isn't it true," the lawyer hit him with the next question, "that you put your hands on the trooper's gun?"

"I instinctively pushed his gun when he pointed it at my chest, yes, and I used only one hand, my right hand," Dallas got in quickly. "He had me by my left wrist. I made contact with the barrel of his drawn gun with my right hand."

"And didn't the gun fire immediately following this, shooting Trooper Schmidt in the chest?" The lawyer's eyes stared right through him.

"Yes." Dallas bowed his head.

"How much time would you say elapsed between the time Trooper Schmidt first spoke to you and the gun fired?" asked the lawyer.

He saw for himself in the video, Dallas huffed. "It all happened in a matter of seconds," came his rehearsed response.

"And isn't it possible that perhaps your hand touched the trigger in this rapid altercation?"

Not tho' the soldier knew
Someone had blunder'd:
Theirs not to make reply,
Theirs not to reason why,
Theirs but to do & die,
Into the Valley of Death
Rode the six hundred…'"

Dallas chuckled at Channing's poetry recitation. *I sure didn't need to enroll him in school here. Channing's the master of self-education, no doubt. Good thing Mitchell never said anything more about it.* Dallas entertained the thought of figuring out how to get Channing his GED. *He'd blow that test out of the water, I'm sure, and maybe it would come in handy for him in the future.*

Breaking Dallas's train of thought, Channing stumbled across his line of vision, gasping, "The sarin is getting thick…" He pretended to pass out and collapsed in the dry grass in front of Dallas, imaginary battle ended. The weary soldier lay breathing heavily for a few minutes, then rolled onto his stomach to face Dallas. "Did you get your paycheck?"

"Yep," Dallas replied, standing up to poke at the fire. "Now we can buy more groceries. Hopefully, I'll start making more after I've been working for Mitchell a little longer. I think I understand what my mother meant when she would mention 'living paycheck to paycheck' - just trying to cover the basics each month. Maybe someday, I'll be able to run a shop myself. Cars are really the only thing I know enough about to possibly make into a career." He sat back down in the lawn chair, watching the leaping flames.

"Maybe I should get a job, too," Channing mused. "I've been working on a few ideas for some projects, and maybe I could sell the finished artwork to help earn some money, after I collect all the supplies. But you know what I'd *really* like to do? Rule my own kingdom."

Dallas cocked an eyebrow.

"It would be a special country," Channing continued, faraway look in his eyes, "made up of all those little towns in Florida that I love. I'll have to figure out a way to buy Florida or something. Only good people can live there with me, like you, of course, and Mitchell, and Father Benedict. And there will be no pollution, no crime…"

Dallas shifted in his seat and gave a slight cough.

"No corruption," continued Channing. "I'll design all the signs,

"I know for certain that I didn't touch the trigger," Dallas answered firmly and couldn't help continuing, "but as I told my lawyer, the trooper's finger was on the trigger the whole time, and I saw that as a threat."

"Are you saying, Mr. Malone, that Trooper Schmidt pulled the trigger *on himself?*"

Dallas met the man's hard stare. "Yes, although I don't think it was intentional."

"So you are saying that his *accidental* pulling of the trigger was the result of the scuffle which *you* started?"

"Yes," Dallas mumbled, eyes down.

The prosecution fired the next question at Dallas. "Why did you resist, run from armed law enforcement, for such a minor crime as shoplifting?"

"I made a snap decision," Dallas began his unrehearsed response. "I was afraid that if I got arrested, Channing would have gone to juvenile detention for being in on it with me, or he'd be put into foster care, and he..." Tears welled up in Dallas's eyes. "He was emotionally fragile, from being abused all his life. I was trying to protect him, and I made a rash judgment."

"So all the crimes you committed, you claim you did them in an attempt to protect your friend? Do you understand that your impulsive decisions are what cost your friend his very life?"

"Objection," called out Dallas's lawyer. "Mr. Malone is not on trial for the death of his friend."

But the damage had already been done. Dallas dropped his chin to his chest, tears flooding his eyes, and the accusation drowned him. *Yes, I killed him! I killed Channing with my own stupid choices!* His body shook, racked with sobs.

Dallas's lawyer stood again to further deflect the kidnapping charge. Dallas had tried from the start to keep Channing out of the theft, and his role was irrelevant to the charge of manslaughter. Channing's mother had not even claimed his body for burial, the lawyer pointed out, more evidence of his justifiable reasons for leaving home with his friend, who was only a year past eighteen himself. The minimal age difference lessened Dallas's responsibility for Channing, and there had been no intent to kidnap. The lawyer's argument was strong.

But all Dallas could hear was his guilt for Channing's death. *None of the charges matter to me — nothing could be worse than having led your best friend to his death, the best friend who was like your little brother, who you'd made yourself responsible for!* Dallas's composure was annihilated for the rest of the trial, every subtle jab from the prosecution about his recklessness like a kick to the gut. *Nothing matters now! What kind of sick fate is this? What kind of insane, hot-headed impulses were these that came so naturally to me — under the guise of protection — that ended up killing Channing instead? Channing, who I loved above all people in the world?* Dallas's body was consumed with violent sobs as he accused himself. *I killed him. I killed Channing!*

"Hold it in; just get through this," his lawyer coached in his ear, but Dallas was wrecked. Hitting a lower low since Channing's accident and the arrest hadn't seemed possible, but it was happening. His guilt for Channing's death proclaimed by strangers who didn't even care about him personally made it all the more true. *Now I know without a doubt that I'm to blame for Channing's horrific end! I'm gonna be locked in prison with myself, where self-loathing can consume me. I just want to die, to beg them to execute me and put me out of my misery!* A dull sense of responsibility told him not to act like a complete idiot while his lawyer was trying hard to help him. *I'll have the rest of my life to wish I was dead,* Dallas consoled himself inwardly with a sick, bitter satisfaction. *I deserve it. I can never feel okay ever again, and that's what I deserve.*

The sentence was read, barely registering with Dallas. *I know I'm staying in the clink, so what do the specifics matter?*

Dallas was convicted as guilty on all counts except kidnapping. His sentence would amount to four years total, with the possibility of parole after three.

"It was the best outcome we could hope for," his lawyer commented in a low voice as he packed up his briefcase.

Hope? Dallas nodded dutifully, devoid of emotion. As he was being handcuffed to be taken back to the prison, he reminded his lawyer about the holy card that should have been removed from Channing's body. Other than this one thing, Dallas had no further requests. There was nothing else — it was all over now.

Dallas lay on his back, staring blankly at the ceiling a few feet above him. He'd settled into a mindless routine that propelled him involuntarily through the days, lacking the motivation to care about anything. The one activity he did consciously — doing pull-ups in the exercise room — had been accomplished today. He mostly kept to his cell, sleeping or staring at nothing, crying silently when his mind slipped into thinking about things. Thinking and feeling only brought unrelenting pain. Dallas's cellmate, John, had gone outside for yard time. Dallas refused. *I'm not worthy to see the light of day.* It would only be a gut-wrenching reminder of Channing's love of the natural world. Dallas's face was set like steel. He had barely spoken since the trial — not to John when he was assigned to his cell after his sentencing, not to anyone at meals. He complied with the correctional officers in stoic silence. Dallas was mechanically moving through the days.

There were voices in the hall, then the creak of the cell door swinging wide. John's footsteps penetrated Dallas's mind, but he remained motionless. He felt John's eyes boring into him but refused to look back.

John cleared his throat. "There's some stuff we hafta talk about."

Dallas swung his eyes towards John but stayed on his back on the top bunk, knees bent with feet flat near the end of his mattress. His cellmate had been incarcerated several months already. John spelled out specific cell etiquette like being quiet after lights out, use of the shared toilet, and general privacy courtesies. Dallas reddened at his cellmate's candid words. *There's no privacy here, only in the ugly recesses of my mind.* He understood that John must be hearing him at night when he sobbed to himself in his bunk. Dallas acknowledged John's words with shakes and nods of his head, passively agreeable.

Having opened conversation, John pressed for more. "I'm here for armed robbery," he stated. "How about you?"

Dallas looked away. "I'd prefer not to talk about it."

"Sure, okay." His cellmate shrugged. "I mean, I already know the basics. People talk. Just tryin' to make conversation."

"It's nothing personal," Dallas grumbled. "I just don't want to talk about anything." He turned on his side to face the wall and hoped John wouldn't push him any further. *I'll have to talk to the guy more eventually. Four years is a long time. I don't want to get to know anyone, though. I just want to be left alone with my misery.* He decided to fight harder to stifle his nocturnal crying after this.

Dallas sank slowly as days drudged by. He ate the bare minimum. His pull-up routine kept his mind numb for a brief half-hour each day. Dallas had always identified with the sentiment of being alone in a crowd, but now it had meaning at an even lower, more isolating level than ever as he moved through the hallways, seeing nothing.

One day, Dallas noticed a Catholic priest passing by his cell. His stomach fluttered, and he thought of Channing. *It would make him happy if I asked for a priest to visit me.* Then Dallas recalled with bitterness how he had cried out that Channing needed a priest at the scene of the accident, and how nobody had done anything about it. Dallas gritted his teeth. *I couldn't even get that last request granted on Channing's behalf. Maybe a priest would condemn me for my terrible sinfulness, which is what I deserve.* Slipping back into his state of berating self-hatred, Dallas forced himself to try to sleep.

He couldn't. Days passed with no letup in Dallas's despair. He cursed the overhead lights, yanked the blanket over his head, and squeezed his eyes shut, brain tormenting him with his guilt. *Channing should've been the one to live! He had so much more promise than me. He loved life, genuinely loved it despite all the garbage he'd been through. It's so unfair; I can't stand it — he died while I lived! I can't go on. I hate this; I don't want to live. I'd rather die than know Channing is dead and that I caused it!*

His pulse hammered in his head. *Just kill yourself. You're no good.* Dallas couldn't climb from his pit of wretchedness. *I don't even want to try. I have to end this misery,* he convinced himself. *But how, with the guards watching?*

For the rest of the day, Dallas lived inside his mind, obsessing with the idea of ending his life. *Maybe I can attack a guard or another prisoner or attempt to escape so they'll shoot me down in the process.* But there was a slight twang of guilt over forcing somebody else to have to be the one to end his life. *I've gotta do it myself — alone. I'm the lowlife jerk that got myself to this place. I've shouldered my own burdens my whole life, and I'm not about to dump this one on somebody else.*

Four weeks after his conviction, thoughts of suicide consuming him as agonizing days crawled by, Dallas devised a plan to hang himself. He was so steeled to the idea that he should be dead, had no right to still be breathing, that he didn't think he'd have to resist any urge at self-preservation. *I'm done with life.* Dallas grimaced with a twisted kind of satisfaction, knowing he would have to suffer, dying in pain and confusion as he slowly deprived himself of oxygen. *I can't die an easier death than Channing. It has to be more painful for me than it was for him, because I deserve the worst suffering there is. This is the only way I can make up for Channing's death.*

That evening after lights out, he lay talking to Channing in his mind one final time as he waited to make sure John was deeply asleep. *I'm so sorry, Channing, so sorry! I just don't know what else to do. I don't deserve to live. I killed you! I wanted so much to protect you, to give both of us a halfway decent life. I failed, and it cost you your life! I don't give a crap about the trooper*

I accidentally killed, either. I'm absolutely despicable, Channing, and I don't know what you ever saw in me as a friend. I ran you to your death! You would've been better off with your no-good mother, because then at least you'd still be alive. You're dead, dead forever! I can't even breathe without hurting so bad when I think those words. Oh God, I killed you, Channing! It doesn't matter that I didn't mean to, because you're dead, and nothing will ever bring you back! In his mind, Dallas pictured Channing's body as it was in that last moment, lifeless and broken on the street, killed in some sick irony by a tractor-trailer. It was like some demon had taken something Channing had found joy in and used it as a weapon against him. *I'm a failure,* Dallas insisted to himself over and over. *And I'm the demon.*

He shook with silent tears and gut-wrenching pain, hoping his cellmate wouldn't wake up. Finally, he slipped into the silent state of numbness that had become his new norm, unfeeling and unthinking, only harboring the dark emptiness inside. *If hell is real, it can't be any worse than this.* Hazy images from Channing's reading of Dante's *Inferno* flashed through his mind. *I'm already in hell.*

An hour of complete stillness passed, then Dallas slid down from his bunk and stole across the cell. Moving with quick determination, he climbed up the bars of the door and tied one pants leg to the highest horizontal bar. He suspended himself with one arm while slipping the other pants leg, already tied into a slipknot, around his neck. Dallas recognized no sadness, no fear, no anything other than the blackness within himself in that helpless moment.

As he tightened the unconventional noose around his neck and prepared to let go of the bar, a memory blazed uncontrolled through his mind, and Dallas froze. *You've taught me so much about God.* Channing's voice, ringing clearly into Dallas's ear... A tear formed, and Dallas's breath lurched in his chest, then he squeezed it back and hardened his heart. "No, I didn't. I let you down, Chan," he whispered. "It's over."

At that instant, loud expletive shouts interrupted Dallas, and John grabbed his legs from below. "Suicide! It's Malone! Somebody, get the hell in here!!"

Dallas cursed and kicked at John.

John clung to his thrashing legs and lifted him up, snarling, "Stop it, ya freaking idiot!"

"Leave me alone, dammit!" Dallas let go with one hand and hit John in the face.

The hallway lights shone bright, other inmates shouted angrily as they were roused from sleep, and a couple of correctional officers came tearing down the hall and unlocked the cell. One cut Dallas's pants from the bar, and the other wrestled him into handcuffs as John dropped him to the floor, taking a kick to the thigh in the process. Dallas struggled and writhed, blinded by rage. The tightness of the cuffs tugging against his wrists told him he had failed, and he finally gave up.

The two COs ordered Dallas to step into his shoes. As he sullenly complied, John stood in the doorway and blocked their exit. The cellmates locked eyes. "Don't ever try any crap like that again, Malone. You think I wanna wake up to your dead corpse in here? Ya selfish jerk." Dallas glared tight-lipped as John stepped aside to let them out.

Dallas dragged his feet but didn't resist as he was escorted through the hallways. The stares of other inmates leering at him as he passed each cell burned into him. The guards walked him to a stark cell—no furniture, no toilet, no bars—Dallas was surrounded by four smooth walls, a floor with a drain in the center, and a steel door equipped with a one-way window. The COs stripped him of his clothes and handed him a paper gown.

"We're watching around the clock, so trying anything else is futile," one warned. Dallas covered himself, then collapsed into an exhausted, degraded, shaking heap on the floor in a corner. He'd drained himself emotionally, mentally, physically. He fell into a fitful sleep.

When he awoke, Dallas jolted upright and instantly remembered everything. He scowled at the glaring lights, his immediate instinct a seething rage that John had stopped him. *I could kill John too—kill him first, then kill myself!* Dallas leaped up and paced back and forth in his enclosure, then whirled and kicked at the door. His sudden and unexpected sleep had refreshed his thinking, and for the first time in weeks, he was angry, really angry at somebody other than himself. He stood in the center of the room, breathing heavily. *I care about something.* A funny sensation welled in his throat. Dallas had forgotten how it felt to care about anything except his own desire to die.

His last thought before John had grabbed his legs to stop him bombarded him. *Channing.* "Did you do that, Chan?" Dallas quavered aloud. "Did you do that to give John a couple more seconds to save me from myself?"

The officer stationed outside the door called, "What was that?"

Dallas fell silent. *Channing, that was you trying to save me, wasn't it?*

Channing, who had always looked up to Dallas, always trusted him, always stood by him even when he was in the wrong—not always agreeing with him, but remaining loyal nevertheless... *would Channing want me to kill myself? Channing, who saw beauty and truth in little pieces of his life despite all the terrible things that happened to him, would he want me to hate life so much that I chose to make a grand exit? No.* Dallas breathed with a thin ray of hope. By hating life, he was despising Channing's wonder at it. *I can't dishonor Channing's memory that way.* Dallas set his lips in a tight, stubborn line.

But oh, the misery of having to live with this! Dallas's stomach lurched. *The terrible ache, the awful guilt, the waking up and immediately struggling to breathe because the tightness in my chest is so strong it feels like I'm dying! But enduring it is my punishment. Living with myself will be a pain worse than being a quitter. I have to suffer. I deserve it.* The storm rose until Dallas gave in to the heaving sobs. He cried for knowledge of having to endure a life without ever seeing Channing again. He cried for his final image of him, dead in the street, and for the fact that nobody would ever know his incredible personality the way Dallas had. Dallas cried for the loss of his one true friend, and finally, he was truly mourning. A weight was shed from his soul as he convulsed in gut-wrenching sobs. He cried so hard he threw up, and still he couldn't stop.

Dallas cried it all out for over an hour. Less than a day earlier, he'd thought that his body was completely numb from having nothing left in it, but his bouts of intense grief were only beginning. *The one reason I'll have for living will be to endure suffering for Channing's sake. Death would be a coward's way out. I deserve to live in pain for this, forever. How's **that** for truth?*

Dallas remained on suicide watch for 36 hours. His food was brought to him, and he wasn't allowed anywhere without a correctional officer, not even to use the bathroom.

A queasiness fluttered in the pit of Dallas's stomach as he trudged along the hall, being led back to general population wearing a clean uniform. *What will John's reaction be towards me?* The focus on another human being's point of view was new and sudden. *I'm feeling again. Feeling worried about something is better than feeling nothing.*

John was silent as Dallas entered their cell. He gave him a sideways glance as the CO left.

Dallas leaned motionless against the wall. "I'm sorry," Dallas said to his back.

John turned around and faced him, still saying nothing.

"You were right," Dallas admitted. "That was a despicable thing of me to do in a shared cell."

John shrugged and turned to go.

"And… thanks," Dallas finished, thinking how lame he must sound.

John finally spoke. "Yeah. Nobody needs to see that, and nobody needs to go that way, either. Gotta just stick it out while you're in here." He turned and left the cell.

Dallas sank onto the chair, not hungry, and debated whether he should even bother heading to the cafeteria himself when a CO approached. "Malone, your lawyer's here to see you."

Dallas bolted upright. *My lawyer?* The case was over, and the man had no further obligations to an inmate who couldn't pay him a cent. He followed Officer Greg Murphy to the visiting area. *Would they have called him because of my suicide attempt? Are they gonna charge me for that, too?* The CO stepped outside the door, and Dallas was left alone with his lawyer.

"Dallas, some good news to get you through," the lawyer started. "It's not going to get you out any sooner, but—" He paused to pull something from his shirt pocket— "I got it for you." He held up a small rectangular piece of paper.

Hardly daring to believe it, Dallas reached out a quivering hand and accepted the holy card as if it might burst like a bubble. Gaping, he turned it over tenderly in his hand and gazed down at it. The Madonna and Child smiled up at him. *Channing's holy card.* Tears welled in Dallas's eyes as he ran his fingers along the edges of the card, memories of that last day with Channing flooding his body.

"Thank you," Dallas whispered, finally looking up at his lawyer. "Thank you so much. You can't know what this little piece of paper means to me! How'd you get it? I honestly thought it was impossible."

"I contacted law enforcement in Ericsburg," began the lawyer, "told them what you'd said to me about the officer who arrested you, how he said he'd put a note in the report about saving the card for you. They pulled the file for me and found a post-it note stuck to it, and sure enough, the officer had written on it: 'Check pockets of victim for holy card, hold for suspect, if possible.' That's a really rare thing for an officer to do, extraordinary, really, and certainly outside of normal protocol. So I was able to use the note from the report to have them pull the evidence bin, and there was the card inside. Since the trial is over, and it's not an item of value, they were able to release it to me."

"It's more valuable than anything to me," Dallas murmured, throat swollen with emotion. "That officer must've been like an angel or something." Images of Channing's death scene and his own arrest hammered Dallas's mind: the blood, the screaming, his crazed struggle to get free, desperate to get to Channing... *That officer saw me in the worst moments of my life.*

"They put him on the phone with me for a minute," the lawyer said. "Officer Kowalski. He remembered the incident clearly. Said he was a Catholic and so he felt kinda obligated to save the holy card for you. And that's not all, Dallas. He said he'd called his priest, told him he had reason to believe that Channing might've been Catholic, based on what you'd said at your arrest and the presence of this prayer card in his pocket. So he had the priest come with him to the grave and say some prayers. The officer told me that as the only Catholic on the police force in that whole county, he thought his being the one on duty when it all happened was meant to be."

Dallas was speechless. This was more than he'd expected. It still stabbed deep inside of him to not be there himself, but now he knew that Channing hadn't been entirely neglected in his death. It was a small measure of comfort.

"So this is why you stopped me," murmured Dallas, staring at the holy card, "so I'd get a chance to see this miracle happen."

"Say again?" asked the lawyer.

Dallas tore his eyes away from the image and glanced up at his lawyer. "I tried to kill myself two nights ago. Channing stopped me. I bet he wanted me to hold out so I could get his holy card back for him. He must've..." Dallas fell silent. *I probably sound ridiculous.*

"Well, I'm glad I could do you this favor." The lawyer rose to leave. "It was almost miraculous to get that card. You're a good kid, Dallas, so keep positive, and you'll come through this. I like you, and you have your whole life ahead of you. Start living for the rest of your life right now, so you'll be ready when you get out. If you need me for anything else, just call."

"Thank you." Dallas shook his hand. "Thanks so much for everything you've done."

As he left the room, Dallas pocketed the holy card. His stomach rumbled, so he headed for lunch before he missed his chance. In the hall, he passed the calendar posted on the wall, and his heart lurched in his chest. *It's Channing's birthday. He would have turned 18 today.* Dallas swallowed hard. Every day felt the same in prison, and he had rarely kept track. *Channing's birthday—I got Channing's holy card back on his birthday.* A wave of bitter grief washed over him. *Channing's never gonna see another birthday. If things had been different, I would've been getting him a cake right now.*

That night, as he tried to fall asleep, Dallas made a promise to Channing. "It's your birthday present, Chan," he whispered as he took up the holy card and looked at Mary and the baby Jesus for the hundredth time that evening. "I'm going to say this prayer every day from now on. At least once every day, for you. For the rest of my life." He tucked the card under his pillow and began to recite the prayer mentally. *Remember, O most gracious Virgin Mary…* Dallas dropped off to sleep to the words of the prayer running through his mind.

Dallas had just finished sweeping in the cafeteria after lunch one day when he was summoned by the words, "Visitor for Malone."

Who'd come see me? He walked to the visitors' area with a faint sensation like hope swelling in his throat. *Could my mother have…* The door opened, and Dallas was surprised by Mitchell's eager embrace and slap on the back and "So good to see you, man!" in a warm voice. They sat down across from each other.

"You didn't have to come all this way to visit me." Dallas fiddled with his hands in his lap. "But I can't tell you how much I appreciate it. The only visitor I've had has been my lawyer. I wouldn't blame you if you never wanted to see me again after finding out what I'd done and that you'd hired a fugitive."

Mitchell waved off Dallas's self-deprecation and frowned. "Does your mother know that you're in here?"

"No idea." Dallas didn't want to think of her now. "I still don't know where she is. I'm really sorry I was such an idiot, caused so much trouble…" Dallas's voice faded as he tried not to recall that awful afternoon.

"I hate how it turned out for you," Mitchell said. "I always enjoyed having you around the shop. Hope you aren't forgetting all you know about cars while you're stuck in here. When you get out, you're planning to do something mechanical again, aren't ya?"

"I haven't thought that far ahead," responded Dallas. *I try not to think.*

"You have real talent with cars," Mitchell encouraged him. "I hate that I can't hire you back this minute, 'cause I sure could use your skill."

"Are things going okay?" Dallas asked.

"Oh, yeah, doing decent," replied Mitchell. "I could use another mechanic on staff, but we're making out okay. People keep breaking their cars, so I keep makin' money." Mitchell grinned.

Dallas acknowledged the joke with a slight nod. *The tractor-trailer that hit Channing, right in front of his shop...* There it was again, thoughts of the accident. Dallas teared up though trying to appear strong.

Mitchell's expression softened. "Dallas, hey, I'm sorry about Channing," he said gently. "I know it's gotta suck so bad for you to have lost him that way, and I don't want to upset you more about it. But just know I'm real sorry."

"Thanks," Dallas answered numbly. Mitchell had always seemed so tough to him, the confident, tattooed man who had been repairing vehicles for over twenty years.

Mitchell reached out and clamped a reassuring hand on Dallas's shoulder.

"I spend a lot of my time in here feeling so much regret," Dallas admitted, looking down into his lap. "I should never have run from the police. It's my fault Channing's dead. He was the only thing I had in the world, my best friend."

"You can't beat yourself up over that now," Mitchell reasoned. "Probably easier said than done."

"It's not as bad as the first month or two, which was such total despair that I just didn't even want to live. But it still hurts like hell. I failed him when I was supposed to be taking care of him."

Mitchell was quiet. Dallas thought maybe he'd talked too much. *But Mitchell met Channing a few times, and to be able to talk to anyone who knew Channing...*

"Hey, so all your stuff you asked me to save from the house," said Mitchell, referencing the semi-coherent conversation that was Dallas's one allotted call after his arrest. "I've got it all, for when you get released. I brought Channing's books with me. I know you said he was a big reader and always encouraging you to take on challenging books. So if you want any of them, they're in my car, and I can leave them here with you - if that's allowed."

Dallas closed his eyes. "Let's see," he said, hands on the sides of his head with his elbows on the table in front of him. "Channing's books... he had *Orthodoxy*, his all-time favorite. Also one called *Mere Christianity*. And the *Catechism of the Catholic Church*, a heavy, bulky book he stuffed into his bag somehow. And a *Lord of the Rings* book. Am I remembering correctly?"

"Yep, I found all those," Mitchell answered. "You knew him well. Want me to give you any of them, or wait till you get out?"

Dallas deliberated. "Yeah, I'll take the *Mere Christianity* book if they'll let you give it to me," he said. Something made him consider more. "And… how about that *Catechism*, too. *Orthodoxy* was too special to him; I can't risk anything happening to that one, so you keep it safe for me. I hope the stuff isn't taking up too much of your space. I really appreciate you going to get it all."

"It's not in my way at all," Mitchell said. "I'm glad you had the wherewithal to ask me to get it for you. I cleared out everything, even the little stuff like your road atlas, a pair of sneakers, all the clothes…"

"Channing's Airwalks, right?" Dallas asked softly, the gruesome memory coming to him of Channing running barefoot to his death. He swallowed down the nauseated feeling.

"Yeah, the shoes are Airwalks," Mitchell replied. "So, what happened to your boots?" Mitchell had admired Dallas's bulky combat boots from the first day he walked into the shop. He'd made comments about how they were like a part of Dallas — he never saw him without them.

"Supposedly, I get them back when I'm released," Dallas explained. "They stick all your personal belongings into a bin, and it sits in storage, waiting for you. I love those boots, but I'm just grateful that Channing's stuff is accounted for. He loved those Airwalks. I'll come take it all off your hands - in about three and a half years, that is."

"That's the spirit," Mitchell encouraged him. "You're young, Dallas. You can make a turnaround when you get out. You've got a lot of promise. Don't you forget that, okay?"

"Sure." Dallas shifted, uncomfortable. "I guess I'll survive." *And Channing wanted me to read that book.* Now it was one small thing he could do for him.

As he exited the visiting area, Dallas hoped the books would be approved quickly. Mitchell would drop them off with the appropriate person on his way out. After working his kitchen job not quite a month, Dallas wondered if he had enough money saved to buy a combination lock in the commissary, which would keep the books safely secured in the personal locker in his cell. Having a few of Channing's things in his possession restored a small amount of power to Dallas in his otherwise helpless condition. *I'll take any consolation I can find right now.*

Three weeks after Mitchell's visit, Dallas dropped from the pullup bar in the recreation room. He still hadn't struck up conversations with any other inmates besides John. He just wanted to be left alone. As he sat down at a rowing machine, a group of four guys exchanged whispered comments. Dallas could sense their stares but kept his eyes down and ignored them.

"Yo, Malone, how's it going?" boomed a voice.

Dallas glanced up, shrugged, and kept rowing.

"What, you too good to bother talkin' to us?" accused Maddox, a tall, muscular inmate who had a reputation for being an instigator.

"Don't have anything to say." Dallas stared straight ahead.

"Oh, is that so? You always walkin' around here ignoring everybody, thinking you're better than anyone else? Can't lower yourself to speak to nobody?"

Dallas gritted his teeth and rowed harder. "I'm no better than anyone. Just don't want to talk."

One of the taunters stooped and grabbed something from the floor, and the others laughed and high-fived him. "Look what I got, yo!" he jeered. "Here's why he won't talk to any of us low-lifes. He thinks he's high an' mighty, and we're all goin' to hell! Now you'll talk, Malone—you gotta beg us if you want it back!"

Dallas's eyes shot upward. His stomach leaped into his throat when he saw the guy they called Pulaski waving a small rectangle of paper in the air. *Channing's holy card—it must have fallen out of my pocket!*

"Give it back," Dallas said in an even voice, feet planted on the floor on either side of the rowing machine.

"Hey, that's a start," Maddox gibed. "But you should hafta fall on your knees before us, show how holy you really are! The baby Jesus here might start cryin' if you won't beg us politely." The gathering crowd sniggered and clapped, delighted at having Dallas cornered.

He rose and stepped towards the group of rowdy inmates. "I'm not gonna beg you," he growled. "That's my card, and you *will* give it back to me."

"Finders, keepers!" laughed Miller, snatching the card from Pulaski. The youngest of the group was always side by side with Maddox. He passed it over his head to a guy behind him called Smith, who was jabbing him in the back asking to see it.

What is this idiocy—are we back in middle school? Anger boiled inside Dallas, nearing panic level. He clenched his fists at his sides and bared his teeth. *I can't lose Channing's holy card!*

Smith raised the card above his head and motioned as if to tear it in half while the others laughed and jeered.

Dallas snapped. In an instant, he was on Smith, snarling. Dallas knocked him flat on his back and punched him relentlessly in the face, rage exploding through his fists, rabid over the sight of this guy pretending to tear up Channing's Memorare card. Smith's grip on the card loosened, and Dallas snatched it as he was grabbed from behind by the three other guys. He writhed and twisted, but they dragged him off Smith, who was bleeding from both mouth and nose, gasping to catch his breath and holding his abdomen. Adrenaline coursed through Dallas's veins. *I won't give up Channing's card for anything! Nothing's gonna let me be weak enough to lose it again, nothing!* He stopped fighting but gripped the card like steel, poised to attack again if any of them made the slightest move for it. Two guards entered the room, summoned by the sounds of the commotion.

"Malone beat the crap outta Smith!" Miller's heated words rang out. Smith was sitting up and spitting out blood. "He just went psycho and jumped on him! J-Cat belongs in the ding-wing, that's what!"

"They took something of mine and wouldn't give it back!" Dallas accused through clenched teeth, glaring as the officers separated them.

"Yeah, we picked up his stupid Virgin Mary baby Jesus card, and he went ballistic over a little prank," Maddox scorned.

"I don't think you understand what this card means to me," Dallas said, voice rising. "I'd rather *die* than give it up! It's *not* a joking matter to me!"

"Malone, you did that to him?" asked Murphy as he motioned to Smith.

Dallas nodded.

"Are you prepared to come with us quietly and cooperatively?"

"I am," Dallas responded coolly. "I'll only resist anyone who tries to touch this card again." He was still seething inside, but fear gripped him over the ultimate fate of Channing's prayer card.

The other CO, Bruce Hudson, smirked. "Better not get too attached to it, Malone, if it's what caused you to get so violent. We don't let you keep stuff that incites fights in here." Another two officers appeared in the doorway.

They're ready to deal with me if I struggle. Dallas glanced from one face to another. His fight-or-flight response was going haywire, and he tried to breathe so he wouldn't explode.

"I'll go with you calmly," Dallas said, struggling to keep his composure, "but please, I'm begging you… this card is all I have left. I can't make any promises for how I'll react if I lose it. But I'll go right now with you to solitary, no problem. You can keep me there for a week; I probably deserve that. I don't wanna make any trouble." He offered his hands, wrists together, so they could handcuff him, still clutching the holy card as he trembled with the anguish that it might be taken from him.

Suddenly, Smith spoke up. "Let him keep his baby Jesus card. He's right—we started it."

Hudson cast a wary look at Smith's battered face but made no move to take the card from Dallas. He twisted Dallas's hands behind his back until he winced, then put on the cuffs and propelled him out of the room, followed by the other guards. Dallas heard Pulaski saying, "He begged the COs. I guess that's good enough, huh?" followed by snickering laughs.

Hemmed in by the officers, Dallas grew edgier as they moved towards H Unit. Hudson still had the cuffs in his grip and shoved Dallas from behind, then yanked him back again in a twisted game of tug of war. Dallas stumbled, his pulse pounding in his ears with the rough handling.

"I swear, there's no need for all four of you unless you plan to touch this card," Dallas warned them as he tried to keep his footing. "This is the only thing in the world I have that I'd fight for, and you'd have to *kill* me to get it." Inside his head, he screamed at himself, *Shut up, idiot; you'll only make it worse!*

His inner voice had been too late. Out of view of the security cameras, Hudson seized Dallas's shoulder from behind and slammed him up against the hall wall.

Dallas struggled to get free as two other guards held him against the concrete block surface, Hudson jabbing him in the back with his elbow. Pinned, Dallas desperately gripped the Memorare card between his fingers where his hands were restricted behind his back. *I can't lose Channing's holy card; I can't!* Hudson's hot breath slithered down Dallas's neck like a serpent from hell.

"How you gonna fight for it when you're cuffed, scum?" The guard's hand brushed across the prayer card.

He'll rip it! Dallas pushed back helplessly against his three captors.

Suddenly, Dallas writhed in pain. As Hudson bent back his wrist, Dallas screamed in agony. He struggled in vain against the men pinning him to the wall. Hudson had one strong hand against the back of Dallas's neck while the other hand twisted his wrist without mercy. The pain was blinding, and Dallas's grip failed him.

Hudson slipped the card from his possession with ease and handed it off to Murphy, the one CO whose hands were still free. "Trash it," said Hudson with cold cruelty. "You're gettin' a lesson, Malone. Never think you can win in here. You're pickin' fights with the big boys now, and you can't win. You try, and I'll *break* you."

Another guard strode down the hall towards the commotion as Murphy retreated. Dallas, breath caught in his throat, saw the card in the officer's hand, his whole life now, disappearing down the hall. With a deep cry of rage, he forced his body back against the COs who had him against the wall. He thrashed his legs, trying to kick out and break free so he could run down the hall after the precious card, but the strength of the officers against his back was overpowering. They dragged Dallas towards a doorway, Hudson swearing at him. They were already in H Unit, and it was just a matter of getting him through the door and into the tiny cell.

Dallas fought it with every ounce of his strength, scrabbling for a grip on anything as he was dragged towards that gaping doorway, but Hudson was right — he couldn't win against the three of them. *But I'll go down trying to the last breath! I said they'd have to kill me, and I meant it with all I have in me!* Like a snarling wild animal, he brashly threw himself against the guards, trying to elbow and kick and even bite them. Dallas was shoved through the doorway into the room, the heavy door slamming behind him.

Channing's holy card is gone, on its way to be destroyed! It's all I had, all that's left of Channing now! Dallas let loose with howls and guttural yells that rose from an animal part of himself, blinded to all reason. He threw himself against the steel door for that key piece of connection with Channing. Dallas backed up and flung himself again, screaming and seeing red in his fit of fury. He barely registered the searing pain in his wrist, still handcuffed behind his back. His shoulders took the brunt of his temper as he alternated sides, ramming into the heavy solid door at full force, his screams fueled by hatred with every slam against the barrier.

After a few minutes, he could make out the muffled command of a correctional officer from the other side of the door. "Settle down in there, you hear me?"

Dallas heard, and it infuriated him even more. He kicked the door madly, threw his chest against it, tried in futility to force his way through somehow. Inside, he was a wreck. The depth of his desperation took control of his body, the one thing he had left to cling to now ripped from him, never to be seen again, *never*. Dallas refused to let his rage burn out, knowing he'd give in to bitter sorrow if he ceased. He added words to his feral screams, and with every kick or shove of the door, he spat a string of obscenities at the guards.

"Hudson, you bastard, I'll KILL you!" Dallas bellowed. "I'll *gut you* the second I get out! You'll pay for destroying my only hope! I don't care if I die as long as I go down makin' you PAY!"

After an hour of uncontrollable rage, Dallas's hoarse voice weakened, but he refused to give up. He'd ignored several calls from the hall outside telling him he was making things worse. He couldn't allow himself to sink into the hopelessness he knew would come if he couldn't keep it buried under his blowup.

The rattle of keys in the lock surprised Dallas, and he tensed to impulsively knock over whoever it was in a mad dash through the doorway and down the hall, a crazy last-ditch effort at getting his holy card back. The door opened, and Dallas lunged like a rabid beast against Hudson, hands still cuffed uselessly behind his back. The muscular guard snatched Dallas by the shoulders, threw him to the ground on his back, and stepped on his neck with a large boot.

Dallas gasped and gagged, struggling underneath the pressure of the heavy foot. His vision faded out of focus as he barely made out the sneering expression on the smug face towering above him. He writhed desperately in a pointless exercise of trying to free himself from this monster dressed as an officer. Just as he was about to black out, Hudson removed his foot and rammed a knee into Dallas's chest, keeping him pinned down. Dallas flung a hate-filled, guttural yell at the man ruining the last shred of his pathetic life.

"If you don't cut out your ridiculous temper tantrum hissy fit, I'm gonna make your life a living hell!" Hudson growled. He jerked Dallas's shoulders up from the floor, then slammed him back against the hard concrete.

Dallas felt a hot pain shoot through the back of his head, yet he still struggled and spewed curses at the hated guard, but his energy was running low.

"You hear what I said?" shouted Hudson, his red face in Dallas's. "You're *mine*. I'll break you, lowlife!" He spat in Dallas's face, then stood up and kicked him in the side.

Dallas gasped as the wind was knocked out of him.

Hudson yanked Dallas back to his feet as he fought to regain his breath, one tight fist gripping his shirt collar.

Dallas felt the side of his head slam against the wall once, twice, three times. He struggled weakly and shouted with each abusive hit, but by the third one, he had no more fight left in him. Dallas surrendered.

Hudson gave him one final ram into the wall. "That's right, shut up and stop resisting, wimp. I hear you again, and I'll be back on you before you know what hits you!" He lifted a slumping Dallas by his right upper arm and shoved him to the ground.

Dallas crumpled in a heap, gasping for breath and feeling as if his entire body had been put through a meat grinder. He threw up suddenly and lacked the physical strength to even move out of his own vomit. He wondered hazily if his wrist was broken, if his ribs were broken, and the last thing he remembered before losing consciousness was that blood was trickling into his eye.

When Dallas came around, his eyelashes were so matted with blood that he couldn't open his eye at first. Still cuffed, he couldn't even reach up to feel the damage from the abrasion above his left eyebrow. Conscious thought flickered as Dallas assumed he'd suffered a concussion. He rolled to one side and winced, all the muscles in his abdomen screaming in agony as he forced them to move his body. A smear of blood against the wall came into focus as he caught a glance at where his head had been slammed against the rough surface.

His legs had fared best in the assault, and Dallas willed himself to get to his knees and then to his feet. Stumbling as he rose, Dallas leaned against the wall, gulping in mouthfuls of air, his head spinning. He staggered to the bed and sank onto it, supporting himself with a shoulder against the cinder block wall.

Dallas sat motionless for several minutes, catching his breath and letting his memory return. "I lost Channing's card!" he wailed bitterly. Dallas flopped onto the hard slab and curled up into a ball, defeated sobs racking his exhausted body, every gasping cry agony to his bruised ribs.

Being in "the hole" wasn't physically so bad when compared to the pain inflicted by Hudson, but towards the end of the first day, Dallas understood why it was used as punishment. *I'm starting to go crazy.* There was nothing in the solitary box of a room besides a toilet and a sorry excuse for a bed frame built into the wall and floor. Nothing was visible through the solid steel door. But the worst of it was knowing Channing's Memorare card was gone. In the past couple months since he'd had it, the card was always with Dallas, just as it had always been in Channing's pocket. The loss of it crushed him. He seethed at himself for taunting the COs over it after the fight. *If I'd kept my big mouth shut, maybe they would have let me keep it! I'm such an impulsive moron!* The thought of it being thrown into the garbage made him feel sick inside.

After 23 hours, Dallas was allowed one hour to walk around, directly supervised by a different CO from yesterday's four, but the trip to the H Unit shower and back was all he could handle physically. His fit of rage against the steel door had taken much of his strength, and then the beating he'd received from Hudson... Dallas gritted his teeth as he remembered his utter helplessness, thrown to the floor, pinned by his neck, slammed against the concrete block wall. Catching a glimpse of himself in the bathroom mirror following his shower, he noted the damage done to his left temple. He felt broken at the sight of what another man had been able to do to him and glanced away, cheeks burning.

Dallas's heartbeat quickened, and anxiety swelled inside him like a balloon about to pop as he was returned to solitary confinement. The idea of the next 23 hours triggered a panicky feeling throughout his body. Exhausted but tense, he sneered at the glaring overhead fluorescent light that was kept on nonstop. Emptiness was all that Dallas faced as the solid door slammed behind him. He dragged himself across the floor, head and wrist both still throbbing from his injuries, and curled up on the hard, empty bed, pining for Channing's holy card. "I have nothing now," he whispered to himself. He murmured the Memorare over and over, imagining Channing saying it along with him like they had their last evening together, until Dallas could hear Channing's voice in his ears, but the loss of the tangible reminder, the miraculous card... Dallas was engulfed by the rising deep depression and the thoughts of wanting to die again. *No!* he told himself angrily. *It's your punishment to live a life of suffering now. Losing the holy card is just one more kick while you're down. You deserve far worse for what you let happen to Channing!*

The next couple of days dragged. Dallas alternated between staring at the walls, crying over his loss of the holy card, rocking, sobbing for Channing, and fitful bouts of sleep that never lasted more than an hour or two. Occasionally he heard shouting from down the hall and shuddered at what might be happening between other inmates and the staff. He was still weak and achy from Hudson's assault on him. At one point, he found himself in a half-asleep state, talking to Channing aloud, and then realized where he was and that Channing was dead. *I'm starting to hallucinate.*

With about 24 hours left and his strength returning, a fit of desperate rage came over him, and Dallas flung himself around the cell, kicking the bed, toilet, and door. A CO banged on the door and called to him to knock it off, which only made him angrier as he recognized Murphy's voice.

"You took my prayer card, and I *hate* you for it!" he screamed through where the door met the frame. "I hate you all; you hear me out there?!?" He kicked the door again. Dallas's wrist and ribs had improved, but his head still throbbed, made worse by his near-constant crying, and his gashed temple blazed hot.

"I—WANT—THAT—PRAYER—CARD—BACK!" raved Dallas, ramming the door with every word. He wanted to fight, retaliate—lying around crying and going crazy would consume him otherwise. He screamed the phrase over and over, but the correctional officer on the other side of the door no longer called out to him.

"Gone to get Hudson to keep me in line?" Dallas shouted. "GOOD! I'm ready for that scumbag!! He can come fight me TO THE DEATH! I WANT MY PRAYER CARD BACK!!" But Hudson didn't come—nobody did. Dallas finally wore himself out and sank onto the floor against a wall, trembling and sobbing until he fell into the deepest sleep he'd experienced in days.

Dallas jolted at the sound of the door opening. He glanced up, head hazy from his solid slumber.

Murphy entered the cell and shut it quickly behind him.

Fury built inside Dallas as he struggled upright. He glared at the man and sputtered, "*You*... Did you hear what I said?! I want my..."

Murphy squatted down on Dallas's level. Something in his expression gave Dallas pause. He wanted to punch him in the face, but his hesitation gave the officer a chance to speak.

"Your prayer card is safe," Murphy said in a low voice, stern and serious eyes meeting Dallas on his level. "I want you to cooperate with me and stop acting like a maniac in here, because the card's *not* been destroyed. It's safe in my car. I didn't throw it out — do you understand what I'm telling you?"

The anger ran from Dallas's face as what Murphy was saying registered. He trembled with emotion and collapsed back to the floor, sobbing. "It's safe... It's safe... It's all I have..." he said between heaving cries. "I need it! It's all I have! Give it back to me, *please!*"

Murphy pulled Dallas upright, firm but not rough, and looked him in the eye. "You heard Hudson telling me to trash it. You need to give that CO a wide berth from now on. You understand what I'm sayin'?"

Dallas nodded and gulped for air, relief mixed with shock and skepticism. "You really have it?" he whispered hoarsely. "It's really safe? Channing, Channing's prayer card..." Dallas broke down crying again.

Murphy's voice was reassuring. "Yes, I have it safe for you. I'm on duty tomorrow when your time's up, too. If you can behave yourself until then — well, you can't make a show about it to Hudson if you don't want him to destroy it — but I'll give it back to you when I come to let you out."

Dallas stared in disbelief, tears halting suddenly. "You would... but, why? Why would you be nice to me?"

Murphy replied, "Look, it's not about you, but I couldn't ever trash a holy card. I'm Catholic. That card could've been blessed for all I know, and you can't just destroy a blessed object. And if it's the one thing in here that gives you hope... well, a man needs God in a place like this. Some COs here like to strip inmates of all hope, like a twisted punishment. I'd rather all of you guys were rehabbed, myself. Some are beyond help, I know — that's just reality. But if you can use that holy card to cling to your faith..."

"I'm not even a Christian," Dallas whispered. He immediately wished he hadn't said it as Murphy's eyes widened in surprise.

"Then how is it you've got a holy card — one you'd die to defend?"

Dallas bowed his head. "It belonged to my best friend, and... he's dead now. He believed in God, and he carried that card around with him constantly. It was on him when he died." Dallas raised his eyes to meet the officer's. "So maybe you can understand how much it means to me. And I'll be grateful to you if you'd give it back to me, because it's more than I deserve." Dallas's face burned in shame as his tears began again.

Ignoring Dallas's blubbering, Murphy gave him a thump on the back and stood up, saying, "Okay, so you act straight, and I'll see you same time tomorrow." He backed through the door, kindness in his eyes.

The last day in isolation was made tolerable by the hope Murphy had given to Dallas. *I'm going to get Channing's card back,* he told himself. *I really am! I can make it.*

Disconnected from general population, Dallas didn't even know what time it was, and he alternated between pacing like a caged animal and trying to sleep. The silence and starkness of the tiny cell made him feel that the walls were closing in on him. He went through paranoid fits of panic. *What if Murphy's just messing with me, making a cruel joke? What if he's just as awful as Hudson?* Dallas teetered near a nervous breakdown as the minutes dragged by. He murmured the Memorare under his breath obsessively, a desperate attempt to calm his raw nerves.

When the cell door opened for the last time after his 72-hour punishment, Dallas scrambled to his feet, hand going to his empty pocket by habit.

Murphy stepped into the room. He pulled the Memorare card from his pocket and placed it in Dallas's hands. "Here it is. You got off lucky with Smith admitting their wrongdoing, or else there's no way you'd be getting it back. The incident won't be forgotten. If that card makes you such a hothead that you attack anyone who comes near it, then next time, I won't give it back. It'll be gone, especially if Hudson responds to the fight. If I'm not on duty, then I can't stop him from tearing it to pieces, you know." He opened a set of handcuffs and reached for Dallas's wrists. "I'd advise you to let me put it safe in your bin of personal belongings, or for you to secure it in your cell locker."

Dallas stood frozen, tears streaming down his cheeks. "Thank you," he whispered through trembling lips. "Thank you." He cradled the holy card close in his front-cuffed hands, and Murphy guided him by a shoulder and shut the door behind them. Head down, trying to breathe deeply, Dallas walked away from that hellish isolation.

Back in his cell, Dallas slipped into his bed, the mattress a luxury. *My blanket… my pillow…* He hugged the thin, institutional blanket to his chest and squeezed his eyes shut. Then he lifted the Memorare card and stared at it hard, in a trance, still amazed that Murphy had given it back to him. *I have to keep this hidden from Hudson going forward, and I shouldn't carry it on me all the time, as much as I need to have it close to me. I can't risk losing it ever again.*

"How was the hole?" asked John as he came in.

"Inhumane torture," Dallas said flatly. "And I don't have anything else to say about it."

John fell silent a moment. "So Smith looks like hell." He attempted to stifle a huge grin. "He was in the chow hall the day after, admitting he started it and saying now he knows you're not some pansy pushover. At least you got some respect from him, even though he still thinks you're an aloof, smug..." Here John threw in a couple of choice nouns that Dallas knew didn't refer at all to his parentage in this case yet sounded like half-compliments, having come from Smith. "Don't think he'll mess with you again. But you better lock up that baby Jesus card. Word's got around that you'll die before you give it up. Bet there's some guys willing to put that theory to the test."

"Who?" Dallas pushed up on one elbow, eyes ablaze.

"You know who," John returned. "Maddox especially would love taking advantage of that. He gets a thrill out of pressing people's buttons to see how far he can go before making somebody snap... or making them his boy."

Dallas's stomach churned. "I'll think about locking it up," he answered.

"And you better watch your back around Hudson," John added. "Everyone's heard Murphy one-upped him. They went to the warden, arguing over it. Apparently, Murphy said it was sacrilegious to throw away a prayer card, so they didn't make him do it. Made a case that Smith started the fight, too, not you, and so the warden decided you could keep it. Hudson, that dude's got a real chip on his shoulder. He's gonna have it in for you even more now that his authority got yanked from under him. Murphy thinks three days of solitary is punishment enough for gettin' into your first fight. But *man*, you got lucky."

John sat down on the one chair in their cell and leaned way back, watching for Dallas's reaction.

Dallas sighed. "Yeah, I think I'll just keep my head down and avoid people in here."

"That's smart. You're learning how things work around here real fast, Malone."

Late that afternoon, Dallas walked to the commissary. He considered whether to buy one of the tempting snacks or to save his money for a combination lock. *Twelve dollars – I doubt I even have ten saved yet.* When Dallas asked what his balance was, his jaw dropped: somebody had made a fifty-dollar deposit into his account. *Mitchell.* A strange lightness rose inside him. Dallas bought a combination lock, got an ice cream and a few snacks, and took them back to his cell. He placed the snacks and holy card inside his locker and attached the lock. *There. I feel better with it locked up safe from jerks who might want to take it.* He couldn't bear the thought of it going into storage with his boots and clothes and wallet, even though it would theoretically be safer there. *I need that piece of Channing near me. Doubt I could make it another week without it, let alone a few more years. Years...*

Day after day dragged on. Things weren't getting better, but at least they weren't getting worse. Dallas's grief over Channing's death was a gaping hole in his heart, raw and empty, unchanging. He did his kitchen job well each day, continued working out, and otherwise drudged through the days.

Inside, he wanted to kill the guys who teased him about "the baby Jesus card." So far, he'd bit down their passing taunts, repressing his rage as long as they couldn't touch it. When he left his cell, he locked it up for safekeeping. Smith steered clear of Dallas. His face had healed from the thrashing Dallas had given him, although the bruises had lingered for weeks.

One day Dallas returned to his cell after a workout to find the two books of Channing's that Mitchell had brought stacked on the shared desk. He ran his hands over the covers, picturing Channing holding these very books. Dallas opened *Mere Christianity* and swallowed the lump in his throat. *Reading this won't bring him back.*

Over an hour later, John's voice interrupted him. Dallas snapped his head up with the realization that he would miss dinner if he didn't go now. *This book kinda makes sense.* He reluctantly dog-eared the page and set it in his locker. *Is this what Channing felt as he learned more about Christianity?* Dallas remembered that fleeting thought he'd had, that Channing might become a monk or a priest. *He really understood this stuff, like it had come naturally to him.*

Dallas devoured the rest of the book that evening. Unsure why it had kept him turning the pages, he laid back on his pillow with his hands behind his head. *I didn't understand a lot of that. I should read it through again, more slowly.* Dallas remembered how Channing had said that C.S. Lewis was connected to the other authors he admired, Chesterton and Tolkien... *Catholics.* Dallas's mind snapped back to a screaming, frantic Channing and the emergency baptism Dallas had given him, an event he'd not processed yet, and relief washed over him—he had at least cooperated with Channing's final request, albeit begrudgingly. *Might as well start reading this Catholic Catechism, too. Maybe learning about what Channing had become so passionate about will help me feel closer to him again and remind me of stuff he tried to tell me – when he was alive.* Dallas scowled. *I should've listened to him better.*

Dallas grabbed the *Catechism of the Catholic Church* and hoisted himself onto his bunk. The small print was daunting, and it was written in a numbered paragraph format. *Not exactly leisurely reading.* He sighed and started to close the book, but handwriting inside the front cover caught his eye: *Father Benedict O'Malley, Cathedral Basilica of the Immaculate Conception.* A phone number was underneath. *The priest who gave Channing this book that day we stopped off in the cathedral... This is the book that had the holy card inside.* Dallas's mind was invaded by images: Channing's stained glass... collecting old bottles together for his artwork... the look Channing would get on his face when concentrating on a project, biting his lower lip as he worked... how tiny and awe-filled he'd appeared as he stood in the center aisle of that massive cathedral, staring up at the immense windows...

Dallas felt himself spinning and gasped for breath. He slammed the book quickly and lay down on his bed, burying his head in his pillow to stifle the sobs.

Dallas exited the room where his hair had been clipped short and ran a hand over his head, a measure of subconscious reassurance. Maintaining his same hairstyle with a once-a-month barber visit somehow made him feel like he still existed. If he couldn't have his clothes, his boots, his earring, then at least he could have his haircut, a small consolation.

As he estimated the number of haircuts until his release, Dallas counted the months since he'd been arrested. *I hope Channing'll recognize me once I finally...* The automatic thought was a cruel trick of his mind. Dallas's face reddened, his stomach churning inside him like a steaming cauldron. He quickened his pace, desperate to be alone before he blew his lid. He trotted down the hall, burst through his cell door, and lost control within the safety of a rare moment of privacy. Dallas punched the concrete wall beside his bunk, releasing a fury of self-loathing over the uninvited and misleading intrusion. *What the hell is wrong with you?!* he screamed at himself, drowning out the physical pain. *He's dead!! You're never going to see him again, ever!* Dallas's knuckles were a raw, bloody mess. He didn't care. He despised what he was becoming—a man with no purpose, with nobody in the outside world waiting for him to get out of here.

That night, Dallas clutched the Memorare card in the hand that throbbed with pain, telling himself he deserved it and more. He ran through mindless repeated recitations beneath his sullen message of self-punishment. *More payback for what happened to Channing.*

When Dallas woke up, his knuckles were a mangled crust of dark, dried blood. He tucked his hand against his side when he caught John's stares as they left their cell for breakfast, but his cellmate had already noticed.

"What the heck did you do to your hand?" he gaped.

"Nothing," Dallas grunted.

"That don't look like nothing. Who did that to you?"

"Did it to myself."

"Dude, you really messed yourself up!" John sounded concerned. "It looks like you took a cheese grater to your knuckles! How'd you do it?"

"Punched the wall," Dallas answered flatly. They had reached the line for breakfast.

"Who made you mad enough to do that?" John pressed.

"Nobody, I was mad at myself," Dallas huffed. He heard his voice getting louder. "I hate what happened to my best friend. I *hate* myself for it!"

A few guys in front of them had turned to gawk at Dallas's bitter explosion. John glanced aside and cleared his throat, edging away slightly.

"You know what I did?" Dallas raved, not caring that he was making a spectacle of himself. He threw his arms wide. "I was so stupid and impulsive that I..." Dallas couldn't bring himself to say the words now that all eyes were on him. "This place is my punishment for being such a moron, but it's not enough. This," Dallas said, holding up his raw and swollen hand, "*this* is more punishment. I get to live with myself and my guilt *forever!*" As the rant spilled from Dallas, the others around him shuffled their feet and exchanged glances and snickers with raised eyebrows. Dallas spun around and stalked off before he lost all control of his mouth, or before he started blubbering... *again.* He wrinkled his nose in disgust. *I'm pathetic!*

Too frenzied to eat now, he slammed the door to his cell behind him, eliciting a stern warning from down the hall. Dallas didn't care and slammed it again just to make his point — to whom, he wasn't even sure. He flung himself into his bed, allowing the hard bitterness to take over so he wouldn't shed tears. He examined his swollen, red hand with a sick satisfaction, wondering if he'd broken any bones.

Suddenly, Dallas heard his door open. He turned over, but before he could react, a guard grabbed his shirt and dragged him off his bunk. Dallas crashed to the floor. Bruce Hudson towered above him, eyes glaring.

"I *told* you not to slam that door!" he snarled. "Looks like you don't learn easy." Hudson kicked Dallas in the shins.

Dallas winced and huddled over his legs, shielding himself against the blows of the CO's boots.

"That's right, cower on the floor, sissy," growled Hudson, and he knocked Dallas in the side of the head with the back of his hand.

Dallas snapped and jumped to his feet, lunging at his antagonizer.

Hudson was too quick. Years of prison work had honed his reflexes and hardened him from sparing a shred of mercy. He seized Dallas by the upper arms, spun him around, and slammed him against the cell door, pressing his chest into unyielding bars. "You wanna slam your door, huh?" Hudson said low in his ear. "Well, I'm gonna give you that chance." He snatched Dallas by the back of his shirt and yanked him backward, opening the door with his other hand. "Slam it," he ordered.

Dallas stood alert, fight instinct activated, with arms slightly out at his sides. He glowered at Hudson and didn't budge.

"I said, slam the door!" shouted the guard. A few passing inmates paused in the hall to see what was going on.

Dallas lowered his eyebrows at the man in pure hatred. "Make me," he sneered in a hushed growl.

It had been the stupidest response he could have made. A split second later, Hudson forced him back against the wall, giving him a knee in the gut. Dallas gasped to regain his breath, and the CO spun him around to face the door again.

"Wrong answer, Malone. Now you'll do as I order you, or I'll drag your sorry excuse of a life over to solitary." Hudson wasn't backing down. The threat of going in the hole did it for Dallas. Sullenly, he gave the door a pathetic shove until it latched.

Hudson flung the door back open. "Harder!" he yelled. "I said SLAM it!"

Dallas seethed inside at his humiliation in front of the gathering crowd in the hallway. He gritted his teeth and slammed the door.

"Again!" commanded Hudson, forcing the door back open into Dallas, who met it with his good hand and threw it shut with a clanging rattle.

Hudson paused, staring at Dallas's damaged hand. An evil smile slowly spread across his lips. "So you did that to yourself, huh?" He grabbed Dallas's hand and examined it up close. Dallas winced, trying to pull away, but Hudson's grasp was like iron. "That's real pretty, Malone, real pretty. You shoot your mouth off like a raving lunatic about punishing yourself and, well, since I'm a nice guy, I'm gonna help you out with your self-hatred." In one swift movement, he put Dallas's injured hand on the doorjamb and slammed the door hard on it. Dallas couldn't hold back a scream of agony. He heard a snapping sound from his pinkie finger and knew it was broken.

"And now it's your turn," Hudson said coldly, opening the door once again. He snatched Dallas's throbbing hand and forced it back against the doorframe. "I'll just help you out and hold it here for you, in case you chicken out and can't punish yourself the way you know you deserve."

Dallas, boiling with fury, figured he had nothing to lose. *My hand's already mangled, so I don't even care!* Dallas stared Hudson down with an icy glare and slammed his door hard on his own hand, cringing and biting his lip to stifle the scream that wanted to escape, feeling his ring finger likely joining in the same fate as his pinkie. He turned away from the guard, gasping and cradling his throbbing hand and feeling like he was about to throw up.

Hudson's face steamed at the show of toughness, and he yanked Dallas away from the door.

Just then, John's voice came from outside the cell. "What the... get outta my house, Hudson!"

"Your cellie's just learning things the hard way," sneered the officer through the bars. "Finished punishing yourself, Malone?"

Dallas glowered at him and said under his breath, "Never."

But Hudson was distracted by John forcing his way through the door. "Get out, I said! I want some peace and quiet."

Hudson dropped his grip on Dallas and turned on John, driving him back through the door and into the hall again. He turned and locked the cell door from the outside, trapping Dallas in.

"Nope, you've got some free time to roam around a bit, Johnny Boy. Your idiot cellmate's confined to quarters for a few hours. Take a long walk." Hudson strode off, the group of onlookers parting to let him through.

Dallas stepped forward, gripped the bars of his cage, and erupted in fury. "I *hate* your *guts*, Bruce Hudson!!" The CO was almost all the way down the hall and made no reply other than menacing laughter.

The gathered crowd threw sheepish glances at John and Dallas, then dispersed, all but Maddox, who had approached partway through the incident.

"Get the crap outta here, Maddox," John said. "Show's over." He stalked down the hall in the opposite direction from Hudson, muttering, "Locked outta my own cell! Why the hell am *I* punished?"

Dallas stood inside, staring Maddox down as he strutted back and forth outside Dallas's cell bars.

"Punishing yourself, I hear." Maddox smirked. "If you need more punishment, you just come on over and get some from me any time — I've got enough for you and Miller to share. Such a tough punk you are, cryin' like a girl in your bed after dark. Yeah, I hear you from my cage," he added. Maddox and Miller's shared cell was across the hall diagonally.

Dallas stiffened and turned his back on Maddox, crossing over to his locker. He undid the combination lock and took out Channing's prayer card.

"Ahh, askin' the baby Jesus to help you," Maddox sneered. "Maybe he can punish you too, send you straight to hell where you belong!"

Dallas hoisted himself with his good hand and perched on the edge of his bed, staring blankly at the card in his hands. "Maybe so," he responded in a flat voice and laid down, turning towards the wall.

With time to himself, Dallas read *Mere Christianity* over and over. Book open on his lap and elbows on his knees, he sat on the chair in his cell, feet planted wide, trying to focus. His gaze fell on his pinkie finger as he turned the page. The broken bone had healed crooked. The penitentiary doctor had splinted both pinkie and ring fingers, chiding Dallas for not having his hand examined sooner. It was John who had forced him to go to the doctor about it after the door-slamming incident. Dallas didn't tell the doctor that part. "I did it to myself," he'd said, which was largely true anyway. *At least it's my left hand, but why am I such an idiot?* A few of the hand bones were fractured too, and the three middle knuckles were scarred from his assault on the wall. Dallas was beginning to think he might leave prison with more scars than he'd come in with, following 19 years of dabbling in daredevil feats that had resulted in several already.

He flipped back to the start of the chapter titled "Forgiveness." The repeated readings had become a mental torture that drew him in. *I haven't forgiven myself for all that's happened.* Dallas bit his lip, realizing he couldn't even begin to forgive anyone else if he couldn't first forgive himself. At least, that's what he was getting from the book. *But I don't deserve forgiveness,* he argued, *and I really can't see why I should forgive other people, especially people who hurt Channing. So why is this book bothering me so much?*

Dallas glanced up as somebody passed in the hallway, eyes alert for John's return, then hunched over the book again. "I have not exactly got a feeling of fondness or affection for myself, and I do not always enjoy my own society," he read. *Hit the nail on the head there. And this says loving your enemies doesn't have to mean that you think they're nice people. But do I love myself? After what I let happen to Channing?* Dallas wasn't sure he could even *like* himself now. He sighed, furrowed his brow, and read on. The book said that sometimes people "imagine that forgiving your enemies means making out that they are really not such bad fellows after all, when it is quite plain that they are." *So if I can get to the point of forgiving my mother, and Channing's parents and bullies, and...* Dallas grimaced as he sensed a shadowy image of the father he'd never met. *At least I can still think they were bad people who did bad things.* He exhaled slowly, finally thinking he might see a glimmer of what Channing had meant about forgiving his parents while hating the evil things they had done to him. *But aren't I just as awful?* Dallas wrestled with himself. *I killed both Channing and another man by my foolishness!* He gritted his teeth and forced himself to read on.

"I don't think myself a nice man, but I know that I am a very nasty one," Lewis had written. "I can look back at some of the things I have done with horror and loathing." *Like me. So, I'm supposed to see myself as a bad person who's done some terrible things, yet still be able to forgive myself because I'm supposed to love myself? And that I should therefore forgive other people who were bad, knowing I've not been so great myself?* It made a lot of sense, but Dallas couldn't get his head around how to really believe it. *I don't love myself, and nobody else ever would either if they knew all my history, so I sure as heck don't feel worthy of forgiveness.* He shut the book with a huff.

"So over in H Unit, did you see any of the guys on death row?" John and Dallas were getting ready for bed.

"No," Dallas answered slowly. "I know they're in there, but I wasn't thinking of it. Why?"

John shrugged, eyes down. "It just bugs me to think of the death penalty and them sittin' here in this same facility, locked in solitary waiting to die. One guy's up for execution next week, you know."

Dallas's face was stoic. The last execution here had been the same day he'd arrived last May, a man just 22 years old who'd committed a murder at age 19. Biting his lip, Dallas rose and took the *Catechism* from his locker. He hesitated in front of John.

"There's something I read recently about the death penalty," he began, glancing at his roommate. John's face was open, so Dallas flipped pages and continued. "It's in the 'respect for human life' section. Apparently, the Catholic Church teaches that the death penalty should be reserved for extreme cases, where it would be hard to prevent more innocent people from being killed by the murderer. And that killing is different from murdering. As much contempt as I have for myself, I know that my crime was killing, not murder. Anyway, the idea here is that neither deserves to be intentionally deprived of life as punishment, because it's not 'in conformity with the dignity of the human person.' I don't exactly know what that means..."

John snorted. "Dignity? Hell, we lost any dignity we had the second we came through those doors. We're subhuman in here."

Dallas nodded in silence. *And Hudson is trying his hardest to ensure that I feel utterly stripped of all dignity.*

"Sorry I brought it up, man," John added, flopping onto his bunk. "I mean, reminding you about goin' in the hole. I'm just so glad it's not me on death row, ya know?"

Dallas stepped on the chair to climb up to his bunk. *H Unit. H is for hole, H is for hell...* He closed his eyes, seeing the doors lining the H Unit hall. *Were the death row inmates in those other cells, maybe one locked up right next door to me?* He opened the *Catechism* to a section on forgiveness and tried to concentrate for the few minutes left before lights out.

Forgiveness, he read, shows that love is stronger than sin. Dallas scoffed at the statement. *Evil holds so much power over men; I know firsthand.* There was a strong drive to choose the way that was easiest, felt best, or worked to one's advantage, no matter how much it hurt him or others. *And yet, I really did love Channing. I know it was the strength of that love that drove me to want to protect him. But I took the wrong actions in my misguided efforts,* Dallas scolded himself. *I only listened to what I thought was best. But I did want the best for Channing, and isn't that what this says love is — willing the good for the other?* Dallas knew this much already, deep inside his conscience.

"Liberation in the spirit of the Gospel is incompatible with hatred of one's enemy as a person, but not with hatred of the evil that he does as an enemy." Dallas didn't know what "the spirit of the Gospel" meant, but that first word, liberation... *that means freedom. That means you're a prisoner until you can forgive an enemy as a person while still hating the bad things he's done.* An uneasiness stirred in the pit of Dallas's stomach. "I'm a prisoner of *myself*," he whispered. "I'm my own worst enemy." His suicide attempt flashed through his mind.

"What was that?" John asked from below.

"Nothing." Dallas buried his face in his pillow, weeping. He gripped the Memorare card and took slow breaths. *I have to stop hating myself. Channing wouldn't want that. And what else do I have to do with my time in here? I'm gonna try, Channing.*

Life stagnated over the next few months. Dallas lay awake each night after murmuring the Memorare to himself, the words "I don't hate myself" droning on repeat in his mind, for Channing's sake. *But I still feel enslaved to my own judgment, my anger, my utter disgust at life, and everyone, at everything!* he fumed, fed up. *What am I doing wrong?! It's like there's a huge hump in front of me, and I just can't get over it. I want to be motivated to live again, to find simple enjoyment again, like Channing had.* Dallas told himself he ought to go outside for rec hour, but he couldn't force himself to take the steps. His desire to move forward wasn't strong enough to conquer his apathy – or his fear. *Trying to live again is to leave Channing behind, and I just can't bear to do that, not yet. It's unfair to him!*

Dallas kicked off his blanket and adjusted his pillow, then held the Memorare card a few inches from his face, squinting at the image in the dark. *You saved my life, Channing. I know you did. You'd want me to try to be happy, to be a good person, to really live. But Chan, I* can't! *I can't go on with my life without you alive. I just don't* want to.

Call the priest.

Dallas's eyes opened wide. *Did I imagine that, or did I really hear it?* The priest whose phone number was written in the *Catechism... But that would be crazy. I'm a random stranger who met him once. It would be stupid to call him out of nowhere.* Dallas scowled at himself in the dark. 'You're being stubborn,' came a voice that didn't seem to belong to himself. Dallas huffed and rolled over, shutting his eyes tight and trying to turn off his brain. Sudden thoughts of Channing, his final moments being filled with adrenaline-pumping fear, then the truck... Dallas felt the all-too-familiar tears running down his cheeks. *Remember, O most gracious Virgin Mary...*

Dallas remained stubborn for several more weeks, shoving down the pestering little nudge to call the phone number written under Father Benedict's name. But Dallas felt hollow. *I look* hollow, he realized, staring into his reflection in the bathroom mirror. *I still have three whole years left in here!* A whole year without Channing now, a whole year in prison had passed. He grabbed his towel and walked back towards his cell. Dallas cracked — he had to call that phone number and talk to that priest. *What do I have to lose?*

Once his phone request was granted later that day, Dallas stood with hesitant fingers hovering over the buttons. He took a breath and punched in the number, then listened to it ringing. A woman's voice answered.

"Uh, is this the Cathedral Basilica of the Immaculate Conception?" he asked.

"It is," responded the voice. "You've reached the church office. How may I help you?"

"I was hoping to speak to Father Benedict," Dallas said.

"I can schedule an appointment with him for you," the woman responded. "Is there a time of day that works best for you?"

"Well, I, um… can't do that," Dallas mumbled, running his free hand through his hair before blurting, "I'm calling from prison." *Why did I have to add that part?*

"Are you a member of this parish?" the church secretary asked.

"No, it's just that I met the priest maybe a year and a half ago, on a trip through Denver, and he talked to me and my friend. He gave my friend a book, the *Catechism*, and I… well, I just need some advice, but I don't know if he does that sort of thing, and… I mean, I… I don't mean to be bothering you…"

What made me just assume that the priest would answer and happen to be available for a leisurely chat? His face flushed pink. *I have no idea how priests or churches work.* Dallas heard a muffled voice in the background, the secretary's "Hold a moment, please," and then more distant conversation. Another minute passed, and Dallas heard somebody pick up the line, and a man's voice said, "Hello, this is Father Benedict."

Dallas's voice stuck in his throat at the rapid turn of events. He sank down onto the stool in front of him.

"Hi, Father Benedict," Dallas managed. "This is going to sound strange, probably…" He paused a moment, uncomfortable.

The old priest spoke. "The office secretary to whom you were speaking told me that somebody was calling from prison, and that you and your friend had met me before. I believe I remember you. Dallas, is it?"

Dallas almost dropped the phone. *How could he know it was me?*

"How did you remember my name?" Dallas managed to ask. "That's, um… that's incredible. Yeah, my name's Dallas, Dallas Malone. You remember me and my friend, the one who was looking at the stained glass windows?"

"Yes, your friend Channing," replied Father Benedict, voice enthusiastic. "How is he?"

It hit Dallas that he'd not prepared for this conversation, either mentally or emotionally. Everything spilled out.

"Channing's dead. It's been so awful. He was hit by a truck, and I've been locked up since it happened. The book you gave him — I have it here in prison, and your name and the phone number are written inside it, and, well, I just… I don't have anyone to turn to. I'm just so lost without him, and so something made me call…"

Dallas trailed off, and when the older man spoke, his voice quavered with emotion.

"I'm terribly sorry to hear of Channing's death," he said. "I… didn't expect to hear that." The priest paused.

"Channing told me he wanted to become Catholic the day before he died," Dallas threw in, not knowing how else to break the silence.

"I had thought he might," replied Father Benedict gently. There was another pause. Dallas wondered if he was supposed to reply to that.

"Dallas," came the soft voice again, "I have some things to say to you, and I can tell you have a story about what happened to Channing and yourself. An in-person conversation might be best. And prison ministry is one of my passions, so please don't think it is at all off-putting for me to come visit you there."

Shocked, Dallas paused before stuttering, "B-but, I'm in Oklahoma."

"If you would agree, I can arrange a visit there within the next few weeks," answered the priest without missing a beat. "I don't want to pressure you, of course, but your calling me is no coincidence. Channing has been on my mind over this past year. And Dallas, whatever you have done, I am not here to condemn you. Know that, and be not afraid. If you need to talk, I will come and listen."

The man's voice was so gentle, yet Dallas squirmed. *How could he remember us so easily? Why has he been wondering about Channing?*

"Yeah, a visit would be nice. But I understand if it's too much trouble, because it's more than a full day's drive."

"I am all too glad to come," responded the priest. "God has put something into your heart for you to call me. Face-to-face conversation is always more meaningful when you are isolated. Can you wait for me until the end of this month? If you have some urgent needs, I can address them right now."

"No, I'd appreciate an in-person visit. I can wait." Dallas swiveled on the stool. "Somehow, the idea of that is, well – this might sound weird, but you met Channing; you remember him. Speaking to anyone who has ever talked with him before would be a real comfort to me."

"My son, I will be praying for you that God gives you strength in this difficult time," said Father Benedict. "I will be praying for Channing's soul as well. The Holy Spirit has urged you to reach out, and your cries will not go unheeded. God loves you, Dallas."

Dallas muttered thanks and goodbye before hanging up. *That was kinda weird… the whole conversation. Is there a God? Why did I call in the first place?* Dallas felt like he was groping blindly in the dark for anything that reminded him of Channing. All he could do now was wait and decide what he needed from the priest when he visited in a few weeks.

FATHER BENEDICT

Dallas walked alongside Officer Murphy towards the visitors' area where Father Benedict waited. His stomach was flipped upside-down, and he twitched with anticipation.

As Dallas slunk into the room, the priest rose, smiling and extending both hands across the table. His warm hands clasped Dallas's. "It's good to see you."

Cheeks warm at the priest seeing him in his prison uniform, Dallas nodded and slid into the plastic chair. He tingled all over as he imagined his visitor's scrutiny of his appearance: hand battered and scarred, cheeks hollow, eyes weary and hardened.

Father Benedict lowered himself into his seat again. "I am so very sorry about Channing's death," he began, "and I have been praying for the repose of his soul daily. I know you two were so close and that you cared for him deeply."

Eyes down, Dallas nodded, still in the dark as to how this priest seemed to know so much about Channing and him.

"So, would you like to tell me all that has happened first," asked the priest, "or do you want me to tell you why I was able to remember you so clearly?"

"Yeah, I'd like you to tell me that right away, if you don't mind." Dallas made eye contact and waited.

Father Benedict returned the gaze. "I wasn't surprised to hear you say that Channing had decided to become Catholic," he began. "So, it was about a year and a half ago when I met the two of you, yes? I remember it was about two weeks before Lent began, late January or early February, was it?"

Dallas nodded again and mumbled, "That sounds about right, yeah."

"And you two had come into the cathedral to admire the stained glass. And I gave Channing the book you now have, the *Catechism of the Catholic Church*."

"Yeah, it's in my cell." Dallas shifted in his chair, edgy with a desire to have all the answers immediately. "Channing picked it out as one of just a few books he brought along when… when we had to pack light and leave my car behind."

"A couple months after meeting you two, I received a phone call from Channing," the priest continued.

Dallas's jaw dropped, and he snapped his head up at attention. *I had no idea...*

"He said you had settled in Minnesota," said the priest. "Channing wanted to ask me a few things about what he'd read in the *Catechism*. Our conversation showed that this was a very intelligent, deep-thinking young man."

"Yeah, that's Channing, for sure." Dallas smiled. It was a foreign sensation.

"He was searching for Truth, and he told me how he was noticing it in many places," Father continued.

"Yeah." Dallas nodded. "That's something he tried talking about to me more and more, the closer... well, in the months leading up to... to his death. He said that everything was becoming clear to him, like he could see so obviously what the truth was. Me, not so much. He'd try explaining things to me, but I just can't always see what's true and what's not."

"Channing was a very clear thinker, and he was making all kinds of connections between Church teachings and what his reason was telling him," the priest said. "Having read Chesterton, he had a very good basis for understanding rational thought in conjunction with the Christian faith. I told him I would be glad to answer any questions for him, seeing how seriously he was taking his faith journey."

"And did he call you again?" Dallas asked.

"Yes, three times more after that," Father Benedict responded. "The last time, he confided that he had almost decided about converting to Catholicism. I told him that when he was ready for sure, I could help him determine the steps to take in receiving instruction before being welcomed into the Church as a baptized member of the Body of Christ."

Dallas was trying to follow this, with his memory of Channing's explanations and the little he'd gleaned from his recent attempts with the *Catechism*. But he did remember this part about how Channing had hoped to be able to find a way to get to a Catholic parish in a nearby town to take a class.

"He never called back to say he was ready," the elderly man said, shaking his head, "and now I know why." The priest's eyes got misty.

Resigned to his own bouts of crying, Dallas made no effort to hide the tears streaming down his face. *Somebody else cared about Channing.* The realization swelled inside him until he felt he might burst, and his entire body shivered.

"So is Channing in heaven?" The question escaped through his sniffles before he knew his brain had formed the question.

Father Benedict pursed his lips. "Do you believe in God, Dallas?"

Dallas looked away. He still wasn't sure, but the things Channing had said to him about God, the things he'd been reading these past few months in prison... He took a breath, lacing and unlacing his fingers on the tabletop in front of him.

"I used to think I didn't," Dallas began slowly, "and then, when Channing was still alive, I just didn't know whether to believe in God or not. When Channing died, I was sure he couldn't be real. It was so, so awful. It still is, really. Then I decided I hated God for letting things happen the way they have, and that's when I thought maybe he does exist after all. So, I guess I *might* believe in God. But I sure as heck don't understand him. That's why I asked that about Channing, I guess. I mean, I *know* Channing believed in God. He believed in him the day he died, right before his death, I know for *certain*." Dallas hesitated, unsure if he wanted to tell Father Benedict about the bizarre emergency baptism in the water spigot. "But even if I'm not sure myself, it somehow makes me feel just a little better to know that he did."

"Dallas, we can trust in God's loving care and in his all-knowing and all-powerful attributes. You have been reading the *Catechism*?"

"Yeah, some." Dallas picked at a loose string on his shirt cuff in his lap. "I want to ask you a couple things about it, actually. I want to feel close to Channing again by learning about what he had discovered."

"You may come across things there about salvation, and that baptism in the name of the Father, and of the Son, and of the Holy Spirit is the only way God has revealed to us for salvation — going to heaven, that is. But as God may have ways only known to him, and as he exists outside of time and space, and as he could see into Channing's heart and know what was there... Catholics believe there can be such a thing as 'baptism of desire.' Channing revealed to us his desire of becoming a baptized Catholic. Therefore, we can leave his soul to God's loving care with confidence."

Dallas couldn't hold it back now. "He *was* baptized," he said in a quick, low voice.

Father Benedict's eyes widened. "Was he? But he hadn't been raised in any faith and wouldn't have been baptized as a child."

"No, I mean, he was baptized right before he died," Dallas said, eyes staring into his lap and cheeks growing pink. "I... I baptized him."

Silence hung in the air between them, and Dallas was afraid he'd done something terribly wrong. *Maybe it's a sacrilege for somebody who doesn't believe in God to baptize anyone.* He stole a glance at the priest's face, expecting fire and brimstone but saw instead that he was both smiling and crying.

Dallas hesitated and then began describing what had happened, falteringly at first, then spilling it out as the event replayed through his mind, as clear as the day it had happened. He heard Channing's desperate plea, saw his own hands splashing the water frantically over his friend's head so they could hurry and run, run from the police...

"He asked me to do it. *Begged* me to. And I said the words he told me to say," finished up Dallas in a hushed tone. "I said, 'I baptize you in the name of the Father, Son, Holy Spirit.' So, was that real? Did it count as an actual baptism?"

Father Benedict nodded with calm eyes. "It did count, most certainly. Although we could trust Channing's soul to the mercy of God without baptism, the fact that he wanted it so badly as to beg you to do it..." The priest cleared his throat and dabbed at his eyes. "Thank you, Dallas."

Dallas shifted uncomfortably and shrugged his shoulders. "But I did it begrudgingly. I didn't believe in it myself, really. I guess it brings me some peace, knowing I did something he was so desperate for, if that's what you mean. Like, it could make him happy before... before he died... and I didn't even realize at that moment that less than ten minutes later..." Dallas turned away from the priest, shoulders shaking with the sobs that had come with his memories.

The priest sat in patient silence, eyes closed and head bowed. "Channing had a very intuitive nature, as you surely noticed yourself." Dallas nodded through his tears, and Father Benedict went on. "There was something quite spiritual within him, and I noticed it from the moment I saw him in the basilica that afternoon." He paused and wiped a tear from his eye. "Channing had the intuition to see the danger he was in and to know he needed to request the sacrament of baptism. The Holy Spirit urged him to make that last request of you, Dallas, and allowed you to be willing to confer the sacrament upon your friend. Yes, Dallas, the chances of heaven are quite good for Channing. While God alone knows the state of a soul after death, he has given us so many reasons for hope in Channing's case. We can and should still pray for his soul, but to be consumed with worry over whether he is in heaven now... Be at peace, Dallas."

Dallas let out a long, shuddery sigh, followed by a shivery tingle up and down his spine. He leaned his face against his hands, elbows resting on the tabletop, eyes closed.

"Another thing you will find in the *Catechism* is how Catholics believe that, in order for a man to gain heaven, his soul must be free from sin. A baptized Catholic would come to a priest and go to confession in order to have his soul cleansed."

"I've heard of that, yeah," Dallas said. "To ask forgiveness for your wrongdoings, right?"

"Yes," the priest answered, "and we believe it is truly Jesus forgiving sins, and he merely uses us priests as instruments, to be his hands and feet here on earth. So, of course, not yet receiving specific instruction on joining the Church, Channing couldn't make a sacramental confession to me or any other priest. But baptism washes away all sin committed up until that point, and so God, through your actions, also forgave Channing of all sin. And Dallas, I can tell you from my conversations with him that he was certainly sorry for his wrongdoings."

"Channing didn't have any wrongdoings," Dallas said with a scowl. "It was all me. *I'm* the one who led him into wrong." *And then I conferred a sacrament on him that made him a Christian and forgave him of his sins at the same time, according to this priest... Catholics are kinda crazy.* Dallas's head spun.

"Oh, I'm sure you may be able to guess some of them yourself," Father Benedict said. "He told me the two of you were closer than brothers."

Dallas closed his eyes and heard Channing arguing with him on the side of the road, Dallas tired and grimy from repairing his car. "He did regret calling me a jerk after I blew up at him for wasting money on books when we were desperate for food," Dallas mused. "I mean, he apologized to me for that himself. And I had to apologize for yelling at him."

"He did tell me that very story." The priest smiled. "It shows that you were both willing, for the sake of the other, to admit your faults and forgive each other. Dallas, he also told me that something had happened to cause the two of you to flee from the police."

Color drained from Dallas's face, the sudden turn in the conversation leaving his mouth dry. "What did he tell you?" he managed, the horrific scene of the accidental shooting invading Dallas's thoughts, the state trooper's blood soaking into his shirt...

"He didn't tell me the details," the priest answered quickly.

"Remember how I said that I am not here to judge you? Only God can do that. Channing was worried about you. He told me you had a serious accident that was weighing heavily on you and that the police would arrest you and possibly him as an accomplice if they found you. Channing asked my advice on whether it was right to hide from the police. He said he trusted you to look out for him, but he was worried for your soul. He wanted to make a confession to me and asked if he could make one on your behalf too, for the sake of both of your souls. Of course, it doesn't work that way. But I did advise him to put his trust in God and ask him directly for forgiveness for the time being, and that if he really thought what had happened was an accident, then God could see that, and the severity of a crime is lessened when we weren't able to fully consent to it or didn't understand the gravity of the wrongdoing."

Dallas was openly weeping, palms to his forehead and fingers scrunching in his hair. "No, I didn't fully understand, but I do now!" He sniffled through his tears. "I didn't consent to being thrust into the world to fend for myself suddenly by my mother. But I was 19; I should've been able to handle it because I was an adult! And I didn't understand the severity of trying to run from armed law enforcement, but I completely understand how serious that is now, beyond a shadow of a doubt! I thought I was protecting Channing: from his mother, from hunger, from arrest and juvenile detention... but I got us into worse trouble with all my bad decisions! And I... I got Channing killed in the end." Dallas buried his head in his arms on the table.

Father Benedict was silent and grasped Dallas's shaking shoulder with one hand.

"I suppose I need to explain how it all happened," Dallas said after regaining his composure, head still on his arms. "The whole awful story." He pushed himself up and took a breath. He told the priest everything, starting with their homelessness and leading all the way to Channing's death. As he narrated, Dallas interjected what he should have done instead. He should have kept a steady job after graduation. They should have stayed in Nevada, gone straight to the homeless shelter there, even if it meant separation in two different shelters. Should have tried harder to catch fish. Should have offered to wash people's windshields in exchange for money or food. Should have pressed themselves to hold out longer without eating. A whole list of now-useless should-haves.

Father Benedict listened without interruption, nodding.

Finally, Dallas sighed, and his shoulders drooped, emotion draining out of his body. The thorough retelling had sapped him. He closed his eyes, the silence in the room physically surrounding him.

"Dallas," the kind voice began. "It is true that you made some rash decisions. It's also true that you were—still *are*—really no more than a child yourself. Legally being an adult magically at the age of 18 doesn't give much leeway for growing into your responsibilities, and I can see that they were thrust upon you rather unexpectedly. And you expected more of yourself than anyone your age could properly handle. You have grown in wisdom to be able to see that while you made what you thought were the only decisions possible at the time, perhaps things could have been done differently. We can't torment ourselves with past failings that we cannot change but only learn from experience and make better choices moving forward. And, son, I am so very sorry that you have had to learn these things in the hardest way imaginable. You have suffered the greatest loss you could have endured: your very best friend. He loved you so much, Dallas, and he was sure of your loving care for him too, so sure that he didn't judge your choices as being rash or impulsive. All Channing said to me repeatedly was that you were acting in what you thought was his best interest. That you wanted to protect him. He knew that. He also knew underneath it all that you were making serious mistakes, and it bothered his conscience. But he credited you for doing your very best at the time."

"My best got him killed," Dallas said miserably. "And it was because I thought I was the only one who could help him. I was the responsible one, the 'adult,' who had to get us into a better situation. Father Benedict, was that pride? Trying to bear the weight of it all myself and not letting Channing help deal with anything? At first, he wanted us to go turn ourselves in; explain it was all an accident. He was right. He was *right!*" Dallas pounded a fist on the rickety table. "I didn't listen to him, because I thought I knew better. I thought that I'd go to jail and he'd go to juvenile detention. I thought he wasn't strong enough to handle that. I was trying to keep him with me at all costs. I was selfish and proud by assuming he couldn't make it without me. I was so stupid! We could've survived a few months apart in shelters while we got on our feet. I was so blind to the logical things to do, the *right* things. I've been tormented by the fact that my stupid choices are what killed Channing." Dallas was whispering now. "Four years of prison is a light punishment compared to what I've done. I killed my best friend."

"Dallas, your burden is so heavy." The priest sighed. "You took much responsibility on yourself, and you still can't set down this heavy load a year after Channing's death. It may have been prideful of you to call all the shots, but do you think you were trying to be the one and only for Channing, selfishly trying to have his friendship all to yourself? Or did you feel as if his issues from his family background were such that he would have difficulty managing on his own? Did you do it out of love for your power and control over him, or out of genuine concern and care for him?"

"I did it because I was worried about him, yeah," Dallas said. "But… well, I guess I've always liked to be in control. The night before he died, right before telling me he had decided to become Catholic, Channing told me I needed to let him share the load. I hadn't even considered doing that before. I hadn't thought of him as capable at all… and I don't know, maybe he wasn't. He never got the chance to show me. But I didn't know how to take less of it on myself."

"While you certainly have some responsibility for your wrongdoings, Dallas, it lessens your culpability that you were young, that your mother had left you with nowhere to go, and that Channing had experienced a past that left him quite childlike in many ways."

Dallas's eyebrows shot up in surprise.

"Oh, yes, Dallas, I noticed his mannerisms and how, in some ways, he seemed much younger than he really was. It was only natural of you to want to take on the role of big brother. And you didn't know God. Had you known God, you could have given some of that burden over to him. Did you realize that was something you could do?"

"I'm so used to just doing everything for myself." He shrugged. "Nobody else has helped me much my whole life, and I just felt obligated. But I *wanted* to help Channing. I would've done anything for him. Is it prideful of me to still wish I had died instead of him?"

"That is a natural response to feel," the priest responded. "You are still early in your grief over Channing. This will be with you all your life. It will get easier over time, the pain will dull, but you will always have it. I would like nothing more than to help you start turning it over to God if you are willing to try that."

"How?" asked Dallas helplessly.

"It won't happen all at once," he answered. "But if you'd like, I'll keep meeting with you. Your intentions were never malicious, but you see the harm that resulted from them regardless. The circumstances you were put in were very difficult, Dallas, and God knows what was in your heart and that you are sorry for any outcomes of your decisions. True sorrow and repentance are all he asks of us when we have made mistakes, both for sins committed with full planning and consent and those where you only realize how detrimental they were in hindsight."

Dallas had pulled out Channing's prayer card. He held it up to the priest. "This was in Channing's pocket when he died. Since I've had it, I've made a commitment to say the prayer on the back every day for him." Dallas gazed at the card in his hands, his precious treasure. "The night before he died," he continued, his voice cracking, "Channing taught me this prayer, the Memorare. We recited it over and over until we fell asleep. It was the easiest I'd fallen asleep in months. The enormity of my crimes and hiding from the police weighed on me so that I couldn't get to sleep most nights for hours. I'd been trying to hide it from him, but that night I finally let my guard down and agreed that I'd let Channing share the burden with me. And then, when he told me he wanted to become Catholic... well, I thought maybe he'd become a priest, even." Dallas swallowed the lump in his throat and shook his head. "How could God just let him die when he had his whole life ahead of him? And right after he was trying to teach me more about him, teaching me to pray? Some kind of sick way for God to thank him, that's for sure." Dallas felt his face redden with anger.

"None of us can make sense out of suffering on this earth," the priest offered, bowing his head. "God doesn't cause it, but he allows it to happen. That's so hard for us to understand. But it causes us to lean on him desperately and rely on him more."

"Or to turn our backs on him completely," Dallas shot back, an edge of hostility in his voice.

"That is a choice we can make, yes," answered Father Benedict, pulling at his beard. "God gives us free will and won't force us to love him or follow his laws. It's more meaningful when you *choose* to love, even when it is difficult."

Dallas's heart lurched at the connection. "You mean like the way Channing chose to love me. He knew what I'd done was wrong. And still, he stood by me. He was worried about my soul, you said? That I'd just hold in my guilt and never seek forgiveness for it?"

"Yes, something like that," the priest responded. "Channing told me in our last phone conversation that he saw the toll it was taking, as if you were imprisoned by your secret. And he seemed so ready to convert, which is why I was surprised and concerned when I never heard from him again. The not knowing was easier for me, but now I can share this burden with you, Dallas. I cared about Channing and the promise he showed. He was an incredible young man to make so many connections without any formal religious guidance, and you were so blessed to have him in your life. I know the weight of it all is difficult for you to bear. And Channing wanted to help you to bear it, wanted you to know God, to make your burdens easier, to seek the forgiveness that would give you peace."

"He was so much smarter than me," Dallas said, shaking his head with a half-smile. "He could tell it was eating me up inside, even though I tried to keep it hidden from him. I was finally ready to treat him like a man… then poof, it was all over. I want Channing—if he's able to see me here and now—I want him to be able to *respect* me. Be proud of me. See me happy, or at least content. See me making better decisions. My stumbling across your number, calling you, and finding out that Channing had been talking to you… it's like puzzle pieces coming together or something, like it all *means* something. I want to find some answers, Father, especially about forgiveness, and love, real love. I just can't love myself right now; hell, I don't even *like* myself. Oh gosh, I shouldn't have cussed in front of a priest." Dallas blushed.

"I know the vocabulary is rough in here," Father answered. "Nothing I haven't heard before."

"Channing didn't like me cussing," Dallas reflected. "Probably reminded him of his parents cussing at him. Bad habit I picked up. I could've tried harder to hold it back, for his sake. He really accepted me despite all my faults."

"And he thought the same about you," Father Benedict said.

"Yeah," Dallas answered, nodding, "he sure did. He told me so. He was so good at expressing his gratitude. And I don't know if this sounds crazy, but I feel like maybe he's still trying to communicate with me, like he wants me to… to find God like he did. Channing's already intervened in my life once since I've been in here." Dallas hung his head as he mumbled the details of his attempt on his own life. "Since then, I've imagined Channing chiding me for it, saying, 'Hey, Dallas, don't you remember when I read Dante's *Inferno* to you?' The ones who committed suicide—they became trees for eternity in hell. The images were so gruesomely clear to me as he was reading it aloud that night, sitting on the shore of the beach. But then, when I was in the thick of it, about to hang myself, I couldn't even appreciate that; it wasn't even a blip on my radar to be afraid of what I was about to do to myself. I was too deep in my own head with self-pity. He was giving me so much to ponder and learn, and I'm too boneheaded to use it until it's too late. So he had to speak to me directly, and good thing he did. I know I'd be dead right now if his voice hadn't popped into my mind just then. I would have lost both my life and my soul itself," he whispered with a shudder.

"He left a huge impression on your life, Dallas," the priest reflected. "Maybe one of God's very special purposes for Channing's life was to allow him to draw you closer to him."

Dallas frowned as he pondered the priest's words. "I don't know if I like that," he said. "God 'using' Channing. To help *me*. What about him? Why didn't God care that *he* died a horrible death, right in front of my eyes, and when he was so young? I'd rather have been used to save Channing!"

"When death is unexpected, we feel that it isn't fair," answered Father Benedict. "And it isn't. But Channing's life, regardless of how short, was a beautiful gift. A *beautiful* one. And it was a journey for him, from a difficult childhood, into an acceptance of himself and a contentedness he found because he could rest in his knowledge of God. And so, because he found that peace and that truth, you might say he lived a full life."

"And I'm still lost, so I'm stuck here," Dallas mused with cynicism in his tone. "But yeah, I see what you're saying. Channing appreciated everything; I mean every little thing. He really had learned to like himself. And me... yeah, I spend most of my time disgusted with myself." Dallas lowered his head.

"We weren't meant to live this way," the priest said. "I know it's hard to accept yourself, to live with the bad things of your past. You were left to live for a reason, and it is one you may never fully understand in this life. When you feel hopeless because you can't do anything for Channing here on earth anymore, remember the thing you can do: you can still pray for him."

"Can I pray for somebody when I'm not even sure if God is really there?" Dallas asked. "I don't want to be a hypocrite or act like prayer is some kind of magic."

"That's very wise, Dallas," mused the priest. "But if you have doubts, the very best thing *to* do is pray. Love and faith are choices, not feelings. It's nice when you feel strongly about something, such as the presence and the reality of God. But everyone has doubts from time to time, and some people have many doubts. It is the *choice* to push through anyway, to persevere, that is important in those times of doubt. That's not being a hypocrite; that's being steadfast. There is a story in the Bible where a man says to Jesus, 'Lord, I believe; help my unbelief!' That is a perfect prayer to make when you have uncertainties about faith. God will hear your attempts."

Dallas shifted uncomfortably in his chair, cracking his knuckles. "That's sort of how I feel, maybe," he began. "I... I've never read the Bible before. I mean, like never even once. I get the basic idea that Jesus died on the cross for us. I've heard the Noah's ark story, Adam and Eve... I hate to admit I don't know much more than that, and maybe bits and pieces Channing would talk about in the past couple of years. I mean, the last couple of years he lived..." Tears welled up in his eyes. "I believe; help my unbelief. I never heard that before." He pursed his lips.

Father Benedict smiled. "I don't know if I'm talking too much, Dallas, but maybe I'm giving you some things to think about. And it can be a long journey. We can't expect to find peace with ourselves all at once. Do you need a break? I understand if it is getting to be too much."

"I'm good, thanks," Dallas responded. "I'm sick of feeling this way about myself. I'm just glad to hear that maybe there's hope for me, that maybe something's trying to get through to me."

"Would you like to pause for a drink and snack?" asked the priest, motioning towards the vending machines. "My treat."

"Sure, that'd be great." Dallas's mouth watered. "I haven't had a soda since before my arrest."

Dallas and Father Benedict each selected a snack, and Dallas got a Coke as well. They sat back down after stretching.

"So what was it you heard Channing saying, if it's not too personal for you to share," the priest asked quietly, "that stopped you from taking your life?"

The memory flashed through Dallas's mind. *Channing's voice. His innocent, clear tone...* "It was something he said to me on the last night of his life, and I heard him as if he was repeating it in my ear just as I was about to hang myself. He told me," Dallas said slowly, eyes on the candy bar in his hands, "that I'd taught him so much about God." He raised his eyes until they met Father Benedict's and waited for his response.

The priest reached out and patted Dallas's hand, eyes teary. "You made sacrifices for Channing, and perhaps he identified that with the way Jesus sacrificed himself and with the unconditional love and acceptance of God the Father. Your friendship, despite its human imperfections, was a way God was trying to reveal himself to the two of you. You gave hope and goodness to Channing as best you could, and in the end, you began to allow him to do the same for you. And you can continue to allow him to help you."

"You mean, even now, after his death, I can allow Channing to continue to lead me? Like, really put some effort into following Channing's example of contentedness? Because Father, he was so content, despite all the rough stuff he went through." Dallas cleared his throat. "He was so… so *earnest* about God. I rarely let him lead, felt guilty if I dumped any decision-making on him, but – that last night especially – I was finally seeing how he was onto something, something big. And so now, if I can still let him lead me somehow, to a truth I've balked at for so long… if there's really a truth…" Dallas fell silent, ruminating on his jumbled thoughts. *I can't be stubborn anymore. I have to give in, or else I'm gonna break. Channing wouldn't just want me to be alive… he would want me to truly live. I want to feel close to him again, and then maybe I can learn how he was able to accept himself, to be happy.*

"Father, I…" Dallas hesitated as the priest leaned towards him. "I think I *want* to believe in God, to have some hope, but I'm just not sure how. What can I do while I'm stuck here serving my term?"

"Keep reading the *Catechism*," the priest responded. "And I will send you some things: a Bible, first of all. Read and ask questions. Write down anything you want to ask me. You can call me, and if you'd like, I will come back to visit you again next month."

"Yes, thanks," Dallas said hopefully. "It's been so good to tell somebody else about everything that's happened, to be able to talk about Channing. And I'm glad to know he was reaching out to you, Father. I appreciate you being there for him. He was growing up and really coming into his own and on the verge of so much…" Dallas choked up, unable to continue.

"And you miss him and mourn the loss of seeing the full version of himself that he was becoming," Father Benedict said softly. "I have great peace from knowing that Channing wanted to commit himself to following Christ and joining his Church. I hope that even if it doesn't feel like it right now, that your role in it, your willingness to fulfill his desire for baptism, will one day give you lasting peace too."

Their time was up. As the priest stood to leave, Dallas rose with him and clasped his hand across the table. He walked back to his cell, deep in thought.

Dallas lay sprawled on his belly across his bunk, reading through the *Catechism* and jotting down questions in a notebook. He was making his way through the thick volume, a smile flickering across his face each time he came across Channing's handwritten margin notes and underlining. He furrowed his brow and applied himself to the next section. Some of it was really challenging to understand, but much was making sense.

John entered the cell, whistling. When Dallas didn't look up, John stood at eye level beside the bunk.

"You've been real quiet the past few weeks," he commented. "What's up?"

Dallas, breaking away from the page in front of him, glanced at John and answered, "Just got a lot on my mind." He shielded his notes with his arm, unwilling to reveal to his cellmate his attempts at serious religious study.

"You just seem calmer lately," John commented. He turned away and busied himself with something in his locker.

Dallas turned over and curled up towards the wall, cradling the book and trying to direct his attention back to the tedious paragraph in front of him.

Father Benedict had sent three books: a copy of the Bible, *The Everlasting Man* by Chesterton, and a collection of lives of the saints. Dallas had focused on the Gospels last week, trying to gain some insight into how Jesus brought the faith to humanity as God made man, fully God and fully man.

John was in a chatty mood. "What's the current book?"

"Just the *Catechism of the Catholic Church*." Dallas tried to sound nonchalant.

"What's it about?" John continued.

Dallas sat up and swung his legs over the edge of the bed. "This section's on heaven, hell, and purgatory."

"Purgatory?" John wrinkled his nose. "That's, like, the Catholic do-over, isn't it?"

"Not quite," Dallas said slowly. "It's like a place of purification. This says nothing sinful can enter heaven, so as sinful people... I don't know if I believe any of this, anyway," Dallas added with a shrug, glancing at John's questioning face. He turned back towards the wall.

Purgatory had sounded strange to him, but it was making more sense, especially once he read the parts of the Bible that Father Benedict had pointed him towards as evidence for the need for prayers for the dead.

He'd spoken to the priest over the phone a few times since their meeting, and Dallas sensed from their conversations that not everything was perfectly black and white — that God was a God of mercy and that there were reasons for hope. Before, he had just assumed it was a split-second thing, going to heaven or to hell. But the concept that for God, there is no time as we know it and that our prayers could assist somebody years after their death... it was mind-blowing and gave Dallas a vague peace about Channing. But he was embarrassed to say so to John.

The tiny flame enkindled in Dallas was preferable to no flame at all, so he decided to persevere. He prayed upon waking, at meals, and at bedtime, even though he still mostly doubted God. *Remember, Channing said God probably likes our fumbling efforts.* And with this memory, Dallas sensed he'd made a connection, like his feet were hitting solid ground here and there.

The bad moments still came, nearly every day, some worse and longer than others. He still felt like a part of his body had been torn from him when he missed Channing. He still cried at least a few times a week over his death, agonizing over why he had been spared. He improved at pushing aside the feelings of self-loathing when they came, but he was aware of them at a low simmer beneath the surface. *Channing wants me to have peace, and he thought God could give it to me.* Dallas wanted this for Channing more than himself, he realized. *I wonder if that's wrong of me.*

He asked Father Benedict about it at their second in-person visit.

"Ultimately, God wants us to have faith in him because we realize we need him, we desire to worship him, and we want to save our souls." Father raised his eyebrows and asked, "Are you concerned that you are wanting a relationship with God only because you'll feel closer to Channing?"

"Yeah," replied Dallas. "Is that terrible of me?"

The priest made no response.

"Well, I guess I also want to learn more about Christianity because Channing was so smart," Dallas added, "and if he thought it was right, then maybe it is. In deep things, I usually trusted his judgment. He followed my judgment on shoplifting and running from the cops, and my judgment failed him. It's like maybe I can make it up to him by trusting he was right in this. But those aren't the right reasons to believe in God, are they?"

"It is an understandable reaction," Father Benedict said softly. "But God desires a relationship with each one of us. Channing had his own relationship with God, and you were beginning to see that firsthand. It isn't wrong of you to come to God in this way, though, Dallas. You may be doing it more for Channing than for yourself and for God right now. Our job on earth is to help each other get to heaven, and Channing was trying to do that, whether he knew it or not. But if you focus on trying to know God, then you can build that relationship with him. Channing may be the one that led you to start down this path, but he can't be the one that keeps you here. That has to be between you and God."

"So, it's okay if Channing's experience was what enkindled the fire for me… but something else has to keep it burning?" Dallas saw in his mind an old memory of the two of them sitting beside the campfire in the woods at the outskirts of town.

"An excellent way to put it," Father Benedict said with a smile. "You have to keep it burning through your own efforts. Even when it doesn't feel easy, you just keep making that choice to believe in God, that he loves you with a perfect love."

"Lord, I do believe; help my unbelief," Dallas murmured. He swept his gaze back up to the face of the priest across the table from him. "I've been saying that a lot to myself lately. Even wrote it down and taped it to my wall by my bed."

"I'm glad it is helpful." Father smiled.

Dallas sighed. "I still don't feel like I'm able to forgive myself, though," he confessed.

"Do you see yourself as a sinner?" the priest asked.

"Definitely," Dallas replied. "I do bad things all the time."

"Then give yourself over to God's hands," persuaded Father Benedict. "If you cannot forgive yourself, you must throw yourself to the mercy of somebody more powerful than you."

More powerful. The phrase sent shivers through Dallas. "Somebody else can be in charge," he whispered, slumping back in his seat.

Father Benedict sighed and nodded.

The load lightened as Dallas began to realize he didn't have to be—couldn't be—his own savior. *I've gotta give that over to somebody else. And maybe—just maybe—I can accept God's forgiveness, even if I can't forgive myself.*

DOWN IN A HOLE

"You seem like you've lost your old restlessness, or at least, it's not so strong as it was before," John observed one day late in autumn.

Dallas realized that John was right—he had been pacing around their cell less in recent months, opting to sit with his nose in a book instead. Father Benedict's regular visits were a spark igniting fire, giving Dallas glimpses of the reason behind Catholic doctrine. He finally felt like he might be starting to believe because it was true and not just for Channing's sake.

He responded, "I guess part of it's that I've become resigned to my fate here. And the other half of it is… well, I think I finally believe in God, for real."

"Shoot, I knew you believed in God ever since that baby Jesus card incident," scoffed John. "Why else would you have gotten so defensive over it?"

"Because that prayer card belonged to my best friend," Dallas said, "and he died the day I got arrested. I got it back miraculously and wasn't about to lose it."

"Miraculously, like an act of God?" asked John. "See, you've believed in him all along."

Dallas shrugged. "So, what do you think about God?"

"Eh, not much, but I believe in him," John answered. "I mean, *somebody* must've made the world and all. So yeah, I think there must be a God."

Dallas smiled at his cellmate's laid-back response. But being on decent terms with John was comfortable.

Dallas crossed himself and dug a spoon into his oatmeal. He was sitting alone, his norm. Lost in thought, Dallas reveled in his solitude, sipping a cup of black coffee in silence, surrounded by a murmur of voices.

The clatter of a plastic tray hitting the table directly across from him startled Dallas, and he jumped, dropping his spoon. The pasty prison-grade oatmeal glopped into his lap, and he muttered a curse, glaring up at the owner of the other breakfast tray.

Maddox jeered down at him. "This seat taken, holy boy?" he asked, plunking himself into the spot.

Dallas gave a silent stare in return. The hairs rose on the back of his neck as his muscles tightened defensively.

Miller slid into the seat next to Maddox, fake grin plastered across his face. "We got a new friend?" he asked his cellmate.

"Depends." Maddox jutted out his chin. "Don't think he wants to be friendly with the likes of me, know what I mean?" He flashed a wicked smile at Dallas and nudged him in the shin with his shoe under the table.

Dallas kept his eyes on the bland sustenance in front of him and made no reply.

Maddox gave him a harder nudge.

Dallas bit his lip, refusing to take the bait.

Miller elbowed his cellmate and whispered to him, and they both turned their heads. Dallas glanced over to see what had caught their attention. The chow line was dwindling, and two COs stood alongside the last of the inmates. Bruce Hudson was one of them. Maddox and Miller glanced knowingly at each other. *They're up to something.* A tightness grew in Dallas's chest.

Maddox left his seat and sidled up alongside Hudson, mouth moving animatedly.

Kiss-up. Dallas glanced at Miller, still seated diagonally across from him and beckoning another inmate over.

"Hey, it's the baby Jesus guy!" said Pulaski, sitting down beside Miller, who laughed raucously at the joke.

Dallas felt his face getting warm, and he ground his teeth behind tight lips. *Why can't they just leave me alone? Now I know how Channing felt. Except I can trounce every one of them, at least.* An aggressive satisfaction built inside him.

Just then, Maddox sauntered back to the table with Hudson alongside him.

"Looky here; we're makin' a new buddy!" Maddox announced. "Except the Hermit's much too good for any of us. Always prayin' to himself..." He glanced at Hudson for approval.

Hudson gave him a half-smile. "Shut up, Maddox." He turned to face Dallas.

Dallas refused to make eye contact and continued to shovel the lukewarm oatmeal into his mouth.

Hudson rounded the table and straddled the bench, all his focus on Dallas. "So, think you're better than everyone?" Hudson mocked in a threatening voice.

Dallas dragged his eyes up to the CO, who leaned in close, and he made no effort to hide his contempt. "Maddox says so, boss." He went back to his eating.

The guard's face flushed red at Dallas's stoic response, and he pounded the table with one fist. Trays and dishes rattled with the thump. "Maddox says something else, scum," growled Hudson in Dallas's ear. "In this institution, we put down riots before they can get started."

Dallas snapped his head up and glared into Hudson's fierce eyes. "What's *that* supposed to mean?"

"I mean you goin' around asking for help with your plan to attack the COs tomorrow!" spat out Hudson. "I don't tolerate that crap on my watch."

Dallas was seized with rage over the lie Maddox must have told about him. "You have a grudge against me already, and Maddox is exploiting it!" he said, hostility rising in his voice, his breakfast tray forgotten. "I never planned any such thing!" Dallas faced the officer now, poised, as Hudson stood up above him. Dallas rose to meet him face to face, lip curled.

"And you'll get away with no such thing, 'cause I'm shuttin' you down now." Hudson towered over Dallas at six feet four inches, glowering down at him. "Come with me to your cell for a shakedown."

Dallas shot a menacing look at Maddox, who had come around the table behind Hudson, glowing in his smugness.

"He's a LIAR!" Dallas roared, lunging towards Maddox.

Hudson was between them and grabbed Dallas by the arm, jerking him towards the door. "Lash out like that again, and I'll teach you a lesson you'll never forget!" he snarled.

The horror of returning to solitary confinement coursing through his body, Dallas bit his lip and willed himself to walk alongside Hudson, but he couldn't help from turning his head back and yelling again at Maddox, "Filthy *liar!*"

"You'll shut up if you know what's good for you," Hudson growled as they exited the cafeteria, twisting Dallas's arm until he winced. "Or do you need a reminder of what happened last time?"

Dallas forced down his desire to attack the guard and made himself resume his sullen demeanor. *Don't give him the satisfaction of getting a response!*

John wasn't in the cell, a fact Dallas soon learned was to his disadvantage. Hudson shoved Dallas through the door.

"Bend-and-spread," Hudson ordered. "You know the deal by now."

Dallas did. He closed his eyes and took himself elsewhere mentally for the strip search that was no less degrading than the many he'd endured since his arrest.

Dallas pulled his uniform back on as Hudson barked at him to sit down in the chair while the room was searched. The guard tore the sheets off both beds, then lifted the mattresses, examining underneath.

Dallas, eyebrows lowered and arms crossed, stared at Hudson's back. "What exactly do you think you're gonna find?"

Hudson spun around, eyes full of contempt. "Anything that can be used against you," he sneered, then struck Dallas on the side of the head with the back of his hand. Dallas flinched but kept staring hard at the guard, refusing to be intimidated.

"You got a shiv or a shank hidden in here?" asked Hudson. "Best to just fess up if you do. Maddox heard you asking some others to get in on your little plan. Tomorrow morning, 7:30 sharp, in the chow hall. Real cute, Malone, planning to shank the COs. Ain't nothing that hasn't been tried before."

Dallas snorted to suppress a sarcastic laugh. "You know Maddox would lie to his grandmother, right?"

Hudson retorted, "Better safe than sorry. And," he added, turning back towards Dallas after shaking out all the sheets and inspecting the area around the toilet and sink, "at least he's not a self-righteous SOB like you. That attitude don't fly in here." He stepped closer to Dallas and leaned down, right in his face.

Dallas braced himself for impact, staring the man down with an icy glare.

"Open your locker," Hudson demanded, standing up straight again.

The color drained from Dallas's face, and he saw the sick glee Hudson was getting from his fear. Dallas glanced at where Channing's holy card lay safe inside, and his stomach lurched as he clenched his fists, remembering how fiercely he'd defended it before. *I'd still die to protect it*, he vowed.

Dallas took a deep breath and steeled his will, narrowing his eyes at Hudson. "No." He folded his arms across his chest again, feet planted firmly against the floor.

"Open your locker!" Hudson snarled again.

"No!" shouted Dallas.

The officer was on him now, jerking Dallas up from the chair and pressing him against the locker, an elbow in his ribcage.

"I think you wanna change your mind, you stubborn little..."

Dallas spat in the CO's face. Hudson stepped back and wiped it off with his forearm. His eyes blazed, and his cheeks puffed out, but then he shook his head, chuckling in a low, eerie voice.

"Boy, you just don't know when to stop," Hudson drawled. "You gonna open that locker so I can check for contraband, or do I need to call for backup?" He tried to force Dallas into a corner, but he obstinately stood his ground, pressing back against the aggressive guard.

"Nobody's gonna back you up on forcing me to open my locker for no reason," Dallas replied, chin jutted out. "You can see what's in it through the gaps."

For a moment, neither man budged, locked in a staring contest of contempt. Suddenly Hudson flashed a smile.

"Okay, have it your way." In a lightning-quick movement, he viciously rammed his knee between Dallas's legs.

The sound of maniacal laughter barely registered with Dallas as he gasped in agony and collapsed to the floor, writhing in pain. Hudson stepped on him and stalked out of the cell. Dallas felt like he was going to throw up and tried to drag himself towards the toilet, but the intensity of the pain made him dizzy. He could only lay on the cold concrete floor, whimpering and seeing stars.

A few minutes later, he pulled himself to his feet and hung on the bars, glaring down the hall. "Didn't get Channing's holy card," he fumed quietly with a hardened feeling of satisfaction, "and that's all that matters." But deep inside, Dallas felt himself breaking from his confinement in this hellhole. For the first time in his life, he was unable to defend himself.

"Don't report it," John advised. "It only makes things worse."

John sat beside the lower bunk. He'd offered to switch with Dallas temporarily so he wouldn't have to climb to the top bed. The mid-20s inmate straddled the chair backwards, leaning his crossed arms on the backrest and staring at Dallas.

Dallas lay in bed, not quite recovered from Hudson's latest assault. He just wanted to stay as still as possible. He'd missed lunch and was dreading the thought of having to limp his way to the cafeteria for dinner. *This is so humiliating! And forget working out today.*

"I've seen it before," John went on. "You squeal on a CO like that, and maybe he gets suspended for a week, twenty days tops. Then he's back, and with an even bigger grudge against you than before. All he's gotta do is show that you threatened him or were so uncooperative he had to use force, and they take his side over ours. We have no rights."

Dallas sighed. He'd already sensed the trouble it would cause to file a complaint against Hudson. It's why he had kept his mouth shut before, after the severe beating in solitary and the door-slamming incident. *Besides,* Dallas conceded inwardly, *I can't hand over my manhood like that! He wins if I admit that I've been bested physically.* He was no match for either Hudson's strength or authority level.

"Sorry, man, I know it sucks to hear that we're powerless in here," John added.

Dallas nodded in sullen agreement.

A few weeks passed. Neither had mentioned Dallas's abuse to anyone, but the silent show of support from his cellmate was chipping away at Dallas's defensive walls. Their conversation today turned towards faith again.

"I've finally figured out that I need God. I can't forgive myself. And so there's gotta be a higher power that can, or else my life is pointless." Dallas stared at the Memorare card as he spoke, held at arm's length above him as he lay flat on his back.

"I figure that serving our terms is earning us forgiveness, right?" asked John, rocking back in the chair.

"No, it's just making up for what we did." Dallas rolled to his side and met John's eyes. "I'll still feel as guilty as ever when I get out of here. A man's dead because I decided to run, and I wouldn't blame his wife if she never forgives me. At least, it's partly my fault…"

John's open expression prodded for more.

"Channing kept saying afterward that the guy should never have pulled his gun to question a couple of petty thieves," Dallas added, gaze swinging to the ceiling above him.

"Channing, that was your friend who died?" John asked, and Dallas realized it was the first time since his arrest that he'd said Channing's name to anyone who hadn't known him before.

"Yeah," Dallas responded quietly. "Channing was my best friend." The old protectiveness welled up inside him, a fierce feeling that surprised him. *Channing's dead — you can't protect him anymore.*

"Well, he was right; no cop should pull a gun to stop unarmed teenagers from shoplifting," John said with a convincing nod. "How'd the guy get shot then? It was an accident, yeah? Do you mind me asking? I mean, all I've known is the bits and pieces I hear. But it's hard to tell what's rumor and what's not sometimes."

Dallas was suddenly struck with the realization that other inmates had been talking about his crime behind his back. It surprised him only because he hadn't noticed. Gossip gave him an uncomfortable feeling, and besides, he didn't care enough about the details of the other men's crimes to want to know.

"If you're curious about the basics, I can tell you. Guess that's better than hearing rumors." Dallas swallowed and closed his eyes. "It started because we had no money, because my mom disappeared. So we needed food, and we went into a gas station to steal some, after we tried begging with little luck. I told Channing to run as soon as the trooper stopped us when he'd caught us shoplifting. It was stupid of me, but he was blocking our path to the door and pulling his gun, I guess as a way of intimidating us into obeying him. It all happened so fast. In my scramble to get away, I ran into him, and he grabbed me with his free hand, and... his gun went off. And killed him. Probably should've been me for being so reckless."

"Well, that sounds like an accident, yeah," John thought aloud. "And so you only got an involuntary charge. Man, you're lucky, though. They're usually a lot tougher on cop killers."

Dallas winced, and John immediately corrected himself. "Sorry, man, I don't mean you *tried* to kill him. Just that when a cop dies in action, they act like it's worse than a regular citizen getting killed."

"So I know that was mostly my fault, yeah, especially since then we fled and were on the run for a few months," Dallas said. "I made things even worse by running. But my lawyer argued that no law enforcement officer is supposed to draw his weapon when we hadn't made any sort of a threat."

"Then you should feel forgiven," John said. "You weren't even fully guilty."

"It's not that simple." Dallas's hands trembled. *Maybe I can't talk about this to somebody who never knew Channing and me back then, even now, almost two years later.* He sat up on the edge of his bunk.

"How'd your friend die?" John asked.

Dallas held his breath, a weight dropping to the pit of his stomach. He realized with irony that John was probably trying to change the subject away from Dallas's nagging guilt, presumably for the trooper's death. There was finally some remorse over the shooting accident, but it paled in comparison to the guilt that still consumed him over what had happened to Channing.

"He…" Dallas took a deep breath, focusing on his hands in his lap. "He got hit by a truck. A tractor-trailer. We were on foot. He was just over an arm's length away from me." His voice quivered, and he swallowed it down hard. "That's the biggest thing I can't forgive myself for."

John was silent a minute. Then he blew out a low sigh. "Wow. I'm sorry. That's real rough."

Blood throbbed through Dallas's veins. That old bitter anguish flooded his heart as he relived the death scene in his mind. Dallas's face reddened as his heart rate quickened. He jumped off his bunk and paced to the door, staring out at nothing.

"So you feel guilty about him dying right there beside you?" asked John.

A numbness had crept over Dallas. *Why did I even start talking about this?* "I feel guilty," he began in a low voice, turning to meet John's eyes, "because I told Channing to run. He listened to me; he *trusted* me. It's my fault we ran into the street. I hadn't learned from before, and we ran from the police again – only this time, it was my best friend who died."

John shuffled his feet. "Man, I'm real sorry. I…" He glanced side to side as if wanting to disappear.

Dallas's grip on the bars of the door tightened. *Stupid, you said too much!* John hadn't forced him to talk. *Have I betrayed Channing's memory or kept it alive by telling a stranger how he died?*

"So my worst guilt isn't about the manslaughter charge that put me here in the slammer." Dallas's face burned, but he was unable to stop the cascade of words racing from his lips. "It's Channing's death, something I can only beg God for mercy about. When you get your one and only friend killed, then you have nobody else to turn to. My last hope, my *only* hope, has to be God." Dallas stumbled over the words, hoping desperately to believe his feeble faith.

Shaky and nauseated, Dallas flung open the cell door and strode down the hall to the weight room. He poured himself into a rigorous workout, pushing his body to its limits to escape the cagey feeling. He beat the punching bag with a white-hot hatred. He did pull-ups so fast he could barely breathe. He only stopped when a CO told him his time was up. He stalked to the showers, still numb, and then went straight back to his cell and climbed into bed. It wasn't even dinner time yet, but Dallas didn't notice. His retelling the story had spiraled him back into depression. *Now John knows how despicable I am, too. This is killing me! Killing me slowly from the inside out.* After Dallas's recent forward progress, he now felt pulled under again, a steady tug of relentless tides, and the thought of this being his life from now on was more than he could bear. He pulled the covers over his head and broke down crying again.

Sitting on the floor with his back against the wall, seeing nothing, Dallas beat the back of his head against the cinder blocks in a steady rhythm. "Love is a choice, not a feeling," he droned in a mumble to himself, but the words rang hollow in his heart. Father Benedict had warned him about possibly losing his momentum after riding a high for several months, but he wasn't coping well with the darkness after glimpsing the light. His fingernails were chewed down to the quick. Dallas hadn't slept more than a few hours a night in nearly two weeks.

John entered their cell, deliberately avoiding eye contact.

Dallas stopped rocking and buried his face in his arms against his knees. For the hundredth time, he mentally tore into himself for revealing his ugly secret to John without considering the emotional ramifications. Dallas heard the shuffling of feet and John using the toilet, then the creaking sound as he settled onto his bunk. Their relationship had been strained since the conversation about Channing's death. *John doesn't understand. And everything's awkward between us now. But who cares anyway — how could anyone like me after what I did?*

The Bible on the nearby desk caught Dallas's eye. A few weeks ago, he had been devouring it and the *Catechism* and his other religious books as a ravenous fire, a deep desire igniting within him, a feeling of being on the right path, the true path. Now he turned to the Psalms and stared at the open pages, but only disgust and apathy gnawed at him. He couldn't reclaim that fire no matter what he tried. *God, you're the only thing I have left to hope in, and I feel like you've thrown me off a cliff, back to my old enemies of guilt and self-loathing. Why'd you let me make progress only to drop me back here again?* Dallas blazed inside. *Channing's dead, and I killed him!* His breaths came rapidly, and he flung the Bible across the room, where it hit the wall and landed with a thud on the floor. Dallas scrambled up to his bunk and ground his teeth on his pillow to stifle his outburst. *I can't ever let myself off the hook, 'cause that'll mean Channing didn't matter. I have to suffer.* He squeezed his eyes shut tight. *I deserve nothing more!*

Only after hearing John leave the cell for lunch did Dallas drag himself out of bed. He plodded to the cafeteria and sat alone, resigned to being his own worst enemy. As he choked down his sandwich, Dallas noticed a group of guys a few tables away, Maddox and Miller among them. They spoke in low voices, glancing over at him and then away. Their occasional howls of rowdy laughter rang out across the room. *They're talking about me.* Dallas shifted in his seat and ate faster.

A moment later, Maddox, Miller, and a new guy Dallas didn't know swaggered towards him from the rowdy group. Two sat down on either side of him, with Maddox directly across. Several men watched from the other table with bated breath.

Dallas tensed up, prepped for trouble.

"So you're lettin' this place break you after all, huh?" started Maddox. "We heard you were crying like a baby again in your bed last night. You gotta toughen up in here to survive, punk. You've been here almost two years now. Surely that means it's time to stop bawling over your dead little friend." The man gave Dallas an ugly smirk.

Dallas snapped his head up and clenched his fists. *What does this jerk know about Channing? What did John say? I was stupid, stupid, stupid to have said a word about any of it!*

"Yeah, you should just get over it," said Miller, seated on Dallas's left. "Ya know, Paddy just got here a couple months ago." He jerked his thumb to indicate the man sitting on the other side of Dallas. "He's done feelin' sorry for himself. It's sink or swim in here, *boy*." Miller prodded Dallas in the side with his elbow.

Dallas stiffened and fought the urge to lash out. He tried to stand up with his tray, but two hands on either side of him yanked him down.

Maddox grinned approvingly at the way his toadies did his bidding. "Naw, you stay right here," he said from across the table. "We just wanna help toughen you back up. I saw what you did to Smith last year, Malone. What happened? You were so tough and hardened, and now you're just a little pansy crying for your friend."

That word. Dallas stiffened up. *The jerks in school used to call Channing that!* Dallas forced himself to stay calm.

"Guys, I don't know what you've heard," he said, trying to keep his growling voice level, "but I'm done here." He tried to rise again, but they pulled him back down.

"Nah, we're gonna *help* you," Maddox said. "Get you back to being the tough cop killer that we heard you were." The others jeered. "You'll just waste away in here if you're gonna cry about your guilty conscience all the time. Although it's more fun for me if you make yourself into a vic." The guys from the other table had stood and crowded close, eager to see

Maddox's abuse directed at somebody else. Their ugly sneers and teeth-bared laughs surrounded Dallas, frozen in his place while electricity coursed through his veins. The correctional officer on duty stood across the room, ignorant that the laughter and upbeat voices masked a brewing brawl.

Dallas was trapped. He seethed inside that John had told somebody, and now these jerks were trying to push his buttons. *I could've handled this more coolly a couple weeks ago, even, but not now. Not when I've sunk so low again. But I WON'T be a victim!* The despair over Channing's death and the stagnated feelings about his newfound faith in God were wearing Dallas thin. These guys were kicking him when he was down, and they knew it.

"Toughen up and deal with the fact that you're a cold, hard killer," Miller whispered in his ear. "You kill a cop; you kill your friend: both are lives ended... but you must've been one hell of a friend!"

As the whoops and jeers rose, Dallas lost it. He turned with a snarl and bowled Miller over, knocking him off the bench and onto the concrete floor below. Both fists flying, Dallas pinned Miller to the ground with his legs, one foot planted on a thigh and the knee of his other leg grinding into his gut. The hand that had taken so much damage proved itself recovered as knuckles met the flesh of Miller's face. All Dallas's misery over the last few weeks of being deep in the pit again, all his pent-up aggression that he'd held back from Hudson in an unnatural denial of the strength of his manhood... it had all come to a head, and Dallas gave in to his primal fury now that his loyalty to Channing was being called into question by these pigs.

Maddox leaped over the table onto Dallas, knocking a tray to the floor. The new guy they'd called Paddy had Dallas's left upper arm tight in his grasp, trying to tug him off, and the surrounding shouts of "Kill, kill, kill!" and "Fight! Fight!" echoed in Dallas's head. He was vaguely aware, as if it were happening to somebody else and yet with full understanding that it was his own fist connecting with Miller's face, that he'd knocked a tooth out of the mouth he'd just pummeled. *Good!* he seethed with a hardened satisfaction as the bloody tooth fell to the floor. No desire to stop the rage within himself, Dallas slugged Miller's face again and again with his unrestrained hand, the sound of each punch revving up the adrenaline within him even more. Maddox was on Dallas's back, grappling to get a hold of his damage-inflicting right fist. Miller flailed his arms, trying to shield his face while managing some jabs to Dallas's gut with one knee.

A minute later, it was over. Three COs rushed in and tugged Dallas off his rival. He was still a wild animal and lunged at Miller again. The officers restrained him, barking their orders. Their muffled yells came to Dallas through a dense fog. He finally gained control of his arms, stopped struggling, and stood hot and sweaty, nostrils flared and mouth gaping in rapid breaths as he glared at Miller's bloodied face. *That bastard, daring to smirk and jeer at me through his messed-up smile! I want to* kill *him!* But Dallas forced himself not to fight against the guards.

A CO turned Dallas away by the wrists so they could slap the cuffs on him. He caught sight of Maddox's silent, taunting smile. He stared right into Dallas's eyes with a coldness, and he hissed, "You maniac! Some friend you must've been to your beloved *Channing*." A couple of other guys nearby snickered and repeated, "Channing," in mocking, singsong voices. *John even told them his name!*

Dallas lurched towards Maddox reflexively. "I could *mangle* you!" he spat. One officer's grip on Dallas slipped, but the other two jerked him back.

"Like you mangled your best friend," sneered Maddox to several approving whoops. Somebody shouted, "I don't think the baby Jesus would approve of that!"

As Dallas strained to get at Maddox, the guards got rougher with him, twisting his arms hard behind his back, forcing one wrist into the cuffs, and shoving him up against the wall, a position and sensation becoming all too familiar. Dallas snarled and shoved, his reason unable to stop his runaway train of rage.

"Calm down, or you're gonna get the taser!" yelled one of the COs as he struggled to get the handcuffs on Dallas's free hand. "Murphy, call for backup, will ya? This guy's 5150; we gotta get him down to solitary."

Dallas fought the cuffing. He tried to elbow the CO in response to his threat, kicking out behind him, growling at Maddox, who still stood by with an evil smirk across his face. Suddenly Dallas was seized with pain, all his muscles tensed up, and he couldn't move. He screamed in agony as the officer got his other hand into the cuffs, Murphy and the third guard supporting his body for the few seconds that seemed an eternity.

"I warned you." The CO yanked the probes from Dallas's back. "Let's go."

He tased me! Dallas collapsed in their grip, but he willed himself not to cry. *Not here, not in front of these jerks!* He regained control of his legs and allowed the officers to walk him out of the cafeteria, sullen and expressionless as terror rose in his throat. *Don't call for Hudson, don't call for Hudson,* his brain ran through the silent plea, heart racing. As Dallas trudged down the hall, the whispered comments and laughter behind him burned in his ears.

Dallas was assailed by the nightmarish memories of his last experience in solitary confinement as they pushed him through the steel door and into isolation. *Don't think about it; don't think about it!* The echoing slam of the door behind him jarred deep down into his bones. *How dare they talk about Channing that way, about* me *that way! They know nothing of our friendship, of my agony over his death — nothing!* Dallas paced the barren cell like a caged animal. He had so much pent-up rage left and nothing to take it out on except the toilet. He bared his teeth and kicked the single piece of stainless steel over and over, heart still racing, but since there wasn't even a seat on it, he gave up on causing any damage. He had to be satisfied with the memory of Miller's wrecked face. *I'm not sorry!* Dallas locked his mouth in a tight line. *I'd do it again in a heartbeat. I'll fight when it comes to Channing, to the death!* He ran in place and did jumping jacks to burn off the rest of his agitation, then finally collapsed onto the hard excuse for a bed.

As he lay panting on the bare metal slab, pain throbbed in his lower ribcage where one of Miller's knees had rammed him. Now he felt it with each rapid breath. His wrist ached from the rough handcuffing. "My fault there," Dallas conceded aloud. He remembered talking to himself when he was in solitary before. "Please, God, don't make me go crazy in here," he mumbled. *God.* Dallas had made the request naturally. *I do believe,* came the glimmer of hope. *And I can't do this alone. I can't help myself. But I can't even tell if God's there anymore!*

"Channing," he begged out loud. "Channing, I'm going to be sorry for the rest of my life! You know I wasn't trying to get you killed, don't you? It's not like those jerks said, it's *not!*" Dallas beat his fists on the bed. "I even took a tasing for you. I'm still defending you, Chan, even though you're dead," he whispered, desperation sinking in. "I'm fighting for a ghost..."

Can he even hear me? Dallas wondered in desolation, rising to pace the cell. *Please, God, please take care of Channing. Please take my words to him so he can hear me. Please take this burden from me! Please let me accept your forgiveness. I know Channing would forgive me because he was such a good person. Not because I deserve it, but because Channing didn't hold grudges. I was so lucky to have him as my friend, so, so lucky!*

Dallas suddenly wanted Channing's Memorare card. "At least it's safe back in my locker," he murmured. Dallas collapsed beside the bed, on his knees with hands folded. "I'm desperate, God," he choked out. "I'm desperate to be able to accept your forgiveness and Channing's both. Lord, have mercy. Lord, have mercy..." His shoulders heaved with involuntary shudders as he sobbed the prayer over and over, interspersed with, "Channing, I'm so sorry." Exhausted and raw, Dallas finally dropped to sleep, slumped against the bed on the floor.

He awoke a couple hours later with his head against the hard edge of the bed and a cramp in his legs. The pain in his abdomen was a perpetual ache. He opened his shirt and grimaced at an ugly bruise below his ribcage. *I've had worse. Miller got the worst of it for sure, and that scumbag deserved every single punch!*

Dallas paced in the tiny cell, dreading the isolation that stretched endlessly before him and attempting to muster up the ability to spend this time in prayer as reparation for failing Channing. But the darkness was right beneath him, threatening to swallow him in sorrow again. It took every ounce of his power not to succumb to it. Dallas leaped up and down from the bed, ran in place, did pushups, anything he could think of to wear himself out, to keep from going back to that dark wallowing place. The fistfight had woken Dallas up, pulled him out of the mire a bit, and now he was treading water, head barely above the surface, and if he slowed down for an instant... *I might drown. I know what solitary does to men — it breaks their wills. I felt it in here before.* Dallas tried to stay strong. *But I just want to sit with my misery over Channing's death and my role in it... No! Keep fighting it!* Dallas moved around the tiny enclosure, manic, for the next four hours, finally collapsing in a sweaty, gasping heap. He fell asleep again.

Dallas kept active as long as he could, but his isolation was to last five days this time. On the third evening, after his supervised shower when the CO shut him back in the cell, with its glaring lights that never went out, Dallas cracked. He didn't have the power to fight anymore. He curled up in a ball on the bed, surrendering what was left of his strength in defeat. *I'm completely and utterly alone! Channing's dead, and God is gone.* Father Benedict's monthly visit had been the day before, and Dallas knew he'd probably come all this way only to be told that he was locked in solitary confinement and not allowed visitors. *It's like I betrayed the only person who cares about me — if he really cares. How could he like anyone as wretched as me? Maybe I'm just his pet cause. I'm doubting God again – doubting if he's even there at all. Maybe this is all there is, pain and suffering and misery and the torture of being trapped with your sorry self for your whole life, and then you die.*

On the third morning, Dallas didn't look up from his place on the bed as his cell door creaked open. He knew it was a meal being delivered, and he didn't care. When there was no further sound, Dallas's spine tingled with the knowledge that somebody was standing behind him, watching him. His muscles tightened, and he heard breathing. His heart thudded faster when the snake-like voice shattered the silence. "I'm waiting for you to thank me, Malone."

Hudson. Dallas squeezed his eyes shut tight. His mind told him to fight, but the rest of his body clenched in terror, and he knew he couldn't resist, only submit in his state of hopelessness. Dallas wasn't himself, and the knowledge that this was the emotional result of his punishment didn't help him muster up anything of his own will, his rationality, nothing. He was frozen, a prisoner of his body's fear response. *Say thank you to him!* his body begged in a silent scream. Dallas opened his mouth and tried to force out the words through dry lips, but he was too late.

Rough hands seized Dallas from behind and wrenched him from the bed like a rag doll. He hit the floor and curled into a ball, shaking. *Who am I?* He couldn't open his eyes and face his abuser, and now Dallas felt the kicks of the heavy boots, and he squeezed himself tighter, breaths ragged and rapid, tears trapped behind his eyelids. *Please make him stop, no, no, please!*

A hand grabbed his neck, squeezing until Dallas wheezed for air. Hudson threw him down and kicked him in the temple.

Dallas's stomach convulsed, and he reeled with a sick dizziness.

Hudson seized him under the chin, and Dallas was forced to look him in the eye. The CO chuckled and then sneered at his helpless captive crumpled on the floor against the wall. "No need to thank me now," he said with a smirk. "I took it from you instead. And next time, I'll expect something more." He spat in Dallas's face and dropped his head against the floor, then retreated across the cell.

Dallas gasped to breathe as he heard the comforting sound of the steel door shutting and the click of the lock. He fell into a hazy sleep.

Dallas declined to come out for a shower the next day. He ceased his frenzied activity and stopped eating his meals, forcing the memory of what he'd allowed Hudson to do to him out of his mind. *Am I getting used to this? Do I feel safer in a cell, in confinement? Do I even have the will to go back out into general population, let alone the world, someday? The real world, without Channing in it?* Dallas's reason was slipping away, unable to intercept his thoughts. He slept restlessly, an hour on, an hour off, interrupted by constant nightmares.

By the next day, Dallas jumped as every sound from outside bombarded him. Paranoid fears that Hudson would destroy the holy card while he was in solitary consumed him. He thought he saw his mother standing in the doorway, then Father Benedict chastising him. Every time someone came to his door, Dallas cowered on the bed against the wall, gripped in anxiety that it was Hudson again. He chewed on his knuckles and paced back and forth to escape the moving walls. *They'll close in on me if I stop for an instant!*

When the 120-hour punishment ended, Hudson opened the door. "Back to general, Malone," was all he said, a flicker of the thrill of power in his eyes.

Dallas lifted his head, tight-lipped, to cover his instinct to cower. Trudging to his cell block, Dallas was tense with worry that the guard would attack him again.

Hudson stopped at Dallas's cell. "See you again soon, I hope," he said, emitting a low snicker before walking away.

Shivers ran down Dallas's spine. *A threat for later…* He quivered as he entered what had become his refuge and went straight to his locker, ignoring his cellmate. He took out Channing's prayer card and huddled in his bed, clutching it to his chest with eyes closed, shaking, lips moving in a silent repetition of the prayer. Dallas's eyes flew open at the sound of John's movements. *I'm not safe anywhere!* He shifted and twitched, although John was clearly trying to ignore him back.

Dallas slept fitfully that night. He mumbled the Memorare over and over without any feeling. Every time he awoke, he bolted upright in his bed, ready to kill whoever might be about to attack him, steal his holy card, or mock Channing. He tried to shake it off, but his racing heart and mind refused to be resettled.

The next morning, Dallas awoke to John's movements and lay like a lump, no motivation to get up.

John paused at the door and cleared his throat. "Hey, man, I'm sorry I told some of the guys what happened to your friend. They noticed you were back to your dark silence, so I explained you had good reason to be down. Guess they leaked it and that predator Maddox heard. Some guys in here are so evil; it's like they have no souls. But you should ignore them. It's no big deal; they're just full of hot air. Bunch of sissy backstabbing girls."

Dallas's hard lesson in prison life—that some men could find a twisted thrill in cutting others down to the very core of their deepest and most painful secrets, the things they most loathed in themselves—left him ripped open wide, raw and exposed to the world in all his shame and depravity. He pushed himself up on one elbow and glared at John. "No big deal?" Dallas growled. "I can't believe you told them my private business! You only made things worse. I have an anger problem when it comes to people talking about Channing. I was a moron to say anything, to even tell you his name." He laid back down and turned towards the wall.

John sighed and walked off to breakfast.

Their relationship was strained after that. Dallas felt betrayed even though he knew that John had intended no malice. He was fumbling to get himself back up to where he was before, several weeks earlier. *Is my life going to be a rollercoaster from now on?*

He stayed in bed all day. When he attempted to pray, his chest tightened, paralyzed in torment that Channing was gone, and he sank, dwelling on all the things Channing would never be able to experience, all the things he'd never create, all the future memories that the two friends would never gain. Dallas opened the Bible and stared blankly at the same page for an hour, unable to make his mind comprehend the words, and then gave up, slamming the book in disgust.

A brief phone call with Father Benedict the next day brought him no comfort. The priest reminded Dallas that even some of the saints had gone through very trying times, periods of extreme challenges to their faith, but it didn't snap Dallas out of the funk. He sat staring at the printed plea on his wall: "Lord, I do believe, help my unbelief" but felt nothing. He begged God in silent, screamed prayers for Channing to be in heaven, happy and whole, but all he could hear in return was a roaring sound like wind across an empty plain. He was succumbing to the abyss. *This will never get better. I will never be okay again. I will never forgive myself.*

Dallas was asleep, a brief escape in a dream. An intense scene wove itself through his mind as he followed somebody down a long, covered breezeway, intricate stone masonry under the shadowy figure's echoing footsteps. It was a priest, dressed in a flowing black cassock, and Dallas followed him into the church in the dream and watched from the back as the man knelt in front of a white marble altar. Everything was in black and white until that moment, when brilliant hues scattered across the smooth floor, streaming through a stained glass window that went up, higher and higher until Dallas got dizzy trying to find its top as he strained his eyes upward...

Dallas startled awake, sweating and bolting upright in his bunk. His eyes gradually adjusted to the light. *I'm in prison. It was just a dream – but was that Channing?* His thought from the night before Channing's death stabbed him in the gut — the inkling that he might have become a priest, leaving Dallas all alone. *He certainly did leave me alone, and it's my fault.* Dallas frowned. *Why do I keep thinking of that memory lately?* It hurt to think that maybe Channing was destined not only to become Catholic but to become a priest. *Did I not only kill him but rob him of that, too?*

"Priest here to see you, Malone," Murphy's voice sounded through the doorway.

The unexpected announcement of a visitor one week later didn't excite Dallas. He lay in his bunk, loath even to get up. *I don't want to sit talking to Father Benedict. I don't want to do anything. I just want to numb myself from this agonizing existence somehow.*

Dallas forced himself up, hurled his pillow back onto his bunk, and dragged his feet down the hall. A dull sense of duty propelled Dallas into the visitors' room, where he collapsed, haggard and silent, into the chair across from the priest and crossed his arms over his chest, hardened eyes cast down at the table between them.

"I'm sorry, Dallas," came the priest's normally soothing voice, but today it only grated on Dallas's raw nerves.

"Being sorry doesn't do any good," he said bitterly, refusing to look at Father Benedict. "It's a stupid platitude. I've said I'm sorry a billion times until I'm hoarse with apologizing, and does it help? No. Channing's still dead, that trooper's still dead, I'm still in prison, and life's still agonizing. If God's really there, he hates me."

"I thought you might need some company and support after what happened," the priest continued, voice low. "Would you like to talk about it? I understand if you'd rather not. Solitary confinement does something inhumane to a man's soul. I felt the need to come sooner to check up on you."

"Talking doesn't do any good," Dallas responded in monotone.

"*Nothing* does any good anymore. Praying helped for a while—I thought things were getting better, but I was just fooling myself. Hearing those guys blame me for Channing's death was like somebody rubbing salt in my wounds," Dallas grumbled. "I'm slowly losing myself in here, a bunch of jerks know what happened to Channing now and are using it to get to me, and…" Dallas swallowed hard. "…and one day I'm gonna walk out of here, and he *won't be there*." The words emerged in a haunting whisper, and Dallas covered his face with his hands. "And I won't be who I was anymore, either."

Father Benedict was quiet for a moment before speaking. "What do you mean when you say you're losing yourself in here?"

Dallas thought about what he meant and loathed himself deep inside. The beatings he'd received from Hudson over two years were wearing him down, breaking him inside, shattering any remaining self-respect he'd had left. He didn't want to admit it to another man, even an elderly priest who he doubted had even been in a fistfight in his entire life.

The muffled voice came from behind Dallas's hands. He couldn't bear to look at the priest in his shame. "I don't wanna talk about it." Dallas was pouting, and he didn't care.

"Dallas, there is no doubt that your incarceration is having an impact on you," Father said softly. "These years will change you, absolutely. You have the choice to grow for the better so that the changed man who walks out of here in another two years has used his time to become better."

Dallas slammed his hands down against the table violently. "But I've lost EVERYTHING!" he yelled. "Anything that made me who I am, it's *gone!* I lost my car, my job, my home, my clothes, my best friend, and then I get locked up in this hellhole, and I've lost all control! I'm losing who I am! I walked in here with only my body, my physical strength, and now I'm even losing that too. If I lose my ability to defend myself, then I don't know what I have left of myself." His voice quieted to a hollow, even tone. "I won't know who I am anymore."

As Father Benedict reached out to pat Dallas's hand, Dallas jerked it back and tucked both hands in his lap. *I'm being a jerk after he came all this way to see me, and I don't even care. Because that's what I am, a hate-filled jerk.*

"It's a very hard thing to feel as if you are losing your human dignity," the priest said. "Prison has a way of stripping that away. But your physical strength isn't the only thing. You have your mind and your will, a type of mental strength, even if you feel as if you have no control over your body."

"Look, you don't know what it's like in here!" Dallas cried, his voice rising again. "I've had the crap beat out of me by a guard. A *guard!* I can't resist much, because even if I was a match for this huge guy, fighting back just makes my punishment worse! He hates me because he wanted to destroy my prayer card after the first fight I got in over it, and another correctional officer got it back for me instead. He wants to make my life *miserable* because he feels like I showed him up! He has it out for me, but I'm terrified of going in the hole again if I fight back. So I let myself get thrown around, ground into the floor, *humiliated* by him! And then, when I see myself in the mirror, I *despise* who I'm becoming. It's like I'm not even a man anymore!"

Father Benedict's eyes widened. "Can you file a complaint against this guard? He shouldn't be assaulting you like that."

"No way," Dallas said evenly. "Like I said, you don't get it! What kind of man runs and tells on another guy who's pushing him around? I've *always* stood up for myself my whole life, and I always used to win. But now..." Dallas bent forward, elbows on his knees with hands laced together above his forehead, staring at his feet.

Silence filled the next several minutes. Dallas wondered if Father Benedict would offer any more advice, or if he'd even want to return after that rant. A slight nagging urged him to apologize, cut the visit short, and go to bed and try to sleep off his bitterness.

Then the priest spoke. "Dallas, you do still have your mind and will, and your will is quite stubborn."

Dallas threw himself upright in the chair and glared across the table, mouth hanging open as he tried to think up a retort.

"That may be all you have right now," Father Benedict went on quickly, "but your tenacity is a powerful tool when used properly. Let God use that in you. When everything else is out of your control, ask him to guide that unrelenting, stubborn spirit inside of you to refuse to break from the toxic atmosphere here. Beg God's assistance to maintain your strong will, because it can't be taken away from you without your consent, not by a guard or anyone else. But, Dallas," he finished quietly, "ask God to help you see when to bend your stubborn will, to flex it to help make you stronger, and yet not to allow it to be broken."

"Stubborn, am I?" Dallas growled. "Yeah, I've been *stubborn* all my life!" He flew up from the chair and gripped the edge of the table in front of him with both hands, leaning down with a sneer. "I don't need a reminder of one of my many faults, thank you very much!" His voice dripped with sarcasm on top of the fury. "God's not giving me any help with *that* character flaw he's saddled me with, seeing as it's what got me here in the first place!" Dallas paced in agitation behind the small table. "My strong will gets me *beat up!*" he continued hotly, flinging his arms wide. "Broken bones, concussions! But at least I still pounded a guy's ugly face for being such a jerk to me, and I don't even care! I'm *glad* I hurt him because at least it proves I still have a little fight left in me. It's every man for himself in here, and I *won't* let myself be at the bottom of the pecking order. Stubborn, yeah! I'm *stubborn,* and look what it's getting me!"

Dallas cursed Hudson and hurled aggressive comments aimed at Maddox and Miller as he kicked the folding chair he'd been sitting in. It clattered to the floor, and he reached to snatch it up again when Murphy was right in front of him, separating him from the table and chair. He'd slid in to intervene practically unnoticed.

"Okay, Malone, you're done," he said in a firm but gentle voice. "You don't wanna make things worse by flinging that chair. Let's get you outta here so you can cool off."

Dallas tried to sidestep the officer, but Murphy moved with him skillfully.

"You gonna cuff me?" Dallas snapped. "'Cause I'm so *stubborn,* I might not cooperate with you?" Dallas shot the seething adjective around Murphy in the direction of Father Benedict, glaring as he spit out the words.

"I don't think you're really gonna make the cuffs necessary, now are you, Malone?" Murphy said. "Come on, man, you know I just wanna help you out. But you gotta cool down now."

Murphy had righted the chair and coaxed Dallas towards the door without a struggle.

Father Benedict stood on the other side of the table, his expression loving with tears in his eyes.

Dallas caught his eye. *Like a father, a real father, looking at his screwed-up failure of a son,* the thought flashed through his mind. Dallas's cynicism pushed the idea away. *He has no obligation to me. I'm probably never gonna see him again after this, and that's my own damn fault. At least I still have enough control to alienate people!* Dallas clung to the power grab, but it didn't make him feel better.

"Dallas, I'm praying for you to hold on, to not lose yourself," the priest said. "And that the changes you do experience are only for the better in the end. May God fortify your will and help you use it effectively. God bless you, Dallas." He made the sign of the cross from across the room in Dallas's direction, eyes closed.

Murphy crossed himself, then put a strong hand on Dallas's shoulder and led him through the door.

As Dallas stepped into the hall, he threw one last glance back at Father Benedict and regretted everything. He hoped the look in his eyes conveyed that, but before he could speak, he was moving down the hall at Murphy's side.

When they got to his cell, Murphy glanced back and forth down the hallway and then stepped inside with Dallas. He looked him in the eye and whispered, "Malone, I know what Hudson's been doing to you. I've seen some of it, you know, and I heard what you were telling the priest. You're right that not much can be done about it—he's got a lot of seniority here. But I'm on your side, okay? You gotta believe that, even though I can't always do something to change the situation. Just don't instigate anything with Hudson, you hear me? Avoid baiting him in any way, like don't even *look* at him when he's near you. Don't give him *anything* he can take as a threat from you. I know he might still single you out, but, man, I promise you I'm trying my best to keep things somewhat balanced in here. Like your priest friend was telling you, bend but don't break. You stand up to that man like you think you can win, and he won't stop 'til he's broken you. Keep your will, but just let him bend it if he's messing with you again. *Don't let him snap it.*"

Murphy was already heading back into the hall as Dallas registered all he'd said. It was good advice, but Dallas, still angry at the world, didn't want to admit it yet. He sat sullen in his cell for the rest of the afternoon. Finally, after dinner, he pulled Channing's prayer card out of his locker and laid down on his bunk. He murmured the prayer repeatedly until he broke down. "I'm sorry, Father," he whispered through his tears. "You were right. I'm a stubborn jerk, and I need to man up on the inside, strengthen my will. It's not just being strong on the outside that counts. I've gotta remember how Channing was and try to have the faith he did. Please, God, help me. I believe in you, but I can't be a better person without help, and I still can't trust that you could care about me, because I'm so bad. I'm too weak. Help me, God."

Dallas fell asleep with the holy card clutched in his hands. He slept soundly all night.

MERCY

A week passed, and the advice of Father Benedict and Murphy began to sink in. Dallas's initial response had been to fight it, but ultimately the truth of what they meant was undeniable. *I need to stop being such a hothead and, instead, just hone my will towards survival in this place.* Dallas knew his reactions could stand some refining. Being stubborn had both its up and down sides.

And the way I behaved when Father Benedict visited… He was concerned and even came back earlier than usual to see me, and I did nothing but complain and yell at him. Dallas sighed. Alone on his knees against the hard, cold concrete of his prison cell floor, forehead against the wall, Dallas pleaded, *Please, God, help pull me out of this funk, and please help me be a better person, a person I can like even just a little bit. Help me get over myself when Hudson roughs me up. Help me focus on just getting out of this place, where that guard won't ever hurt me again.*

Dallas propelled himself through each day by simply doing the next thing. One day almost two weeks later, he dragged his body through the morning, demeanor still depressed, and now sat hunched on his bunk, forcing himself to read from a book of writings of the early saints that Father Benedict had given him. His eyes passed over the words as his brain processed little. Suddenly, a phrase darted out at him: "When I was lying in darkness and gloomy night, wavering hither and thither, tossed about on the foam of this boastful age, and uncertain of my wandering steps, knowing nothing of my real life, and remote from truth and life…" Dallas inhaled the words, lips forming them silently as he read. "And that a man quickened to new life in the laver of saving water should be able to put off what he had previously been; and, although retaining all his bodily structure, should be himself changed in heart and soul…"

A stirring inside his heart pressed him to continue: "For as I was held in bonds by the innumerable errors of my previous life, from which I did not believe that I could possibly be delivered, so I was disposed to acquiesce in my clinging vices; and because I despaired of better things, I used to indulge my sins as if they were actually parts of me, and indigenous to me."

These words were attributed to a St. Cyprian of Carthage, but Dallas felt them burning as his own, deep within his soul. *My pattern is to keep sinking back into despair, unable to stay afloat. And my main vice is an inability to forgive anyone.* Dallas had assumed he was chained to his vices permanently. *But could I really be completely changed, able to throw off my past sins and become a person who wants to forgive? Could that be the way that prison is supposed to change me? Not to lose myself, but to let God change me on the inside?*

Dallas's thoughts cut deep ruts as he proceeded through the routines of the next two days. A stillness moved in, settling inside him, even now as he worked through his rigorous set of pushups in his cell. He'd always valued control: to be responsible and take action were necessities to him. *But control is just an illusion – I know that from Channing's death and my prison sentence. I can make better choices, but I can't control all outcomes. I'm letting anger control me. I'm letting self-hatred control me. I'm letting other people's behaviors, even from years and years ago, control me.* This was the stubbornness in him that needed refining. Dallas had been baffled that Channing could forgive his parents. *Maybe I'm starting to understand now. I'll never move on without being able to forgive — instead, I'll end up driving myself insane. I'll never get out of this dark pit if I can't surrender myself to God's mercy. I have to let go, and yet, I don't quite want to, somehow.*

"What do you want of me? I'm not in control," Dallas whispered, trembling at his admission of weakness as he sat back on his heels. "Lead me, please, God." Dallas's dream swept like the wind through his mind: the priest, the color-infused light from the stained glass windows smattering across a smooth gray altar before the cassocked kneeling man... "I know that's what you wanted of Channing, God, and I'm sorry I ruined that chance," he choked out. "Help me focus on giving myself over to you now."

At that moment, an officer outside his cell interrupted his thoughts and prayers. "You got a visitor, Malone."

Dallas jerked his head up. *Could it be… and after just two weeks?* Holding his breath, Dallas followed the CO to the visiting area.

Father Benedict was waiting at a table. Dallas wanted to rush over to him, but he scuffed the toe of one shoe against the floor and blushed instead.

"Father," Dallas greeted him, "I didn't expect you to be back, especially so soon, after the way I acted last time." Dallas slid into a chair, shame hot in his cheeks and words thick in his throat. "I was acting like a spoiled brat, and I... I don't deserve your kindness."

"It's all forgotten, Dallas," the priest answered. "It's hard in here, almost impossible at times. I prayed you would accept another visit from me. And I've been praying for God's peace to come to you, for you to find it and cling to it when you need it the very most."

Dallas's eyes watered, and he didn't try to hide it. *He's already forgiven me, forgiven my rage when he was just trying to help me.* "I'm so sorry, Father." His voice cracked. "You're my only friend now, and your coming here month after month means the world to me. It's all I have, and I acted like I wanted nothing to do with you. I really want to act better, be a better person. You deserve more from me."

"All I desire is to show God's mercy and hope," the priest said. "Any good that comes of my visits, he does through me. And if you're still not up to talking today, then I would just like to sit with you, pray, and remind you that God will never give up on you, Dallas."

"I'm more than ready to talk now," Dallas agreed. "Last time, I was just so deep in my own head, ashamed of what happened to Channing and enraged at people for taunting me. It was like darkness had engulfed me. I was starting to doubt God's existence again. I know you warned me that feelings are fickle. But man, to have it hit me like that, to feel *nothing*… I guess I took it really badly."

Father Benedict smiled and added gently, "That's where that obstinate nature in you can be a great strength. I'm sorry it hurt you for me to bring it up last time. But when you feel nothing, you can still stubbornly hold fast to a *decision* to power through, to keep believing in God's presence, even though you can't feel it."

"I'm bull-headed enough to give that a try," Dallas conceded with a sheepish grin. "You were right, you know. And I understand you meant it as both an insult and a compliment wrapped up into one. I've gotta separate them and use that stubbornness in the right way. I've been thinking a lot about that, actually."

Father Benedict beamed. "I'm so glad to see you're more positive today."

"Yeah, I'm not quite so down now. I guess that will come and go, huh? But a couple days ago, I had some kind of lightbulb moment or something," Dallas related. "I read something written by St. Cyp-… I don't know if I'm saying his name right…"

"St. Cyprian?" put in Father Benedict.

"Yeah, he wrote something about being in darkness and gloom, and being held in bondage to his sins and vices, but then he realized he could become a changed person, and I think," said Dallas, pausing and taking a deep breath, "I have to let go of my need to control everything because... I *can't*. When I start thinking that everything hinges on me, the darkness takes over, and that's when all my sin comes out. I start thinking I'm the only one I can rely on, that I'm in charge, when in fact, it's those vices that are controlling me! And if I can hand it all over to somebody else's responsibility — I guess that'd be God — then, maybe, my life will be *more* controlled. It's like some crazy backwards thing, that giving up control could actually bring stability!"

Father Benedict smiled. "Much of life, and much of Christianity, is a paradox. Strange, but true."

"Yes, a paradox!" Dallas exclaimed, eyes wide. "I didn't know what he meant at the time, but Channing said that! A paradox!" Clarity struck Dallas, and he marveled at how the priest understood exactly what he was talking about. *Like a ton of bricks, Channing said.*

"It is Truth, Dallas." Father Benedict locked eyes with him. "God has written his truth in our hearts. He's given us a desire for him and given us our senses and minds, and the ability to come to common truths, things that are universal, for all mankind. It's what both you and Channing always searched for."

"And so," Dallas continued, "my vices. I know what they are and that I need to let go of them. Stop trying to control everything through them."

"And what do you think they are?"

"Inability to forgive, quick temper that's easily fueled by rage, and thinking the world depends on me and only me to be in charge. Like, every man for himself. I've never let anyone help me with that, and... I need to let God help me."

"Surrender," the priest said.

"Yes," Dallas answered firmly. "Surrender. Not a giving up in defeat type of surrender, not a fault but a meekness. It's admitting that I need God, that I can rely on him alone. And, wow, what a relief that'll be if I can just remember and believe it. It won't be all on me! I still have to learn to forgive, but maybe I need to allow God to forgive me first. I still haven't accepted that he would."

"I know finding the ability to forgive yourself has been challenging," Father Benedict said. "It doesn't matter who tells you that you're not condemned for Channing's death, that you're forgiven for your accidental role in it — you still cannot forgive yourself. And you've hit on something big here, Dallas." The priest leaned in closer. "You said you can't forgive anyone else?"

Dallas nodded.

"The reason to forgive others is not because they deserve it in and of themselves," the priest said. "It is because they are children of God. They have human souls given to them by our Creator. If you can learn to see God in others, maybe you can start to see him in yourself. Each person on this earth, including those who have wronged you or Channing, was created in his image and likeness. They have made mistakes, as we all do. Some of their mistakes may have hurt you. But if you can see other sinners as worthy of forgiveness, maybe then you will be able to forgive yourself. Can you look at others as real persons? Can you look at another human and focus on his humanity and think of what you can do for his soul?"

Dallas's eyes widened in an open stare. "N-no," he stammered, "I guess... I guess not. Like, even with Channing, I... I don't know if I thought that deeply about it. I mean, I saw his humanity, more than anyone else's, but that the same humanity is in everyone, even my enemies... like, Miller, the guy I punched recently. He has a mother and father somewhere. He had a childhood. The same God who made Channing made him, and... and me. I have vices, just like he does. But God made us all... and so I should forgive Miller for what he said to me because it would be seeing his humanity, and using my own humanity to do so. It's almost like I can... I don't know, feel a weird connection with him, almost like a kinship, when you put it that way. Man, this is deep stuff." Dallas sighed and ran his fingers through his hair. "I have to forgive him, don't I?"

Father Benedict nodded.

"Even if he doesn't feel sorry?" Dallas asked. "Even if he's *glad* he made me so angry; even if he thinks mocking me over my best friend's death is funny?"

"Even more so because of that," the priest said, laying a palm on Dallas's hand. "When you forgive him, you are not saying that what he did was right. You are giving your hurt up to God. You are releasing yourself and your emotions from the situation. You are showing mercy to one who doesn't deserve it by any merits of his own, just as God does for each of us. Just as you want to be able to feel Him do for *you*."

"And then... then will I be able to forgive myself?" Dallas asked, raising his eyes to the priest's.

"It will become easier as time goes on, the more you forgive others," Father Benedict responded.

"But do I have to feel truly, fully sorry for what I did to him in retaliation?" Dallas frowned. "I'll apologize for attacking him, but, I mean, it's wrong, isn't it, to feel this... this *satisfaction* at having beat his face in with my fists? I even knocked one of his teeth out! And I don't feel any remorse for it! Isn't that wrong?"

The priest paused a moment. "Your apologizing and forgiving him for his part is the first step. And if he returns your apology with an insult, forgive him and walk away. Don't allow him to enrage you. Should you apologize for punching him? Yes. Should you *feel* sorry about having done it? Maybe you can't right now. You might feel some mercy for him as a fellow fallen man. But remember, Dallas, feelings can't rule us. Choices are what matter. You can *choose* to apologize. You can acknowledge that punching him was wrong. But to feel badly about having done it... well, we can't always force ourselves to have perfect contrition. And I will admit myself, I can see why beating him up would have felt really good." The priest showed a flicker of a grin on his face, his eyes twinkling.

Dallas nearly laughed aloud. "Yeah," he admitted. "Yeah, it felt great to pummel his face. And yes, I know it was wrong, I know I shouldn't have done it, and I really am going to try harder not to do that again, to anyone."

"That is enough for now," Father Benedict said. "God sees your attempts and knows you are trying as much as is possible. So that's a recent offense. How about those bigger grudges inside you, built up over the years? Like your parents? Can you forgive in those deeper, long-term cases?"

Dallas tensed up just thinking about it. "Channing and I talked about forgiving our enemies," he said slowly. "He was able to forgive his parents, but some of the stuff they did to him when he was younger was just awful, like *despicable*. And he said a lot of what you just said, Father, about how forgiving them isn't like saying that what they did was okay. You know, I've never even met my own father, but my whole life, I've... I've *hated* him. I've held a grudge my whole life over a man I've never even seen. I know nothing of him except that he left my mother after he found out she was pregnant with me. How do you forgive somebody you've never even known?"

"You don't have to do it in person," the priest said, "especially if it isn't physically possible. If they haven't asked, then you aren't doing it for their benefit. You forgive because it is the right thing to do and because you are trying to be a better person yourself. You are showing God your appreciation for his willingness always to forgive *you* whenever you forgive somebody yourself."

"So I just have to pray about it, huh?" Dallas asked. "And I don't have to really feel as if I *like* the people I forgive?"

"Just as you want God to forgive you for your wrongdoings, even when you don't like yourself," Father Benedict responded. "And yes, that takes a lot of prayer and quiet contemplation."

"Which is something I have plenty of time for in here," Dallas said with a grimace. "Might as well make the most of it, right?"

"Certainly," Father Benedict answered. "An excellent attitude to have. Your term is about another two years, yes?"

Dallas nodded, eyes downcast.

"I know the darkness can be overwhelming in here." The priest looked Dallas in the eye. "But if you can use this time to build your relationship with God through prayer and spiritual reading, and to pause before any interaction with another person within these walls… if you can respond not to their actions, but through the image of the man you want to become, and because of who God is, then you will begin to feel peace."

"What can I do, like in the heat of the moment, to remember somebody else's humanity?" Dallas questioned. It sounded good in theory, but he didn't know if his gut instincts would cooperate.

Father Benedict pursed his lips. "Well, what you said about each person in here being somebody else's son, or brother, or best friend… that is a very insightful thing for you to realize, Dallas. So, when you look at another person, you can try to remember this: that person may be a Channing to somebody else."

Dallas felt as if the wind was knocked out of him as he realized what the priest had said. *Each person in here might be just as precious to somebody as Channing had been to me.* The image of somebody else pummeling Channing in the face and knocking out his tooth sickened him, and he hung his head as tears burned behind his eyes. "I *am* sorry I punched Miller now; I really am," Dallas murmured.

Father Benedict patted Dallas's hand from his seat across the table.

"Will I ever stop crying over this, over losing my best friend in that horrendous way?"

"It will always hurt." Father Benedict rested his chin on folded hands. "The pain and sadness will dull with time, but they will always be with you. They are your cross, and you can embrace that cross by asking God to bring good from it. Knowing the depths of your own pain, you can decide to alleviate another person's pain by forgiving him—whether he accepts it or not at the time—and by showing him kindness and compassion. We must try to see Christ in others as well as behave as Christ would towards them. Christ crucified is our example of a heart-wrenching pain, a deep human suffering, and we can identify with that as we bear our crosses in life. Christ forgave them for doing it to him—even though they didn't apologize or feel any contrition. He is our example."

The image was powerful, and Dallas nodded. "I'm going to think it over the rest of this evening, of who I need to forgive in here and who I need to apologize to," Dallas said, drumming his fingers on the tabletop. "I know I have to forgive John. He didn't mean to make trouble by telling a few of the other guys about my history. He just wasn't thinking."

"So perhaps he will be easiest to forgive," Father Benedict suggested. "Start with him."

"And guys who deliberately started fights with me?" Dallas questioned. "I should forgive them, but how do I get past my anger?"

The priest replied, "Well, you don't have to stop feeling anger over what a person did. Pray for the strength to direct your anger in a positive direction. Do that right before approaching a person. It takes self-discipline, especially if you anticipate that your apology will be scoffed at or that your forgiveness will be rejected. Expect ahead of time that the person will not receive your words well and practice your reaction in your mind. Walk away before anything escalates."

The thought of Hudson flashed through Dallas at the word "escalates." His eyes flitted towards the door and then back to the priest, and he cleared his throat.

"Um, Father," Dallas began, voice lowered. "There's one person in here who it would be best to *not* forgive... at least, not to his face."

"You're referring to the correctional officer who has mistreated you?" Father Benedict furrowed his brow. "Which officer is this?"

Dallas nodded and sighed. "You might not be able to believe it, but remember the time you were visiting me in here, and how that inmate growled like a wild animal at some little kid who was waiting with his family for a visit? The guard who got in the guy's face and then apologized to the kid and gave him a candy bar - *that's* the guard. The same one who's been rough with me. But, come on. If I walked up to him and said, 'I just wanted to tell you I forgive you for ramming my head against the wall, stepping on my throat, spitting in my face, slamming my hand in the door, and racking me in the… uh, the genitals…" Dallas blushed. "Anyway," he continued quickly. "He'd think I was mocking him or being a smart-mouth."

Father Benedict's eyebrows lifted. "He's done all those things to you?"

Dallas nodded meekly, face burning.

"Dallas, don't take this the wrong way," began Father Benedict, "because I'm not calling into question your ability to protect yourself under normal circumstances, but if this employee assaults you in such a way again, then you should consider reporting it."

"I can't."

"Why not?" asked Father Benedict. "He used his position to inflict violence on you. It was unprovoked each time?"

Dallas glanced off to the side. "Well, I was probably being a little cocky sometimes." He remembered how he'd behaved after Hudson had handed off his holy card and told Murphy to destroy it. "So, well, I don't feel like I can file a complaint against him. I went berserk when he took Channing's holy card, and after they locked me in solitary, as he was coming into the room to get me to calm down, I lunged at him. So, while his reactions to me have been way out of line, he could also make a case that I started it some of the time. I wasn't really violent to him outright, but maybe in self-defense, and in reaction to his taunts…" Dallas sighed a frustrated sigh. "He's got authority, so if I do the slightest thing wrong, it'll probably seem like any force he uses is acceptable. I mean, *I'm* the criminal here. I've given up my normal rights."

The priest was nodding thoughtfully. "I see the quandary you're in. But I don't like that he's attacking you. He slammed your hand in the door, you said? Did your fingers break?"

Dallas held up his left hand. "Just the pinky." He pointed to where it was slightly crooked and then to two small scars. "Well, and the ring finger broke too, but…" Dallas paused and pulled at his collar, looking away. "Well, that one didn't break until I slammed the door on it myself."

When Father Benedict furrowed his brow, Dallas gave an embarrassed half-smile. "See what I mean about me being cocky, a smart aleck, to him? He ordered me to slam it on my hand myself after he'd done it once, and I stared that man down and put all my strength into crashing that steel door closed as hard as I could on my own damn fingers." Dallas sighed. "Stupid of me to show off like that, though. It was excruciating, and I actually heard the ring finger snap. So while it was still his doing,

I didn't have to slam it so hard. I was definitely trying to win that battle of wills."

Father Benedict examined the hand closely, lips pursed. "Did the doctor look at it?"

"Oh yeah, he did," Dallas responded. "X-rayed it and splinted the fingers."

"And the doctor didn't seem to care that a correctional officer had been the cause of this?"

Dallas dropped his eyes and paused. "I didn't tell him."

"Didn't he want to know what had happened?" asked the priest.

Nodding, Dallas answered, "Uh-huh. I told him I'd slammed my hand in the door. Which was true."

Dallas had slid down in his seat, and Father Benedict pressed him no further on the issue. Instead, he said, "You certainly don't need to forgive this man to his face, no. I see you must tread carefully in this challenge. I'll pray especially for you to be spared any more of his cruelty."

"I'm planning to just keep my head down and not draw his attention," Dallas said. "And I appreciate the prayers. Somehow I don't think he's going to leave me alone so easily." Flashing a reassuring smile in response to the priest's concerned expression, Dallas said, "Don't worry about me. I'm stubborn, remember? I won't let him get me down."

Father Benedict sighed and returned the smile. "I know you will have to work out problems like this the best you can, Dallas, and I have confidence in your abilities. You know, I see something extraordinary in you, always have since you called me out of the blue." He reached out and clasped Dallas's hand. "And I'm so glad you did. I know God has great plans for you, Dallas."

A shiver coursed through Dallas's body as he wondered what the priest saw in him. *I'm nothing remarkable — that was Channing, right?* Maybe it was because Channing had seen something in Dallas, and Father Benedict knew how special Channing was, with his intuitive spirituality that had finally begun to draw Dallas in, even after his death. *I'm really not that special. Father Benedict is just being supportive.* He brushed the praise aside and focused instead on his gratitude for this man's willingness to invest in him.

Their time was about up. "I'm so grateful you didn't give up on me," Dallas said earnestly. "I'm really going to try to do better, to not get into fights, and to ask people for their forgiveness."

He stood to go. In the doorway of the visiting room, Dallas turned and met Father Benedict's gaze, then faced the corridor with his head held high.

Dallas and John had barely spoken in the weeks since Dallas had come out of solitary. Dallas paced the floor before breakfast, then forced himself to get it over with. "Um, John?"

"Yeah?" John was bent over, putting on his shoes, and didn't look up.

"I wanted to... apologize to you," Dallas said haltingly. "I'm sorry I got so mad at you for telling some of the other guys about me. I know you didn't mean to cause any trouble, so... I forgive you for it."

John glanced up with flushed cheeks. "Uh, yeah, no problem. It's no skin off my back." He turned and left the cell.

Dallas leaned his head back against the wall and closed his eyes. *This isn't gonna be easy. But remember, it's okay if you don't get a positive response.* He would have to wait a few days before he'd gather the courage to try apologizing and offering forgiveness to anyone else.

Smith would be first. The two of them hadn't spoken since the incident over a year previous, successfully avoiding interaction, although they'd made wary eye contact from time to time across the cafeteria or weight room. Dallas waited until breakfast was almost over one morning and then approached the table where Smith sat laughing with two other guys. One was Pulaski, the guy who had picked up the holy card from the weight room floor and started the whole thing. Dallas inhaled deeply as they eyed him. He read mocking expressions of contempt and curiosity on their faces.

Dallas spoke from across the table, hiding his sweaty palms. "I wanted to say something to you guys. I just thought I should apologize to you, Smith, for punching you last year. And... I want to thank you for telling the COs that you started it so they wouldn't take my prayer card away from me for good. And... I forgive both of you for taunting me about it."

The three inmates stared with dropped jaws. Dallas prepared to turn and walk away when Pulaski spoke. "Nobody asked for your forgiveness, Malone," he said in a cool voice, eyes the color of steel. "It was all just a joke anyways. I ain't got nothing to be sorry for, so I sure as hell don't need your forgiveness."

Dallas shrugged. "I'm still giving it to you." He turned on his heel, knowing he'd end up saying something boneheaded if he stayed, possibly something that could lead to another fight. Butterflies swirled in his stomach, reminding Dallas he was out of his comfort zone.

As he strode away, Pulaski's yell assaulted him from behind. "Still think you're better than anybody else in the place, dontcha? I don't know why, 'cause the baby Jesus sure thinks you belong in hell for bein' in love with your dead best friend. That's a sin if I ever heard one!" Snickers followed his insults, and Dallas stalked out of the room as a correctional officer moved towards the jeering group.

Dallas jogged down the hall, seething inside at Pulaski's words. *They didn't have to accept my apology, but to hurl lies and insults at me...* It took every ounce of his strength to keep distancing himself from them rather than to give in to his temper, to turn back and beat the crap out of Pulaski. *They're somebody's sons, somebody's brothers, somebody's friends.* He approached his cell. *They might have somebody who cares as much about them as I did for Channing. And if they don't, well, that's even sadder and more pitiable.*

Dallas flopped on his bed with Channing's holy card, breathing hard. *Calm down, calm down.* He repeated the prayer as he clutched the card, twice, three times, a dozen times. He could still feel his heart racing. Finally, he jumped up and spent an hour in the weight room working off the pressure he'd bottled up inside of himself, then headed to the showers. Dallas ignored the smirks from a few guys who'd witnessed the incident in the cafeteria, got cleaned up, and went to get his hair cut. It was his scheduled appointment day, and it always made him feel better to get it cropped short again. He couldn't believe the speed at which it grew.

As he passed the calendar, Dallas glanced at the current date and tried to process the fact that his birthday was next month. *I'll turn 21 in prison.* The thought was like sand slipping through his hands. He tried to brush it aside.

After lunch, he spent a long time in his cell, reading and praying. *I need to humble myself. I can't let comments from other guys in here fire me up. I need to just turn the other cheek. Surrender. It's a show of strength, not weakness, not to let it get under my skin. Please, God, I'm begging you to give me this gift, this ability to appear meek, which takes incredible strength.* The strength needed to possess self-control had to be stronger than the anger and the fighting in him. *Another paradox.*

Dallas didn't see Smith or Pulaski again for the remainder of the day. An odd sensation of peacefulness crept into his heart. *I released the power I'd been letting those guys hold over me. I don't need them to accept my apology or my forgiveness. I've turned it over to God.* It was a burden off his shoulders, off his very soul. As he lay down in his bunk that night, Dallas breathed out a heavy sigh as if he'd just completed a long day of hard and satisfying physical labor. He shrank small under the covers with the uncomfortable self-scrutiny that he'd been one to hold bitter grudges all his life. The hope of breaking free from layers of contempt gave him a new lightness and freedom — and even control — that he'd never imagined would come with surrender.

On the way to breakfast the next morning, Dallas wheeled around at Smith's voice calling his name. *Uh-oh.* All his muscles tensed. *Is he gonna make me regret saying anything yesterday?* Dallas answered Smith's address with an emotionally flat, "Yeah?"

The two men stood a few feet apart in the hallway, eyeing each other warily. Dallas whispered a prayer to himself to contain his instinct to size up the potential fight like a tiger ready to spring on its prey. Smith, in his mid-twenties and a bit taller than Dallas's nearly six feet, had a thicker build and was heavier than Dallas, who, despite his constant working out and natural upper arm strength, maintained a more modest muscular figure. He'd been lean all his life, and the unappetizing prison fare hadn't changed that. Dallas wasn't scrawny, but the two men standing face to face didn't seem so evenly matched to the outward eye. Smith appeared able to best Dallas in a fight, but Dallas knew from experience that Smith's upper body strength was no match for his. He tried to push this barrage of thoughts out of his mind. *I'm not going to fight him if I can help it. Just breathe — you can't keep falling into traps.*

Dallas waited, poised to receive a hurled insult, but Smith merely said, "Thanks, Malone. For what you said yesterday. It's in the past, man. No hard feelings." He almost smiled, then turned and walked away.

Dallas stood awestruck. Smith had accepted his apology and his forgiveness. It hadn't been necessary, but it brought Dallas more peace to know that Smith wasn't harboring a grudge against him as well.

Dallas was putting off apologizing to Miller. Their altercation was more recent, and the damage Dallas had inflicted more severe, so the feelings were still strong. To prepare himself mentally, he reread the chapter on forgiveness in *Mere Christianity*. As he turned the same pages that Channing had once turned, Dallas smiled at the peace he felt in connecting with those same words now, well over two years later. *Now to just put them into action.*

"It is made perfectly clear that if we do not forgive, we shall not be forgiven," wrote Lewis. "There are no two ways about it." *I have to forgive all those who have wronged me. I can't fully know God's forgiveness until I do.* It was still difficult to forgive somebody who didn't want it and wasn't sorry, but Dallas knew he must.

That Saturday morning, Miller caught his glance from across the cafeteria. Dallas's pulse quickened when the man with the blatantly obvious missing top tooth sauntered up to where he stood in line for breakfast. Seeing Miller's mouth up close stabbed at Dallas's conscience. *Might as well get it over with.* He opened his mouth, but Miller spoke first.

"I hear you apologized to Smith the other day," he began in a sarcastic voice. "But what about me?" He jerked a thumb towards his chest. "You playin' favorites in here? Bad idea. *Really* bad idea, Malone."

Dallas met Miller's stare. "I've been considering how to best apologize about what I did to your tooth. So I guess now's as good a time as any." Dallas took a deep breath. "I'm sorry I hit you, man. I was furious over what you said to me, but I shouldn't have..."

"So beg me for my forgiveness, Malone," sneered Miller.

"I won't beg you," said Dallas in an even tone. "But I ask that you forgive me for attacking you."

"No," returned Miller, and he spat on Dallas's shoes. He stood glaring, as if daring him to argue about it.

"That's okay," Dallas forced the words. "I forgive you for what you said." He tried to turn and walk away from the breakfast line, but Miller caught his wrist. Dallas jerked his arm free and wrestled his physical reaction into submission as the storm threatened to surge.

"I ain't askin' you to forgive me!" Miller snarled in Dallas's face. Suddenly Maddox was there, backing up his cellmate. He'd appeared out of nowhere.

"Got a problem, Malone?" Maddox said, voice incredulous and body language all swagger.

"No." Dallas fought to keep his voice calm. Maddox was much bigger than Dallas, both broader and taller at well over six feet. "I'm just apologizing to Miller for punching him. And I forgive both of you for what you said."

"You *forgive* us?" Maddox said, eyes wide and mouth gaping. Then he shook his head and curled his lip as he stepped closer to Dallas. "You can't do that, man. We didn't ask you for no forgiveness about what we said about your precious Channing. We ain't sorry for saying you killed him, because you *did*. You know your cellie squealed all about it to everybody."

"That's what I said," Miller added. "You can't forgive me if I ain't even sorry!"

"All I'm doing is offering it," Dallas stated through clenched teeth. "Channing would want me to forgive you." *So would God.* About to explode from the bombardment of repeated jabs, he forced himself to turn away again, but this time Maddox sidestepped to block his way. *Get out of here; get out of here now!* Dallas's brain screamed at his body, tense and flooded with endorphins poising him for a fistfight.

"Nope, you don't get off that easy!" Miller shouted, barging between the two men. His eyes were like ice in his red face. "Why don't you try hittin' me again, huh?" He thrust his face inches from Dallas's, chest to chest. "You scared that Maddox can molly-whop you? That I've got somebody to back me up, and *your* only friend is dead? Come on, take a swing at me, Malone!"

Dallas clenched his fists behind his back so hard that his knuckles felt numb. He was about to give way to the rage that had built up inside him. Propelled by a supernatural force, he backed towards a doorway. Miller reached around and grabbed his forearm, and Dallas yanked away furiously.

"Not gonna defend your dead friend this time?" Maddox taunted from beside Miller. "Won't take care of your business and fight? What kind of man *are* you, Malone?"

"He ain't a man," put in Miller. "He's an inhuman killer! We don't want your forgiveness, Malone! We don't want your friendship 'cause we don't wanna end up *dead!*"

"Then what are you doin' trying to get yourself thrashed again?" came a growl from behind Dallas. It was John. Dallas's shoulders sagged before he registered that John had made a threat on his behalf.

"I'm not gonna attack him again," Dallas told John, pent-up frustration escaping in his voice. Glancing at Miller and Maddox as he backed away further, he added, "I'm just offering an apology and forgiveness, but you don't have to take it, and I'm *not* going to be provoked into a fight. But I *will* protect myself in self-defense if I'm forced to!" Dallas turned on his heel, fuming, and headed for the door. Miller's mocking voice and Maddox's sinister laugh rang through the air behind him. The last thing he heard was John telling them to knock it off. Dallas glided down the hall, cheeks burning, praying that John wouldn't get into a fight on his behalf.

He sat on the chair, mentally kicking himself for letting those guys get to him, for allowing himself to miss breakfast because of them. And he was conflicted at having left John to face them alone. *I'm a coward.* Dallas swung an arm at nothing. *Surrender*, the word floated softly through his mind. *No, I know I'm not a coward. That's a lie of the devil, trying to drag me down by questioning my strength. It took a lot of strength to walk out of there, more than it would've taken to give in and beat the crap out of Miller again.* Dallas's stomach growled. *Offer it up*, he heard a voice say inside him. *For Channing, and for Miller and Maddox, who are somebody's brothers, somebody's sons, somebody's friends… well, maybe, if there's anybody else who can stand them.* Dallas closed his eyes and took deep breaths. He jumped up and splashed cold water on his face.

The cell door opened, and John came in. He pulled a biscuit from his pocket and handed it to Dallas, grinning.

"Hey, thanks," Dallas said in surprise.

"Couldn't let those jerks deprive you of your chow," John said. "Man, I thought you were gonna let Miller have it again. That idiot doesn't know when to back off! It's like he wants to lose his other top tooth. Maybe he wants them to look even."

Dallas stifled a laugh. "I wanted to smash his face again, believe me," he admitted. "And to prove to them that I'm not scared of Maddox, that I could kick his…" Dallas bit his lip. "It took all my strength to get away before I lost control of myself. They didn't do anything to you, did they?" His eyes scanned John for any signs of damage.

"Nah," replied John, "just warned me that being friends with you would get me killed. Like I'd wanna be 'friends' with Maddox in exchange for his sick-earned protection?" He rolled his eyes. "I told them to shut the hell up about Channing, or they'd have to answer to me. They kinda skulked away after that. It's *you* they're after, for some reason."

"Don't fight with them, okay?" Dallas pleaded. "It's only gonna make things worse. I've done what I could, and I want to just move on and forget about them. And Maddox is sort of friendly with Hudson, I've noticed, and you know…" Dallas's face reddened. "I don't want to give that guard even more of a vendetta against me."

"Well, let's hope they let you forget about them," John said. "But I bet they're gonna keep it up, hoping to make you crack. Maddox is crazy if he thinks he can make you hold his pocket like Miller does, though. Hey, don't go to the chow hall without me anymore, okay? They're less likely to pick at you if you aren't alone."

Dallas gritted his teeth. He knew it was probably true. "Sure, thanks."

"I've struggled hard to keep my temper," Dallas admitted to Father Benedict at their next monthly visit. "But somehow, by the grace of God, I've kept from exploding. These two guys who have it out for me tried to draw me into a fight. I wanted to lash out at them so bad. They still taunt me, but I just walk past without looking at them, and so far, I've avoided any more confrontations."

Father Benedict smiled. "It must have taken great restraint to hold back when you wanted to hit them, but God gives you a superhuman strength, does he not?"

Dallas nodded. "Every time they do it, I try to silently say a prayer, asking God to give peace to them and me both, because I guess they must have a lot of pain inside them to be the way they are. I kind of pity them that they don't seem to understand right from wrong. And one of them abuses the other; everyone here knows it. Controlling my temper has been a huge challenge. I guess I never realized how little self-control I had before."

"How have you been able to refocus yourself in the heat of the moment, to remember to turn to God instead of your fists?" asked the priest.

Dallas cracked his knuckles and looked at his hands, thinking. "I've started being able to see others as real people, and even put them ahead of myself sometimes," he began. "It's been eye-opening. Like, I've been so occupied putting myself down, hating myself for my mistakes, and now that I've started trying to see the humanity in other people, it's... I don't know. Logically, you'd think putting others ahead of yourself would mean you hated yourself even more. But it isn't working like that. I'm just less focused on myself than before, so I'm not dwelling on hatred of myself. It's like I was being *selfish*, being so wrapped up in hating myself. When I missed breakfast to avoid that fight, I offered it up as a sacrifice for them instead of seething over the fact that I let myself be intimidated out of a meal. I still don't like to think of them getting the best of me, but not getting so angry over it just makes me feel better."

Father Benedict smiled. "Dallas, I'm so glad. You are seeing what God can do in our lives when we live as Christ shows us. And it honors Channing's memory when you treat others as you would have treated him. Treat yourself with that same courtesy, and self-forgiveness will follow."

"So I've been reading more and more of the Bible, and I've gone through a lot of the *Catechism*," Dallas continued. "I've read and reread *Mere Christianity* and *The Everlasting Man* and the saint book you gave me. So, if I decide I want to convert – like, join the Catholic Church and all – what steps would I take? Here in prison, I mean?" Dallas looked earnestly at the priest.

Father Benedict tilted his head to one side. "What is prompting this?"

"I want to make a commitment to God. And Catholicism is just so logical." Dallas opened his hands wide on the table. "I've gotten so much peace in the last few weeks. Except, well, I haven't tackled trying to forgive people from the past who hurt me and Channing. I know that's gonna be harder, and I don't think I can deal with that yet."

"It's okay if that takes some time," answered the priest. "As for deciding to become Catholic, if you continue to read and to pray and you make that decision, then I could give you private instruction during our regular visits. Normally, you would attend a weekly class at a Catholic parish, and then you would be received into the Church at the Easter Vigil Mass. But while incarcerated, we would evaluate how prepared you become throughout the rest of your sentence. There are options for giving you the sacraments that we can explore if it comes to that point before your release. Do you know what you would like to do or where you want to go after this, in a couple of years?"

Dallas's mind was pensive. The repeated dream flashed into his mind. It happened at random times when he was trying to focus on something else, and it was starting to annoy him. His thoughts would always turn immediately to how he may have robbed the world of a future priest when Channing died. He pulled his mind back to the question at hand. "I don't know," Dallas reflected. "I could maybe work for Mitchell again, but I'm not sure I want to live in Minnesota. We got there at the tail end of January, and it was way too cold for my tastes. I mean, Nevada was cold too, but not like that. And I know I'm not going back *there*." Dallas shrugged. "I haven't thought much about it, but I know I need to. I'm saving everything I earn, so I should at least be able to pay rent somewhere for a couple months while I'm starting a job. But I need to come up with a plan of where to begin. So, yeah, auto mechanic job, I guess. I enjoy the work and already know a lot about it."

"Would you consider living in the Denver area?" asked Father Benedict. "Or do you have ties to anyone elsewhere, another friend or family member you want to be near?"

"No, not really." Dallas sighed. "Denver could be a possibility, but I guess it depends on the cost of living there." The thought of Central Florida flashed through his mind, and he suppressed a smile as he recalled Channing's near-obsession. "You see," Dallas continued, "before my arrest, I loved to take road trips, just take off and drive. Me and Channing would go to whatever place struck my fancy when I was looking through the road atlas. And we'd get there, and the destination wouldn't be what I'd made it out to be in my mind. Channing asked me about it once — like, what was my purpose? My mentality was, okay, I met my goal, checkmark — time to move on. I was really, *really* restless. No amount of roaming could truly satisfy me. And now — I think Channing saw it in me too, maybe even subconsciously — I think I was looking for God. I need something to ground me. Channing was trying to show me that, but I just couldn't understand it then. But I do now. I realize I *need* God, and his Church left here on earth for us lost humans is the way to find him and to rest in the stability it can give me."

Dallas sat motionless, half-wondering if those words had come out of his mouth.

Father Benedict's face glowed with a fond expression.

They sat in silence for a few moments.

"If you want to start now, Dallas, I can come up with a plan for helping you to learn about joining the Church. I can bring specific study materials for you next month, if you want to use this time to ponder it and make sure you are ready to make those steps. Your insight is very keen," the priest noted, "and your growth in wisdom is quite impressive."

"Amazing how all this prison time helps a guy to think about stuff, huh?" Dallas cocked an eyebrow.

"Truly, Dallas, you are wise beyond your years," replied the priest. "How old are you now?"

"I'll turn 21 on Monday," Dallas responded. "Some way to spend my 21st birthday, huh? I'll be a full-fledged adult, I guess. It's surreal. In some ways, it seems like it's been a thousand years since Channing was alive and I was free, and yet I still feel the same age. But I know I've been changing in here." Dallas looked up into the face of his mentor. "Yeah, I'd like to have private instruction about the Catholic faith. I mean, I feel like you've already been giving me some of that. I appreciate you giving so much of your time, Father. I would have wasted away in here if it weren't for you. I mean that."

Father Benedict smiled. "You have so much promise, Dallas. God has great plans for your life, even if they aren't clear to you right now. You are on the right path."

Before he left, Father Benedict prayed with Dallas and gave him a blessing, as he always did.

Dallas left the visitation room. *All right, God. If I'm really supposed to become Catholic, let me know it somehow. Help me see that it's not just me hanging onto any thread connected to Channing.*

Channing. The ache of his loss was still bitter. But Dallas was resolved to offer up that sadness for Channing's soul. He silently thanked God for Father Benedict's guidance.

INKLINGS

Dallas was sprawled across his bunk, engrossed in a slow reading of the crucifixion from the Gospel of John. He was serious about studying, moving forward instead of merely treading water with his head barely above the surface. He came to the part where Jesus was condemned to die, and the people had brought him before the governor, Pontius Pilate. When Pilate spoke the line "What is truth?" Dallas bolted upright.

That was me! Dallas thought, breathless. *I asked Channing that same exact question, with the desperation over our lack of food coming to a head.* A kinship with humanity crept over Dallas. *Does everyone have the same struggles and ask the same questions?* He remembered a Chesterton quote Channing had recited from time to time: "We've found all the questions that can be found. It is time we gave up looking for questions and began looking for answers." *Am I really at that point now?* Dallas knew the main, big-picture questions. And they had answers, logical yet mysterious answers, that he was finding in Catholicism.

If the man who condemned Jesus to death struggled with the same questions, then can I truly be forgiven? Dallas felt sorry for Pilate and wondered if that was wrong.

At their next visit, he asked Father Benedict about it.

"Is it bad that I sort of identify with Pontius Pilate?" Dallas asked directly. "I see myself in him. At least, more how I used to be, when I was so skeptical." Dallas related to Father how he had asked the same question as Pilate had about truth. "Is it possible that God could've forgiven even him — the guy who essentially *killed* God?"

The priest answered, "Yes, it is possible. We do not know what Pilate may have done privately before the end of his life. That is between him and God. We can only know that the saints are in heaven, but we cannot definitively state that anyone is in hell. We are sure there are souls there, absolutely, and many of them at that, but as to who they are specifically, we cannot know. But we can be assured that if Pilate or anyone else involved in Jesus's death sought God's forgiveness for his sins and was truly repentant, then he could have been forgiven, because God is all-powerful and all-merciful. Remember the Roman centurion at the scene of the crucifixion. There is no sin too great for God to forgive."

A new lightness seeped into Dallas's soul. "Then," he said slowly, "I might be able to finally believe that God can forgive me, too."

Father Benedict replied softly, "Of course, God can forgive you. He wants to forgive you; he wants only what's best for you, for each member of his creation. And God is changeless. He always waits to accept our changes for the better, for us to turn from our fickle ways and back to him. Because he never changes, he will never abandon you, Dallas. He is always and eternally waiting for you to come to him, like the father of the prodigal son. In the book of Hebrews, we are promised that Jesus Christ is the same yesterday, today, and forever."

Dallas drew in a sharp breath and closed his eyes. *This is it,* he understood at last, *this is the stability Channing was talking about. I've been disappointed by people all my life, but God… Will he really always be there, changeless, ready to accept me if I come to him?* Dallas quickly swallowed down the negative emotions that rode in with his thoughts of his parents. *I have to believe he'll never leave.* He opened his eyes and looked at the kind face of the priest. "Never-changing," Dallas whispered with awe. "That's exactly what I need."

Dallas scrubbed the bottom of the huge stainless-steel pot, scraping away the last stuck bits of breakfast. He peered inside, inspecting to make sure it was clean before passing it to the inmate on his right. Pedro had begun his sentence six months earlier. The man silently accepted the pot and ran it under water to wash away the suds as Dallas started on the utensils with the lathery scrub brush. The two had been on kitchen duty together for the past month but hadn't ever struck up conversation. Dallas hummed mindlessly as he worked.

Pedro spoke to him suddenly. "You're the one who has a priest come to visit you, right?"

Dallas stopped humming and turned towards Pedro. "Yeah, that's right."

"He must be a really good priest," Pedro commented.

The two men continued the dishes in silence before Dallas responded, "He is. I'm grateful for his visits. He's real good to talk to." *Where is this going?* Dallas concentrated on the whisk in his hands, hardened raw egg clinging stubbornly to the wire.

"He must have a good effect on you," Pedro said. "You're happier lately."

Dallas scrubbed the whisk mercilessly. "Yeah, I am. I guess if you noticed that, maybe I'm making progress. I've been trying to become a better person, and he's helped me a lot. It's hard, though." He didn't know much about Pedro other than he kept himself out of trouble, quietly remaining at the fringes, but he seemed genuinely interested.

"It must be nice to have a holy man to talk to," Pedro said. "What's he done that's helped you?"

Dallas paused. "Well, you seem like you're an observant type of person. Am I right?"

Pedro shrugged. "I guess so. I don't talk a lot, so I notice stuff."

Dallas passed him the whisk to be rinsed. "So you noticed how I wasn't such a nice guy when you first got here."

"I noticed you seemed real angry sometimes," Pedro said. "Especially when other guys would push your buttons. But you don't let them bother you so much now. So I thought maybe it was the priest helping you somehow."

"He's been a big encouragement," Dallas admitted. "He's helped me understand what it means to turn the other cheek. Some of these guys, it's like they've made it their mission to be thorns in other people's sides, and for a while, I just let them enrage me. I thought if I deferred to them, it showed I was weaker than them. I couldn't stand the idea of that."

"I wondered about that when I saw Maddox steal a roll off your tray last week," Pedro said, handing Dallas a towel. "You didn't go after him." They stepped over to the wet dishes and began drying them side by side.

Dallas's face grew pink. "It still burns me inside when they do things like that, but yeah, that's the sort of thing I've stopped fighting back over. I'm trying to see things in a different light now. If it's that important for them to throw their power around, then it doesn't hurt me to let them have their way if it can prevent a fight. I can make the sacrifice."

Pedro stacked the dry dishes in silence.

Dallas pursed his lips as he hung the towels up. *Does he think I'm a pushover, a wimp?*

Then Pedro spoke. "That's probably the best way. It's Christlike. You know, even to hand over your roll when you see them coming, before they have the chance to bully you for it."

Dallas's eyebrows shot up. "That might be going too far, Pedro," he scoffed. But then he paused. Dallas had been deferring his place in line for the showers and weight room lately, letting others go ahead of him, although he hadn't yet made the offer to Miller or Maddox. *Was Pedro's suggestion really any different?*

"It keeps you out of fights and stuff," Pedro replied, "but I think you still come across as too strong for Maddox to do any more to you than little things like that. And you said sacrifice. Well, maybe it makes us better to give stuff up like that in here."

Dallas nodded. "I see what you mean. It's just another little dying-to-self thing, really. I'll try that, giving away my roll when I see him coming. When I think about it, I'd feel like more of a man if I'm handing it to him directly instead of just letting him swipe it."

Pedro grinned. They grabbed the full trash bags and carried them into the hallway.

The light blinded him as he stepped into the yard for the first time in over two solid years. Dallas trembled as a lump swelled in his throat, the mixture of emotions and memories of his past outdoor experiences tumbling over him. He took slow, deliberate steps across the concrete to the other side of the fenced yard to where some stray weeds grew at the edge. He knelt and touched them. *I haven't felt anything natural and living like this in so long.* The warmth of the sun spread over Dallas's back, the tickle of the breeze teased his face, and sounds serenaded him in their foreign familiarity: the birdsong, the buzz of insects, even the sound of motors coming from cars on the nearby highway were like old friends to him, reunited after a lengthy absence. *Why did it take me so long to come outside again?*

A mockingbird landed on a high branch of a pine tree outside the fence. It went through its repertoire of mimicking calls, and Dallas studied it in recognition, mesmerized, as it sang for sheer joy, simply because that is what God had made it to do. Dallas was still watching it when footsteps announced someone's approach.

Smith stopped behind him. "Hey, Hermit, you finally made it to rec time," he commented. "What made you come out?"

Dallas glanced over at Smith, then back at the bird. "It was just time."

"Good for you, man," Smith replied. "Gets depressing to never see the light of day."

They watched and listened to the bird in silence. After a few minutes, Dallas said, "I always took things like this for granted before I was in here."

"That bird's out here all the time, or one just like it," Smith remarked. "Wonder what kind it is."

"It's a mockingbird," Dallas answered automatically. *Thanks, Chan.* "Used to see them a lot when I was younger, in Nevada. Channing said they live pretty much all over the whole country." A few crows landed in the grass beyond the fence just then, drawing Dallas's eye towards them.

"Was he an expert on birds or something?" questioned Smith.

"He was an expert on a lot of things," Dallas said with a wistful sigh, and he found himself wondering if ravens lived in this part of the country. Channing had once shown him the difference between the common raven and the American crow, and he had been able to recite Poe's *The Raven* from memory with a lilting voice that Dallas missed acutely. He bit his lip as he studied the crows, recalling how Channing would greet them using their Latin genus name: *"Hey, corvids!" The corvids were his favorite…*

"Well, I wouldn't have really torn up that prayer card," Smith admitted, bringing Dallas back to the present, "but I see why you reacted to my teasing. It was mean of me, plain and simple. And I'm sorry that you lost your best friend. I lost my only brother, sort of, so I get where you're coming from. He was everything to me when we were kids. Like, when something reminds you of him – like that bird. You know what reminds me of my brother?"

"What?" Dallas asked softly, his throat aching.

"Milky Way candy bars," answered Smith with a faint grin. "They were his favorites. I'd sneak into the kitchen cabinet and get them for him when our mom wasn't looking. And then I'd take the blame when she noticed, 'cause he was younger than me. Stole them from the store for him, too. I'd do all kinds of crazy junk for him."

Dallas was silent a moment and then offered, "If it helps you to talk about him, you can tell me. Or not, if it's too much for you."

Smith blinked. "Yeah, it's pretty tough to think about still, so mostly I don't. He lost himself to drug abuse. He got into all kinds of bad stuff, started arguing with everyone in the family when we tried to help him, and we haven't heard from him in about five years now. I don't like to get my hopes up, so I don't talk much about him. I knew you'd understand, though, Malone, so thanks."

"Sure, man," Dallas responded. Inwardly, he said a prayer that Smith's brother was alive and okay somewhere and that they'd find each other again one day. *How would I feel if I didn't know Channing's fate, whether he was even alive or dead?* The thought made him shudder.

The two men headed back across the yard in nonchalant discussion, Dallas thinking Smith a pretty decent guy. Hudson stood just inside the open door, so Dallas kept his eyes down, Smith's presence a welcome distraction while he slipped past.

Lined up along the inside wall as they waited for the remaining stragglers, Dallas turned to continue the conversation when Hudson seemed to come out of nowhere, brushing against Dallas and stepping on his foot before tumbling to the floor. Dallas wheeled around and stared open-mouthed at the guard, who jumped back to his feet, face red. Before he could figure out what had happened, Dallas was thrown chest against the wall, Hudson's cruel hands pinning his wrists, an elbow in his back. The other inmates in the line stepped back, giving Hudson a wide berth.

"You think you can just stick out your foot and trip me like that?" sneered Hudson. "Guess you *like* the hole. You're comin' with me." Dallas, squirming inside at the familiarity of wrists being handcuffed behind back, suppressed his urge to throw all his weight in reverse and fight off the unjust assault. *I didn't trip him at all! He stepped on me on purpose to make it look like I tripped him!* Dallas desperately sought out the strength of his will to force his burning body to cooperate so he wouldn't make things worse.

"I don't think he tried to trip you," began Smith, stepping forward, but he was shot down by a barked order.

"I know you're gettin' all buddy-buddy with Malone, so shut up, Smith!" Hudson scorned. Smith backed up and was silent. He made eye contact with Dallas, who read in his expression that he knew it was a complete set-up.

Maddox stood several men ahead in line. He spoke up in the officer's defense.

"I saw him stick his foot out," he offered to Hudson. "Looked like he thought it was a pretty clever gag as you fell. I'll vouch for you if he tries to make up some fake story, Hudson."

The CO jerked Dallas by the cuffs away from the wall. "Thanks, Maddox," he said, sounding half-friendly, half-disdainful. "If I need somebody to ride my leg, you're the first I'll ask." He shoved Dallas hard in front of him. Then he turned back, a sudden idea spreading across his wicked face.

"Hey, Gap-Tooth!" he called. Miller stuck his head out from the line where he'd been standing alongside Maddox, nervous eyes darting between the CO and the floor. "Let's show Malone he's not the only one who can rough people up, huh? Stick *your* foot out in the hall."

Miller's glance flitted uncertainly between Hudson and Maddox, and then a mean smile spread across his face. "Sure thing," he responded, voice smug, with Maddox elbowing him, goading him on with a gleam in his eyes.

Hudson shoved Dallas towards Miller's outstretched foot. In silence, Dallas braced his feet. Hudson's neck bulged at the defiance, and he stomped around Dallas and yanked him forward by an elbow, forcing him to stumble across Miller's shoe. Hands cuffed behind his back, Dallas was helpless to break his fall. One knee hit the floor, slowing his descent, but his shoulder and the side of his face still came down hard on the solid concrete. Dallas heard Miller's and Maddox's chuckles amidst Hudson's raucous laughter above him. An uncomfortable shifting filled the hall, and murmurs rose among the other men in line.

Scrambling to his knees, Dallas caught the glance of Smith, who gave him a slight nod in sympathy. Hudson grabbed Dallas by the wrists and jerked him back on his feet.

"I don't think you fell quite as hard as I did," he said, voice dripping with sarcasm. "You sure didn't bust out any teeth on that hard floor. How's about we try that again."

Hudson shoved Dallas across Miller's foot in the other direction. He tripped, caught himself with the other foot, and almost stayed upright until Maddox stuck out his foot too and hooked Dallas's leg out from under him. He went down again with no chance to recover, slamming his mouth and chin against the solid floor this time. Dallas grimaced but didn't give them the satisfaction of hearing him make a sound, humiliation burning in his cheeks.

"Guess you're pretty useful after all," Hudson said to Maddox, and then without warning, he let a foot fly into Dallas's ribcage. Dallas gasped with the sudden trauma but bit his bleeding lip. He got to his knees, then to his feet quickly, Smith helping him by one arm. Hudson was on them in an instant, ordering Smith to back off. He threw Dallas up against the wall again.

"Had enough, Malone?" he sneered behind him, jabbing Dallas in the back until he had to writhe from the discomfort. "Still got all your teeth, but we can make up for that in solitary, now, can't we? Let's go, everyone!" he barked at the group, pushing Dallas ahead of him alongside the string of men marching single file along the cinder block wall of the hallway.

Dallas willed himself to take firm steps. It was unfair, a punishment based on a complete lie, and he fought weakly against the brewing storm inside. *Don't give in to the anger. Turn the other cheek, be stubborn. Act like you don't care that you're going in the hole for no reason. You've survived it twice before; what's another session?* Dallas kept up his internal coaching all the way down the hallway.

At the main cell block, Smith cast Dallas a forlorn parting glance but then winked at him at the last second before Hudson hustled him down another hallway towards H Unit. Once out of sight of everyone, Hudson swept a foot under Dallas's step and brought him to the floor unexpectedly, then let loose a barrage of hostile kicks. Dallas rolled over to shield himself from the attack, but with each ragged breath he sucked in, he was sure he had at least one broken rib already. Dallas protected his abdomen with his arms and knees from Hudson's heavy boots, but the correctional officer changed tactics with a swift kick to his face.

Dallas almost exploded. *I'm trying to be cooperative even though I haven't done a thing wrong, and turning the other cheek is getting me pummeled!* His jaw throbbed, and blood ran from his nose and dripped from his chin onto his uniform. He struggled to a stand and prepared to defend himself with his feet, his hands shackled and useless. But Hudson merely grabbed him by a forearm and walked him into H Unit, saying, "Let's go. I'd say a full week in the hole oughtta teach you somethin'."

They passed a bright yellow door, then Hudson unlocked one beside it and shoved Dallas through. He blocked the doorway, smirking, as Dallas's glance darted furtively around the tiny cell, memories of his past punishments like demons invading his mind.

"So you got a buddy to look out for you now, stand up to me on your behalf?" Hudson said in a cocky, taunting voice. "I'm jealous, Malone. Smith better stay outta this if he knows what's good for him."

Dallas returned a cold, mute stare. He stood in the middle of the room, compliant but refusing to look beaten. His side was killing him, but he breathed through the pain with each slow, shallow breath. The unbearable tickle of his own blood on his face was a silent torment, no relief possible with his hands still locked behind his back.

"Nobody here to squeal on me now, though," Hudson snarled, "nobody to take up for ya, Malone. And ya know, you just don't look remorseful yet. I don't see any suffering or groveling—just that look of pure hatred for me in your eyes." He stepped closer. "I must not be trying hard enough."

Dallas stood his ground and said evenly, "I don't hate you." *That's true. I hate what he does to me, but for my peace of mind, I'm trying to forgive him.*

A slithery smile spread over Hudson's face, pure evil commandeering his eyes.

A sickness grew in the pit of Dallas's stomach at that depraved look. "Oh, you *will* hate me, after I get through with you." Hudson took slow steps towards his captive, the low, creepy words settling themselves in Dallas's ears. "I think I'll keep you company here all night, really get to know you better. Most guys don't get that special favor on their last night in here, spend it all alone with their sorry selves..."

Dallas backed away, heart pulsing in his ears, and he hit the wall, trapped between a toilet and a bed. Hudson grabbed him by the shoulders and spun him around. Dallas flinched for impact, but Hudson fiddled with the handcuffs, and they fell to the floor with a rattle. Then he turned Dallas around to face him again. Leaning in close, Hudson glared into his eyes. "Take your pants off," he whispered in a chilling voice.

Dallas's mouth fell open and he froze. It felt as if the bottom had dropped out of his stomach. He knew this was no routine strip search. An icy fear ran down his spine at the twisted abuse the guard might be planning, and it was all he could manage to find his voice and say huskily with as much force as he could muster, "You're one sick..."

Just then, two COs appeared in the open doorway. "What's going on, Hudson? Need some backup?" It was Murphy's voice. Hudson spun around to face the newcomers, and Dallas succumbed to his shaking knees and slid down the wall in collapsed relief, back against the concrete and knees drawn up against his chest. He shivered violently and whispered prayers of thanks that Murphy had interrupted the assault.

"I don't need your help, no." Hudson sounded annoyed. "What gave you that idea? I've got everything handled here."

"Had a report that we might need to check this out," the other officer added, glancing around the cell warily. "And the fact that you're locking him in LL..."

"It's unoccupied, so why not?" Hudson's response was laced with defensiveness.

Footsteps sounded in the hallway, and then a third man was peering into the cell. Dallas recognized the warden.

"Step out here in the hallway with me, Officer Hudson. Malone," added the warden through the doorway, "I'm going to be back shortly to talk to you, too."

The heavy door shut, and Dallas found himself alone, the sound of the lock echoing in the empty chamber.

Dallas was brought out of solitary an hour later. John and Smith nearly knocked him over for the details as he entered his cell, but Dallas slipped past them to his locker. He retrieved his holy card and held it close, eyes closed, then dropped to his knees. John and Smith gave him some space. Dallas's chin was badly scraped from the fall against the floor, his lower lip was split, and a purple bruise was growing on the side of his nose and cheek from where Hudson had kicked him. Although the guard had failed to knock any teeth out, Dallas was wiggling one lower molar with his tongue, wondering if the root had been damaged enough that he'd eventually lose the tooth. His abdomen was wrapped after having been examined by the doctor, confirming two cracked ribs.

After silent recitation of the Memorare, Dallas sat on the edge of the chair and invited Smith and John to move in close. "Murphy brought the warden just in time," he told them in a hushed voice. "I don't know how bad it would've gotten if…" Dallas shut his eyes against the spinning room before continuing. "The warden came in, asked me for my side of the story. He said he had details of what happened in the hallway when we came in from the yard." Dallas looked at Smith and cocked his eyebrow expectantly.

Smith thumped his chest with one fist. "Well, I couldn't let that scumbag get away with throwing you in solitary because of a dirty lie!" The anger rose in his voice. "Yeah, I told him *exactly* what happened."

"Thankfully, there was a security camera further down the hall, and it caught everything from a distance, but clear enough to back up all you must've said," Dallas told him. "Warden said he still couldn't be sure if I'd tripped Hudson intentionally, but that it sure looked like I didn't. Hudson's gonna be pissed, though. He's been put on leave for a week."

"That punk comes back and tries to rough you up again, and I'll let him have it!" threatened Smith, eyes blazing. John shifted his glance between his feet and the faces of the other two men, then added, "I'll watch your back, man. We can report anything we see, anything that looks like he's abusing you or anyone else. If the warden's on your side this time, any more ammo we can pile up against that bastard will be another nail in his coffin."

"I don't know why they keep him on staff here anyway," Smith complained. "I've heard stories, man. He's abused more than just you, Malone. Seems he picks a new pet favorite to torment every few years. Kramer, he's been in this place for like a million years, and he's told me some stuff about Hudson that would make your hair stand on end. Crazy, sick, malicious stuff."

Dallas closed his eyes, stomach churning. *I don't doubt it.* Opening them again, he added, "The good news is that the warden won't let him supervise me directly anymore. Hudson will have to call in other COs to deal with me if necessary from now on. There's been too many incidents between us already, so the warden decided it's better this way since, as he put it, there's 'something personal' between us. Smith, man, thanks for going to Murphy for me." Dallas blew out a relieved sigh as he leaned his elbows against his knees. "I pray Hudson doesn't take revenge on you, though."

"So what makes him such a lowlife bastard?" wondered Smith aloud.

Dallas was about to second the question when John spoke up.

"I've been here longer than either of you guys," he began in a low voice, "so I've heard things too, about his history. People say he was abused by an uncle growing up. All kinds of stories, some probably exaggerated, but if they're even half true, then the guy did some heinous things to him. And now he takes it out on people here who threaten his power. Being a CO makes him feel like he's in control, and so he throws his authority around because he can. He's doin' to guys in here every dirty, despicable thing his uncle did to him."

Dallas felt a tinge of pity for Hudson as he identified the same need to maintain power and control. *But he's doing it in a depraved, wicked way. It's no excuse for how he's treated me, but maybe I can sort of understand a little what's wrong with him now.* He thought of Channing's childhood, how his best friend had suffered so much abuse from his own parents. *Channing rose above it, though.* Dallas felt a swell of pride.

"Anyway, I'm real glad to hear he isn't allowed to take direct charge of you again," Smith said, interrupting Dallas's thoughts. "But we got your back still, Malone. Those wimps Miller and Maddox won't have anybody to run to with their panties all in a bunch, makin' up lies about you. But they might try startin' stuff with you. What do you say, John?" Smith leaned towards him.

"Yeah, we're on it," John agreed. "I still wouldn't trust Hudson, though. Just the fact that he's allowed back here in a week… he could corner you alone, dude. You can't let him have the chance. He's got it in for you more than anyone. You're his target."

Dallas sighed. "I guess he's still not over the fact that Murphy went above him to get this prayer card returned to me. He can't handle the thought that his punishment didn't stand." Dallas twirled the card between his fingers. "Hey, that's twice you've stood up to him on my behalf, Smith. Thanks, man."

"It was my fault he took that card away from you in the first place," Smith returned. "And I just hate to see unfair punishments."

***

"Father, I'm ready," Dallas spoke earnestly. "Could we start going over everything I need to know?"

"You are ready to take a serious look into Catholicism?" asked the priest.

"Yes," Dallas said firmly. "I want to become Catholic; I *know* it. And I want to know everything I can about it so I can make a solid commitment and join the Church. I've served over half my term now, so less than two years, and I'll be out. I want to be prepared."

"We can start now," answered the priest. "You sound eager to begin."

"I've been reading the *Catechism* closely," Dallas added. "There's so much I want to talk to you about. It's like a huge puzzle with all these pieces, but they're starting to fit together for me. I was reading about confession yesterday, and I get how it might free me from being stuck in the same bad behavior all the time. I want to be able to let stuff go."

"Confession is a healing sacrament, but there will be no need for it at first," Father interrupted. "If you join the Church, all your past sins will be washed away at your baptism."

"You mean I can't confess my crimes, receive absolution for them?" Dallas crossed his arms, dissatisfied.

"It is a beautiful desire in you to want to make a heartfelt confession," Father Benedict said. "God gives us baptism as the primary way to receive his forgiveness for our sins. Remember how I told you that Channing was cleansed of sin when you baptized him? Confession is there for our failings after baptism. Your crimes will all be erased at the moment of your baptism. God sees your contrition and offers you his grace through this initial sacrament."

"Wow." Dallas exhaled. "That's a relief, but how do we know it for sure?"

"Adult converts often find the sacrament of confession to be a beautiful comfort," the priest said. "I'll write down some Bible passages for you to look up later, and you can begin to see the origins of the sacrament, so we can discuss it more next time. What do you know about the Eucharist, Dallas?"

"Just what I've read: that it's truly the Body and Blood, Soul and Divinity of Christ." Dallas straightened and folded his hands on the table. "I don't understand it, but I believe it somehow. At least, I *want* to believe it. Channing talked to me about several aspects of the faith, like forgiving your enemies and why Mary is important and how the Church has never changed its fundamental teachings because of being inspired by the Holy Spirit, but he didn't ever get the chance to explain to me about the Eucharist. Maybe he didn't have a full grasp of it himself, or he thought I'd scoff at it – which I probably would have. He went to Mass once, you know, in the cathedral with you. So, do you think you could help me understand the Eucharist?"

"It goes along with what Channing told you about the Church never changing her teachings," Father began. "Since the earliest days, Christians believed the Eucharist was Jesus's actual body, re-presented in a non-bloody sacrifice, *made present again*. The original Greek text of the Gospels makes this clear, that we were to physically eat the body of Christ, truly present under the forms of bread and wine. The word for it is *anamnesis*. The phrase "in memory of" is used in English because there is no direct translation for making one and the same thing present again."

Dallas furrowed his brow. "So like Channing told me before, and I've heard you say it too: God exists outside time and space. So his sacrifice can be one and the same both historically and at each and every Mass, so it's real—not just a symbol of one event that happened in the past." He cocked his head. "But we're not re-sacrificing him at each Mass. The *Catechism* says it's a non-bloody re-presentation and that he only died once. Right?"

The priest beamed at him. "You've got it!" he said. "Your understanding is amazing, Dallas!"

"Really?" he asked, raising both eyebrows. "But... but it's so simple somehow."

"Most people find it to be one of the hardest teachings to accept," Father Benedict said. "Even when Jesus said to eat his flesh, his followers claimed that the saying was hard and questioned who could accept it."

"But Jesus just repeated himself," Dallas said. "I read that a few days ago, in the Gospel of John. Jesus meant it."

Father Benedict's face glowed. "I don't know that I've ever seen anyone understand the Eucharist so quickly and put it into words as succinctly as you've just done."

Dallas's cheeks felt warm at the praise. "It must be because you're such a good teacher, Father."

The season changed — Dallas's third autumn in prison, but the first he observed by the changing leaves and cooling outdoor temperatures. He walked to the cafeteria, glancing at the calendar on the wall, and listed in his head all the major milestones occurring during his incarceration. *Channing's 18th birthday, my 21st, and the world about to turn over to not just a new century, but a whole new millennium...*

Dallas sat down with his tray, followed by Pedro, then Smith across from him. John and a few other guys joined them a moment later.

"So what's this Y2K thing I keep hearing mentioned?" Dallas asked the group.

"It's gonna be the end of the world, man," one told him. "All the computers are gonna, I don't know, explode or something. People are hoarding food and stuff."

"It's just that these huge computers that run everything weren't designed to roll over four whole digits at once," John added. "Not the end of the world, but it's supposed to screw up a bunch of stuff big time."

Dallas's brow furrowed in skepticism. "I don't get it."

"You wouldn't, Hermit," ribbed Smith. "You have no clue about what's happening in the outside world."

"He's not so reclusive as before," John said to Smith.

"Hey, you guys are the ones who sat down with me..." Dallas began, raising both hands.

"Yeah, 'cause you don't look like you'll bite off the head of anybody who looks at you anymore," Smith retorted.

Dallas smiled and slathered jelly on his biscuit. It was weird to be at a full table, but good, too. "I do get the significance of entering into a new millennium," he observed. "Not everyone gets to see that in their lives."

Chatter escalated about the doom and gloom predictions, but Dallas slipped back into his mind, pondering the passage of time. He finished his meal and entered the kitchen to work on clean-up. Time seemed to drag in prison, yet Dallas realized it was moving forward at an alarming speed. It just kept going on — *without Channing. He's frozen in the past, perpetually 17 years old.* Dallas sighed and murmured a prayer for Channing. *How can he be dead? Sometimes I feel as if he's just waiting, somewhere outside these solid cement block walls.* All that waited for Dallas was a grave to visit. He pushed back the temptation to slip into wallowing in his sorrow. "Lord, have mercy," he whispered aloud, picking up a scrub brush. "I do believe; help my unbelief."

"What's that mean?" Jasper Gaines pointed to Dallas's prayer, still posted on his cell wall. The sixty-year-old inmate, nicknamed the Old Man, had come by Dallas's cell, staring at his shoes and mumbling something about wanting to talk.

Dallas listened to the man's story of how he wanted to believe in God but had lost his faith years ago. He was nearing the end of his term: twelve long years, and he admitted feeling adrift and unsure of what would happen upon his release.

"I just want to have some peace, but I don't know how," Jasper admitted. "I saw your sign on the wall. I know the story of you carrying around that 'baby Jesus card,' as some of the guys say, and that you have a priest come visit you regular. So I thought maybe you'd be able to give me some, I dunno, advice or something. Where'd you get that idea from: I believe; help my unbelief?"

Dallas told him the story from the Bible. "It pretty much sums up what it's like to be a flawed human being," he tried to explain. "We can be pretty skeptical when life doesn't go the way we want, when bad junk happens to us, and when we can't see God with our eyes. It makes it hard for us to believe there could be something that's all-good, somebody who wishes well for us, when he doesn't swoop in to save us from all the bad in the world. So we want to believe, but we can't… at least, not perfectly. And if God is truly all-powerful, then he's gotta be the one to help us believe."

"So why does bad stuff happen to good people?" Gaines asked.

Dallas pursed his lips. "Well, give me an example."

Gaines listed off offenses committed against him over the years.

Dallas prodded for more, and Jasper got around to describing his crime. The cracking in his voice and the emotion welling up through his hardened exterior was like a mirror to Dallas, reflecting a common struggle.

"I know why *that* bad thing happened," the Old Man mumbled. "Because I decided to do it. It's my fault. I guess I've been not believing in anything good because I wanted to blame something else for not stopping me from committing those crimes. But I guess that's why bad things happen. 'Cause people decide to do them."

"And that's why I decided I needed God," Dallas told him. "We do bad things without God's help. And yeah, sometimes bad stuff happens that wasn't anyone's fault. Or, it's your fault, even though the bad that happened wasn't what you intended." *Like accidents.* Dallas squeezed his eyes shut for a second. "That's when we really need help believing that we need to rely on something bigger than ourselves to get through bad things, and hoping that there is this perfection called heaven and that it's our real home after getting through the pain and challenges on earth."

"How do you keep believing?" Gaines asked.

"It's a constant challenge," Dallas admitted. "You just have to decide to do it. And you have to decide again every day sometimes. You saw what I was like when I first got here, right?"

"You were a mess." The Old Man shook his head. "I can hardly believe you're the same guy. I've even seen you smile at folks now instead of poundin' them for lookin' at you. That's why I came to you, 'cause it's clear to me that *something's* changed in you. I'm still gonna call you The Hermit though. 'Cause you're not so much of a loner anymore that nobody can approach you, but, you know, hermits were like these wise men who lived alone talking to God and who could give good advice. Like a quiet leader type. That's the kind of hermit you seem like to me."

Dallas grinned. "Okay, Old Man."

"I don't want to trouble you none," the man said. "But you're good to talk to, Malone. Malone the Hermit."

"No trouble at all, Old Man." Dallas clapped a hand on his shoulder. "Been good to talk with you. And I don't know all the answers, but I'll listen if you need it. And if you wanna borrow my Bible any time, you're welcome to it."

Jasper smiled as he turned away, nodding and humming to himself.

Dallas listened to the phone ringing and tapped his foot. He only used his money to make calls as a last resort, and this was too embarrassing to say to Father Benedict face to face. *Please pick up,* he prayed. Father had given him his personal phone number at the rectory.

"Hello?" answered the priest.

"Hey, Father, it's Dallas."

"Dallas, good to hear your voice," Father Benedict said. "Nothing is wrong, I hope?"

"No, no, I'm fine," Dallas rushed. "It's just that I had some questions that couldn't wait for your next visit… um, if you have a few minutes to talk, that is."

"Certainly," answered the priest. "I have a couple hours before confessions and Mass."

Dallas felt his cheeks redden and blurted, "I read in the *Catechism* yesterday that, um, this certain sexual action is wrong. It doesn't involve anyone else, so I don't understand why."

The brief silence seemed much longer to Dallas. Then Father Benedict asked, "What is the purpose of this action?"

Dallas scratched the back of his head and stuttered, "I, uh… I just want to know, is it really a sin, and why."

"Then tell me what you think its purpose is," repeated Father.

Dallas glanced over his shoulder and lowered his voice. "Well, because it feels good. And to blow off stress. It doesn't hurt anybody, and all the guys in here do it. It's like an understood rule that you give your cellmate privacy for stuff like that every day."

You say it doesn't hurt anyone," mused the priest, "and at first, that appears to be accurate. But it hurts the person doing it."

Dallas raised an eyebrow. "How so? I figure it's a little thing that helps us get through the monotonous days of imprisonment."

"So you see it as a form of self-entertainment?" asked Father Benedict.

Dallas didn't answer. Somehow Father Benedict's phrasing had made it seem like a crude and pathetic exercise.

The priest continued, "God gave humans the gift of sexuality, and he did so to unite and create families. When you reduce it to a single person acting alone, then it becomes selfish. You're using it as a false escape from reality, a mindless succumbing to your base instincts with no thought to the purpose of God-given male and female complementarity. I have a book about the Theology of the Body — a phrase used by Pope John Paul II — and it explains more about God's design for our bodies. You can read over it and think on it."

Dallas chewed his lip. "So… if it's a sin, then I have to stop, right?"

"That should be your goal, yes," Father Benedict replied. "It can be difficult to curb a habit, especially one that is a coping mechanism in a bad situation. But working at conquering those temptations is a great exercise in self-mastery."

"Ah, my stubbornness again, huh?" Dallas asked, grinning despite himself.

Father chuckled on the other end of the line. "Yes, denying oneself of fleeting pleasure for the gain of virtue is a great strengthening of steadfastness in faith."

Dallas sighed. "I guess I still don't see what's so wrong about it, because it just seems natural, biologically speaking."

"What is the biological reason for sex?" interrupted the priest.

Dallas furrowed his brow. "Well, at the most basic level, it's to continue the human race."

"And bonding a father and mother together gives their offspring the best chance at survival and advancement," Father Benedict added.

"Yeah, it doesn't always work that way, you know," Dallas grumbled, scuffing a toe against the floor.

"No, in this fallen world, it does not. But it was God's plan for the best outcome, and humans don't always follow the natural law. Many people treat others as a commodity, with sex as a selfish pleasure. It deforms the meaning when it becomes solely about self-gratification, and that is detrimental to a civilized society as well as to human souls. Human dignity is about so much more than the passing physical pleasures of this world."

Civilized society... world pleasures... soma... Dallas lit up. "Father, it's like in *Brave New World!*"

"You've read it?" asked the priest.

"Channing read it aloud," Dallas replied, "and it was disturbing, but I couldn't quite put my finger on why I thought so. I remember Channing saying, 'These people are so bored, even though they're constantly entertained.' I think I get it now. They were just takers, consumers. Channing was always happiest when he was learning or creating something. Is that what you mean by 'human dignity,' sort of?"

"Learning, creating, working, all are ways to actively use the bodies and minds God gave us in ways that respect our dignity," Father Benedict replied. "It is more challenging for you than ever, being in a place where you have fewer opportunities. You can find your dignity in giving your all to work and prayer, in your studies, and in looking *outside* yourself for ways to help others. Dallas, you're showing more and more that you are not a selfish person at heart. I will pray for you to overcome this temptation and to use your body in ways that glorify God and serve others in appropriate ways. Don't give up—try again even after you fail."

"Thanks, Father. I guess it sorta makes sense. I'll look forward to learning more when you bring me that book."

"It will give you a good understanding of the Catholic view of male-female relationships," Father Benedict added. "Women bear the brunt of much of this world's sexual dysfunction. When sex is reduced to a selfish pleasure, then women are treated as objects and are left struggling to raise children alone."

A memory intruded on Dallas's thoughts. *The only time my mother gave me an outright expectation...* Her crass directive hit Dallas from a buried place inside. *"Don't go around hopping into bed with girls. That's not what makes you a man. Keep it in your pants—got it?"* It had been the extent of the sex education she'd given her son, but the words had stuck in his fourteen-year-old mind. *She didn't want me to be like my father.* The realization jarred Dallas deep inside. He lowered his eyebrows. *And I won't be.*

He blew out a sigh. "Okay, thanks, Father. I just had to get your take on it, and… well, thanks."

"I'll see you in a couple of weeks, my son," Father Benedict replied before they hung up.

Dallas leaned against the wall, waiting in line at the commissary. He had been thrifty with his growing balance, saving for his release. Once a month, he splurged for a couple of six-packs of sodas, and there was an unspoken understanding among the other inmates that if they asked him, Dallas would give them one with no expectation of payment or favors — a rare instance in the typical ways of prison life.

Whispering and keeping their distance, Maddox and Miller followed Dallas as he strode back to his cell, sodas in hand. He set them in his locker. Maddox, hanging through the bars from the hallway outside the cell, said, "So, Malone, I hear you give those drinks away to your road dogs." Miller jeered alongside with his gap-toothed grin. "Which leaves *us* out."

"I give 'em to anybody who asks," Dallas replied, guarded but trying not to sound hostile.

"Betcha wish you could give one to *Channing*," mocked Miller in a singsong voice. He and Maddox laughed wickedly.

Dallas gritted his teeth. He whispered a prayer for Channing inside to push down the seething. "Since I can't," he said slowly, "I'll offer them to you two instead."

Maddox spat on the ground outside the cell. "So's that like how you offer your forgiveness, huh? Your forgiveness, as if it's some wonderful gift you lower yourself to give to people who don't even want it?"

"I just offer a soda to anybody who's interested," Dallas responded, ignoring the attempt to change the direction of the conversation. "If you don't want one, you can kick rocks."

"Okay, we'll take 'em," Miller said, arm extended into the cell.

Dallas, face emotionless, handed them each a can through the bars.

Maddox added, "But it don't mean we accept your forgiveness." With that, he opened the can and poured the soda straight onto the hall floor while he stared coldly into Dallas's eyes. He and Miller laughed as it ran in a stream to a low spot and into a grate on the floor.

Dallas watched his money go down the drain. His arm and shoulder muscles tensed, and he chanted to himself, *Turn the other cheek; ignore them.* He turned his back abruptly, hiding how he really felt.

"Remind you of the life of your punk friend, Malone?" crowed Miller. "Gone?"

Dallas clenched his fists. He climbed into his bed with a book and a Coke for himself, refusing to look at them. He was trapped, but he couldn't get out of there without going past them. *And I don't think I can manage that without becoming violent...*

Just then, the cell door swung open, and John entered. "Boss coming, jerks," he said. "Better beat it quick and head back here with a mop to clean up your mess, ya filthy pigs."

Saved by John again. Sure enough, a correctional officer had been close behind. Maddox and Miller tried to brush off what they'd done, but they were made to mop up the floor and then sent on their way.

"What'd you give those morons sodas for?" John screwed up his face in disgust after the two had slunk away. "That's your money, your own hard work!"

"I'm just trying to keep things smoothed over." Dallas rubbed the back of his neck. "It's only a little money."

"Next time, I'm coming right behind you to the commissary, and then let's see them try *that* again!" John said heatedly. "You shouldn't feel obligated to give anything to them!"

"I don't feel obligated." Dallas had an edge to his voice. "It's just something I hafta do if they ask, okay?"

John glanced aside and shrugged. "Well, okay, but I don't want those jerks intimidating you." Dallas held his breath, a kettle filling the tiny cell with a built-up pressure about to blow. John met his eyes. "Hey, let's go work out. You want to?"

Dallas leaped down from the bed. "Definitely." They headed to the weight room, where Dallas worked off his aggression in a sweat of physical exertion.

Dallas closed the *Catechism* and grabbed his notebook. He'd just been summoned to the visitors' area. He put the book inside his locker.

John spoke to Dallas's back with his eyes glued to his television. "You sure have spent every waking moment studying and reading all that Catholic stuff lately. You're gonna know enough to become a priest yourself."

Dallas halted in the cell doorway. He turned towards John and leaned on his elbow against the doorframe. "*Me*, a priest? Nah." He brushed off the words. The memory of Channing telling him eagerly about his decision to become Catholic over their coffee in the restaurant in Minnesota flashed through Dallas's mind: *the first time I predicted a religious calling for him.* The thought had so entwined itself into him, it was almost as if Channing himself had confided this plan to Dallas. *But he didn't.* Dallas stopped himself. *Maybe I've been projecting thoughts onto Channing that weren't there. How could I even be sure he would've taken that path?*

He debated explaining to John and then decided against it. That dream of following a priest into a church filled Dallas's mind again. *I had it last night, come to think of it. Maybe it isn't Channing in that dream at all. Maybe it's about finding a home in the Church as a member myself.* Dallas turned and headed down the hall towards the visitor area.

As he sat down across from Father Benedict a moment later, John's comment reverberated in his head. Dallas scoffed. *I'm unworthy even to be considered for such a calling.* A funny quiver crept up into his skin from deep inside him, like butterflies in his stomach, only it was everywhere in his body all at once.

"How have you been?" the priest asked Dallas.

"Really good, Father." Dallas shook off the sensation and focused on his mentor. "Every day, I'm telling myself that God is true, and I'm getting this contentment I've never known before. And you've become a father figure to me — another thing I've never had. Learning about God as Father along with your example is giving me real stability for the first time in my life. I get what Channing meant now about stability in the truth. It was like the blind leading the blind with me trying to rely on myself to take care of him, instead of looking to God. I'm trying to talk to God often and live by his standards. I feel so much gratitude when I realize how Channing paved the way for me."

"A beautiful way to remember your friend," the priest spoke gently. "The peace and stability you are discovering because of Channing's nudges are real, and they lead to God himself."

"Something bothers me, though." Dallas sighed. "I have this fear of Channing's memory fading, like I'm leaving him behind. I've started writing down memories to cement him in my mind. I realize it's an improvement that I don't constantly cry, or lash out all the time, and yet it feels *wrong* somehow. My pain over him is different lately. Sometimes I'm shocked how it almost feels like it happened to somebody else, and I'm removed from it, on the outside and looking in."

"Grief has a progression," the priest answered. "It is still there, and the intensity likely will return, but it does gradually get to be a more distant grief. It is also normal to be afraid to move in that direction. You don't want to dishonor a person by thinking you aren't grieving enough."

Dallas nodded. "Channing was worth a lifetime of raw pain. I'm not saying everything's easy and pleasant now—I mean, come on, I'm still locked up in here with very little control over my life—but it's like an ache now instead of a punch to the gut. I feel guilty for not crying naturally over him as often. I thought it was my burden to bear, my perpetual punishment, to feel despair forever, every waking moment, as a way to make it up to him. You know, something to 'offer up' for him and for my own sins."

"God doesn't want us to remain in constant despair," Father Benedict said. "You will have more pains throughout life to offer up. Your sadness for Channing may come and go in the future. You will always miss him and have regrets, but you are learning to live alongside those, like an open wound becoming a scar over time. And you have been trying to put others ahead of yourself, yes?"

Dallas nodded.

"Focusing on other people can change our grief, too," Father Benedict murmured. "It is not that you are thinking less of Channing—just that you are thinking less of *yourself*. When you think more of the people around you and extend the same compassion for them that you had for your best friend, then naturally, you focus less on your misery. Dallas, you have a real natural leadership inside of you, a quiet but strong presence that is becoming more refined. Have you noticed it? I think it has always been there—it showed itself in its underdeveloped but fierce way with how you felt for Channing—but in what you've told me about your recent interactions with others, it seems to be growing."

"I'm not the leader type, really," Dallas said modestly. "I'm pretty introverted." He picked at a hangnail on his thumb as he spoke.

"That makes you a good listener," Father Benedict said. "There is a calm strength about you in these last several months, and from the way some of the other inmates have sought you out to talk, they are sensing it too. People are drawn to truth naturally, but even more so to your quiet way of presenting it. Your brief but encouraging words to fellow inmates, your subtle deferment to others to go ahead of you, the way you respond in kindness even to the hateful actions of others - those things *do* something, Dallas. They show something true to other people. They express what Channing saw in you all along..."

A strange numb sensation crept over Dallas, and he knew what the old priest was going to say. He held his breath and closed his eyes, waiting for the words, words that had saved him from destroying himself.

"Your humble actions, your way of quietly serving others — these things teach people so much about God." Those words were already ringing in Dallas's ears, the observation straight out of Channing's mouth on his last night alive. Tears formed in Dallas's eyes. *I'm not worthy of this.* It was never his intention to teach anyone about God — *I'm far too messed up and ignorant to be able to do that.* That had been especially so when Channing had said it. That was when Dallas didn't even think there *was* a God. *And yet, Channing recognized truth merely by how I treated him. God had written it into my very life, without me recognizing it.* He took an awe-filled breath and opened his eyes.

"So, God's had a plan for me," Dallas said slowly, "for my life, this whole time, when I was just trying to do the right thing for Channing, in my impulsive and completely confused way... and even in prison, deciding to focus on the humanity of these other lost guys around me, while I was lost myself. God is in everything, using our unintentional actions to impact other people. I wish..." Dallas choked out the next words. "I wish I could've told Channing how much *he* taught *me* about God. Imagine that—he learned about God from an unbelieving me, and I learned about God from him without realizing it at the time. It's crazy! I thought he might've had a religious calling. I wish he'd been alive to see me realize that the love of God is what I was really searching for. I can finally just... *breathe.*"

Father smiled. "The sadness of missing Channing and the joy in the gift of faith he gave you are all intertwined now."

Dallas nodded and wiped his nose with the back of his hand, trying to stop the tears. "I'm confused, but I'm grounded at the same time. I feel kind of... scared, nervous, but also that the Catholic Church contains the fullness of God's truth. Maybe it's another paradox or something, all I'm feeling inside."

"Why do you think you feel nervous?" probed Father Benedict.

Dallas looked away, a flush rising in his cheeks. *John said it outright, and is Father Benedict hinting at it with his comments about me quietly showing God to others?* Was the priest Dallas was following in his dream... *himself?*

These ideas are nuts! Dallas argued inside. *It's gotta be my pride talking— I'm not worthy to be a* priest! *Me, a felon! But could it be? All this time thinking it was supposed to be Channing... could it really be* me *the Holy Spirit is calling?* Dallas squinted, trying to picture the outline of the priest from his dream.

"What is it, Dallas?" asked Father Benedict again.

"I think I'm just having some prideful thoughts," Dallas replied, shaking himself. "I don't need to dwell on them. I'm just overwhelmed with emotions about lots of stuff. I, um… I'm really feeling good about working towards becoming Catholic," he finished lamely.

Father Benedict flashed a grin, a mischievous glint in his eyes.

Dallas furrowed his brow. *Does he know what I'm thinking?*

The priest said, "Just think and pray on what I said about the strength of your quiet leadership, my son. I wonder what God may want to reveal to you in all this."

Mixed-up thoughts swirled through Dallas, nauseating him as he walked back towards the cell block. It was almost dinner time, but he had to calm down his mind first. His thoughts raced through all kinds of extremes. *I feel so sure yet so confused.* Was Father Benedict seeing it in him too? Could he see another man's calling? Was it all a hallucination — grandiose, wishful thinking? *I could never measure up to having a true religious calling! Surely it'll go away if it isn't real.* Wishing the weight room was still open, Dallas returned to his cell and jogged in place.

The thoughts didn't go away — they only became more persistent. Dallas lay awake a long time each night, unable to settle into sleep. He recited the Memorare dozens of times, sometimes hundreds, before drowsiness finally overcame him. His mind was turned on constantly, like there was somebody else talking to him inside his brain. Dallas had learned how to pray the rosary and ran through it mentally during those sleepless nights. He argued with the voice in his head, tried to reason with it, tried begging it to leave him alone and find somebody better than him.

Dallas kept the invading idea at bay during daylight hours by keeping busy. He headed into the yard alongside Smith, a camaraderie growing between the men. Color had crept back into Dallas's skin to chase away his pale pallor.

Breathing in a gulp of fresh air, Dallas scanned the yard for the mockingbird, which had found a mate. He pulled some bread scraps from his pocket. Some of the other inmates laughed at him for wasting part of his meal, but many were fascinated at his friendship with a bird.

"Didn't hermits tame wild animals sometimes?" Smith joked as the bird approached Dallas's outstretched hand to take the offered bread.

"You really are The Hermit. So what's his name?"

"His name?" Dallas questioned. "I dunno; I haven't named it."

"It should have a name," Smith said decidedly. "Can I name him?"

"Sure, knock yourself out."

"Okay, his name's Andrew," Smith said. "Hey, Andrew, how's the chow today? Same ole, same ole, huh?"

Dallas had to smile to see this tough prisoner talking to a mockingbird. "You named him quick. Why Andrew?"

Smith gazed beyond the spiraling razor wire towards the horizon. "My brother's name," he mumbled.

Dallas grew quiet as he thought about their previous conversation.

"Hey." Smith looked up at Dallas. "Would you, um, pray for my brother for me?"

"I already have been." It was true. Dallas mentally listed Smith's missing brother when he went through his prayer intentions every night. "And you should pray for him yourself, if you haven't been."

Smith blushed and scuffed a shoe against the dirt. "Eh, I don't really know how..." He trailed off and then turned back to Dallas. "You just seem, like, *holy* or something. You're different than you used to be. It's hard to put it into words, but... you're a real man, Dallas."

Dallas. It was the first time somebody else in the penitentiary had addressed him by his first name.

"Anyway, I just figured maybe God listens to people like you," Smith went on, "because you're good to everybody, even that despicable prison wolf and his spineless cellie..."

"I think God hears all of us," Dallas interrupted, not wanting to think about Maddox and Miller. "We just don't realize it. I can't always feel it myself, to tell you the truth. I still have doubts that creep in. But I just have to believe that God is there."

"Know what?" Smith asked. "Some days I get scared thinkin' of my release. Like, what will I *do* with myself? Where will I go, and who'll hire me? I don't know, man. I wish I had just a little bit of your calm trust, and that I felt like if I prayed, it would help."

Dallas had those same fears. He tried to ignore them, but an uncertain future loomed ahead of him as well. *The priesthood...* The vision of the priest from his dream, standing in front of an enormous stained-glass window, elevating a golden chalice in his hands before dropping to his knees... *I'm not even a baptized Catholic yet,* he chided himself, as if it were some forbidden fantasy he'd been reveling in. *But I know for sure that priest in the dream isn't Channing now. He even has my silhouette…* Dallas blinked his eyes to shoo the vision away, then turned to face Smith. "I know what you mean. I don't know what I'll do, either. We've just gotta hang in there and trust that things will work out for us."

"Well, Hermit," Smith said offhandedly, "we all know you're gonna go become a *real* hermit when you get out, right? Like, a monk or something. Except you shouldn't because then you'd be all hidden away in some mountain cave."

Dallas was amused despite the uneasy prompting he was getting from all these signs of his imagined vocation. "What'd be wrong with me hiding alone in a cave? Sounds kinda nice. A retreat away from the whole world, the peace and quiet, being your own man completely…"

Smith stepped closer to Dallas, his mouth in a thin line. "What would be wrong with that?" he repeated. "Malone, you've got a real gift with other people, and *everybody's* noticing it. You're like a connection between God and some of us guys in here. It'd just be a shame to let it go to waste, is all." He watched Dallas for his response.

Dallas had none. He was outside himself looking in again. Only a light breeze rippled across the flat terrain, yet somehow it sounded like he was in a wind tunnel. He stared back at Smith, speechless.

"I really appreciate you praying for Andrew," Smith added. "If he ever comes back home, after we're outta here, I'm gonna have to look you up and introduce him to you. He would like you, Dallas."

Smith turned and walked away.

Dallas stood, taking in the sound of his own name again.

Alone in his cell that evening, Dallas paced. "Okay, God, what is all this?" he asked into the air. "Level with me. What do you really want from me? I *can't* become a priest. Maybe a monk, but too many people depend on priests. To know the right things to say, to be a shepherd to people… to take the place of Jesus here on earth! I could *never* be as good as Father Benedict. I mean, some days, I barely understand it all, but I know somehow I firmly *believe.* But who would let an ex-con become a priest anyway?" Dallas froze, then fell to his knees and sat back on his heels. He begged for an answer to come in the stillness but heard nothing. Dallas heaved a sigh and stood back up. He tried again.

"Channing?" he said softly. "Can you hear me? Can you ask God what I'm supposed to do? I don't wanna put myself up on a pedestal or anything. You knew all my flaws." Tears welled in Dallas's eyes, and he blinked them back. "Am I making all this up in my head?" he whispered desperately. "I can't discern if this is real or not. Channing, is it God talking to me? Or am I just going nuts in here? I wish you were still here so I could really talk to you. You'd know what I should do. You were closer to God then than I am now." Dallas gripped his prayer card tightly in his hand.

Tell Father Benedict.

Dallas had been resisting this. He gritted his teeth.

Tell him.

"Channing?" Dallas asked again, eyes glancing up. "Should I tell him? Is that you? Or is it God? Or am I inventing all this myself?"

Dallas climbed into bed early. He tossed and turned, then finally gave in. *Okay, okay. I'll talk to Father Benedict.* Satisfied with his submission, Dallas's brain allowed him to sleep.

"Father, could God call an ex-con to the priesthood?" Dallas spit out his question as soon as he sat down, thrusting it at Father Benedict like a hot potato. His eyes were in his lap. *What a way to start our monthly meeting,* Dallas groaned inwardly.

Silence filled the room, all but the clicking of the wall clock. "Of course, he could, if he desired that man to become a priest," Father Benedict replied slowly. "God can do anything. Your question might more accurately be: would a former convict be allowed to become a Catholic priest? Is that what you are asking?"

"I guess so," responded Dallas. He still couldn't make eye contact, fidgeting with his fingers in his lap. "I'm embarrassed to tell you this, but it's just that I keep having these crazy thoughts, and dreams, and even these weird encounters with some of the other guys in here. I'm probably just making it all up, exaggerating it."

"Well, perhaps, although you couldn't be making up the encounters with other people. Do you mean how some of the other men have come to you for advice lately?"

Dallas nodded. "One of them said he thinks I'll become a monk, except that I shouldn't hide away like that because I could do more good by helping people connect with God. I don't know what makes him think that; I could help people in other little ways, surely. But since I had already had the thought – like, a *persistent* thought bugging me, almost like a fire inside me – well, it's strange that this guy brought it up. And my cellmate, he made a priest comment too…" Dallas threw a helpless glance across the table.

Silence followed for a few moments, and then Dallas spoke again. "I've been dreaming vividly about it for months, sometimes every night for a week straight at a time. But I'm not good enough to be called to something so sacred. I mean, I'm not even Catholic yet! If I really think I have a calling to the priesthood, then am I just making more of myself than I really am? Somebody who's done the things I have... I wouldn't even be allowed to become a priest after I'm out of here, right? So why am I being harassed by this dream and these thoughts?"

Father Benedict smiled. "So have you been thinking about what I said, about your calm, strong leadership that has emerged over the nearly three years of your being here?"

"I've been thinking about it nonstop!" Dallas scowled. "About what it means for my future. Maybe I can just help people know God through doing prison ministry. Surely God can't mean for me to be a *priest*, right? It's my ego making me even consider that, right, Father? God could never choose me as worthy of being... well, like you."

"God has called some unlikely men to the priesthood before," Father Benedict replied. "St. Augustine led a terrible life before his conversion, but he even became a bishop. And St. Ambrose was made bishop within a week of being baptized and ordained a priest! The people felt so strongly about him being their bishop that it was viewed as God's will."

"But they didn't kill anyone," Dallas argued. "*I* did."

Father Benedict said nothing for a moment, just stared. Finally, he spoke. "Dallas, what do *you* think God is telling you? Really, deep in your heart?"

Dallas threw up his hands. "I don't know! I'm so new at all of this anyway. How do I know if it's something from God?"

"Tell me this," the priest asked. "Do you *want* it to be real? Do you want to become a priest?"

Dallas's emphatic gut reaction jumped out of his mouth ahead of his thoughts. "No, not really! I mean, I don't *want* it, like for my own personal desire. I'd much rather *not* have that kind of responsibility. I'd rather go off quietly and pray by myself and have a peaceful relationship with God. And that's what I've been trying to do, but it's almost like... well, if it *is* God doing this, it's like he's *pestering* me! It's unrelenting! I feel like I'm avoiding something, trying to hide. And I can kinda do that for now, in prison. But before too long, I'll lose the safety of these walls. Weird for me to say 'safety,' huh? As long as I'm in here, I don't have to make a choice about what to do with my life beyond trying to be a good person and to follow God. I've got this internal pressure to take on more responsibility once I'm released. And that's…" Dallas trailed off.

"Scary?" asked Father Benedict.

"Exactly." Dallas gulped. "I'm… afraid. Afraid of making the wrong decision, but even more afraid about always having to put other people ahead of myself. I guess I want to be a little selfish with my life. To think I might be called to minister to other people, all the time… I mean, in here, there's no escape. I don't mind helping these guys when they need somebody to listen, because I have nothing else to do. If I feel like I want to be guarded with my time once I'm free, well, priests aren't supposed to be selfish, so maybe I'm not called to be a priest?"

"Maybe you aren't," the older man mused, "but then again, maybe you are. God asks us to do uncomfortable things, to give more of ourselves than we naturally want to do. The question for you is whether this is the thing he wants you to do with your life. And it is okay to have doubts, Dallas! It's normal! You don't have to know for certain right now. The important thing is to be open to this, to see if it is truly a call. Simply pray, 'Lord, I am open to your will. Help me know what you desire of me.' You have time. Things will become clearer for you after you've been out of prison for a bit, too. You have, how long, another year still to serve your term?"

"Yeah," Dallas replied. "Another year and a few months, minus whatever good time I earn. But I'm eligible for parole in a few months, at the three-year mark. Doubt they'll let me out early, though."

"And after your release, you would still need a bachelor's degree plus another four years of studies to prepare you for the priesthood. So, why not take the pressure off yourself for now? Focus on becoming Catholic first. You are joining the universal Church, Dallas! That's a huge thing! Let's get you there first."

Dallas nodded, and his heart clenched.

"I'm not trying to discourage you from considering the priesthood," Father Benedict continued, "not in the least! And I am not at all shocked by it. Sit with the idea, keep it in mind, as you complete your sentence, as you move into life after your release. You will see over the next few years where God wants to lead you. This could be a true call, a beautiful and holy vocation to the priesthood, and if it is, it will not go away after you become Catholic. It will gradually grow within you, to where you cannot ignore it. How long has this inkling been within you?"

"A few months. I guess that sounds silly now," Dallas said. "Such a short time, and I'm acting like it's been this huge unrelenting thing."

"Well, it has been unrelenting for these few months, has it not?" asked Father Benedict. "It has probably felt very urgent for you."

"Yeah, it has," Dallas said, "but what's a few months?"

"A few months could be a passing feeling, or it could be a powerful flame igniting a call for your future."

"Sounds like the potential for a romantic relationship," Dallas reflected.

Father Benedict chuckled. "That's very insightful of you. Becoming a priest is similar to making a commitment to a spouse. You are dedicating your life to someone, not just on this earth as you would in marriage to a woman, but for all eternity. So you want to be sure of it. Time will help you with this, Dallas, and down the road, if you still feel like God is pestering you — because he will if it is what he wants! — then I will be here to support you. Your crime does not automatically disqualify you for the priesthood, so don't waste your worries over that. There are all kinds of things that would be considered, such as your growth since the commission of the crime and your intent at the time. But let's not get ahead of ourselves. I have some fantastic news for you!"

"What's that?" Dallas looked up.

"I have received permission from the bishop of this diocese to allow you to begin accessing the sacraments of the Church," the priest said, his expression warm. "You may receive the sacraments of initiation next month and become a member of Christ's Church, if you are ready. I believe you are."

Dallas was floating on air. He wasn't expecting this yet.

"I have no further materials to give to you," Father Benedict continued. "We have discussed all the important points. I want to make sure you have any other questions answered today, so you are prepared, and next month, you may be baptized and confirmed, and you may receive the Eucharist for the first time."

"I... I'm stunned!" Dallas said. "You mean I can become Catholic while I'm serving my term? I don't have to wait 'til my release?"

Father Benedict smiled. "Dallas, I meant it when I said you are wise beyond your years. You have grown so much, learned so much. With God's help, you are fighting to master your foolhardiness and unhealthy passions. You show a deep, intuitive understanding of the faith and a strong desire to follow Christ as a member of his holy Church. I believe you are prepared, if you are ready to make the commitment."

Tears of joy welled up behind Dallas's eyes. "Yes," he said softly, "I'm certain of this. Becoming Catholic is everything to me, committing myself to God through the Church he left us."

"I will speak to the warden about arranging it," the priest promised.

"Thank you, Father," Dallas whispered. "I want this so much. I've been on a path of restlessness all my life. 'All roads lead to Rome...' and I finally found the road!"

"You have true direction now." Father Benedict smiled. "So, I will get all the details set with the bishop and will let you know the date."

"I'm in awe that I'm going to be able to participate in the Mass." Dallas trembled. "And receive the Eucharist!"

"I earnestly look forward to your coming to Mass with me in the basilica in Denver sometime after your release," Father Benedict said, "full circle from the day I met you there."

Dallas tingled head to toe with warmth. "Absolutely," he said with a smile. "I guess I still need to decide where I'm gonna live once I'm out. I need to focus on that before being concerned over whether I'm being called to anything big, huh?"

"God will make all clear to you in time." The priest smiled. "Pray for his guidance. Think ahead a year from now. Do you know who will come pick you up at your release?"

Dallas chewed his lower lip. "That's something I hadn't thought of at all. I don't even know. I mean, I guess I should've made a few more friends or something." Dallas felt his ears growing warm.

"Would you want to try to locate your mother?" the priest asked quietly. "Would she come to pick you up?"

Dallas hesitated. "I don't know how I'd even find her. She was distant, secretive, and as soon as I could fend for myself, she would go days without coming home. She left me food or cash, and I'd get myself to school – I was on my own a lot. We drifted further apart as the years passed. We just... didn't have much of a relationship. When she disappeared, it sounded like maybe she was mixed up in something bad. She made it clear that I was old enough to take responsibility for myself." An empty ache stirred inside Dallas. "And she didn't plan to come back."

"If you would like me to try to find her, I will," the priest offered.

"No, no, please don't," Dallas said quickly. "I don't think she wants to be found. She might not even be capable of coming to get me — she was in bad shape financially. She wanted me to be independent, so I wouldn't want to burden her, anyway. I really have nobody... nobody else to fall back on."

"You do have someone," Father Benedict said. "I will come get you if you'd like, Dallas, when you are released."

Dallas gazed into the kind face. "You would do that for me?" he asked in a small voice. "I really am alone, so... I *need* you, Father. You've meant so much to me and have been such a good example. But I don't want to take advantage of you."

"You wouldn't be," the priest said. "I would be honored to be the one to pick you up on that joyous day."

"Thank you so much," Dallas replied, relief coursing through him. "I promise I won't be all needy and rely on you for everything," he added. "I'm going to get a job and be responsible for myself. I gotta start a new life while I'm figuring out what God wants of me."

The priest smiled. "I have confidence that you will be able to do just that. It will take some time, but you will find your way. And I am happy to provide support when you need it."

"Well, how else do I need to prepare myself before next month?"

"You can choose a confirmation saint," replied the priest.

"Done," said Dallas, leaning back in his chair. "St. Cyprian of Carthage."

"Ah, yes. You were touched by his words. An excellent choice," Father Benedict said.

"I know a little about him from the book of saints you left with me," Dallas said. "I'd like to learn more about him and other early Christians, those who risked their lives for their faith. But, yeah, that quote of his jumped out, lit a fire under me, like it had been spoken to me at that precise moment of darkness."

"And he was an adult convert, just like you," Father Benedict added.

Dallas nodded, shaking off the internal shivers. *Adult... is that what I am now?*

A few days later at breakfast, Pedro approached Dallas's table. Assuming he was coming to ask for his bacon—everyone quickly took advantage of the fact that he'd given up meat entirely for Lent—Dallas held it out.

Instead, Pedro asked, "Is it true that the Catholic bishop is coming to say Mass and baptize you?"

"That's right," Dallas answered, relinquishing the bacon to Pulaski, who snatched it with a smirk as he strode by.

"Do you think I could come to the Mass?" Pedro asked. "See, I was baptized Catholic and made my first Communion, but then my family fell away, my parents got divorced, and I haven't ever gone back. I should probably go to confession sometime before receiving the Eucharist. But I would like to just go to Mass again. It's been so long..."

The genuine ache in the request stirred Dallas's heart. *Maybe Pedro's time here has urged him to look for meaning, too. Maybe this is a step back onto the path for another lost soul.*

"Definitely," Dallas responded. "I'd be glad to have you there. It's not just about me. It's scheduled for the Saturday after Easter. I didn't even realize you were Catholic. I thought nobody in here was."

"Thank you," Pedro said. "The only other Catholic I know of is one of the COs."

Murphy... I'll invite him, too.

Dallas cleared his tray from the table. Rather than becoming more nervous as the day approached, a peace had enfolded him—the knowledge of making the right decision and that God was real. He passed Maddox and Miller on his way to the door, subconsciously cushioned from their taunts. Hands in pockets as he trudged down the hall, his only sorrow was that Channing was missing. Dallas would complete the journey without his best friend by his side, the one he'd helped to become a Catholic in his final moments of life. *Another paradox — that I was the one to have baptized him! Me, in my depraved, sinful, impulsive state.* Dallas swallowed a lump in his throat. *I'll always be so grateful to Channing. I owe him so much. And he's already completed this journey, God willing. I'm only beginning.*

CLEANSED

Dallas arose on Saturday at the end of Easter week. Tingling with anticipation of what was going to happen to him this evening, he showered, shaved, and put on a clean prison uniform. He ate a light breakfast and planned to spend the rest of the morning in silence to prepare his heart, mind, and soul for his first Mass.

He jotted in his journal, putting thoughts to paper on how mercy was working in his life on this vigil of Divine Mercy Sunday, when John got his attention. "Malone," he said for the third time. "Hey, you in there?" The flow of ink across paper paused, and Dallas lifted his chin. John grinned. "Sorry to interrupt. I've thought about it, and yeah, I'd like to be there for you today."

Dallas's heart warmed. "Thanks. That means a lot to me, man. You know, I might not be here, making this move in my life, if it weren't for you."

"You wouldn't have done it," John said with a wave of his hand. "You'd have chickened out."

Dallas wasn't so sure. He didn't even want to think about his suicide attempt two and a half years earlier.

"So I've never been to a Catholic church service before," John said. "What should I know before I go in there, so I don't look stupid?"

"I've never been to a Catholic Mass myself," Dallas replied, "but I'll tell you what I know. There are verbal responses, but if you don't know them, it's okay to just listen. You sit, stand, and kneel at certain times, although we won't have any kneelers. I guess I'll just kneel on the floor." Dallas screwed up his face, trying to picture what it would be like. "You just follow along with the sitting and standing. And only Catholics receive communion."

"Why's that?" John asked. "I grew up in a Baptist church, and when they had communion — the Lord's Supper, they called it — everybody could have it."

"It's different for Catholics," Dallas explained. "Catholics believe the bread and wine actually become Jesus's very body and blood. It's not just a symbol or a remembrance. He's truly physically present in the Eucharist in the bread and wine."

John squinted. "Where did Catholics get that idea?"

"From the Bible," Dallas said, "in the Gospel you're named after. It's in chapter six if you ever wanna read it." Dallas turned back to his writing.

He didn't want to get into a theological debate with a friend.

John shrugged. "Okay, maybe I will, sometime."

In the yard after lunch, Dallas glanced towards the door. *Almost time to go in, and then…* His gaze returned to his open Bible. Dallas flipped pages until he found the verses Channing had read aloud to him that last day in their yard by the fire: *Psalm 118.* As Dallas read it over and over, the meaning seeped in from the words that had effortlessly hit Channing as so relevant and important. "Give me understanding, and I shall live," Dallas whispered with a shiver.

Smith watched out for Maddox and Miller all day as an unrequested favor. "I'm not gonna let those punks spoil your big day," he'd said firmly. Dallas appreciated the gesture. Smith would attend the Mass, too, along with Pedro, John, Gaines, and Murphy.

It was time. Dallas and the other four inmates were escorted down the hall by Murphy and another officer.

Father Benedict stood at the doorway. He gave Dallas a beaming smile, then took Pedro aside to hear his confession before everyone entered the room.

Dallas shook hands with the bishop, who told him Father Benedict had nothing but good things to say about him. Dallas felt the warmth of a blush on his cheeks.

"Father Benedict is a wonderful servant of God," the bishop added, "and I'm so grateful for his ministry to you here."

"He is an amazing priest," Dallas said sincerely. "He's helped me to find a great gift through the Church: the truth of God."

They took their seats in the bare room-turned-sanctuary. Father Benedict rose to concelebrate the Mass with the bishop. A portable baptismal font stood before a simple table covered with a white altar cloth.

The Mass began. The now-familiar words were a balm to Dallas's soul. He slipped into the reassuring rhythm of participating in the prayers and responses, his months of practice aiding him, as naturally as if he'd been doing it his whole life. Pedro, seated right behind him, murmured responses in Spanish. *It must just stick with you,* Dallas mused.

Even in the absence of a real church building, the lack of music, and the presence of the guards, God was there. For once, Dallas had no sense of his being an awkward outsider among a group. He was a part, welcome, whole. *This is all so very right.* Dallas gazed at the small gold crucifix on the makeshift altar. *I am loved. God became man like us and died to save the world from sin. I'm about to be forgiven.* The words breathed inside Dallas, finally. *God forgives and accepts and loves me.*

Father Benedict stood to give the homily.

"God has one deep desire, and that is to pursue each and every one of us, to draw us into closer relationship with him. We are his children, his creation. He is the loving Father who forgives us of any wrongdoing, if only we acknowledge and confess our sin by asking God's pardon. All mankind wrestles with suffering and sin, and the Church offers us a way to hand all that over to the One who is more powerful than all — to a God so big and so powerful that he can take on our sins, no matter how terrible, and wash us clean again. This is precisely what baptism is about to do for Dallas — to rid him of all sin of his past life, to make him a new creation. Now, baptism isn't a magic trick done to us by God that frees us from all earthly struggles — life will still bring its challenges in its imperfection. There is a need to keep returning to God after slipping back into sinfulness, because he is always waiting with open arms for us to come back to him in confession. Speak to God often, know he is your friend and your savior for eternity. This prison environment reminds us more than any place on earth that this world is not our true home, only a temporary place on the path to our home forever in heaven. St. Augustine rightly said, 'Our hearts are restless, O God, until they rest in you.' Dallas, you are accepting God's rest today to fill that longing in your restless heart. You are about to begin your new life."

Dallas stepped forward. His hand subconsciously went to his pocket to touch the worn Memorare prayer card tucked inside. *I hope you can see this, Channing. Thank you! Thank you so much.*

Dallas barely heard the words as they seemed to float to him. The bishop asked Father Benedict questions. A white taper flickered, held by Dallas's mentor priest. The tiny flame mesmerized Dallas. Suddenly the words rang clearly in his ears.

"Do you reject Satan?"

"I do." Dallas's response came without hesitation.

"And all his works?"

"I do."

"And all his empty promises?"

"I do."

After making his baptismal promises, Dallas leaned forward over the font. Reflecting up at him from the shallow pool was Channing in mirage, water streaming down his wavy locks from Dallas's hand, his frantic face transformed to peace in an instant at his baptism. The first cool stream of water flowed over Dallas's forehead, drops scattering the image in the font.

"I baptize you in the name of the Father…"

More water pouring, running water, trickling from Dallas's eyebrows…

"And of the Son…"

A third stream of water from the shell-shaped scoop in the bishop's hand…

"And of the Holy Spirit."

Dallas opened his eyes and lifted his head. His wet hair above his forehead stuck up slightly, and the bishop dabbed a towel on his head. Father Benedict's face glowed in the brightly burning flame of the candle held aloft, and Dallas pictured Channing by the fire pit, flames flickering as he read aloud from the Bible while the bishop's words filled him: "You have been enlightened by Christ. Walk always as a child of the light and keep the flame of faith alive in your heart." Time froze for a moment, and then it passed too soon as the candle was extinguished. He returned to his seat. A couple of the guys behind him clapped him on the shoulders in congratulations.

I'm forgiven! The warm knowledge washed over Dallas, inside him, surrounding him. *God forgives me! Even when I know I don't deserve it, he forgives me. Even when I can't forgive myself, he still forgives me.*

Dallas approached the bishop again and was anointed with the sweet-smelling chrism oil, and, using his chosen saint name, the bishop said, "Cyprian, be sealed with the gift of the Holy Spirit." Dallas, fully initiated into the Catholic Church, was sacramentally joined with all others who had received these very same sacraments from the hands of the successors of the apostles, the earliest followers of Christ. He was suddenly reminded of Channing waxing poetical about being united to all other coffee drinkers throughout history, and Dallas smiled with damp eyes. That had been a simplistic foreshadowing of something far greater — *the greatest thing on earth, Christ uniting his creation with him through baptism in his Church and nourishing us with the Eucharist.* Dallas quivered in anticipation of his first reception of the Word made Flesh.

As the Liturgy of the Eucharist began, Dallas dropped to his knees on the concrete floor. Silently, the other four inmates and the officer did the same behind him. *This is the moment when God himself willingly comes down to earth, bridging the space between here and heaven.* That God would enter a filthy prison, a holding pen for the worst of sinners, and choose to be with his people humbled Dallas to breathlessness. Trembling, he couldn't take his eyes from the priest and bishop standing behind the altar, the simple bread and wine about to be transformed through the power given them by God, Christ's sacrifice made present again. As the bishop picked up the host, Dallas could feel his own fingertips quivering.

Words were spoken, the host was elevated, all heads bowed. *I'm clean and pure, totally ready to receive the Eucharist for the very first time.* The words of the bishop flowed, familiar yet new, and the responses rolled off Dallas's tongue. The order of the Mass had already become a part of him.

Father Benedict beckoned Dallas, and he rose, tingles running up and down his spine, drawn forward, barely aware of Pedro beside him approaching the bishop. Dallas dropped to his knees before Christ in the Eucharist, invisible weights pulling him down. He gazed up at his mentor priest. Tears trickled down Father Benedict's cheeks as he held the Eucharist aloft before Dallas and said the words, "The Body of Christ."

"Amen," Dallas whispered with reverence, and then he received the Eucharist. He rose and stepped back to his seat and knelt once again on the floor. Silent sobs shook his shoulders. *I'm home, really home! God has forgiven me; God has come to me in the simple form of bread.* Dallas cried, a mixture of warmth welling up in him combined with the fact that Channing couldn't have come with him. *But he's already home, if God wills it. He went ahead of me. Channing led this time.* Dallas bowed his head low and prayed fervently for Channing's soul.

A small reception followed the Mass, and the men remained in the room for the next half-hour to enjoy sub sandwiches, chips, and drinks. Father Benedict had even stopped at a grocery store bakery and bought a cake. Murphy stepped over and congratulated Dallas.

"I can never thank you enough," Dallas said to the correctional officer as he withdrew Channing's holy card from his pocket, "for not taking this prayer card away from me permanently that day when we got into a fight over it."

Smith joined them.

"Hudson definitely thought we should have," Murphy admitted. "I couldn't throw away a sacramental, of course. And I don't like putting guys in the hole. I know what it can do emotionally. I knew you being in there just thinking you'd lost it would be punishment enough and then some. Hudson's not happy until he breaks somebody down completely. And maybe some guys need that to turn a corner in here; I don't know. But I can see, and I've known since you were first incarcerated, that you don't wanna start up trouble and hurt people just out of meanness. If that card led you to finding faith in God, then I'm even more convinced it was the right thing to give it back to you."

"And I can finally pay Smith back," Dallas teased, "by getting him a change of scenery and some cake today." Dallas nudged him with his elbow playfully.

"Are you kidding?" Smith said. "This sandwich from Subway is the payback for me. I haven't had one of these in ages. It tastes like a million bucks. Never would have thought we'd be here like this 'bout two years ago, huh?"

Dallas grinned.

Finally, the room was empty except for Dallas and Father Benedict.

"I got you a little something, Dallas." Father Benedict held out a book of the complete writings of St. Cyprian plus a small box.

Dallas removed the lid and lifted out a silver crucifix on a chain and two saint medals: St. Cyprian and St. Francis of Assisi.

"I checked on the protocol on jewelry," the priest said.

Dallas's hand subconsciously felt for his missing earring. "Thank you," he said, holding up the crucifix by its sturdy chain. "We're allowed to wear small cross necklaces in here, but no more."

"That's what I learned," Father Benedict replied. "So I'll hold on to the saint medals until your release, but if you'd like, you may take the crucifix now."

"Dallas ran a finger over the engraving on the medals. "St. Cyprian is obvious, but why St. Francis?"

"Because Channing had said he would choose Francis as his confirmation saint," Father Benedict said softly. "I suggested him because Channing had much in common with him—namely, that childlike trust and joy over simple things. I bought it," the priest's voice dropped low, "about a month after having spoken with him last. I hoped we would come in contact again so I could give it to him, and now, well… I have, in a way."

Dallas was speechless as he held up Channing's medal, glinting in the light. "I'll be honored to wear them all together when I get out of here," he murmured. He handed the medals back to Father Benedict and clasped the chain with the crucifix around his neck.

"Speaking of your getting out," the priest added, "you have a parole hearing coming up soon, yes?"

"Yeah, in about two months," Dallas replied.

"Let me know the date, and I will come speak on your behalf," offered Father Benedict.

"I'd appreciate that," Dallas said, "but I don't know how much of a chance I have. The judge specifically ruled that I couldn't get parole until I'd served three years. Most times, you're up for parole after a third of your sentence, except for really big things, and they take the death of law enforcement seriously. I may have blown my chances with my poor behavior in here the first year or two, anyway."

"Even more reason to have me attend," the priest said, "to describe how much you've grown in the nearly two years since I first started coming to see you. I'm so very happy for you, Dallas, that you have found truth, found God, and allowed his great gift of mercy to come into your life."

"Father, I don't know how to thank you," Dallas said, voice cracking, "for pulling all this off for me. I have hope. I have a new life! It all feels so right, and after losing Channing, I never thought I'd feel anything ever again."

The old priest smiled. "And remember our talks regarding feelings," he said. "It's wonderful how you feel right now, yet feelings can rise and fall. The important thing is riding out the falls because of the choice you made and the actions you engage in—*that* is what brings stability through life's inevitable ups and downs. *That* is how to be a real man, one who keeps his commitments."

"Lord, I do believe; help my unbelief," Dallas whispered with a smile.

Father Benedict returned the smile, gave Dallas a congratulatory hug, and bade him farewell for now. Dallas was escorted back down the hall, wearing his crucifix and chrism and feeling every bit a new man.

As they slid into their bunks that night, John commented on the events of the day. "Hey, man, I'm real glad you figured out God, got some peace for yourself. You sure aren't the same pitiful kid I yanked down off those bars more than two years ago. You'd really never been to church before today?"

"Nope," Dallas replied, "besides this vague memory of a funeral in a church, my mom's mother, I'm pretty sure, when I was really young."

"Today's sure was different than what I grew up with," remarked John. "I got baptized when I was eight or nine years old, and they dunked me all the way under the water — my whole body. But I s'pose it's the same God and all."

Dallas smiled secretly from the upper bunk. John believed in God, but he had a very casual way about it.

"I appreciate that you came today," Dallas said.

"It was interesting, with the candles and that holy oil," John said. "Dang, you smell good from that oil. I've been smellin' it all evening. I might just climb up there and sniff you all night."

"Weirdo," Dallas scoffed. "Try it, and you'll find your butt on the floor so fast you won't know what happened."

John laughed wildly from the bunk below. A CO passing by warned them to quiet down. *The smell* is *heavenly, though,* Dallas silently agreed. *I don't even want to take a shower and have it wash off. I'd love to smell it forever, for the rest of my life...* He drifted off to the comforting scent, running through the Memorare in his mind.

Maddox and Miller stood shoulder to shoulder, a blockade to Dallas's path to breakfast the next morning.

"Now, don't he smell like holiness itself?" Maddox jeered.

"He always gotta be better than everyone else," Miller said, wrinkling his nose.

Dallas sidestepped them and kept walking.

"You better look at us when we're talkin' to ya, Malone," Miller said from behind.

Dallas strode down the hallway, eyes pointed forward.

"Got yourself baptized, huh?" Maddox continued. He and Miller followed close on Dallas's heels. "What for, so you can go to heaven? Don't wanna go to hell and be with your dead buddy?"

Dallas jerked to a stop, fists clenched in his pockets, then forced his feet to go again. *Please, God, help me ignore them!*

Maddox took his slight pause as an opening and yanked Dallas's necklace from behind. "What's this? Magic charm that shows you're special?" The chain tugged at Dallas's throat, and he gagged before pulling free. *Don't fight them; don't fight them!* Another voice, deep and primal, urged him to knock them both to the ground and punch the crap out of them.

Dallas jogged to the cafeteria entrance, where a CO eyed Maddox and Miller at the door.

"Something going on here, fellas?"

Breathing a sigh of relief, Dallas slipped into the breakfast line. *Thank you.*

He sat down across from Smith and Pedro and gulped his lukewarm coffee. Pedro caught Dallas's flushed face and tight lips. "What happened?" he asked.

Dallas sighed. "Just the typical." He jerked his head over his shoulder towards where Maddox and Miller were slinking into the room with the officer closely following.

"They confronted me in the hall with their typical nasty talk," Dallas said. "CO saw Maddox grab my necklace. Not sure if he was planning to break it or to strangle me."

"Man, they're idiots." Smith shook his head. "I learned quick not to mess with you, Hermit. Sounds like they wanna get *real* messed up." He flashed a wicked grin at Dallas.

"I wanted to hit them," Dallas confessed, "but I'm trying to keep control of my temper. They know just how to push my buttons, though."

"Maybe they won't stop 'til you've had it out with them both, given Maddox a thrashing too. Miller's scared of you since you bashed his tooth out. That's why he clings like a wuss to his predator cellie. You gotta put Maddox in his place, so he knows for sure you'd kick his keister. He thinks he's tough stuff, but you'd pound him. No question. Speakin' from personal experience with your fists, that is," Smith finished with a jesting smile, rubbing the place on his jaw where the bruise Dallas had given him had lasted for weeks.

"Hey, I don't want to be reminded of that," Dallas said, his face getting hot. "I lose my cool way too easily, and I've been trying to be better. It's such a release and feels so good in the moment to just give in to the rage, but I can't live my life that way."

"But he may never leave you alone until you show him you're a hell of a lot stronger than you look," Smith continued, waving his toast around. "Apparently, he needs to learn firsthand, 'cause Miller's ugly toothless face don't seem to remind him."

Pedro set down his fork. "Don't fight him, Dallas," he said.

"It's not against you guys' religion to fight in self-defense, is it?" asked Smith incredulously.

"No," Dallas replied. "Still, better to avoid it when possible. If a group of them tried to check me or something, then yeah, I'd fight back to protect myself. They know that, but I don't wanna broadcast it like it's an invitation, you know?"

"Okay, we just gotta put ourselves between them and you, then," Smith decided. "What do ya say, Pedro?"

"Sure," Pedro replied. "We can make a buffer for him."

"Yep," Smith said, crossing his arms over his chest. "We're not gonna let them bother you, Malone."

Dallas gave a slight smile. He had friends here.

"I'm up for parole in a couple months," he mentioned. "Probably won't happen, with the two major fights I've been in since I've been incarcerated and the way I've pushed back against Hudson. I do have some good time built up, though. So even without getting parole, since I've been keeping myself under control lately, then I may be able to get out several months ahead of the four-year mark. I don't want to jeopardize that."

"You've been like a whole new person in the past year," Smith said. "You should get parole based on how huge a change has come over you."

"Eh, maybe." Dallas shrugged. "I'm still really a hothead at heart, but telling myself that every human being is created in the image of God has changed my perspective enough that I've at least kept my anger from bursting out as violence."

"Well, we're gonna make it where you won't have to get into confrontations with them if you don't want to," Smith pledged. "Don't walk around alone, okay? Make sure one of us, or John, is with you. Or that you're in sight of a CO at least – one who's actually a human being, that is, not Hudson. Now there's a creature not made in God's image."

Dallas knew what Smith meant and sighed. "Even him, man. I've been trying to see him that way. He was, but he's gotten corrupted. Fortunately, I haven't had trouble with him recently."

"Well, we got your back, Malone," Smith said with a pound of his fist on the table. "We'll watch out for Hudson, too." Pedro nodded, eyes serious.

Over the next several weeks, Dallas had the priest dream again. Some nights it woke him multiple times, over and over. He prayed to know what it meant, more and more certain that the man he saw each time was himself. He used simple, repeated words: *Show me what you want of me, God. Show me your will for my life.*

Despite the changes most of the inmates and correctional officers had noticed in Dallas, he tried not to get his hopes up about the upcoming parole hearing. *Do I even want to get out that soon?* Not having a firm plan in place for his life was frightening. He called Mitchell.

"I hired on this guy about a year ago, and he's been real steady," Mitchell explained. "So I hate to say it, but if you get out in a month, I doubt I'll have a position for you. Sucks, 'cause I would hire you in a second if I needed another guy. But, hey, if you don't get paroled, then once your release date gets close, check back with me again. Even if I still can't use you in the shop, you gotta come pick up your stuff, and it'll be great to see you again."

"Yeah, I'm looking forward to that. Thanks." Dallas tried to cover his hesitancy. He wondered how it would feel to walk back into his old life again—a life that had been drastically altered just moments before his arrest. *It won't be at all the same.* Dallas privately acknowledged that his fear of leaving prison went a lot deeper than not knowing where he'd work and live.

Dallas began searching the country in one of his old favorite ways: poring over road maps in an atlas from the library cart. He knew he wouldn't return to Nevada. Father Benedict had mentioned Denver, but Dallas's remaining self-respecting ego couldn't handle the idea of appearing dependent on the priest for support. He wondered how he'd even get himself to Minnesota to see Mitchell. *This place is making me helpless.* He scanned the Minnesota page vaguely, lips pursed. *I don't have to manage anything for myself in here, and suddenly, I'll be thrust back into real life, having to figure out how to do the basics as an adult.*

Dallas flipped the page in the atlas with a sigh. Maybe he would go south just a bit, into north Texas, near where he and Channing had initially fled following the robbery gone bad... Find an auto parts store or a mechanic shop that would hire him in a town in north Texas, find a cheap apartment to rent, and then...

Dallas closed his eyes. *Then, figure out if I have a vocation.* The call to the priesthood followed Dallas out of his dreams and into his consciousness at least a few times a day. When he tried his hardest to tune the thoughts out, that's when they assailed him even more relentlessly.

"Okay, God, I'll look into that at some point, I promise," Dallas prayed. "But I hafta get a job first, to make sure I can integrate back into society and take care of myself. Please help me do that first." He turned pages until he found Texas. With no other connections anywhere, it was as good a choice as any. Loneliness seeped into Dallas's heart, but he pushed it away quickly. *You'll be fine. You're a loner, remember?*

It was the morning of Dallas's parole hearing. Father Benedict had arrived the day before and heard Dallas's confession. He fell asleep renewed and lighthearted. But the dawning of the next day brought butterflies in Dallas's stomach. He was searched and escorted by armed officers to the back seat of a law enforcement vehicle, too nervous to enjoy the sensation of speeding down a highway for the first time in three years.

I probably won't be granted parole, and that's okay. Dallas walked down the hall of the unfamiliar correctional facility with two guards behind. *Maybe I shouldn't have pursued it — or did I even have a choice?* Dallas shrugged. He had practiced what to say and knew the parole board would ask uncomfortable questions. Father Benedict would be there as his allotted person to speak on his behalf. Mitchell had written a letter to the board in Dallas's support.

He entered the room, wrists shackled, head bowed. He kept his eyes on the floor, but the presence of Trooper Schmidt's widow filled the space. It was what Dallas had most feared confronting. *I only hope my remorse looks as genuine as it feels.*

The parole board sat at a table in front. One member addressed Dallas. "Please recount the crimes for which you were convicted and describe how you have bettered yourself during your incarceration."

"My first mistake was shoplifting," began Dallas in a low voice. "I should have gone to a homeless shelter when I had no place to live and no money, but I chose to steal instead. The third time, when I got caught, I found out just how wrong it was to run from the police and how bad things like that can backfire and end in tragedy. I should've stopped, shown Trooper Schmidt what was in my pockets, and taken whatever the consequences would've been. Instead, I ran, and I regret deeply that it led to a man's death. It happened just over three years ago, and everything has changed since that day. I was 19. I'll turn 23 in a couple of months now, and I never want to make such an impulsive decision again. If I had cooperated, there wouldn't have been any struggle, and the gun wouldn't have accidentally fired. I have deep remorse over what happened to Trooper Schmidt. If I hadn't shoplifted from the gas station and then struggled to escape, then Mrs. Schmidt's husband would still be living. I can never make that up to her, and I will always be sorry for my actions."

He couldn't look at the young widow. Tears burned Dallas's eyes, and he hung his head. *It doesn't matter that he shouldn't have had the gun out. I still should have obeyed him.*

"Mr. Malone," asked a member of the board, "what is your present opinion on the proper way to interact with authority figures?"

Images of Hudson's cruel face invaded Dallas's mind suddenly. His body trembled, and he gulped down the memories of being kicked in the face and side, pinned against the wall… *Think of Murphy as authority, not him!* Swallowing again, Dallas steadied his quavering insides with a firm voice. "Authority is always to be obeyed. It doesn't matter if I think I'm in the right—I'm supposed to cooperate with their orders. I've been trying to do that with the correctional officers and the warden, especially in the last two years. I'll admit that my first year in prison was like a blurry nightmare. I needed to be incarcerated as long as I have because it's given me time to think about the gravity of what I've done and to learn to cooperate with authority."

"Please tell us the rest of your offenses for which you were convicted."

Tears streamed down Dallas's cheeks now. "I ran from the police, across state lines. Then when I was tracked down, I ran away from my place of employment to avoid being arrested. I'll never stop regretting that. I should've turned myself in. As a stupid kid, I didn't see that my choices were getting me into worse trouble, and…" Dallas gulped. "And putting my best friend's life at risk. He died in the chase. A truck hit him, and…" Dallas glanced at Father Benedict seated across the room. The priest's head was bowed, lips murmuring silent prayers. "And if I had just let them arrest me, then he'd still be living today," Dallas blubbered. He stared at his lap and wiped his eyes with his sleeve. *Crying like this probably doesn't make a good impression on the board.*

"And you continued resisting arrest once the police had you handcuffed?" asked a member of the board, consulting some papers on the table before her.

Dallas nodded. "I did. I was distraught by seeing my friend's sudden violent death and went kinda nuts. I know the arresting officers deserved my respectful obedience, and they were good to me, truly. I deserved to be tased or knocked over the head, but they were firm while not being rough with me. I can see that now, and I should've stopped fighting them."

The board members exchanged glances and a few murmurs, and then the man at the end of the table addressed Dallas. "Mr. Malone, please tell us why you believe yourself to be ready to be admitted back into society."

Dallas kept his eyes down. *You're not ready,* came an admonishment inside him. *Will I ever be ready?* Dallas inhaled. "I won't ever deserve my freedom, but I believe my time in prison has been good for me. It's given me time to reflect on my mistakes, and I've gone from simply despising myself to gaining a true understanding of how wrong my actions were, and I despise those actions now. I used to think I could control everything, do whatever I thought was best regardless of the law or anything else. I've learned that I don't know everything. My time in prison has humbled me. I've been focusing on getting control of my impulses, especially in this past year. And I believe in God now and was baptized a few months ago. My punishment has led me to surrender my will to God. Since I've started to accept God in the last year, I've looked for him in others incarcerated alongside me, to forgive them and treat them as my neighbor, following Christ's example." Dallas fell silent, wondering if he'd spoken too long.

"But, Mr. Malone, the time prior to this past year, approximately the first two years of your sentence – you acknowledge you've had a few infractions?"

Dallas nodded and closed his eyes. The papers from his file, spread out on the table before the parole board, contained all those details. The incidents rang in his ears as the man read them out: A suicide attempt. Fistfights. A verbal threat to kill another inmate. Talking back to an officer. Slamming the door to his cell. Resisting COs while being escorted to solitary confinement. Throwing himself against the door screaming at COs while locked in solitary confinement. An assault that knocked out an inmate's tooth. Resisting handcuffing until having to be tased. Dallas's face reddened at the reading of his rap sheet, each black mark on his record echoing in the room. The board had every reason to consider him as violent, a threat, with the bruises and black eyes and missing tooth he had inflicted on others.

"I regret my responses to other inmates and to some of the officers," Dallas began. *Don't think of Hudson's unfair treatment of you!* He gritted his teeth behind closed lips. *This isn't the place to throw blame. They only want to see how I've improved myself.* "I haven't had any infractions in over a year now. I've learned that I can't overreact the way I had been at first. I've attended anger management classes and focused on getting control of my temper. I think it's paying off, and I'm learning to treat other people with respect. I regret responding to others with my fists. I'm so ashamed I knocked out another guy's tooth. That was an overreaction to his teasing on my part. You might have a record in my file there," Dallas continued with a motion of his hands, "about an incident in which a correctional officer was wrongly accusing me of something, how he was roughing me up and I didn't resist. Even though he was wrong, I was trying hard to respect his authority. I've also walked away from other inmates when they've taunted me instead of getting into fights with them."

A shuffling of papers and a pause. "Finally, Mr. Malone," the board continued, "please speak of your plans for the future. What will you do upon your release?"

Dallas cleared his throat. This part was going to be a hard sell. "I don't have a job lined up yet, but I want to seek employment as an assistant auto mechanic. I believe you have a letter from my last employer stating he would hire me back if he had an opening. I, uh, have a friend here with me today who's going to help me find a place to live and find a steady job when I get out, and... I want to be a productive member of society. I came into prison a kid, and I'll be leaving an adult, and I'm determined to act like one." Dallas sighed internally. *I sound so lame.*

"You have no family members with whom you could live starting out?" inquired a member of the board, peering over his glasses.

"N-no, sir," stammered Dallas. "My only relative was my mother, and she... I don't know where she is. She disappeared several months before my arrest."

The board thanked Dallas for his statement and called Father Benedict forward. "You have two minutes to describe to this board why you believe the felon ready for release on parole."

Just two minutes. He came all the way here for two measly minutes.

"Thank you for your time," began Father Benedict, as dignified as ever. "I first met Mr. Malone prior to the commission of his crimes, and I have gotten to know him well during the past two years while making visits to him in prison. The difference in this young man from then to now is like night and day. It is quite phenomenal. You have all the details of his offenses and the early days of his sentence, and you can see how much he has grown and matured in the past two years. I had the pleasure of welcoming him into the Catholic faith a couple months ago following many heartfelt discussions on his growing belief in God and his Church. Mr. Malone is a quick learner, a willing student in all that I have brought him to read, and his remorse contains a genuineness as informed by his newfound belief in God's love. He has held down a job in the cafeteria, and you can see in his file the amount of good time he's built up for his exemplary behavior since his last infraction. Other inmates have sought him out for advice and spiritual guidance of sorts, commenting on how different he is now as compared to when he began his sentence. I am committed to helping this young man make a fresh start upon his release. You can see from his last employer as well as his prison work experience that he has an excellent work ethic, willing to take on extra tasks, and his attitude with the staff has been a positive one overall. I am glad to vouch for him and the strides he has made towards reform. I believe he has shown an unlikeliness to engage in criminal behaviors in the future, as these have been one-time mistakes of immaturity that have been hard-learned but learned deeply nonetheless. Thank you."

Dallas shifted in his chair at hearing the priest's praise. *What a generous and holy man he is, And without Channing, I never would've met him.*

"Ms. Molly Schmidt, you may speak now."

Dallas's heart lurched in his chest. The trooper's widow had elected to address the board directly. Dallas had desperately wished she would have somebody else read her statement.

"Ladies and gentlemen of the board," she began with a hint of emotion masked by cool confidence, "I urge you to allow the convicted felon, Mr. Malone, to receive the full weight of his prison sentence by serving out the remainder of his term. My late husband, a young man committed to preserving the peace, had been a state trooper only eight months at the time of his death. We'd only been married just over a year. I lost my husband, and law enforcement lost a brave man who would have gone on to give many more years of service to the people of Oklahoma. His life was cut down by a reckless and irresponsible young adult—yes, *adult*, only three years younger than him. You heard that right—my husband was only 22 years old. The reckless actions of a nineteen-year-old homeless vagabond killed a responsible, employed 22-year-old. An entire lifetime with him is missing from my future now. The children we hoped to have will not exist. I will never be the same. His parents and siblings will never be the same. A piece of my life is gone, missing, never to be replaced. You have heard evidence here of Mr. Malone's impulsivity. You have accounts of numerous incidents of misconduct since he has been imprisoned. The lesson of deference to authority is often hard-won, and I propose that some young men need more severity than others to learn that lesson fully enough to be able to make appropriate responses to their anger and impulses. Mr. Malone was given a sentence of four years, and shortening that sentence by a fourth of its duration, as this parole board is considering, sends the wrong message to the people of Oklahoma. A sentence should mean something. The citizens of this state need a clear message of no tolerance for resisting arrest by law enforcement officials. Mr. Malone's insubordination to correctional officers on a few occasions and his aggressive responses to other inmates alone should make him ineligible for parole today. He has not demonstrated a clear, long-term ability to obey authority and control his temper, which is needed in a civilized society. So I implore you, please let justice be served for my husband and for all officials who have to handle impudent young criminals who pose a danger to them and all citizens by fleeing instead of cooperating." Her eyes welled up with tears.

Dallas made himself look at the woman's face as she spoke. His eyes overflowed. Hearing how she desperately missed her young husband nearly brought him to his knees. *I can't blame her at all for wanting me locked up permanently,* he derided himself. *I can never make it right, no matter how long I serve. I'm so, so sorry, and yet I can't fix it now; the consequences are what they are, for her husband and for Channing both.*

Molly Schmidt caught Dallas's gaze and locked her eyes with his. Her eyebrows lowered. An invisible power paralyzed Dallas, and he stared back into the face of a woman whose life he'd helped to ruin. His throat went dry, and his heart dropped into his gut. Nothing could wrench his eyes from her pain.

Molly pointed at him. "You killed my husband," she growled low, "and I can't ever forget that, ever!"

"Ms. Schmidt, please, I remind you to only address the board in your comments," the man at the end of the table spoke up as Dallas broke down crying.

"I'm so sorry for resisting!" sobbed Dallas, trapped in that shattered stare. "I'm so sorry your husband died! I don't deserve parole!"

"Mr. Malone, that applies to you as well," barked the board member. "You may not address the victim's next-of-kin directly."

Dallas nodded his compliance and ducked his head, ears burning with shame, heart thumping wildly. *She won't ever forgive me; she won't!* For the first time, Dallas's regret focused entirely on this tragedy, one equal in its gravity to the loss of Channing's life. The depth of the consequences of his actions cut Dallas down to the bone and laid him wide open and exposed for all his sin, all his depravity. *This is what Father Benedict meant. I know I'm forgiven by God, and I believe it, but the temporal effects of sin remain. Please, please Lord, take all my sufferings over this, let me offer them up for that poor woman, please Lord, please be with her, give her comfort, and never allow me to act so rashly again…*

The board's verbal recommendation was to deny Dallas parole. The official written decision that would come later was unlikely to be different, and Dallas blew out a sigh of ironic relief that he would probably be serving the rest of his term. He spoke briefly with Father Benedict on the way out.

"Thanks for being here, Father."

"Even if you aren't granted parole," the priest said, "I'll only see you a few more times before your release date, and isn't that a blessing to look forward to?"

The parole board had reminded Dallas that the credits he'd earned for good behavior while incarcerated had added up, leaving him with only four more months to serve if he continued to fly right and didn't lose any of this "good time." Dallas groaned inwardly, knowing he needed to make some decisions either way.

"Have you decided where you'd like to live after your release?" Father Benedict asked.

"Yeah, Texas," Dallas responded, deciding for certain at that moment. "North Texas. I'll have to choose a town, but I guess wherever I can get a job. I'm gonna set up a meeting with the reentry people. Supposedly, they can help me line up a job right before release, or at least get me some interviews scheduled. Gosh, I don't even know all I'm supposed to do. Like, my driver's license, for one thing. I'm sure it's expired by now, and it's a Nevada license anyway."

"I'll help you get yourself started," Father Benedict assured him. "North Texas is only two or three hours from here. Do you have some money in your account?"

"A few hundred bucks," Dallas answered. "And they give you some as you get released — 'gate money,' they call it — maybe another hundred dollars, from what I've heard other guys saying."

"You may have just enough to find yourself a place to rent," Father Benedict said. "Dallas, you know I will be glad to help you with all of this."

"I'm grateful to you," Dallas acknowledged. "I can admit I won't be able to get started all by myself." It was a humbling feeling.

The CO motioned that it was time to leave. Dallas had to walk past Trooper Schmidt's widow. He wanted desperately to apologize to her again, but he bit his tongue and kept the rules of the parole board. He bowed his head to avoid eye contact and mouthed a silent prayer for the repose of her husband's soul, squeezing back more tears.

Back in his cell that evening, Dallas tossed and turned. It had shaken him to see the wife of the man whose life he had taken. He tried to pray, but his mind wandered. All the events that had led him deeper into trouble and pain played on a loop in his head, culminating with Channing's horrific death. Dallas fought to push the gruesome images from his mind. He gripped the Memorare prayer card under his pillow, urgently whispering the words over and over until he fell asleep.

BROKEN

"I'm happy for you, man, but it'd be a lie to say I won't miss having you around," Dallas said as he shuffled the deck of cards. "Hope my next cellie's half as decent a guy as you."

John's release date was scheduled for the end of the week. Dallas had been denied parole as expected, but the board's written decision encouraged him to continue behaving as he had most recently and commented positively on his improvements.

"Hope I can handle reentry okay," John said, picking up his cards as Dallas dealt them. "Living with my dad will be weird, but I'm thankful he'll take a chance on me. I wanna do better, for Gwyneth's sake. I'm determined to be a real father to her." Gwyneth was John's five-year-old daughter, and John would finally see her again after four years.

"I'm never gonna forget how you stopped me when I was about to hang myself," Dallas admitted. "I thank God you happened to be here, 'cause I don't know what might've happened if it had been somebody else."

"I still say you wouldn't have gone through with it, but hey, if I could help, then I was glad to do it." John shook Dallas's hand firmly with his free hand. "It's the pits in here, especially early on in a long sentence like yours or mine. I can't believe I'm about to get gated out, man. Don't lose hope yourself — you'll be right behind me, you know. What, November, December?"

Dallas nodded as he drew another card. "Yep, Saturday, November 28, if I calculated it right and get my maximum good time between now and then. Get to celebrate my last Thanksgiving in here, and then, God willing, and I can keep my temper, I'll be free."

"Bummer about missing Thanksgiving by a hair," John sympathized. "Then you hafta wait a whole 'nother year before a real Thanksgiving meal. The stuff they serve in here is like rubber turkey covered in paste. Three Thanksgivings of that should be punishment enough."

"The fourth one won't kill me." Dallas chuckled with a shrug. A pang pricked him inside as his attention wandered from the card game. *I wonder what a real Thanksgiving meal is even like.* His mother had never made one.

It was a few days after John's release. Dallas was outside for rec time, deep in a friendly racing match against Smith, with Pedro as judge. Dallas had just eked it out in the last moment with a crazy dive ahead of Smith to cross a finish line toed by Pedro when the on-duty CO motioned at Dallas.

"Cowboy wants you." Smith nudged Dallas and nodded towards the new officer, Wilson.

Winded from running and brushing the dirt from the front of his uniform, Dallas held up a finger and turned, jogging over to where the guard stood. This was Wilson's first time on yard duty while Dallas was out, and all the men knew he had a backup on the way, one who was making sure he learned the ropes. Sometimes the rougher inmates would try to take advantage of a new officer.

"Malone," Wilson said. "Just got radioed that you're needed in the kitchen. Better get yourself down there."

Dallas sighed and wondered if he'd missed something at cleanup. Maybe the kitchen staff had some extra work, like food needing to be unloaded. But shipments usually arrived in the morning. Dallas scratched his head as to why he was being summoned.

"Could you tell Smith and Pedro?" Dallas asked Wilson. "Don't want them to think I chickened out and came up with a fake excuse to get out of running races against them." He gave a smirking smile.

Wilson returned it warily. "Sure, I'll tell 'em."

Dallas turned and entered the building, trotting down the empty hall in the direction of the cafeteria. As he passed a corridor branching off to the right, he felt strong arms suddenly grab him from behind and yank him into the narrower hallway. Dallas yelled out, but a gloved hand covered his mouth, stifling his alarm. He bit down hard, instinct demanding that he fight, but the owner of the hand was unfazed. He dragged Dallas around another corner, overpowering his flailing limbs. As they passed through a doorway, Dallas made a desperate grab at the doorframe, clinging to it by three helpless fingers before his grip was wrenched free as he was hauled into a dark storage room. A cold echo of steel and sudden blackness — the door had been shut.

It's Hudson! Dallas panicked, the hair at the back of his neck standing on end. He had known it must be the second those rough hands had closed on him, and the low, menacing voice at his shoulder confirmed his fear as he was pinned against the floor by the guard's full weight.

"I hear you'll be gated out pretty soon," Hudson snarled in a cold, purring whisper in Dallas's ear as he handcuffed his wrists behind his back. "I'm gonna miss my favorite jailbird. Thought I'd spend a little 'quality time' with you, know what I mean? We can make these last few months count, so you don't *ever* forget me, hmm, Malone? Or hey, maybe I can speed up your escape from this place for you. How about leaving in a *body bag*?" As he spoke, he tied something around the back of Dallas's head — a gag. Dallas's eyes widened as all the things Hudson might be planning to do to him flashed through his mind, each more gruesome than the previous. *How will anyone ever find me? How long before they even notice I'm missing?*

"Scared, Malone?" sneered the malicious guard as he jerked Dallas to his feet. "It's about time. I'll just go nice and slow, then, enjoy myself, so you can wet your pants in fear over what's coming and to give you time to realize exactly *why* you deserve what you're gonna get." A sole lightbulb further back in the storage room was the only illumination, and Dallas could make out the twisted expression on Hudson's backlit face, demonic. He gave a sudden kick to Dallas across both shins, and as his legs were knocked out from under him, he staggered and nearly hit the floor. Dallas could see that once again this would be no fair fight. *It'll be a bloodbath.*

Hudson emitted a low, wicked laugh, grabbed Dallas by the shoulders, and slammed his back against the wall, breath heavy in his flinching face. "Yeah, I'll sure hate to see you go," he said with a crooked fake smile. "I'll have to pick one of your buddies as my new favorite. Hmmm… how about Pedro?"

Lightning flashed in Dallas's eyes as he bared his teeth and foolishly struggled to fight back. One swift punch in the gut from Hudson had him sliding down the wall where he crouched helplessly, subdued.

"Glad you decided to have a seat, Malone," Hudson teased. He pulled up a chair from a corner and sat down a few feet away from Dallas, staring at him as he leaned forward, palms on his knees. "Figure I have time to tell you why you've earned this special treatment." His eyebrows lowered. "It's for all the times you've one-upped me, Malone — or tried to and failed." That evil grin again. "I've hated you since the day you got Murphy on your side. Two Jesus freaks thinkin' they can trample on my authority. That was your first mistake, scum."

Hudson stood and paced slowly back and forth in front of Dallas. Suddenly, he turned, and Dallas realized too late what had happened as a pair of handcuffs whacked him on the side of the face. Hudson had pulled them from his pocket and was using the cuffs like nunchucks on his victim. The hard metal ring flew at Dallas from the other direction, and he winced and turned his face, but they hit his ear hard, and he heard ringing in his head. Before he could recover, a flash of metal hit him square in the face, and Dallas felt a searing pain in his nose and cheekbone, and he tasted blood.

"Then when you decided you'd play tough guy, stand up to me with your little door-slamming showoff trick," continued Hudson, "that wasn't cute, Malone. It just made me madder."

Dallas knew it and felt the adrenaline surge through him as he tried to shout, "I won; you lost!" He mumbled and sputtered, but the gag prevented him from communicating, and another whack from the handcuffs, this time in his left eye and temple, was delivered by Hudson in response to Dallas's darkening eyes.

"Don't you get all defiant on me," the guard said coolly. "You know, part of the reason lowlifes like you get thrown in jail is so you'll leave here broken, not wanting to act like thugs again. I still see the attitude in ya, Malone, even with the sickening comments I hear some of the other COs sayin' about how good you've become. Well, you're *not* good — and you *still* haven't learned your lesson, now, have you?"

As he spoke, Hudson sidestepped to avoid stumbling over Dallas's desperate foot sweep that struck and almost knocked the guard off balance. Wide-eyed with flaring nostrils, Hudson brought a heavy boot down with all his force on Dallas's shin in retaliation. Dallas bit down hard on the gag and winced.

"You're gonna lose this time, and big," Hudson snarled. "Your attempts at fighting back are pathetic. You're gagged and cuffed and on the floor, and nobody knows where you are. You got nothin'."

Dallas knew he was right. *Trying to fight back is making it worse. There's still so much more he could do to me, and nobody's near to see or hear!* He drew his quivering knees up to his chest and closed his eyes, screaming desperate prayers in his head.

Hudson crouched down in front of Dallas and leaned in close. "Then havin' your friend squeal on me for tripping you, and that jerk Murphy comin' to show me up *again*. You got out of punishment in solitary, and me — well, I looked like a fool, bein' put on leave for a week. You seem to like trying to destroy a man's ego, Malone. Well, when I get done with you, you're not gonna feel like a real man ever again…"

Dallas felt his head slam back against the cement wall and saw stars. He refused to open his eyes and look at his aggressor now, racing through the fervent barrage of mental prayer.

Hudson unleashed a string of vile profanities on Dallas, each a more degrading attempt at ripping the notion of his manliness to shreds.

Dallas's head collided with the wall again and again, dizzy and distant.

"I'll give you one last chance to beg for mercy." Hudson released his grip on Dallas's hair. The gag around his head went slack. "Admit your defeat, that you're a *nothing*, and maybe I'll make this a little less painful for you."

His mental faculties groggy, Dallas fought for clarity. His mind was struggling to form prayers. *If I die right here, please God, take my soul... and please somehow use my death for good.* The gag hung under Dallas's chin, and he realized Hudson was waiting for him to speak — to grovel and beg him to stop.

Mustering the last ounce of his strength, Dallas squinted at the blurry figure and said hoarsely, "I'm not gonna hand over my dignity. If you want it, you'll have to take it yourself. I forgive you for whatever you're gonna do, and may God have mercy on—"

Dallas was interrupted by a smack in the face from Hudson's hand. Blood was still flowing from somewhere — Dallas couldn't tell the exact source — and he caught a glimpse of it on the gloved hand as it was withdrawn. His head throbbed, and he was dimly aware of Hudson dragging him away from the wall by the legs, leaving his abdomen exposed, and then Dallas took a kick in the gut. He doubled over with pain and was yanked upright again, receiving another kick that narrowly missed his face and instead hit his shoulder. Hudson made up for the miss with a solid punch to Dallas's nose and another to the stomach. Maniacal laughter rang through the echoey room as Dallas slumped back against the wall, brooms and buckets on either side of him. The floor tipped drunkenly, and Dallas suddenly leaned forward and heaved. *Did I just throw up blood?* Dallas was hazy as he tried to focus through his swollen eye in the dimness. *If I'm gonna die, please, Lord, let me be worthy of heaven, let me see Channing there soon! I accept whatever pain is in store for me, just let it be quick, please God...*

Hudson lifted Dallas by his collar and forced the gag back into his vomit-tainted mouth, then shoved him down into the chair in the center of the room. One hand reached up and yanked the pull chain to an overhead light, the sudden glare blinding. Dallas squinted and flinched to avoid the beam which Hudson was angling directly into his face.

"Yeah, you're helpless, Malone. Helpless and completely terrified,"

Hudson hissed. "Can't even look at me, can you? Don't want to see what's about to end your miserable life? Well, not too soon... I'm gonna enjoy the fun we're having for as long as I can drag it out, make your last memories real special. I do believe I've made up my mind that at the end of this, you're not gonna survive."

Fire rose inside Dallas, and he clenched his fists behind his back and lifted his head. The sweaty red face of the devil stared him down, and he met the threat with a hard glare, teeth clenched tight on the gag in his mouth. *Yeah, I'll stare down death.* Dallas made the decision in stoic silence. *"I gave my back to those who beat me, my cheeks to those who tore out my beard, my face I did not hide from insults and spitting. The Lord God is my help, therefore, I am not disgraced; therefore, I have set my face like flint, knowing that I shall not be put to shame... For it is a great glory to adorn the life of eternal salvation with the dignity of suffering: it is a great sublimity before the face of the Lord, and under the gaze of Christ, to contemn without a shudder the torments inflicted by human power..."*

As the memorized words coursed through Dallas like rushing water, Hudson spewed out every sickening threat of torment his mind could devise, cursing and jeering at his captive victim. Dallas winced as his shins were kicked again and again, his lips barely moving with the murmured prayers, his ears registering Hudson's icy intimidations but letting them fall away. The foreboding shouts hinted at even worse degradations to come. *He can take my body, but he can't have my soul...* A smack in the face, a punch in the gut left Dallas sucking in a gasp for precious oxygen. *"All day long my enemies taunt me, they burn with anger and use my name as a curse..."*

Hudson's raspy breath was in Dallas's face, the blazing, venomous eyes inches from his. A resigned peace issued from the windows to Dallas's soul, his mouthed prayers still inaudible, and he wasn't hearing the screaming taunts flying as spittle into his face anymore. *"Even though I walk through the valley of the shadow of death, I fear no evil, for you are with me..."* The deranged correctional officer snatched him up by both shoulders and put a knee in his stomach, then turned him around and bashed him head-first into the wall. He jerked him back and rammed his head into the unforgiving concrete again. The last thing Dallas was semi-aware of was his head hitting the cinder blocks once more, and then he was out cold.

Muffled voices came to Dallas through a swamp that hung in the air all around him, and he struggled to look around and sit up. One eye was swollen shut. An unidentified force pressed him down onto his back again, and Dallas flailed his arms in a frenzy to fight back. *My arms are free!* was the only thought coursing through him with a swell of adrenaline.

The lights were bright overhead, and Dallas was pressed down again. The voices around him became clearer. He opened his good eye and saw somebody who wasn't Hudson, and the fight in him relaxed. He strained to understand the voice.

"This is the doctor. Don't struggle," a voice finally broke through the fog that was Dallas's brain. *The doctor… Thank God, I'm alive.* Dallas fell back, an oblivious sleep overtaking him again.

When he woke up fully, Dallas was in the prison infirmary, in a bed in the corner of a darkened room. He tried to get up, felt horribly dizzy all of a sudden, and leaned over, throwing up on the floor. A doctor was by his side a second later, urging him to lie back down. But Dallas wanted to get up. *I survived, apparently, but what else did Hudson do to me?*

"How… how did I get here? What happened?" Dallas asked the man who was checking his vitals.

"You suffered a concussion, and your collarbone is broken, so you need to lie still," the doctor directed. "I want you to think about what happened if you can, and the warden is going to be in to talk to you later, if you feel up to it."

Dallas wasn't sure what he felt up to. He'd never felt so weak and sick in his life. The room was spinning, his head like a sloshing fishbowl. He submitted to what his body was begging of him and lay back against the pillow, succumbing to sleep.

When Dallas woke again, his head was clearer. He tried again to shift into a sitting position. The room remained stable this time, but he winced with the pain from his shoulder. Short, tight breaths told him of his damaged ribs, and his shins were killing him. Ice packs strapped on them hid the damage that had been done by those heavy boots, and Dallas cringed. *I don't even want to look.* His left pinkie was splinted, and he assumed it had been broken — *again.*

The doctor entered the room at his stirring and asked him how he felt.

"I can think straighter now, I think," Dallas stated, his words an obstacle course in his brain as he spoke them. "Uhhh… and I'm starving. Can I have something to eat?"

"Well, that's a good sign," the doctor said with good humor. "I'll send for something from the cafeteria. I'm not surprised, because you've been sleeping off and on for nearly 24 hours."

The meaning of the words slowly puzzled together for Dallas. He had no recollection of the passage of time.

"Do you feel up to speaking to the warden soon?" asked the doctor. "He wants to hear all you remember about how you ended up this way."

Dallas nodded. "But how did I get here?"

"That will become clear as we piece together what happened," the doctor assured him.

Dallas didn't argue and considered how much he should say. *If I tell the truth about what happened and Hudson still gets away with it, then I won't survive the next attack. But will others end up taking this same kind of abuse — or worse — if Hudson remains on staff here? Could this evidence finally get him fired?* He shuddered with the memory of the guard's chilling body bag threat.

Over the next hour, Dallas ate what was brought to him and then tried to move around the room. He gathered the courage to look at his legs — they were black and blue under the ice packs. He could bear his own weight, but each step shot searing pain through his shins. He hobbled to the bathroom. Confronting himself in the mirror was crushing — his eye was swollen shut, his upper lip was puffy from where Hudson had busted it with the handcuffs, and there was an ugly gash on his cheek along with severe bruising. There was a puzzling red mark on one side of his neck that felt like a rugburn. His shoulder was wrapped to protect his broken collarbone. *I look terrible.* Dallas pulled his gaze away in disgust. *I lost. Big time.*

The doctor caught him limping back to the bed. "Don't try to walk without help," he chided. "We might have to get you some crutches. Your legs are seriously injured."

Dallas didn't have to be told that. He suddenly just wanted to be left alone. He was utterly shattered, inside and out. Struggling to get back onto the bed with the doctor's assistance and snarling that he could do it himself, Dallas turned towards the wall and closed his eyes. *What else did Hudson do to me after I blacked out?* Dallas shuddered, wrapping his arms tightly around his abdomen and drawing his knees up close. *What else am I going to find out?* Clear images from the beginning of the struggle flashed through his mind and became increasingly hazy. He tried to recall each punishment Hudson had inflicted on him, and he felt more and more degraded. The vulgar threats the guard had strung around

Dallas loomed in his memory, growing more real in his imaginings of all he couldn't recall. Dallas's head pulsed with pain. The place where Hudson had whacked it against the wall repeatedly was tender to the touch, and the throbbing radiated from that spot until his whole head was pounding. He didn't want to think about how wretched and broken he felt. Dallas fell into a restless sleep.

When he awoke a few hours later, Dallas's headache was fading. The sun was getting low in the late afternoon sky through a narrow window in the corner of the room. Against the doctor's advice again, Dallas pushed himself up on his good shoulder and slid out of the bed. He hobbled to the second-floor window and looked out. The yard lay below. It was empty this late in the day, and he guessed it was nearly the dinner hour. Heat waves rose from the dry earth in the August afternoon, and Dallas, for the first time, remembered that his birthday had just passed last week. He hadn't given it a second thought. *I'm 23 now,* he told himself, unable to believe it.

Dallas was still at the window watching Andrew, the mockingbird, perched on the fence below, singing its heart out. He lost himself in thoughts of his old life. All of a sudden, someone cleared his throat behind him. Dallas turned around to see the doctor and the warden.

"Mr. Malone, you aren't supposed to be up without help, remember," the doctor said. "You could make the significant damage to your legs worse."

Dallas limped to a nearby chair and sank down, appearing submissive as his heart pounded in his throat. "So level with me — how bad are my legs? Nothing's broken?"

The doctor came closer and pulled up a nearby stool. "No, none of the bones in either leg are broken, miraculously. The swelling has gone down some since yesterday, a sign of beginning healing. But you need to stay off them."

"I'm ready to know what happened, how I got here," Dallas said bluntly, glancing at the warden's knowing look.

"We're hoping you can detail all that you remember," the warden stated. "You passed out, as you've probably realized, but I want to know what happened before that because from the looks of your injuries, a criminal report needs to be filed."

"I don't want to make any trouble," Dallas muttered. "But I also don't want this to happen to some other guy in here."

"That's why I need to know specifically what happened," the warden said, "because there has been another similar incident of violence in the past 24 hours. Tell me who did this to you, Malone."

Dallas's eyes flashed with anger. "Who else was attacked? Was it Pedro?"

The doctor and warden glanced uneasily at each other and remained silent.

"Tell me, was it Pedro?" Dallas almost shouted, alarm rising in his voice. "What else happened?" He tried to stand but accidentally bore weight on his bad shoulder while pushing himself up and collapsed back into the chair with a wince.

"You'll find out all that's happened soon enough," the warden replied grimly. "Right now, I really need your cooperation. If the attacks are linked, then this could mean serious punishment and charges being filed against the perpetrator. There was no surveillance camera in the storage room where you were found unconscious. It will be based on your word alone and the details surrounding the time of day, where all the inmates and correctional officers were known to have been located at that time, and then this second attack. The injuries were of a similar nature."

Dallas had angry tears welling up behind his eyes but refused to let them escape. His heart pumped wildly with suspense. "Just tell me if it was Pedro!" he sputtered. "Pedro was threatened by the person who did this to me. Or was it Smith?"

The warden relented. "Both Pedro and Smith are fine."

Dallas closed his eyes and blew out a sigh of relief for his friends, but still, his heart raced. *Somebody else has been hurt, and now I'm gonna be made to detail the humiliating account of my failure to defend myself. But if this could protect others from that corrupt guard once and for all...* Dallas swallowed his pride and opened his eyes.

"Okay, I'll talk," he began in a low voice, eyes on the floor. "I was out in the yard. Wilson, the new CO, told me he got a radio call asking for me in the kitchen. But the kitchen staff didn't really call for me," Dallas added, glancing up. "It was a setup. I went into the hallway, and as I passed near where that storage room was, I got grabbed from behind and dragged in there, with a hand clamped over my mouth. I knew who it was the second he grabbed me..."

Dallas stared the warden down, trying to read the man's mind. *Does he think it was Hudson? Or has the slimebag come up with some kind of cover to pin this on somebody else?* Dallas saw expectation in the warden's eyes. The man had taken his side the last time Hudson had attacked him. Maybe this was the evidence needed to prove Hudson's instability as a correctional officer.

Dallas mustered up his courage. "It was somebody who wasn't supposed to be alone with me anymore." His tone grew hostile. "He'd backed off since his last attack, but he hates me. He told me so, and that's why he did this, to punish me. He said he was gonna kill me, long and drawn out. It was Bruce Hudson."

The warden said nothing, but Dallas saw a slight change in his demeanor. The doctor sighed.

"Is that who you think attacked somebody else?" Dallas pressed. "Are you gonna tell me who he hurt now?"

The warden closed his eyes and tilted his head downward, as if in thought. The doctor cleared his throat. It dawned on Dallas that he'd been alone in the infirmary all this time. *Surely if the other man was beaten as badly as me, then he'd be in here too. Or was it so bad he's been removed to a hospital?*

"Where is he?" he asked, deep dread swelling in the pit of his stomach. "Where's the other guy Hudson attacked? Why isn't he in here?" A chill ran down Dallas's spine.

"I think you've guessed that already." The warden avoided eye contact. He crossed to the window and stared out, shoulders slumped, before sinking into a chair facing Dallas. "This has been a rough few days, Malone, and it's weighing on me. I want to put Hudson away for good, get him out of here, and into prison where he most likely belongs for the mounting evidence of abuse. Will you help us out by telling everything he said and did to you?"

Dallas nodded, throat dry, and he couldn't stop the next words that whispered from his mouth. "Hudson killed a guy, didn't he? Who... who was it? Who'd he kill?"

The warden stared steadily back into Dallas's eyes. "Jasper Gaines died yesterday. He was beaten for what Officer Hudson called insubordination and then transferred to a hospital under threat of suspected heart attack. He passed away in the ambulance."

Dallas clutched the arms of the chair as the room spun. *Hudson iced the Old Man...* Only last week, Dallas had sat across from him at lunch. They'd had a conversation about prayer, Dallas remembered clearly. He and Pedro had been considering starting a prayer group for anyone interested, and they'd ended the conversation with Gaines agreeing to come and try it out. Dallas closed his eyes and put his head to his knees, trembling. He'd escaped his threat of death, but now it was Gaines in the body bag.

"We are investigating Officer Hudson for his possible role in leading to that death, and if he's the one who inflicted this damage on you, then I need to know all the information, Mr. Malone."

The words barely registered with Dallas for a few moments. A man was dead. Could he have done something more to have prevented it? Should he have pressed harder when Hudson was given the mere slap on the wrist and then returned to his job? Dallas wracked his brain for memories of any negative interactions between Hudson and the Old Man. Had Gaines been another of Hudson's targets, and he'd covered it up out of shame? Did he already have a heart condition that was exacerbated by Hudson's harsh treatment of him?

"What did he do to Gaines?" Dallas found himself asking.

The warden sighed. "I can't reveal those details. But what you tell us can have an impact on the next steps we take."

"Hudson's not here, is he?" Dallas's eyes were wide and darting, body tensed up as his fingernails dug into the arms of the chair. "He's not in the prison right now? When's he allowed back?" Cold fear shot from his heart to his head as beads of sweat formed on his brow.

"Currently, he has no return date set," the warden explained. "He's been given a mandatory leave while we figure this all out. But if you're worried about him retaliating…"

"That's *exactly* what I'm worried about!" Dallas snapped back. "I was told he wouldn't be able to be alone with me again, after what he did to me in the hallway that day and then beating the crap out of me when he took me to solitary for no reason!" Dallas's whole body shuddered with the memory and what might have happened if Officer Murphy hadn't intervened when he did. He swallowed down the churning nausea in his gut.

"All I can do is offer you my sincerest apology," the warden said in humility.

"Before I talk, I need you to promise me he's not coming back, *ever*." Dallas set his mouth in a tight line and crossed his arms across his chest. The old fight in him was coming back, and he rallied inside with the strength that he'd not been defeated. He was still in the game.

"It seems pretty certain, from the evidence so far, that Officer Hudson will no longer be permitted access to this facility," answered the warden.

"Or any other ones, I hope," Dallas said in a biting tone. "Okay, so if I tell you it was him that did this to me, describe the way he beat and humiliated me, then you think he'll be put away somewhere, so he can't have any power over others to abuse them?"

The warden nodded. "Yes, your testimony will be important here. We need to have documented evidence."

Dallas took a deep breath. "Okay. I told you how he dragged me into the closet..."

The warden took down notes as Dallas narrated back the terrible events as he could remember them. The doctor showed the warden evidence of the abuse resulting from each part of Dallas's story and confirmed that his examination was consistent with the expected injuries from each violent act that had been inflicted on his body. Dallas told everything he could remember Hudson saying to him, face burning crimson as he repeated the vulgar, humiliating threats.

"The last thing I remember is him slamming my head against the wall. It must've knocked me out. I don't remember anything else until I started to come around here in this room." Dallas stared at the doctor and warden expectantly. "I want to know what else happened to me," he said, trying to push down the fear in his voice. "I have this burn mark on my neck, and I don't remember how that happened. I don't remember how my finger broke, either, but he was stomping on me and kicking me plenty, so I might not've even noticed when it happened. And how did I get found?"

"I can fill in those details," the warden responded. "You're correct that the kitchen staff didn't summon you. Officer Wilson says it did sound like Hudson's voice on the radio, and he didn't yet know that Hudson's direct authority over you had been revoked. And that's my fault. He should have been informed right away. I hadn't realized what kinds of abuse Officer Hudson may have been inflicting on people. He's been here longer than me, and some things have been coming forward that imply he's been abusing his power for a long time over his years as a CO. Again, I apologize. We want to reform the system so that this won't happen again, to anyone."

"So how'd somebody figure out where I was?" Dallas pressed, ready to get the gruesome details over with.

"Smith started hounding Wilson when you'd been gone for over a half-hour. Wilson told him to check in the kitchen once they got back inside if he was concerned about you." The warden paused and gazed at Dallas. "You've got a good friend in him, Malone. Smith wouldn't relent. He told

Wilson that you weren't supposed to be alone with Hudson and how he'd made it his personal mission to watch out for you, to ensure that never happened. That's when Wilson radioed to check on the validity of what Smith was telling him. He brought everyone in early—we were short-staffed, and the other CO who was supposed to come out there with him had been assigned elsewhere. Smith immediately checked the kitchen. When he couldn't find you, he rose hell. Several COs came running at the uproar—he was turning over garbage cans in the cafeteria, really going wild." The warden chuckled. "After we sorted it all out, I had to go let him out of solitary, where two of them had dragged him for the ruckus he was raising. He got everyone's attention, though— one of the COs went searching for you. Pedro related the details about how you'd been summoned. They discovered that nobody in the kitchen had called for you. By this time, I'd been notified to come on down. When we couldn't get Hudson to respond on the radio, I got concerned. So I started checking all along between the yard and the kitchen. That's how we found you in that storage room. You were out cold, and nobody else was there."

"Are you convinced it was Hudson even without my word?" Dallas asked quickly. "He had gloves on."

"I had my suspicions it was him due to the other details. That's why I wanted to get the name out of you first before saying anything."

"He just left me in the storage room, then?" Dallas felt chilled at the thought of how long he might have lain there unconscious had Smith and Pedro not reported their concern.

The warden couldn't meet Dallas's good eye anymore. "We went in and found you on the floor. Your face was bleeding, and your breath was raspy. Twine was wrapped and tied tight around your ankles, binding your feet together." The doctor pulled up one of Dallas's pants legs at the ankle and pointed out a laceration there. Dallas hadn't even noticed it yet.

The warden continued, voice dropping low. "And the mark on your neck—your pants were tied around your neck."

Silence hung in the room. Dallas's hand went instinctively to the red streak. *Hudson tied my pants around my neck...* Memories of his own hanging attempt three years previous flooded Dallas's mind, and he saw himself as he must have appeared when they'd found him. He didn't want to hear more. Without a thought, Dallas shot up from his chair, ignoring the pain in his legs, and paced, wincing at each step. The doctor came alongside him for assistance, but Dallas brushed the man aside.

"Can I please just have a little of my dignity?" he snapped. The doctor backed off as Dallas hobbled to the window and back again.

"And so you brought me up here then?" he asked the warden, staring at nothing across the room, hands gripping the back of the chair for stability.

"That's correct," answered the warden. "We brought you up on a stretcher and had you thoroughly examined and cleaned up. It's fortunate that none of the injuries required more extensive work."

"So..." Dallas gulped, not wanting to ask but needing to for his peace of mind. He kept his eyes on the floor, face flushed. "Is that it? I mean, you checked me over *completely*, and you didn't find... anything else?"

The doctor tried a reassuring smile. "That covers the extent of your injuries. Don't you think that's more than enough?" he added light-heartedly.

The warden said, "If you're asking whether we found evidence of Hudson carrying out any more of his threats to you while you were unconscious..." The man threw a sideways glance at the doctor, whose eyes suddenly registered understanding in what Dallas was getting at. "No, you had a very thorough examination. It appears that after tying you up, he left."

"What about the writing?" interrupted the doctor. "He didn't mention remembering that."

"Writing?" Dallas asked, glancing from one face to the other.

The warden cleared his throat and shuffled his feet. "You may not have noticed the writing on your chest yet..."

Dallas unbuttoned his shirt and bent his neck to see the words Hudson had scrawled there in permanent marker. *See you in double L, the cell to hell.* Dallas squinted at the strange phrase.

"No man should have his mind messed with like this," the warden continued, shaking his head. "Nothing I say can make up for such sick mental torment, and..."

"What do you mean?" Dallas cut in. "I don't get it. You're saying Hudson wrote this to traumatize me mentally? I don't even know what it means."

The warden shifted his gaze and met the doctor's eyes.

Dallas sensed their surprise at his lack of understanding. He stared at the warden, waiting.

"Cell LL, in H Unit," the warden said slowly. "It's the cell where death row inmates are housed for their last night. It connects to the execution chamber."

The ticking clock on the wall filled the silence of the room. Dallas swallowed and tried to keep breathing. *That's where Hudson took me for solitary that last time, LL.* The meaning of his 'final night' comment hit Dallas all at once. His stomach swirled at the depravity, and he squeezed his eyes shut, but all Dallas saw was that haunted cell, the final stripping away of the humanity of souls condemned to the nearby lethal injection chamber...

"I'm real sorry, Malone. I thought everyone knew about LL. Hudson probably thought you knew, too, and was trying to use it to scare you. As for the reason he left you alive in the storage room... well, judging from your account of what he said to you, it seems he got bored once he'd knocked you out. It's sick, but it sounds like his main interest was in you being aware of everything he was doing to you, as an additional trauma." The warden's sober eyes avoided Dallas.

Dallas heard echoes of Hudson's threats, and he was sickened at the realization that the guard had been planning to return later, once Dallas had regained awareness, so he could have the twisted pleasure of watching him endure more of his depraved torture. Dallas held up his broken pinkie, staring at it, but saw instead an endless expanse of railroad tracks, the figure of a skinny boy with brown, unruly hair hanging to the top of his shirt collar walking along before him, hand dangling at his side with pinkie bound crudely between two popsicle sticks with duct tape... The horror of having experienced a similar bullying, humiliation, and pain that Channing had endured throughout his childhood drowned Dallas, and he shuddered violently as he climbed into bed, mumbling, "I need some sleep." The doctor and warden bowed out of the room without another word before Dallas lost his last ounce of composure.

Dallas lay on the infirmary bed, shaking with miserable sobs that made his sore ribs protest with pain. Unutterable prayers lodged in his throat as the destruction of his self-esteem consumed him. Knowing in his head that he couldn't have won this fight didn't ease Dallas's fallout of complete defenselessness and brokenness. He was in a frantic, out-of-control freefall, surrounded by nothingness, no firm handholds to grab, nothing to break or even slow his drop. *Hudson didn't kill me, but he broke me... just like he said he would.*

Dallas spent the first half of the night shaking and sweating and unable to sleep, his life a parallel with Channing's childhood, running like a horror film through him. *How did he handle it, being powerless all the time, and still get up with a smile the next day—how?!* Dallas wanted to stay in bed for the rest of his life, to give up and sit in bitter friendship with his weakness. Going back into general population still limping and with his face battered was a humiliating thought. *Hudson* wrecked *me. I thought I'd just die in that storage room, but now I'm gonna have to face guys like Maddox and Miller who'll just love to gloat over this, and somehow that's gonna be even harder for me than if I'd just died, because at least then I couldn't be humiliated.* The unknown of what had happened while he was unconscious plagued Dallas. *They said there was no evidence of any more violence to my body, but what if...* He gulped and tucked his arms protectively around himself, shivering at all the violations that could have taken place even while leaving no physical marks.

Dallas forced himself out of bed after a few hours of restorative sleep. *I can't slip back into these old feelings of despising myself,* he argued. *You'll only be a broken man if you don't do something to change it. But that's hard, maybe too hard.* Standing before the filmy bathroom mirror and staring at his complete lack of power, Dallas saw a glimmer of stubbornness in his eyes and caught his breath. *I'm still in there. My humiliation at looking battered, at being beaten... that's not me. Christ was beaten too, but would he have wallowed over how others perceived him because of it? Remember, this faith is the only one in which God willingly chose to suffer as a man, to fully experience and understand pain and humiliation.* Dallas closed his eyes and saw his friend how he'd always remember him, alive with his sheer joy for life despite the way others had treated him. *Channing.* Dallas ached. *His greatest gift to me—my faith. The truth that allows us to be at peace even in the darkness.* Dallas opened his eyes again and looked beyond the bruises, forcing the fight back into himself, the old stubbornness that Father Benedict had told him to shape and direct in a positive way. His challenge was to combine that with his faith and utter dependence on God.

Dallas walked back to the bed and knelt, exhaling prayers. *You know what's best, God. Use me according to your will. Please have mercy on the soul of Jasper Gaines. Please grant me the strength to finish these last few months of my sentence, to not care when people taunt me, and give me the steadfastness to lead the prayer group that me and Pedro have been planning.* Aching to regain the high ground he'd attained before this attack had cut him down,

Dallas focused on the positives of seeing Father Benedict soon, holding Channing's prayer card again, and thanking Smith and Pedro. *This world will never be perfect, but you know who you are in Christ. Don't give up!*

Dallas stood in his cell, collecting himself before heading to the cafeteria. He had just taken his Memorare card from his locker when he heard familiar voices on the other side of the bars. He walked easily to the door, bruises the only remaining evidence of Hudson's brutal kicks.

"Smith! Pedro!" Dallas greeted his friends with enthusiasm and invited them to step into his cell.

"We're not lettin' you out of our sight for an instant, Malone." Smith grabbed Dallas's shoulders and stared at him squarely. "Except maybe when you're sleeping, but that's only 'cause you'll be locked safe in here."

Dallas smiled. "Hey, it's okay. Hudson's probably getting fired."

Pedro and Smith exchanged a relieved glance. "So did they tell you everything that happened?" Pedro asked softly.

Dallas nodded. "Pretty much."

"Then you know about Gaines?" Pedro continued. "It happened less than half an hour after Hudson left you in the storage room."

Dallas nodded again, staring at the floor.

"Makes me sick that it takes killin' a man to get an abusive jackass fired!" seethed Smith. "Malone, you should press charges against the whole institution. Prove that things are so out of control here that a CO who wasn't supposed to supervise you directly was able to beat you senseless, then went and *killed* a man! You could make out big if you win. I mean, just look at your mangled face!"

Dallas gave Smith a withering smile. "Thanks for reminding me of my dashing good looks," he said sarcastically. The swelling had gone down around Dallas's eye, leaving a purple bruise, and the cuts were in various stages of healing. "Really, I'll just be satisfied knowing Hudson's gone and prevented from being on prison staff anywhere else. He's gonna do hard time, too."

"But this whole place needs to be shaken up," Smith insisted, pounding a fist against the frame of Dallas's bunk. "Sweeping reforms! The Old Man deserves justice!"

"Justice will be done if Hudson goes to the slammer." Pedro's voice was assured. "He's going to pay for his actions."

"But somebody should pay for being irresponsible!" Smith raved.

"Come on, don't you think so?" He turned towards Dallas, eyebrows up.

Dallas sighed. "I appreciate your zeal, man, but really, I don't wanna have to rehash all that's happened, over and over again. It was degrading enough to have to tell it to the warden and the doctor. Maybe that doesn't make sense, but… well, if you've never felt totally powerless before, then maybe it's hard to understand. I gotta focus on my gratitude that Hudson didn't get a chance to come back after I came around, because…" Dallas shivered. "Anyway, I already told the warden everything, and he said that I shouldn't have to lay it all out again in a courtroom. They have enough evidence to prove Hudson's wrongdoings and can present all the abuse he inflicted on me and others. Apparently, several other guys have spoken up now. It sucks that it took the loss of a man's life for it to happen, though."

Pedro spoke after a moment. "Did you hear how it happened? With Gaines, I mean?"

"Not the details, just that Hudson roughed him up, and he had a heart attack."

"Yeah, we'll tell you everything," Pedro said.

"In the chow hall," Smith added. "Come on, before we end up last in line."

Dallas nodded. "Just give me thirty seconds, okay?" His eyes went to the prayer card in his hand.

Pedro began, "Remember, O most gracious Virgin Mary…"

Dallas joined in, a warmth spreading through him. Then he secured the card in his locker and headed down the hall between the two inmates who'd promised they weren't ever going to let him down again.

By Father Benedict's next visit, the physical signs of the brutal beating had mostly faded.

"I keep telling myself it's not a reflection on who I am as a man," Dallas said in a low voice, hands folded on the table in front of him. "I realize I have a bit of self-humbling to do still. I can't tie up my self-worth in my physical abilities. But, of course, I want to be able to protect myself and others who are vulnerable."

"That's part of who you will always be," Father Benedict responded. "While remaining humble, you still have the duty to stand up for what's right, and you've always done that physically. Life is a fight, Dallas, but not only a physical one. I see that desire for battle in you as something you will be able to cultivate to serve others throughout your time here on earth, all for God's glory. So this correctional officer won't be returning?"

"Nope, he's been fired and charged criminally," Dallas replied. "After a few years of taking his abuse, now I can rest easy these last few months. Except, it makes me nervous just thinking about leaving. I'm eager and scared at the same time. I'm trying to make the most of it these final months before I'm gated out."

"At my next visit, let's get you ready for that release date, then," Father Benedict said with a smile.

Dallas threw himself into productivity for his final months of incarceration. Following a few extra hours of work in the kitchen, he had done some reading and written in his journal, then headed to the weight room and finally to the showers. Rotating his shoulder to wash his back, he felt the regained range of motion, indicating the full healing of his collarbone. Dallas was lost inside his brain under his four-minute water allotment cascade. *I'm grateful for the changes in myself, but, man, it's wearying sometimes when these guys come to me like I have all the answers. All this responsibility weighs a ton. "Quiet yet approachable," that's how I heard Pedro describing me to another guy yesterday. I guess he's right. I want to stop and listen when people come to me to talk, unlike a few years ago… but, God, it's still uncomfortable, a sacrifice for me. But I guess that's what you want, huh? After all, Father Benedict's done the same for me, and the least I can do is listen to other guys struggling like me. It's gotta be* you *they see, God. Not me.*

He rinsed the shampoo from his hair. That unrelenting feeling hammered in the back of his mind that he was being called to serve as a priest and thus be able to give all the glory — and control — to God. *But that idea frightens me, because I know my time would never be my own again. Is that selfish? Or is it just realistic of me to resist the idea?* Dallas toweled off his hair with a sigh. *Please show me your will for me, God.*

Dallas stepped to the sink alongside Pedro. As he lifted his razor, his critical eye in the bathroom mirror compared the new scar to those above his eyebrow, then gave way to acceptance. He would always carry these marks left by Hudson's abuse. *Thy will be done*, repeated his mental mantra. *It's in the past now, and I've gotta move forward.* Nearly a month had passed since the assault, and Pedro and Smith had been good for their word: rarely was Dallas alone when he was outside of his cell.

"A new guy asked if he could join us today," Dallas mentioned, eyes still on his reflection as he maneuvered the blade around his chin.

"That's great," Pedro answered. "Your new cellie?"

Dallas shook his head. "Nope, TJ's still kinda shell-shocked to be here. He's a firecracker. He blew up, and now he's just silent. I get it, though. He'll come around, hopefully."

Pedro nodded. "Blew up at you?"

"Yep." Dallas turned his head to scrutinize the razor's work. "You know I've been deferring to other guys lately, and maybe I can get to that point with him before my release. But he came in with guns blazing, and of course, a fish has gotta see that his entitlement attitude won't work in here. If I hadn't, somebody else would have put him in his place, and more violently."

"He wanted bottom bunk, huh?" Pedro rinsed his razor under the running faucet.

"Tried to chin-check me for it." Dallas smirked. "I didn't rough him up or anything, but he learned that won't fly when I had his wrist in my grip. Wish I coulda been nicer to him somehow, but I'm not living with a bully for the next couple months."

"It's for his own good in the long run," Pedro said. "So, you have enough rosaries for the group?"

Father Benedict had given Dallas several plastic rosaries to share around. "Yeah. I hope the group is okay with it, even though most of them aren't Catholic."

"I think they will be," replied Pedro. "Remember last week, when Ferguson said he figured Catholics really were Christians, now that he's got to know us. Said he used to think otherwise."

"Yeah, and Smith sat with me yesterday while I prayed the Rosary out in the yard. He said he appreciated the calming effect of listening to the repeated prayers."

"You're doing a lot of good by starting the prayer group," Pedro said. "How many guys have come up to you in the past few weeks asking about it now? Or even just to ask you to pray for them or to listen to their problems?"

Dallas closed his eyes, still. "I don't know." He shrugged modestly. "But we're up to eight guys praying together before dinner each day. It helps me to know that others are offering prayers for my guidance and decision-making about what I should do after my release, too. Thanks for helping me put the idea into action."

"I don't think you hear half of the grateful comments those guys are making about you." Pedro's tone was serious. "It's doing something for us all, Dallas. People are drawn to your genuine personality and your humble ways."

Dallas kept his lips drawn shut. *You're doing something big, God. It's weird for me to be in the middle of it, but it's exactly what a lot of us need in here. Even though I still long for Channing's companionship, there are some great friends alongside me now.*

As they headed down the hallway towards the cells, Pedro made a small noise in his throat. Dallas glanced up ahead. Miller, Maddox, and Pulaski were coming from the opposite direction. Dallas took a breath and offered a small smile without a word.

"Loser Jesus freaks," mumbled Maddox, followed by snickers from his sidekicks.

Dallas bit his lip and ignored them.

"Maybe they'll grow up one day," Pedro commented once they were out of earshot.

"Hope so," Dallas agreed. "Let's offer our Rosary for them in a few minutes." *Father, forgive them, for they know not what they do. You accept me, and that's all that matters, not what they think about me.*

Murphy was supervising the end of kitchen clean up, alone with Dallas for the first time since Hudson's attack.

"I wish something had been done about him sooner," he confessed, watching Dallas scrub out the last of the huge industrial steel pots. "I'd tried to compile enough complaints, but it's real hard to remove a CO with a history of milder attacks or things that don't have video evidence. It took some major stuff to make it obvious that the man was out of control. Wish that wasn't the way it worked."

Dallas paused in his scouring, lips pursed. "I bet your job gets discouraging, seeing these kinds of things and not being able to change it. I guess that's just the way things are in here. I mean, it's prison. It's supposed to be rough."

"Yeah, but not *that* rough." Murphy shook his head. "Especially not when you're trying to do better, improve your life, and you get knocked down for it."

Dallas knew what Murphy meant. "But hey," he added, "I know I was cocky to him at times, and I'll admit that, on occasion, I pressed back harder just to push his buttons, which only escalated things. I'm kind of a glutton for punishment that way sometimes. I tried to be meeker when he got onto me, but... well, I still struggled not to lash back at him."

"It's definitely discouraging," Murphy continued, "but maybe with Hudson gone, I can just get back to the basics of having to break up fights and intervene in suicide threats and figure out if an inmate's lying through his teeth about a pain in his abdomen — the usual stuff. Still, I wish I'd been working that day when Hudson dragged you off."

Dallas put down the dishcloth and gave Murphy a firm handshake, looking him steadily in the eye. "Thanks for all those times you had my back, when you saw him being unfair with me. Or with anyone. You're a good CO, Murphy. Us guys, we've done some wretched things to get ourselves thrown in here, but you... you've always treated me with respect and dignity. You let me be my own man and face my punishment here without ever trying to rub salt in the wounds. You're a standup guy, and I'm glad the others in here will have you after I'm gone. I'll worry about them less because I know they'll be in good hands."

Murphy looked back at Dallas with his typical serious expression. "Glad to do my job, Malone. And it's watching guys like you, who change for the better, that makes this job all worth it. I know you're gonna get out and do right, be good for the world around you. I thank God you survived that day."

"I was prepared to die," Dallas admitted. "I thought he'd go through with it, kill me in the end..."

"God has different plans for your life, Malone," said Murphy.

The two of them clasped hands, clear that an undefined bond had united them over the past three years. Murphy grinned and playfully punched Dallas in the shoulder. "Okay, back to work with ya."

Dallas had kept quiet about his abuse at the hands of Hudson, but bits of the story got passed around nonetheless. He'd let Maddox and Miller's comments about his bruises and bandages slide, allowing them to sting inside while fighting down the desire to lash out. It was the worst in the cafeteria.

Dallas and Pedro headed for a table with their dinner trays. "Let's save a spot for Smith," Dallas said. They paused at a congested spot alongside the table where Maddox and Miller sat.

"Look at the pretty boy, face all healed up," Maddox mocked, and Miller laughed raucously beside him. "Bet you're sad to have all the evidence gone now. Probably liked seein' the reminders in the mirror that you'd been raped by Hudson. You're cryin' since he's gone now and can't do it again, 'cause you *liked* it! Come see me in my cage sometime if you wanna reminisce, sissy."

Dallas tensed up with revulsion, unable to let this one go as Hudson's disgusting words rang in his ears. He stopped short and turned to face Maddox and Miller, dropping his tray with an echoing clatter on the table across from them. The surrounding tables fell silent, all eyes on the potential altercation.

"He didn't rape me," Dallas growled in a low voice. *At least that much I know for sure...*

"Oh, sure, he didn't, sure," Maddox continued, rolling his eyes and elbowing Miller. "Everybody knows what happened in there, Malone. We heard *all* the details of how you were found tied up by your pants – pants that *somebody* must've stripped off you..."

Fire ignited fury inside Dallas.

"But you better watch your back in the showers is all I'm sayin'." The two of them snickered at Dallas with taunting eyes.

He clenched his fists and held his breath, suppressing the urge to react physically, and managed to pick up his tray and turn away, scoffing, "Eff off, you jerks." *Shut up and get away from them!* Dallas had taken two steps when he heard Pedro stumble to the ground behind him, tray and food exploding in all directions. Whirling around, Dallas caught the tail end of what had happened. Maddox had stuck out a foot to trip him.

Dallas dropped his tray back on the table and stalked towards Maddox, fuming with a laser focus. *This is it; he's finally gonna get it! I'll smash his face in and end up doing extra time, and I don't even care and...*

Miller and Maddox jumped up to meet Dallas's threat, and Maddox withdrew something from his pocket with lightning speed, his cold eyes narrowed at Dallas.

A lock-in-a-sock. Dallas clenched his fists at the sight of the improvised weapon.

The growing murmur in the room gave way to shouts of, "Dinner and a show!" "Fight, fight!" A sudden tugging at his pants cuff stopped Dallas short. Pedro, on his knees on the floor, gripped Dallas's ankle, as if he could restrain him by the sheer power of that one hand.

Dallas fought himself for control and won, the wild animal response subdued as his rational brain told him to halt. He backed away from Maddox, eyes not leaving the weapon, then squatted beside Pedro and retrieved a fork. *Don't fight them,* mouthed Pedro as they made brief eye contact. Dallas gritted his teeth and blocked out their taunts. *Turn the other cheek. God created them, too...*

Amidst the whoops from others who'd enjoyed seeing the tumble and the potential skirmish, two COs shouted orders as they approached the table. Maddox slipped the slock into Miller's pocket before the guards reached them. Dallas silently helped Pedro pick up the mess, then the two of them rose to slink away.

"You'll be out of here soon," Pedro reassured Dallas quietly, "and then you never have to see them again." Dallas's cheeks burned, his fists clenched on his tray. *Pedro's right.* He counted it as a victory that he'd not let them get a violent response out of him. *Only by the grace of God.*

"These are a few job options in the area." The man across the table slid Dallas a sheet of paper. "One auto mechanic that's hiring, and a few construction contractors with openings on their crews. Here are the phone numbers so you can start making contacts soon to line up interviews."

Dallas scanned the descriptions of four potential jobs, all located in Wichita Falls. It appeared to be a moderate-sized town in north Texas, had a few Catholic parishes, and was about three hours from the prison.

"Only one mechanic?" Dallas met the eyes of Carlton Brown, the reentry services employee who'd been assigned to him in this final month before his scheduled release date.

"I know that's your preference, but this is the only one hiring," Carlton responded. "But these crews here, two of them will take guys fresh out of high school, no training or anything required. Mostly demo work, on-the-job learning as you go."

Dallas chewed his lip as his eyes were drawn to the next page, a map. Each of the businesses was marked.

"There are several apartment complexes that rent in the range you're looking for," Carlton continued. He pointed to blue dots plotted on the map. "All of them on bus routes. Your employer wants to know all these kinds of details — how you're planning to get to work and anything else to build your case that you'll be a committed employee. And here are the Catholic churches." Carlton handed over another sheet with the addresses and pointed them out on the map.

Dallas scrutinized the list of construction crews. Demolition work sounded like a good way to channel his aggression into something positive. Some days, he felt as if he was barely holding it together when the anger built up inside of him as Maddox and Miller continued their typical verbal abuse. *It's like a tug-of-war, me against my own body, when I command myself not to respond to them. Smashing up walls and tearing stuff out of buildings might give me a good, safe outlet until I get over everything that's gone on in here.*

"If you do get the mechanic position" — Carlton tapped the map with one finger — "you can see how close this apartment complex is. You could probably walk instead of paying bus fares and be able to save up for a car more quickly."

My car! Dallas had pretty much forgotten the abandoned Isuzu near that lake in North Texas, not too far from Wichita Falls. *Maybe…* It was possible the car was still there and possible it would still run. *But it's been nearly four years.* It was improbable he could even find the spot they'd left it in their frantic state that night. He wistfully said a mental goodbye to the last items they'd left locked inside.

Dallas looked up at the man across the table and said, "Uh, well, this sounds like some good info to get me started."

"If you have any questions, let me know," Carlton said. "Otherwise, I won't be seeing you again, so good luck on your future, Mr. Malone."

Dallas rose, tucking the papers into a manila folder. The two men shook hands, and Dallas slipped into the hallway, folder under one arm. *I guess this is it.* He sighed. *I've gotta be an adult now, for real.*

"I'll be back to pick you up in just under three weeks." Father Benedict was beaming at Dallas during their final visitation time. "I have eight days set aside in which to travel and help you get settled in."

"Thank you," Dallas said. "There's no words that can express it. I don't know what I'd do without you to even drive me anywhere." Dallas hesitated. "And about driving… I know it's a long shot, but do you remember how I told you we abandoned my car in the woods on the night of the shooting accident? It's maybe an hour from Wichita Falls, I'm guessing from looking at the map. On the chance it's still there…"

"I can drive you to the place, and we'll look," finished Father Benedict.

"I'd appreciate that," Dallas said. "If by some miracle I find it, I hope I can fix it up. New tires, see what else it needs. It was old, but it was a solid car. It'll be just about another two months, after my release, until the four-year mark since that awful day…"

"Did they ever find the license plate?" Father Benedict asked.

"No. I told them where I threw it," Dallas said, "but since I was found guilty without it, they probably didn't need it for evidence. Maybe they never looked for the car, either. At least, I hope not. It was a remote place, way off any paved roads. But people out hiking may have seen and reported it. I'm not getting my hopes up that it's still there. I know it's doubtful." Inside, Dallas tried to quell the sentimental tingling at the mere thought of his car.

Before their time was up, Father Benedict spoke seriously. "Remember that feelings can be fleeting and that making determined choices to keep faith is what will get you past the inevitable dips. I want you to be aware that you might hit a low place after being released. Many people find the transition to be somewhat of a shock. You will suddenly have freedom after having been told what to eat, how to dress, when to sleep. That can be a difficult adjustment once you're out in society."

"Honestly, that's why running off to become a monk is so appealing to me." Dallas sighed. "But, yeah, I know." He grinned at the priest's twinkling eyes. "That's totally the wrong reason to become a monk. I can't run and hide from life. I keep praying for God's will to be done, and that's all I can do."

Father Benedict was silent a moment. "Do you still find yourself being pulled towards the priesthood?"

"All the time," Dallas answered immediately, "by some unconscious force. I don't want to resist that, but I know I need to prove I can simply make it after I get out of here, hold down a job and take care of myself… and control my temper. I mean, what kind of a priest wants to punch people in the face all the time?"

"You've done well mastering your anger recently," Father said. "I know it takes great effort."

"It takes so much effort, I feel like I'll explode sometimes." Dallas gazed up at the ceiling. "I'll have to watch that closely, maybe find some more anger management classes once I'm out. But keeping others in mind as children of God — who are just as deserving of forgiveness as I am — is the only thing that's kept me from being an idiot and knocking out more teeth. I'm gonna apologize to Miller about that again, one last time. I just hope he can understand that I'm genuinely sorry."

"That's all you can do," Father Benedict agreed.

Smith was waiting for Dallas in the yard when he came outside. "Hey dude, what am I gonna do after you leave? One more week, right?"

"Yep," Dallas replied. "But I'll come back here and visit you and Pedro both before your terms are up. You two stick together," he advised. "I know he's even quieter than me, but he's a good guy, a friend. And the others who've been doing the prayer group with us — watch out for each other, okay? You'll keep going, right?"

Smith stared at his shuffling shoes. "I don't know that we wanna keep it up without you."

"Hey, we do it for God," Dallas reminded him. "For our relationships with God. Not for me. I want you guys to continue it."

"Really?" Smith glanced at Dallas.

"Definitely. Pedro offered to lead it. You gotta stick up for him if anyone tries to bully him about it." Dallas bumped Smith with his shoulder. "He needs your confident swagger alongside his steadfast devotion."

"Malone, you sure got our numbers." Smith pushed back playfully and shook his head. "Man, we're all gonna miss you. Can we come invade your hermitage when we get out, disturb your solitude?"

Dallas laughed. "Yeah, I'll be in Wichita Falls. In an apartment, not a cave out in the desert. You can look me up."

"I will, Dallas," he said solemnly. The two of them clasped hands in an arm-wrestling posture and locked eyes for a moment. The twittering of Andrew, perched high above on the razor wire, broke the silence.

"If I don't get a chance to tell you, lemme say it now." Smith locked eyes with Dallas. "Thanks for offering me your forgiveness. It's made a huge impression on me. While I'm not glad for the reasons we're locked up in here, I am glad it gave us the chance to meet. You're a good man."

Dallas felt a lump in his throat. "Hey, you too," he said softly. "I still regret attacking you that time. I'm glad that apologizing led to our friendship now. And you've done so much to stick up for me during these past couple of years. I'm gonna miss you and Pedro, too."

It was time to head back in. Shivers overwhelmed Dallas's insides as they parted in the hallway. How could it be that gaining one's freedom would be so challenging, even painful?

The final days were a mixture of anticipation and agony for Dallas. Constant thoughts of Channing returned with a vengeance, interrupting his sleep. His biggest concern about being set free was one he couldn't even voice to Father Benedict now. *I'm having to truly acknowledge that Channing won't be there when I get out, that my real life is going to have to go on without him.* For three and half years, time had halted for Dallas, everything arrested, and he felt like he'd walk back out into the springtime of the year 1997 as if it had been yesterday, life just waiting for him to pick up where he'd left it off. In reality, not only had time elapsed, but things would never go back to normal for Dallas. In just a few days, he would have to walk out of here and into November of the year 2000, no longer as a lost and angry 19-year-old but as a scarred and healing 23-year-old man.

He threw himself into prayer during the last jittery, sleepless nights, begging for calm and peace. He prayed to be able to get through the rest of the week and trust that all would be well. He kept Channing's prayer card on him at all times, suddenly seized with irrational fear of losing it again.

After Thanksgiving dinner, two days prior to his release, Dallas lay in the stillness of the night, the Memorare card gripped in his fingertips as he squinted at it in the dark. The vivid priest dream had awoken him again. He closed his eyes and imagined Channing's hands on the card, holding it close, slipping it in and out of his pocket with devout frequency. *This is my most prized possession, and all my recitations of the prayer on the back since the day I received it have helped draw me home to the Church, the home Channing had found right before he died.* Dallas's sobs escaped as vicious heaves.

TJ stirred above him and groggily asked what was wrong.

"N-nothing," Dallas choked out through his tears. "I... I'm just... overwhelmed." Dallas bit down his sorrow. *TJ won't understand when he's practically just started his sentence and feeling like his release date will never come.* He drew in a deep breath. *Jesus, I trust in you...*

Dallas's release time was scheduled for 11:00. Auto-pilot propelled him down the hall for his last breakfast as an inmate, Pedro and Smith treading along on either side. In the cafeteria, Dallas noticed Miller ahead of them in line and took a deep breath. *It's now or never.* He said a little prayer in his mind as he approached.

"Hey, Miller," Dallas began, "I want to apologize again about your tooth. I still feel awful for knocking it out, and I didn't want to lose my last chance to let you know. I'm really sorry, man."

Miller stared, unresponsive. Maddox nudged his cellmate from behind and murmured something, grinning wickedly. As Miller stepped aside, Maddox took a threatening stride towards Dallas.

In his earlier prison days, Dallas would have stood his ground, but this morning he stepped back instead.

"I think you should have to make it up to him before you leave, Malone," Maddox sneered.

"I'd like to do that." Dallas sidestepped him to face Miller again. "Is there anything I can do for you this morning?" he asked. "Would you like my breakfast?"

Miller still stood, speechless, while Maddox shouldered himself back between them.

Dallas backed off again.

"No, the real way to make it up to him is to give him one of *your* teeth, man. An eye for an eye, a tooth for a tooth, right?" Maddox lunged at Dallas and shoved him in the chest.

Dallas held up both hands and stepped away, pulse pounding in his head as he held back. *I can't ruin my chance at getting out today!*

Smith was beside him immediately, voice rising. "You don't wanna do this, Maddox." He stepped in front of Dallas, separating the two men.

Maddox's hands went for Smith's shoulders in his attempt to get to Dallas, but he was suddenly flanked by two COs who seized each arm and pulled him back. Maddox struggled for a second, then froze and spat at Dallas's feet. The guards walked him away, and Dallas and Smith fell back into line.

"Pedro snagged them the second we saw Maddox tryin' to start trouble," Smith said. "We sure as hell weren't gonna let him provoke you into a fight that could get your good time revoked on your last day! Man, the idea makes me *sick!* As much as we're gonna miss you, you don't need to get thrown in the hole on your gate day! The nerve of that jerk!"

"Maybe it was foolish of me to even approach them." Dallas ran both hands through his hair. "Selfish to try to relieve my conscience. It only stirred up trouble."

Pedro spoke. "You did the right thing. You wanted to use your last chance to make your remorse known for the wrong you did to him."

"Yeah," Smith added, "you apologized to me again a few days ago, and nobody got all offended over it on my behalf." He glared at Miller, alone in line ahead of them.

"Guys, please try not to get into it with Maddox once I'm gone," Dallas begged. "I can't bear to think of either of you being put in solitary because of the beef he's got with me."

"Hey, man, I'd be proud to go against him, one on one, for the sake of your honor," Smith said, thumping his chest with a closed fist. "I'd take a week in the hole in exchange for punching that guy in the face."

Dallas sighed. "You're hopeless, Smith. I promise you; it's not worth it, no matter how good those punches feel in the moment. Pedro, I guess it's on you to keep him in line now. Sorry, dude."

Pedro smiled wanly and shrugged. "That's on him. He's a bigger guy than me. All I can do is encourage peaceful responses."

"Okay, so I'll put in a little effort and *try*, Malone," Smith conceded. "For your sake, if you'd really feel better about it."

"I would," Dallas replied. "I don't want you fighting on my account."

"You think he'd hurt me?" boasted Smith with a swagger. "I could take 'im."

"Like the way you could take Dallas?" quipped Pedro, who rarely made snappy remarks.

Dallas and Smith both had to laugh.

"You got me there, man!" Smith slapped Pedro on the back.

They reached the front of the line and grabbed trays. Dallas glanced up as they passed the correctional officers. Wilson and another guard had stepped in to replace the two who'd escorted Maddox out.

Dallas crossed the cafeteria, passing where Miller sat alone. He paused, then set down his tray in the empty space across the table.

"I honestly do wish I could give you back that tooth," Dallas said quietly. "I know this won't make up for it, but if you want it, you really can have my meal. And once you get out, I'll pay for any dental work you get done. Look me up; I'll be in Wichita Falls, Texas. Or you can track me down through the priest at the cathedral in Denver. I mean it." He began to turn away.

"Wait a sec," Miller said, jumping up from his seat. "I, uh… it's okay." His uncertain eyes met Dallas's before darting down again. "I can let it go. I mean, I was kinda being a jerk to you before you hit me. So, uh… thanks." He sat quickly down again.

Dallas stood immobile, studying Miller's nervous response that was free from his cellmate's control. *He accepted my apology.* An uncomfortable pity nagged at him. Dallas knew the unspoken truth of what Maddox did to Miller in exchange for his protection and so-called friendship. Dallas silently slid the tray towards Miller. "Good luck, man," he said softly. "Hang in there." *And enjoy a few days' break from that monster while he's locked up in the hole,* he added silently.

Dallas turned and walked to the table where Smith and Pedro sat with one of the regulars from their prayer group, who tossed him his slice of toast. Pedro offered him a piece of bacon, and Smith passed him his orange juice. Dallas smiled, holding up a hand with a shake of his head. They pressed him to take it until he agreed to half the slice of toast with his coffee. "Guys, I'm leaving today," he reminded them. "I might get to eat some exotic outside food later—so don't worry about me. I can hardly believe this is my last chow in here," he said with a note of sadness.

"Malone, you can't actually be sentimental about it!" Smith said adamantly. "This is awesome—you're gonna be *free!*"

"It's encouraging to us to see your term end," Pedro agreed. "So don't feel badly for us. You did your time, and now we finish ours. It's okay."

Dallas smiled at Pedro. The intuitive man had a gracious way of putting things in a positive light.

Meal finished, the men dispersed from the cafeteria. Dallas had a couple hours before being escorted to the property room to claim his belongings. He powered through one last workout in the weight room, a bundle of raw nerves with anticipation and anxiety over what was about to happen to him. He made each pullup a silent plea for peace as thoughts of Channing bombarded him. *What am I gonna do without him?* Dallas didn't want to face the answer to that question but knew he must. Entering this old yet entirely different version of life would be scary.

Finally, Dallas's aching wrists and arms demanded he quit. He glanced at the clock on the wall. *No wonder.* Dallas had been at the pullup bar for nearly an hour straight. He headed to the showers and let his mind go blank for those few minutes of water rushing over him. *My last prison shower. Tomorrow, I can spend as long as I want in a private shower.* It all seemed so strange to him.

Back in his cell, Dallas gathered the items from his locker. Books, five of them. Notes from his preparation for his conversion to Catholicism. His rosary. His toothbrush, toothpaste, comb, deodorant. His combination lock and two granola bars. He triple-checked his pocket for Channing's prayer card.

It was time. Murphy stood at Dallas's cell door. "Pack it up all the way, Malone." A smile danced in his eyes.

"Bottom bunk's yours." Dallas slapped TJ on the shoulder, who nodded. "Keep your chin up in here, man. You've got my prayers."

Trancelike, Dallas followed the officer down the cell block hall. He passed Pedro, exchanging a huge smile and a passing high five. In a moment, they were moving through doors that had not opened to Dallas in three and a half years.

In the property room doorway, Murphy stopped. "Congratulations, Malone," he said, and with a hearty handshake, he was gone.

Dallas turned to where a plastic bin marked with his ID number sat open on a table before him. It was surreal to see his few possessions there, dormant since his arrest. His jeans and belt, his work shirt with a grease mark still on the sleeve, the t-shirt he'd been wearing underneath. He lifted each item and held it close, burying his face in the fabric of his past. His wallet. Dallas flipped it open to see his expired Nevada driver's license inside, three twenty-dollar bills left from his last paycheck, and a few other paper items: his social security card, the final note from his mother, a few receipts... the last one he'd slipped into his wallet was from dinner at Katherine's Kitchen with Channing, their final night together.

Tears burned Dallas's eyes as he quickly tucked the receipt back into the wallet. He picked up his keyring, with his bronze-colored rental house key and the Isuzu's large silver key attached. The familiar weight and jingle in his hand was like he'd never missed it, as if he'd last grabbed these keys off the kitchen counter only this morning. At the bottom of the box, his lighter and a tire pressure gauge. *That must've been in my shirt pocket. I should return it to Mitchell.* A small plastic baggie contained a digital wristwatch, its display blank, and a small silver hoop, Dallas's earring. He wondered whether he could get the earring into the piercing anymore or if the hole had closed up after all this time. Dallas tucked the baggie into his pocket. Last, he grabbed his black boots, dried mud still crusted in the treads, and lifted them out.

A staff member handed him a bag and showed him into a tiny room where he was to exchange his uniform for his old clothes. It felt strange to dress in private. The jeans fit, slightly looser around his waist. He pulled on the t-shirt and stuffed his long-sleeved work shirt into the bag. He slipped his wallet into his back pocket, keys into the right pocket. He fumbled a moment with the earring, trying to get it back in, and then hesitated, debating whether he even wanted to wear it right now. Dallas dropped it back into the baggie with his watch, then sat down to pull on his combat boots. Left foot, zip halfway. Right foot, zip halfway. Emotion engulfed him at the familiar feel of his old worn boots. It was like he had worn them yesterday a million years ago. He took a few steps in them and swelled with gratitude. *The simple things, like your own clothes and your favorite boots... Thanks, Channing. I really and truly get it now.*

Dallas stepped out of the room as if watching from outside himself. He saw his account balance transform to green bills counted out into his outstretched palm, topped off with his extra gate money. As the next door opened, he caught sight of Father Benedict seated in a chair, waiting. He rose and crossed the room, and the two embraced.

"I'm really out," Dallas whispered. "I'm free."

"Then let's go," the priest said, conviction in his voice. "Let's get you started in a new chapter of your life."

Dallas walked past the last few prison personnel in the room. Nobody held him back. He glided towards an exterior door, no fence outside it. Dallas controlled his movements in calm competence. He strode alongside Father Benedict through the doors of the state penitentiary and towards the parked cars in the nearby lot, a free human being again. He didn't look back.

About the Author

Erin is a Catholic homeschooling mother and a first-time novelist, following a childhood filled with writing creative fiction. She lives with her husband and four daughters in North Georgia. Her passion for vocations became strong when her youngest brother was ordained a priest. Her twenty years of Catholic adulthood have given her time to grow and see what really matters in life with a focus on the good, the true, and the beautiful, and she wants her characters to find and reflect the same. Reading the classics and Church Fathers and especially Chesterton alongside her homeschooled children has informed her current writings.

Erin initially created her characters, Dallas and Channing, over twenty years ago. She was prompted to pull out an old story about them to share with her teenage daughters and was dismayed to realize she had left the characters she loved hanging in hopeless despair. Dallas and Channing were always searching for something, and that something was God all along. The book's direction was suddenly clear, and Erin gave the characters depth and purpose, knowing she owed it to them to develop them further and give them hope amidst their hardships.

Erin is a member of the Catholic Writers Guild, and when she's not writing, she reads aloud to her children, organizes a moms' book club, builds community with her church family, and leads a forest school for local families to get out in the natural world. She enjoys traveling and photography. She can be found at www.authorerinlewis.com as well as on Facebook and Instagram - @authorerinlewis.